PRAISE FOR *DO*

"A fast-paced and enthralling thriller that blends ancient history, magic, and action. Once I started this book, I couldn't stop—and loved every single scene. A masterpiece of story and setting. Highly recommend!"

—*New York Times* bestselling author A. R. Torre

"Fans of James Rollins and Dan Brown will love this stunning new thriller from Jeff Wheeler. *Doomsday Match* is utterly engrossing, a dark and complex tale filled with ancient secrets, adventure, and betrayal. You won't be able to put it down."

—#1 *Wall Street Journal* bestselling author Melinda Leigh

"Jeff Wheeler knocks it out of the park with his supercharged thriller *Doomsday Match*. From the very first scene, you know you're in for an incredible thrill ride full of constant danger and relentless twists—set against a jaw-dropping conspiracy background. Just when you think you've figured out Wheeler's game, he artfully rips the rug out from under the reader, shaking up the plot. If you're a fan of fast-paced, devious conspiracies with a little more than a touch of magic and mysticism, *Doomsday Match* is for you!"

—*Wall Street Journal* bestselling author Steven Konkoly

"The sheer readability and suspense work so well that readers will race through those pages to see what will happen next!"

—TJ Mackay, founder and publisher of *InD'tale Magazine*

FINAL STRIKE

ALSO BY JEFF WHEELER

The Dresden Codex

Doomsday Match
Jaguar Prophecies

The Dawning of Muirwood Trilogy

The Druid
The Hunted
The Betrayed

The First Argentines Series

Knight's Ransom
Warrior's Ransom
Lady's Ransom
Fate's Ransom

The Grave Kingdom Series

The Killing Fog
The Buried World
The Immortal Words

The Harbinger Series

Storm Glass
Mirror Gate
Iron Garland
Prism Cloud
Broken Veil

Landmoor Series

Landmoor

Silverkin

Other Works

Your First Million Words

Tales from Kingfountain, Muirwood, and Beyond: The Worlds of Jeff Wheeler

FINAL STRIKE

JEFF WHEELER

47N⬤RTH

Published by 47North, Seattle

www.apub.com

Amazon, the Amazon logo, and 47North are trademarks of Amazon.com, Inc., or its affiliates.

ISBN-13: 9781662505591 (paperback)
ISBN-13: 9781662505584 (digital)

Cover design by Shasti O'Leary Soudant
Cover image: © Martin Capek, © Vit-Mar, © Drekhann / Shutterstock;
© Gary Waters / ArcAngel

Printed in the United States of America

To Jordan

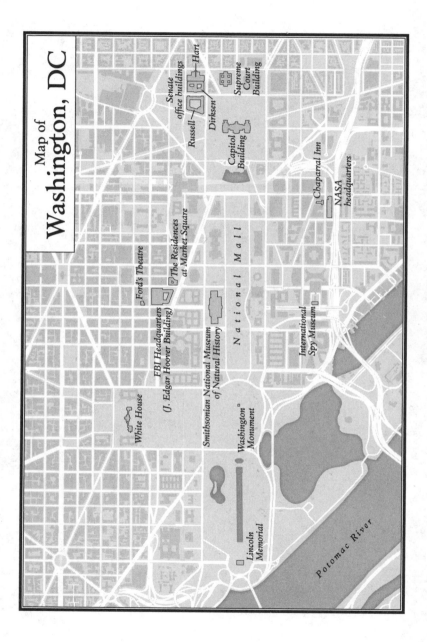

Map of
Washington, DC

White House

FBI Headquarters
(J. Edgar Hoover Building)

Ford's Theatre

The Residences
at Market Square

Senate
office buildings

Russell

Hart

Dirksen

Supreme
Court
Building

Capitol
Building

Smithsonian National Museum
of Natural History

National Mall

Chaparral Inn

NASA
headquarters

Washington
Monument

International
Spy Museum

Lincoln
Memorial

Potomac River

CHAPTER ONE

Qualcomm Institute, UC San Diego

San Diego, California

January 7

"Have you seen the numbers coming out of London? The death rate is becoming exponential."

Dr. Estrada was staring at his own double screen, a cup of lukewarm *xocolatl* near his hand. He rubbed his nose and looked over at his research assistant, Illari Chaska, who was staring at her laptop screen with alarm in her eyes.

"What's going exponential?" he asked in confusion.

"The outbreak in London. Haven't you been following it on Twitter?"

Dr. Estrada lifted the cup to his lips and winced as the tepid drink reached his tongue. He set it down again. "I thought the outbreak was in Spain?"

She ran her fingers through her long, dark hair, the silver rings she wore sparkling under the overhead lights. Her oval face was tight with concern. "That's where it started, but the cases are spiking worldwide.

London, Madrid, New York. Thousands are dying. It's become a pandemic."

Dr. Estrada wrinkled his nose. "I wonder if it started in a biolab. You know they're always working on scary stuff."

Illari shook her head. "The WHO hasn't determined its origin yet, but it started spreading from cruise ships right around Christmas and New Year's. Ten cases. A hundred cases. A thousand cases. Like I said, exponential."

"That's terrible," Dr. Estrada said. If it was growing that fast, it could end up being bigger than the Spanish flu. That should horrify anyone. "Any cases in California yet?"

"Not sure. There's not a single article about it on the CDC's website."

"Then how do you know all of this?"

Illari smirked. "I'm Gen Z. We know things."

That was true. When Dr. Estrada was in college, there'd been no internet, no smartphones. Quite the difference from the research center they sat in now. He gazed around at the wall full of monitor screens showing the LiDAR data he'd been collecting on Maya ruins in Guatemala. None of this would have been possible back then, but here was proof that the impossible could become possible.

The Qualcomm Institute was a joint partnership between the university and one of the biggest tech companies in the world—nearly every cell phone on the planet had some piece of hardware that Qualcomm had designed. The servers in the building were the true breakthrough, though. They were state-of-the-art, running multicore processors custom designed to crunch terabytes of data quickly. Data that the LiDAR technology had produced from his flights over the jungles in the Yucatán—primarily Guatemala.

Grad students like Illari were archaeologists and computer scientists rolled into one. That was the new generation. A group of engineers were making a virtual reality system that would enable users to visit the newly discovered Maya ruins with a headset in an air-conditioned room, something he hadn't thought possible when he was Illari's age.

Dr. Estrada leaned back in his office chair with a creak and folded his arms. "Exponential growth means quarantine measures. Our trip to Belize might get canceled."

His cell phone rang in his pocket, the ringtone a clip from "Smooth" by Santana. Illari shook her head at the "old-man" music and went back to her laptop. The caller ID showed a San Diego area code but no name.

"Estrada," he said, answering the call. Glancing at Illari's monitor, he saw some charts and graphs with data from a website that was unfamiliar to him.

"Is this Dr. Estrada from UC San Diego?" asked a male voice.

"Yes, who is this?" he asked. He switched over to a browser and tapped into the search bar to look for information about the pandemic. Very few articles came up.

"This is Special Agent Foster from the Federal Bureau of Investigation. San Diego field office."

Dr. Estrada's heart clenched with fear. Abandoning his search, he sat up straighter. Sweat began to tingle across his body. Illari looked over her shoulder, brushing her brown hair from her face, and gave him a questioning look.

"Um . . . yes? What can I do for you, Agent Foster?"

Illari's eyes widened with surprise, her nostrils flaring slightly. He gave her a bewildered shrug, trying to play it off, but he was filled with the same kind of dread he'd felt upon seeing a patrol car's lights in his rearview mirror on the freeway a few weeks ago. Except this was worse. Much worse. He'd done something foolish, and he was about to pay for it. His stomach turned sour, and his armpits began to leak sweat.

"Dr. Estrada, do I understand correctly that you do research on ancient ruins? Maya specifically."

"Y-yes. Yes, I do, sir. Am I in any trouble?"

On his last trip to Guatemala, he'd persuaded his pilot to continue north after they were done scanning the Xmakabatún ruins. They'd flown across the Mexican border, to an uncharted and unexplored place within the Calakmul Biosphere Reserve. Because of the dense jungles in that area, there was no way to see it by satellite, but that's where the LiDAR equipment was so powerful. The pinpricks of laser light could penetrate the minuscule gaps in the leaves and hit the ground of the jungle floor, revealing changes in the topography. Like the symmetrical rise of a pyramid compared to an irregular hilltop. Dr. Estrada's research was primarily focused on ruins in Guatemala because of grants and funding provided to that country. The Mexican government had forbidden permission for his research, but the temptation had been too hard to ignore . . .

It had happened over a year ago, right before Christmas. Estrada and his pilot had gotten far enough to see part of a temple protruding from the jungle. A man had been on the ground, looking up at them. It had been . . . disarming. And then a storm had appeared out of nowhere and nearly blown their airplane out of the sky. Dr. Estrada had been in mortal dread that they would crash into the jungle and die, but they'd made it out somehow. He hadn't told anyone about that little excursion. Not the dean at the university. Not his own wife. For months afterward, he'd dreaded getting a call from someone in the US government responding to a complaint from Mexican authorities. Now, perhaps, it had come.

"Why would you think you're in trouble, Dr. Estrada?" asked Agent Foster.

Dr. Estrada lowered his voice and hunched his shoulders. He was sweating as if he were in the server room instead of an air-conditioned office space. "How can I help you, Agent Foster?" His voice was shaking. That made him sound guilty, right?

"If I understand your research, Dr. Estrada, you use laser technology to map ruins in the Yucatán Peninsula. There was a National Geographic special on it a few years ago. I watched the clip."

I'm in trouble. I'm in deep trouble. He took a worried sip from the cup of *xocolatl*, anticipating the coldness but welcoming the flush of energy it gave him. It was a special drink made in the Yucatán. He'd discovered it from an Indigenous tribe that had little contact with the outside world and had purchased the beans and other ingredients so he could make it himself. It wasn't cheap, but it was so much better than coffee.

"Yes. That's my research. I'm with the Qualcomm Institute that—"

"I know, Dr. Estrada. I also understand that your work is primarily out of Guatemala and Belize. But have you ever used your equipment across the border in Mexico?"

Deep trouble. I'm screwed.

"W-why do you ask?" Dr. Estrada said. His hand was literally shaking. Illari was giving him a questioning look that wasn't helping his nerves. His mouth was dry. He needed to use the bathroom very badly.

"You sound nervous, Dr. Estrada. Is everything all right? Are you alone?"

"No . . . I'm . . . my research assistant is with me. Several others. Winter quarter just began, so there are a lot more people here this week."

"I won't take up much of your time, Dr. Estrada. But can you answer my question? Has your research ever covered areas inside Mexico?"

Don't lie to the FBI. His stomach clenched further. If he admitted to it on the phone, he might get charged with a crime. But why would Agent Foster be calling him if he didn't already know? They'd hunted down the plane. They'd probably spoken to the pilot. The bribe that Dr. Estrada had paid to keep him quiet wouldn't be enough for him to lie to the FBI.

"Yes. Yes . . . I have."

He was doomed. His career would be over. All his work would be questioned. He never should have coaxed the pilot into entering Mexican airspace. He cursed himself for being a fool.

"You have?" The agent sounded startled. "And you used your LiDAR equipment?"

"Yes," Dr. Estrada said, wincing, waiting for the blow to fall.

A pause. Then Agent Foster continued. "Have you examined the data? I know that you've found thousands of ruins in the jungle down there. Did any strike you as being exceptionally large or well preserved?"

"Or inhabited?" Dr. Estrada said, half choking.

"You found something."

Dr. Estrada collected his breath. "Yes," he whispered. "I've told no one, not even my colleagues here. Only the pilot knows." He turned away from Illari so she couldn't see his face.

"But the data is there? At the institute?"

"Yes. There are terabytes of data on those ruins."

"Thank you, Dr. Estrada. The information you've provided is very useful. We'll be in touch soon."

"Am I in—" he started, but the call ended abruptly.

"Who was that?" Illari asked worriedly.

"Someone from the FBI," he said. "They want to talk about my research. *Our* research."

"Did it have . . . anything to do with me?" She looked guilty as she said it, and it occurred to him that she might have secrets of her own.

"Not specifically, no," he muttered.

The rush of adrenaline from the conversation and the drink was making his head buzz. He needed to talk to the dean. Having the FBI show up at the university would be controversial. There would be questions asked. His future was at stake.

Illari turned back to her screen, which now shone blue. Seconds later, the wall of monitors all turned blue. Code began to stream across the sea of blue. As Dr. Estrada slowly rose, looking at the monitors arranged on the desks around them, they all went blue. The grad students were gasping in surprise and disbelief.

"What's going on?" someone asked incredulously. "The servers are down. All of them."

The pit in Dr. Estrada's stomach deepened. A moment before, he'd been terrified of having to confess everything to the dean. But this was worse. A data breach was happening in real time. Hackers had infiltrated the institute.

He looked at Illari, who was frantically tapping on her keyboard.

"What's happening?" he asked her.

"Ransomware attack," she said. "They've taken over the institute servers. Everything is locked down."

"You mean the data on the servers can't be accessed?" he nearly shouted in terror.

"How did they get through our firewall?" she said, perplexed. "We have the best security in the world!" She slammed her fist on the keyboard. "It's all locked away."

"But surely the backups—"

Dr. Estrada's throat caught. What if the man on the phone hadn't been with the FBI?

CHAPTER TWO

Ford's Theatre

Washington, DC

January 8

The National Park Service presenter had a clear, strong voice. She stood in the middle of the stage in her uniform, capturing the attention of everyone sitting in the cramped wooden seats. The acoustics were incredible, but that was to be expected. Roth had never been to Ford's Theatre before, but he knew the story she was telling. The story about the assassination of a president.

"John Wilkes Booth was waiting for this line to be spoken. The line that would cause a roar of laughter from the audience. Not that the line itself was humorous. No, the humor was in the *irony* of the line. About a man pretending to be cultured and proving he wasn't. It was just the sort of line that would have appealed to Abraham Lincoln. He died laughing."

Roth shook his head, mesmerized by her voice, by the delicious feeling of being part of history. His twin sons, Lucas and Brillante, were sitting next to him. He couldn't tell whether either teenager was paying attention to the historian. They were looking over at the darkened booth where Lincoln had been shot. Since coming to DC, they hadn't been able to do a lot of sightseeing, not with Jacob Calakmul undoubtedly hunting for them. Their guardian angel, Steve Lund, who owned the private security company Roth had hired to protect him and his kids after they'd survived the death game in Mexico, kept switching their hotels. He was vigilant about providing the security they needed, often in person, but even he realized that the family needed a change of scene from the hotel room now and then. Today, there'd be a double feature because this excursion to Ford's Theatre coincided with a summons to FBI headquarters. They'd taken a long, circuitous route with lots of switchbacks to get there. Lund knew all the tricks.

"'Don't know the manners of good society, eh?'" the historian said with a drawl, pretending to be the actor who had spoken the lines. "'Well, I guess I know enough to turn you inside out, old gal—you sockdologizing old man-trap.'" She paused, her voice lowering to heighten the tension. "As the audience roared with laughter, John Wilkes Booth stepped up behind President Lincoln with a derringer, pulled the trigger, and shot him in the back of the head."

"Oof," Brillante whispered. Lucas elbowed his brother to quiet him.

The presenter's voice began to quicken with urgency. "Major Henry Rathbone noticed the smoke and tried to rush the man. Booth dropped his weapon, drew a dagger, and slit Rathbone's arm to the bone. He then jumped over the balcony and onto the stage and uttered the line he'll ever be remembered saying. *Sic semper tyrannis.*"

"'Thus always to tyrants,'" Roth whispered, spellbound.

"In Latin, 'Thus always to tyrants,'" the presenter said firmly.

Lucas glanced at his dad, eyebrows lifting.

Roth knew the end of the story, but with a few variations. Some thought Booth had broken his leg in the jump from the balcony edge to the stage. It was twelve feet to the floor below. Roth and his boys were in the balcony seating, and it did seem like a dangerous drop. But the presenter said there was evidence Booth's leg had been broken later on, after being thrown by his horse. Many eyewitnesses had seen him run and mount a horse, using the stirrup with his left leg, the one that was supposedly broken.

That detail intrigued Roth. He'd heard the Lincoln assassination story many times, but the presenter's talk had shed new light on it for him. It reminded him of a saying he'd read somewhere: "History is the process in which complex truths become simplified falsehoods."

The presenter described President Lincoln being carried across the street and laid on a bed that was too short for him. And that's where he'd passed away, having never regained consciousness. She received a loud ovation when her speech was finished, and everyone began to stand up to clear out of the theater so the next group of museum visitors could enter and hear the same story.

"Dude, that story was sick!" Lucas said. "It's a bummer that he died, though. What if he'd stayed president?"

The stairwell was narrow and cramped, and they made their way down it carefully. Roth kept both of his sons in front of himself. He was more paranoid now than ever.

"Suki would have loved seeing this theater," Brillante said somberly.

Nearly two weeks had passed since Roth's daughter had been abducted by Jacob Calakmul. The suspense was ripping all of them up inside. Worse: Roth still didn't know whether his wife was alive or dead. Calakmul might have them both, and he certainly wasn't Roth's biggest fan. They were playing the waiting game, and each hour felt like it lasted a year—hence why he'd brought his sons here for a distraction.

As the crowd flowed outdoors, the bite of cold air struck them. It wasn't as cold in DC as it was in Bozeman, Montana, where they lived, but it definitely wasn't California weather.

"If I could travel back in time to any event in history," Roth told the boys, "I would have picked April 14, 1865. So many things went wrong that night. Booth should never have gotten close enough to kill

President Lincoln. Knowing when and how the murder was going to happen, I could stop it all from happening. Like you said, Brillante, the whole history of America altered that night because of John Wilkes Booth and that theater."

"If I could travel back in time, I would have warned us not to go to Mexico in the first place," Lucas said. "Then none of *this* stuff would have happened."

Roth looked at his son, seeing the tightness in his eyes, the worry. They all missed the half of their family that had been carved away. They wanted *answers*. But they were hundreds of miles away from Sarina and Suki, staying in Washington, DC, under FBI protection, trying to sort through an international conspiracy led by a very dangerous man.

Roth's burner phone buzzed in his pocket with a text. He pulled it out and saw it was from Lund. He'd been expecting a message.

I'm behind you. Keep walking straight and then turn left at Pennsylvania.

Roth texted back: *How far away are we?*

The answer came quickly—*3 minutes.*

They passed a Hard Rock Cafe before crossing E Street. And there it was, directly ahead of them, the distinctive building that Roth had seen on episodes of the *X-Files*. The J. Edgar Hoover Building. FBI headquarters.

They crossed the street when the light turned green. The Hoover building was old, having been schemed by President Kennedy and built by Nixon. It didn't look like other federal buildings in DC, with its concrete pillars, small square windows, and memorable overhanging roofline. It was a massive structure with multiple levels below ground and eight to eleven floors above ground. After crossing the street, Roth instinctively looked back to see if he could spot Lund, but there was no sign of him. The man could be a ghost when he wanted to be. He'd spent the majority of his career with the FBI and knew many who worked in the building. But the FBI forced employees to retire early, at age fifty-seven, and many chose to start a new career afterward. Thankfully, Lund had done just that. His commitment to protecting his clients was laudable. He was still fuming that Roth's high school friend, Moretti, had tricked him into handing over Suki.

None of them had suspected the ultimate betrayal, that Moretti, whom Roth had known for decades, had been working for Calakmul all along.

After walking down the sidewalk to Pennsylvania Avenue, they turned left and went to the front of the building. From the corner, there was a row of denuded trees—the leaves long since banished by winter. Looking east, they could see the dome of the US Capitol building.

A man with a big overcoat, a cup of coffee, and a beard reached them. His sunglasses completed the look, and Roth didn't recognize him until he was within a few steps of them.

"Enjoy the museum?" Lund asked after taking a sip.

"It was boss," Brillante said.

"How's Jordan doing?" Lucas asked. Jordan was one of Lund's employees, a younger man who'd left the Army 82nd Airborne. He was a marksman, a sharpshooter. He'd saved their lives in the cabin in the mountains outside Bozeman, even after taking a bullet to the shoulder.

"He's flying to DC tonight," Lund said. "He heals pretty fast."

"Maybe he misses *Monica*," Lucas said, wagging his eyebrows. The boys shot each other matching grins.

Roth rolled his eyes, and Lund coughed to hide a chuckle. They'd all sensed the sparks between Jordan and Monica, although Monica was a consummate professional and didn't give much away. Jordan couldn't keep anything to himself, which was part of his charm. "Agent Sanchez," Lund corrected, "is waiting for us. Follow me."

They approached the main doors of the FBI building and entered through a rotating turnstile. Roth's stomach was doing some flip-flops. They'd come to headquarters when they first arrived in DC, but it had been several days since their last visit, and that had been in the dead of night. Roth worried they were being observed, but Lund continued to assure him that making random changes to the schedule was the best way to prevent being spotted. There were too many people living and working and visiting DC for their presence to stand out in any meaningful way. And Lund's company had set up various fake hotel reservations throughout the capitol to keep Calakmul's goons constantly guessing. Roth had also shaved off his signature beard and started using pomade for his hair, both of which had altered his features dramatically enough that the hotel mirror still startled him at times. The boys had changed their hair too—Lucas's was dyed, and Brillante's was buzzed. They didn't pass as twins on first glance anymore, despite the hoodies.

Agent Sanchez greeted them in the lobby with some plastic visitor badges. "Good afternoon, family." She looked at Roth and tilted her head, her nose a little pinched as if wondering if he was okay.

"Any news?" he asked her in a low voice.

"We can't talk here," she said. "But yes. There's news."

They went through the security checkpoint, where Lund showed the guards the special weapons allowance he'd been given by the director first and then the weapon holstered beneath the jacket as well as a pocket pistol strapped to his calf, both of which they allowed him to keep. That done, Monica took them to a bank of elevators. They filed onto one of them, and she punched the button for an upper floor.

"What time is Jordan's flight arriving?" Monica asked Lund.

Lucas wagged his eyebrows again, but he was behind her, so she couldn't see.

"Eleven tonight. He's taking a taxi to our hotel," Lund said.

"The director isn't happy that you won't tell us which one," Monica said archly.

"Director Wright has bigger problems to figure out than where we're staying. But that was our agreement. Until you find out who else is on Calakmul's payroll, I don't trust any of the regular FBI safe houses."

Monica sighed. "It can't be that many."

"One was too many," Lund shot back. "That was the deal in exchange for our cooperation and for keeping lawyers out of it."

The elevator beeped at their floor, and they emerged into an office area with cubicles and rows of office doors, all facing the exterior windows. The fluorescent lights were dreary. It reminded Roth of one of the old buildings at Hayward State, before it had been renamed, where he'd both worked and gone to college. He'd hated the fluorescents and ratty carpet.

Monica took them to a conference room and held the door for them. Two more special agents were waiting inside.

"Hello, Lund," said Carter coldly.

The dislike between the men was mutual. Roth didn't much care for Carter either. Carter had a perpetually annoyed look on his face. Moreover, he seemed to be a political man, someone who'd worked his way up the FBI ranks through maneuvering and intrigue. Still, they had no choice but to deal with him. He'd been appointed the special agent in charge of the Salt Lake field office after his predecessor was blown up at Bozeman Yellowstone International Airport trying to apprehend Jacob Calakmul.

"This is Executive Assistant Director Brower," Monica said, gesturing to another man seated at the table. He was a big guy, midforties, with all the expressive personality of a sourdough roll. He looked like the quintessential fed—regular suit, cropped dark hair with a receding hairline, and the cool eyes of a man who interrogated murderers.

Roth scratched his chin, feeling out of place.

Lund leaned back against the conference room door. He didn't reply to Carter's greeting.

"Have a seat, if you will," Carter told them. Agent Sanchez sat down across from Brower. Roth took the seat next to hers, and the boys settled in at the far end of the table, looking as sheepish and uncomfortable as Roth felt. Lund didn't sit at all.

The tension in the room was palpable.

"Monica said there was some news," Roth said when he could no longer stand the silence.

"And hopefully she didn't tell you any of it on the way up in the elevator," Carter said. He wasn't in a good mood.

"I didn't," Monica said with an exasperated sigh.

Brower said nothing. He was studying Roth closely, which made Roth even more uncomfortable. Roth began to tap nervously on the table.

"Good clue about the archaeologist," Carter said. "Dr. Estrada did some work with National Geographic on Maya ruins. He's run airplanes out of Guatemala over the jungles and captured mountains of data. Including, it seems, from part of Mexico."

Roth leaned forward in surprise. "That's excellent news!"

Carter wasn't smiling. "Unfortunately, someone else got to him first."

Roth stopped breathing. "What?"

Monica spoke up. "Someone pretending to be with the bureau spoke to him yesterday. He was persuaded to reveal that on one occasion, he and his pilot had crossed into Mexican airspace and found a site that wasn't on any of the charts. Although he didn't relate exactly what he saw to the imposter, he disclosed that something . . . inexplicable occurred over the site. When we interviewed him, he told us that a storm nearly crashed the plane." She gave him a significant look. "He said he's flown through dozens of storms, and this one was uncanny. It literally came out of nowhere."

"Dude," Brillante said, shaking his head. "Like during the games!"

"What did the imposter do?" Roth asked worriedly.

Monica's mouth pursed. "The servers at the Qualcomm Institute at UC San Diego have been hacked and are now under a ransomware lockdown."

"Ransomware?" Roth asked, confused. He'd heard the word before but couldn't come up with the meaning off the top of his head.

"Ransomware is a cryptovirus," Brower said tonelessly. "This particular one is highly sophisticated. They're not asking for money. They're asking for *you*."

CHAPTER THREE

FBI Headquarters—J. Edgar Hoover Building

Washington, DC

January 8

Roth's stomach took another lurch. He kept taking hits, and he wasn't sure how many more he could absorb. The death game. His wife's diabetic coma. The FBI raid on their house in Bozeman. Hiding out in a prepper cabin to protect his kids from Calakmul's men. Then, worst of all, his friend Moretti's betrayal. Calakmul had his daughter and possibly his wife, and he *still* wanted more. He'd never be satisfied until the Roths were all dead, the way he'd thought they would be after the death game just over a year ago.

Monica put her hand on his shoulder, her expression sympathetic. She knew the whole story. She believed him.

"Mr. Roth," Carter said, giving Monica a disapproving frown, "I don't believe that Jacob Calakmul truly expects us to hand you over to him. It's not the policy of the US government to negotiate with terrorists, let alone turn over civilians for them to kill or torture."

"What does he want, then?" Roth asked.

"We were hoping you could tell us," Brower said.

Roth looked at Monica and then back at the stone-faced FBI agent. "And I'm supposed to know . . . how?"

"Jonathon," Monica said to Roth, "Calakmul doesn't fit the profile of regular serial killers, organized crime bosses, or drug lords. Remember the recording you made at the Beck cabin?"

"Yes," Roth answered. Jordan had zip-tied Monica to the kitchen chair. They'd believed, because of Moretti's lies, that she wasn't trustworthy. While she was tied up, he'd recorded his family's story about the Mexico trip. She'd been skeptical at the time, but then she'd witnessed firsthand what a jaguar priest could do. One of them had taken out an FBI helicopter and a sniper team before transforming into a wild animal in front of them. It was the kind of thing that didn't leave room for disbelief.

"We're parsing through every word you said. Our analysts, as well as the CIA's, are trying to connect the dots."

Carter held up his hand. "You're telling him too much, Agent Sanchez."

"We need his help, sir. That's why he's here, isn't it? It was his idea to research the institute at UC San Diego. It might have been weeks or months before anyone thought of it—if they did at all."

"It hardly matters now, Sanchez. They would have contacted us about the attack regardless, and—"

"Mr. Roth," Brower cut in. Roth determined the man's rank was much higher than Carter's when the SAC quickly became tight lipped. "Were you aware that your home was bugged before we executed the search warrant?"

Roth looked into the man's stern eyes. "I suspected it. Yes."

"Why didn't you notify law enforcement back then?"

"Because they had my wife as a hostage," Roth answered darkly. He glanced at the boys, who were staring at the adults with frightened looks. They were just kids. Maybe he should have left them at the hotel, but Roth didn't want to let them out of his sight. Not after Suki's abduction.

"And I advised him not to," Lund added. He'd been so quiet, standing with his back to the door, that Roth had almost forgotten he was there behind him. "I thought, at the time, that Calakmul was just a drug lord looking for money. I didn't realize this was bigger than that until recently. We got a Vivint security system for the house—door locks, motion sensors—but didn't clean the ducts. That's not standard install protocol for a company like that anyway."

Carter pursed his lips. "But if you suspected—"

"We wanted Calakmul to believe that his surveillance wasn't compromised," Lund interrupted. "I provided burner phones and new equipment. All of Jonathon's research into the ancient Maya happened on those devices. That's when he decided to make a trip to Germany to test his theory. As you already know, he wrote a book about his experiences in the death game, changing the names to ensure it didn't show up on any of Calakmul's searches, and published it under a pseudonym. He was sharing information to try and help—to see if anyone else found it and came forward—but in a way that wouldn't compromise his wife or the rest of his family."

Brower's eyes crinkled just slightly. "And so you went to Germany to see this Dresden Codex. The director spoke to the head of the German BND, who was asking questions we're not ready to answer yet. You should have been more open with us about all of this, Steve."

"You and I *both* know why I wasn't," Lund answered defensively.

There was a story behind it. Roth didn't know what it was, but he could feel half the people in the room bristle.

"Can I tell him about the equipment we found in his house?" Monica asked.

Brower nodded.

"It's the same equipment the NSA uses," she said. "High-end stuff. Stuff that even the movies get wrong. The director confronted the NSA about it and learned there was no active investigation happening with your family. No FISA court. Nothing. So we cross-referenced Agent Garcia's cell phone and found a number for a guy who *used* to work for the NSA. A crackerjack hacker. Mexican American from the Bay Area in California . . . where you used to live."

Roth nodded, interested. "Calakmul's been recruiting people from Silicon Valley."

"Obviously," Carter said. "I think we're nearing the boundary of what we can share with Mr. Roth. In the recording, you mentioned seeing people at the death game. Celebrities. Business leaders. Even politicians. Are you prepared to name names?"

Roth glanced at the boys and then at Lund, who shook his head no.

Carter slammed his fist on the table. "We don't have time for games, Lund!"

Brower leaned back in his seat, folding his hands in his lap. He looked patient, unbothered, but his eyes were fixed on Lund.

"You mentioned a ransomware virus," Lund said in a measured tone. "What about the deadly one that's spreading from those cruise ships? Mighty suspicious the way it's spreading. Doesn't seem natural."

Carter's mouth twisted into a snarl. "That is *classified* information. How did *you* hear about it?"

Lund shrugged but said nothing.

"I'm missing some context," Roth said. "Look, I know I don't have security clearance or any of that. But I do know some stuff from my experiences with Calakmul. He warned that violence and disease were coming. Soon. It's possible this virus is his doing. Likely, even. I might be able to help, if you let me, but I need information in order to do that."

"Let me just say," Monica added, "that your cooperation has been useful. Remember the FBI radios in Bozeman, how they were compromised because Garcia was listening in? Someone who used to work for the NSA is feeding Calakmul information. It's like a chessboard, only we can't see all the pieces in play. That's why we need your help."

Brower tilted his head slightly. "Why would Calakmul ask us to turn you over in exchange for removing the crypto lock on the servers? What do you think he expects to come of it?"

Roth leaned back in his chair, and it squeaked loudly. He was uncomfortable and still sweating. "It's probably a magician's trick."

Brower's eyebrows slanted toward each other in confusion.

"Misdirection," Roth said.

"So what is he trying to misdirect us from?"

"Doesn't the server have a backup drive? Any server manager worth anything keeps a backup."

"Of course it does. It'll take three days to recover the data."

"In which time, the hacker will compromise the backup servers too, if he hasn't already," Roth said. "I'm a history teacher, not an IT guy, but it seems logical."

"I *am* an IT guy," Brower said with a tone of anger. His composure was beginning to crack. "If we've lost that backup, there's no way we can find Calakmul's hidden temple. Dr. Estrada flew over it, but he's no pilot. That jungle is too vast for him to pinpoint a specific location like that."

Roth rubbed his forehead. "I don't know what else I can do to help."

"You can give us the names of who you saw," Brower said.

"Off the table for now," Lund countered.

Roth trusted Lund's instincts. "Look, those people are probably back down in Mexico. It would be safer down there right now, especially if he's behind the virus spreading from the cruise ships. Can't you look into who's flown down there over the past couple of weeks?"

"We know Moretti's family is there," Lund said. "Who else is on your list of suspects?"

"We have a meeting with the director in an *hour*, and you haven't told us anything useful!" Carter snarled. "You're wasting our time."

"Tell me more about the virus," Roth demanded. "Is it like small-pox? What is it? I haven't seen anything about it on the news."

Brower looked at Carter and then gave a curt nod.

"If this information gets out, there will be a mass panic," Carter said. "The president has been meeting with his national security team in the Situation Room every Friday to get updates on it and plan a strategic response. The virus may have started spreading on cruise ships, but it's been infecting people in major cities around the world. It's spreading exponentially. These meetings are only going to get more frequent as time goes on."

"What's the source?"

"Unknown, but it's spreading through the European tourist community."

"It started in Cozumel," Roth whispered.

Brower frowned and leaned closer.

"Cozumel," Roth said more loudly. "Do you know how many cruise ships dock there during the holiday season? Calakmul *controls* that island. The virus was started by a . . . a glyph, probably."

"A GIF?" Brower asked, his nostrils flaring.

"No, a *glyph*. Mayan hieroglyphs." Roth pulled out his burner phone and brought up one of the images he'd taken from the Dresden Codex. He zoomed in on it and then showed the phone to Brower and Carter. "In Maya mythology, diseases could be inflicted by the gods through their magic."

Carter looked skeptically at the screen and then back at Roth. "You want us to tell the FBI director to tell the president of the United States that a drawing of a squatting man with a headdress is causing a global pandemic?"

Lund chuckled. "Go for it."

"This is ridiculous," snapped Carter. "A joke."

Roth looked at Brower. "Do *you* think it's real? Monica does because she's seen it. If my daughter were here, she could *prove* it's real. She could levitate your coffee cup right off the table."

"Whether or not I personally believe your story is immaterial," Brower said. He'd smoothed his features again, regaining his self-control. "The director needs to believe it. And right now, he doesn't."

"What about the forensics?" Roth said. "The bullets that killed the FBI agents in Bozeman. Did they come from the guns the agents were carrying?"

"Yes," Brower said flatly.

"So, isn't that evidence?" Roth thundered, gesticulating wildly.

"Agent Garcia is the wild card," Lund said.

Brower glanced at him and nodded once.

"What?" Roth said, exasperated.

"I get it," Lund said, sighing. "The agents' own bullets killed them. Fired from their own guns. But who's to say that Garcia didn't take their guns, one by one, and shoot them and stage the crime scene. You left on snowmobiles with Agent Sanchez. He stayed behind."

"I *saw* it happen," Roth said. "I saw those bullets arc back at the people who'd fired them."

"So did I." Monica had a haunted look in her eyes, and he knew he wasn't the only one who'd lost sleep over what he'd seen.

"And yet, where there's room for doubt, it will fester," Lund said. "Now you see what I had to deal with, every day? Skeptics."

"It doesn't matter that we were eyewitnesses?" Monica snapped.

"Don't get emotional," Carter said.

"But it's okay if *you* do?" she shot back.

Brower rubbed his chin. "Tell us about the Jaguar Prophecies again, Mr. Roth. The translation you got from the student in LA."

"This?" Roth asked, wagging the phone at them. "The stuff you just got done saying you don't believe in?"

"Humor us," Brower said.

"The Dresden Codex contained several blank pages. It's made of bark pulp. I thought it highly strange that it had been preserved for over five centuries with *blank* pages. Well, there's a glyph that made the writing invisible. My daughter, Suki . . . 'counteracted' it? I don't know the right word. She canceled it. I took photos, and the student, Illari, deciphered it and gave me the translation." Roth swiped to another image, one of a piece of binder paper with the translation scrawled out by hand, with a few words crossed out for other ones.

"Just summarize it," Brower said.

"It's a prophecy of Kukulkán, one of the chief Maya gods. It predicts the Maya will be scattered by foreigners. Hint, Cortés and the conquistadors. But if the foreigners don't repent, it says, then a remnant of Jacob—a remnant of the house of Jacob—will trample through a numerous people like a young jaguar through sheep. Sheep can't defend themselves. So, basically, it predicts a reversal of what happened back in 1520. The prophecy was written in the codex, an almanac that helped them track future events, like eclipses and the planets' rotations. Most of the codex is about that kind of stuff. But this prophecy was set to happen after the end of the Maya doomsday calendar. Calakmul told me himself that 2012 was the trigger. It was the beginning of the end times."

"Again, this doesn't help us," Carter said. "It's not actionable intelligence."

Brower looked thoughtful. He leaned forward, interlocking his fingers. "How did Cortés and a few Spanish mercenaries take out the Indigenous population of that land? Was it purely a technological advantage?"

Roth shook his head. "It wasn't any one thing, Mr. Brower. The Spanish brought gunpowder *and* smallpox, which ravaged the population. It's highly contagious, and they had no herd immunity to it. Yes, the Spanish had superior weapons, but they mostly triggered a civil war within the Aztec empire."

"Who was the ruler?"

"Montezuma. Most historians believe Cortés kidnapped Montezuma and then had him killed, triggering the massacre on La Noche Triste. Many Aztec nobility were slaughtered during a feast day. That led to the population rising up against Cortés and the Spaniards. Some say that was the tipping point."

"You sound skeptical, Mr. Roth," Brower said.

"Well, I've researched this quite a bit over the last year. Some newer scholarship suggests Montezuma—or Moctezuma, which is his real name—wasn't afraid of the Spanish but actually lured them into his city as a sort of trophy or prize. Like exotic animals in a menagerie. They were basically under house arrest until they decided to assassinate the king and break out. And, as they say, 'Winners write the history books.'"

"And what's the point of this?" Carter sighed. "We need to prep for our meeting with the director," he said in an undertone to Brower.

But Brower was looking keenly at Roth, his gaze not wavering. "Do you know what exponential curves are, Mr. Roth?"

"I'm a historian, but I also like math."

"They too have tipping points," Brower said. "What we're seeing with this virus is just the beginning of an exponential curve. Once we hit that tipping point, it's going to spread so fast it's almost impossible to imagine what real life is going to be like in the very near future. Like the smallpox epidemic in the sixteenth century. It's difficult for the human mind to grasp exponential things. If we're dealing with a rampant virus that affects every person not immune—which will be nearly everyone on earth *except* a few elite—then when we hit the tipping point and the curve goes vertical, we'll be helpless, our healthcare system overrun, and our military and law enforcement apparatus disabled."

"Exactly," Roth said. "What you're saying is we don't have much time to counter Calakmul's plan before we *can't*."

Brower nodded. "If Jacob Calakmul believes he's fulfilling this prophecy and has been acting accordingly, he may be trying to duplicate historical events. Even if the prophecy isn't real, he seems to believe otherwise."

"There is plenty of room to believe Calakmul has deluded himself." Roth had shared Illari's translation with Monica and knew she'd forwarded it to certain officials.

"In my opinion, he's more than a person of interest. He's public enemy number one. We need to find him. Now."

"Hunting Jacob Calakmul is virtually impossible," Monica said. "He doesn't use modern technology like smartphones or computers. When the SEAL team went to Cozumel, they found the place abandoned."

"You sent a SEAL team to the resort?" Roth gaped.

Monica smiled. "Well, the Department of Defense did. We haven't been sitting on our hands, Jonathon."

"That's classified!" Carter snapped with irritation.

Roth chuckled in relief. Brower was on board. So was Monica. Carter was a holdout, but maybe Carter didn't matter.

"In 1519, Cortés was a nobody," Roth said, tapping the desk. "He was in trouble with the Spanish crown. His own men didn't like him. There's a legend he burned the ships after arriving in Mexico to send the message to the crew that there was no turning back. Just a legend, mind you, and probably a distortion of history. But by all accounts, Cortés and his wife were about as dysfunctional as the Real Housewives families. He wasn't liked, and he's only famous because he succeeded. The turning point was when they tried to assassinate Montezuma." Roth felt the pieces begin to click into place in his mind. He stopped talking, his mind whirling.

Brower was staring at him too. He'd also made the connection. "You're thinking of history repeating itself."

"Like John Wilkes Booth?" Lucas asked from the end of the table.

CHAPTER FOUR

HIDDEN BEACH

MARIETAS ISLANDS, MEXICO

January 8

The yacht left Punta Mita, a private peninsula on the coast of Mexico near Puerto Vallarta. It was one of dozens of luxury yachts that had been in the harbor, ships owned by Russian oligarchs, Chinese billionaires, and the wealthiest of the American tech elites. So far, Punta Mita hadn't been affected by the plague beginning to cascade around the world. There were parties lasting all day and night. Music and dancing.

Jacob would give the final warning tonight. The time had come to retreat to the Maya Riviera. Those who had paid the price would be protected against the end times. Those who hadn't would help feed the fish among the coral reef.

He leaned back in his cushioned seat on the deck of the boat, his shirt open to the breeze. He wore expensive sunglasses against the glare. The golden Maya jewelry on his wrist caught the light, as did the ring on his finger and the Aztec medallion that lay on his chest. It too was of solid gold, made centuries ago. The medallion could be worn out in the open now, marking him as one of the priests of the order. The time for disguises was coming to an end.

Angélica was lounging on a sofa, her skin bronzed by the sun, her beach robe open. Her bare abdomen was completely smooth. The bullet that had nearly killed her had not left a mark. Time hadn't healed the wound. It had *unwound* it. He'd shown her his greatest secret— he'd brought her to Aztlán, to the tree and mountain that could turn someone young again. His own vigor had improved since going there. His feelings for her—the unquenchable desire of a younger man—had barely been slaked since they'd made it back to the Jaguar Temple with their hostage. He'd let Angélica visit his private cenote, built beneath his palace and fed by the man-made canals and natural *aguadas* in the area. That had been a magical night.

Angélica turned her head and looked at him, her blond hair streaming in the breeze. The throb of desire struck again.

"You haven't told me how you will kill the American president," she said, giving him a seductive smile. "Are there to be any more secrets between us?"

A spray of sea water kicked up from the edge of the yacht. The temperature was perfect, the humidity ripe and golden. He eased out of his chair and padded over to her, barefoot. He felt the growl of the jaguar inside him. His magic tingled within.

"You know more than anyone else who has ever been trusted," he whispered, nuzzling her neck with his lips. "My father never shared Aztlán with my mother. You are the first woman to know of it in centuries, I think."

"Centuries? Maybe I should be fearful that I'm the first to know in so long."

He nodded, stealing a kiss from her mouth before pulling away. "Yes, we must both be careful. There are those who would kill for the knowledge. We're almost there."

The yacht was nearly to the island. He'd been there multiple times, of course. It was an uninhabited island where the Mexican military had practiced bombing techniques. They'd inadvertently created an inland beach, inaccessible by land. It was called Hidden Beach—or Lover's Beach, depending on why it was sought out. Surrounded by cliffs and jungle, the beach was the ultimate private retreat. The Mexican government banned tourists from going there because of *environmental* concerns, but in truth Jacob was the reason for the ban. He'd decided to keep it for himself. He owned the Punta Mita peninsula. The luxury hotels paid *him* to lease the land for their hotels and comforts. And the island, which he also owned, was only a fifteen-minute ride from the hub of resorts.

Angélica sat up as the yacht began to slow. In the past, the area had been overcrowded with tourists coming to visit the pristine waters. Without them, the area had begun to heal, the aquatic life reviving.

The captain of the yacht maneuvered to the right spot on the rocky cliff before killing the engine. There was no beach there—it was hidden within the island.

Then the captain killed the engine. "We're here, *jefe*."

Jacob walked to the edge of the yacht. He removed his shirt and tossed it aside. Angélica slipped out of her sheer beach robe, revealing the bikini beneath. Together, they jumped off the yacht into the warm, fragrant waters of the ocean.

"Hold on to my fin," he told her and then used the magic to transform into a dolphin. She hooked her hand on the dorsal fin, and he swept through the waters. The beach was only accessible during low tide. It was a short swim, even shorter for a dolphin. The opening between the rock and the water was barely six feet during low tide. During high tide, the beach was flooded.

Passing beneath the jagged rocks, they entered the secret cove. Jacob transformed back into a man again, and they walked together up the beach. The white sand stretched for hundreds of yards in a circle. The blue-green water of the sea came lapping or crashing up onto it according to the rhythm of the tide. In the cliffs above, they could see the verdant brush of the jungle.

"This is . . . this is so beautiful!" Angélica said, walking around in a full circle. It was just the two of them. No one else.

"This is my gift to you." He clasped her hand and kissed her knuckles. "Hidden Beach belongs to you. So does the Punta Mita peninsula. They're *yours.*"

Her eyes widened with shock.

"A queen has her own lands. Her own domains. Cozumel is mine. The Isla Mujeres I already gave you. And this I give you too. Our secret place."

"I'm . . . I'm overwhelmed," she said. She looked so beautiful in that moment he wanted to give her everything.

"I almost lost you, *cariño*," he whispered huskily. "I want each moment with you to matter." He extended his arms. "No technology here. No spy satellites. I've seen to it that we're safe from prying eyes."

Her mouth parted, the excited smile on her face showing him he'd pleased her with this gift. She was grateful. She was always so grateful.

"Thank you," she said, coming close and kissing him. "Thank you for this."

"You asked me how I was going to kill the American president. I would not speak of it on the boat. As much as I trust *el capitán*, it is not wise to share secrets too loosely."

"So you will tell me?" she asked eagerly.

"Tell me what you know of Huracán."

"He was the rival of Kukulkán of course."

"Indeed he was. The two were great rivals in those days. What was Huracán known for?"

"He was the god of jaguars. Your priesthood comes from him," she said.

"How was he depicted?"

She blinked, thinking quickly. "I don't remember."

"I take away your computer and you forget?" he teased. She always accepted his teasing. He liked that too. "Huracán was one of the creation gods. He was master of wind, fire, and storm."

"Yes!" she said, sighing. "Now I remember. And his foot."

"Some believe he lost it battling a monster. But that's not true. He is depicted with an obsidian mirror on his foot or his chest because he knew the magic of the *smoking mirror*. He is the god of the night sky, the hurricane, hostility, discord, rulership, temptation, jaguars, divination, sorcery, beauty, war, and conflict."

Her eyes sparkled more with each term he said. She wanted to learn the magic of the *kem äm* so she could levitate objects. Control people and things. He could tell she was a little jealous that he'd begun teaching Mr. Roth's daughter, Suki, the secrets of sorcery. Although she'd feigned concern about the price the "innocent" child would have to pay to fully harness the power, he knew it was at least in part because she wished for the magic herself.

"Huracán is mighty," Angélica said.

"Strong enough to defeat Kukulkán, certainly," Jacob agreed. "To rule all these lands. The magic of the smoking mirror bestows the ability to travel *between* mirrors. Years ago, the Mexican government gave certain relics as gifts to the Americans, the British, the Germans, and other powerful nations. The Maya made mirrors out of obsidian. A jaguar priest can walk from mirror to mirror. And there is one inside the White House."

She had a look of wonder as she whispered, "You already have a way inside?"

He nodded, tipping her chin. "Many of my order have been gathering in Washington, DC, to witness its fall. Roth has turned on me. I know he is there. He thinks he is safe. Just as Cortés had Moctezuma murdered, so will I do the same unto their leader. As the prophecy said, *and none can deliver them.* The American president has been meeting with his cabinet because of the pandemic. On Friday, every member will be in the room. All at the same time."

"How do you know this?" Angélica asked.

"I have someone who used to be a college student like you"—he stroked her chin—"someone who works in that false temple. I know about the meeting. I know where it will be held. And that is when I will take him. I will bring him to our lands to execute him, to cut out his heart and throw his body down the temple steps."

"And the other jaguar priests?" she asked.

"They are taking their places now to abduct the other leaders. One day. One strike. First we unleashed the plague on the world's unsuspecting populace. Now we take out their beating heart to show them we mean to rule once again. The new capital of the world will be the Jaguar Temple in Calakmul."

CHAPTER FIVE

Jaguar Temple

Calakmul Biosphere Reserve

January 8

Sweat stung Suki's eyes. It ran down her ribs and trickled down her legs. She hated sweating. But what was even worse was the suspicion that if any of the balls dropped, she would die.

It was surreal actually. Weeks ago, she'd been stressing out about being the stage manager for the high school musical, a role that was almost entirely behind a curtain and out of sight of the audience. Now she was in the middle of a forsaken jungle with no internet, wild animals that would try to kill her if she managed to escape the huge temple complex, and a crazy lady who was forcing her to levitate heavy rubber balls and spin them around the arena all while yelling at her in ancient Mayan.

At least Yoda hadn't yelled at Luke Skywalker. Or whipped him with a reed.

Suki hadn't practiced the Maya magic in Bozeman—mostly because she had still been afraid of it—until that night at Brice's house. She'd certainly never imagined pushing herself *this* hard. The balls used in the death game each weighed about four pounds. She wasn't lifting them with her arms, of course, but lifting them with her mind was real work. The strain and stress of trying to keep five of them orbiting the game court in the ruins simultaneously was . . . totally wrecking her.

The crazy old lady walked around her, speaking in K'iche', one of the native tongues of the ancient Maya. Magic allowed Suki to understand what was said, but she struggled to speak the language herself. She'd thought learning Spanish was tough. Mayan was freakishly impossible. Yet every day she learned a few more words that she used to communicate with the servants who lived at the site of the ancient temple.

"You must focus! Up! Up! Keep them higher!"

Suki's internal conflict had caused two of the five balls to lose momentum, and they'd started wobbling out of orbit. It took so much concentration! And maybe that was the point of the exercise. To train someone from Gen Z how to stick with a single thought for a long time.

"I'm trying," Suki panted, willing the errant orbs back into the pattern.

The old crone didn't speak English. She glared at Suki, circling around behind her. Sometimes she'd whack that reed stick of hers against Suki's legs. It hurt. A lot. But there was no denying the threat of pain urged her to keep things going.

The sun was nearly down. It amazed Suki how every structure at the temple compound had been erected to follow the seasons and the rising and setting of the sun and other celestial bodies. The orientation of the ball court was aligned with the heavens. When she and her family had been tricked into the death game just over a year ago, they'd only spent a few days at the Jaguar Temple. Now that Suki had been there for almost two weeks, she knew the compound a lot better. She'd been able to explore a bit and marveled at the vastness of the hidden temple.

The place where Jacob Calakmul ruled supreme.

The thought of him made her shudder. He'd tasked the crone with testing what Suki could do with the *kem äm*—the ancient Maya magic that made the city glow at night, provided a barrier like a force field against the jungle, enabled her to make rubber balls scoot without touching them, and so much more.

He'd urged the crone to try to break Suki. To see how deeply and quickly she could learn the magic. If Suki were no longer useful, she imagined she'd end up on the sacrificial altar getting open heart surgery for free.

"Do you see it? Do you see the evening star?"

Suki was facing west. And there, just over the tree line of the jungle, she glimpsed it. The Maya called it the morning and evening star, but it was really the planet Venus.

"Je'," Suki answered. That was K'iche' for *yes*. She'd picked that up on the first day.

"See it? Now pull it."

Had she understood correctly? Pull it? As in . . . pull on the planet?

"Jek'?" Suki asked.

"Jik'. Jik' uxlab." The crone insisted. Like tugging someone's hand? But with the breath? That made even less sense.

"Jik' uxlab?" Suki repeated.

"Jik' uxlab. Jik' uxlab," the woman said again, breathing in deeply through her nose. She cupped her hands as if holding a sphere right around her navel, which was exposed, along with a lot of her body because of the tribal clothing worn by the people at the temple. Suki's clothes from Bozeman had been taken away on the first day.

Breathe. Breathe and pull. When her family had been forced to compete in the death game with the Beasley family, Suki had gone into a sort of trance. She'd known she and her brothers and father would all die if she didn't figure out how to use the *kem äm*. The intense pressure of this moment reminded her of that one—only her family's lives weren't on the line. Now it was just her and the old woman in the arena.

Suki stared at the planet, at the speck of light beaming at her from over a hundred million miles away. Seeing the light made her stomach flutter with wonder. She knew it was from the sun reflecting off the planet's surface, crossing all that space.

And then it happened. The right vibe struck her, just like it had that day a year ago. She felt a quiver in her stomach, like a little tugging behind her belly button. The balls began moving in sync with her body, as if they were attached to invisible hula hoops around her. Her mind opened like a flower. And suddenly it was *easy*. The strain of keeping all the balls going vanished. They glided along their various orbits, some with a shorter radius than the others, each in a different pattern.

"*K'amo!*" exclaimed the crone with delight. That meant *good*.

Suki was aware of her entire body in that moment, as if every cell within her had awoken. *Hello, elbow bone. Hello, appendix. Hello, toenails.* Even the sweat no longer bothered her. It was part of her, an essential part of her body needed to regulate her heat and heartbeat. It was a feeling of being alive unlike anything else. She knew some kids at Gallatin High School who liked to vape or smoke weed because of how it made them feel, but even though she'd never partaken in those dubious pleasures, she knew they couldn't compare to this sensation.

The crone reached down and picked up another heavy rubber ball and tossed it to her. Effortlessly, Suki absorbed it into the orbiting balls.

This is so chill, Suki said to herself.

"*K'amo. K'amo!*" the crone said, pleased, walking in a circuit around her.

And then the stick whacked into Suki's legs. Pain cut through the bliss. Suki yelped in surprise, and all the balls thumped down to the dirt, the momentum destroyed. Gravity brought each down instantly.

"Ow!" Suki complained, whirling around and looking at the old woman's vindictive smile.

The crone jabbed the reed stick at her, and Suki backed away so it wouldn't poke her.

"Listen! Learn! Must focus. Even if worried. Even in pain. Many kinds of pain. Burning pain. Illness. Biting pain. Throbbing pain. Fang pain. A pain like being homesick."

All was spoken in Mayan, all understood because of magic. Suki's mind snagged on that last word—*q'atzq'ayil*. She *was* homesick. She missed her brothers. She missed her dad. She missed her boyfriend, Brice. Those were pains that wouldn't leave.

"Drink xocolatl. *Get rest. Enough for today. Go! The master returns to see progress. Do not fail. You fail . . . you die!"*

Suki's legs were still flaming from the surprise blow. She nodded and limped to the end of the ball court. One wave of the hand dispelled the webbing of *kem äm*. A servant approached with *xocolatl*, and she quickly took a sip. The chocolatey drink gave her a burst of energy and focus. It was better and worked faster than espresso.

By the time Suki reached the royal palace, one of the majestic structures in the temple grounds, she could ignore the pain in her legs. Quickly jogging up the steps, she passed by the scary-looking warriors who protected it night and day. One of the warriors leered at her. She wanted to send a floating rubber ball smashing into his face.

When she reached the main level, she went to her private room. Jane Louise was there, using a primitive broom to sweep dead bugs away. Two female servants stood by, holding fans made of palm fronds. That was the only air-conditioning inside the building.

"You're back!" Jane Louise said with happiness and rushed to hug her.

Jane Louise was the youngest of the Beasley children, and the only member of her family who'd survived the death game. Suki had believed the entire family had been executed, but Jacob Calakmul had spared the youngest, using her as a slave in the compound. A drudge. Perhaps he'd have another purpose for her when she was older, but at present she was only nine. The emotional anguish of losing everything and being thrown into a life of service might have been too much for her if Suki's mother hadn't also been spared. Her mom had taken care of Jane Louise.

"I'm starving," Suki said, hugging the little girl tight. "What's there to eat? Any mango?"

"Lots of mangoes." She took Suki over to a wooden table where platters of fruit and skewers of meat had been set out. Suki picked up a slice of mango with her fingers and devoured it. It was so sweet and delicious she wanted to faint. The meat skewers could be pretty sketchy. She never knew what kind of animal she was eating, and the thought of eating a coati was disturbing. They were too cute, Mexico's version of raccoons.

Suki's mom, Sarina, had *disappeared* just before Suki's abduction. The warriors had been searching the jungles for her, but they'd never find her there. She was hidden among them as an old crone. It wasn't a disguising magic. Suki's mom had literally aged forty years overnight, so no one recognized her. Ix Chel had done it—she'd turned her into a crone, one of the goddess's own iterations, so she could evade notice. Jacob Calakmul had been furious about the "escape," of course, and Suki was guarded night and day to prevent her from leaving too. There were always people watching her. Sometimes it felt like even the mosquitoes were watching her.

Suki had only been able to talk to her mother twice since she'd arrived, and both times had been instigated by her mom in the middle of the night. They'd hugged and kissed each other, and even though her mom didn't look the way she was used to, she was still her mother, and being reunited with her made Suki hopeful in a way she hadn't thought possible when she was hustled onto that plane in Bozeman.

Sarina had stayed at the Jaguar Temple because she knew the prophesied end times were coming—although not the prophecy that Jacob Calakmul believed in. No, what was coming was the return of Kukulkán and his followers. Ix Chel had been preparing for it. The goddess would have helped Sarina leave if she'd so chosen, but she'd asked her to stay behind and help—and so she had.

"These are good too," Jane Louise said, picking up a brown-colored fruit and eating it.

Suki took a bite of one. It had a brown-sugar flavor. Nice.

"We're leaving tonight," Jane Louise said in a pointedly offhand voice, going for a banana next.

"What?" Suki asked. As an incentive for Suki to train harder, she'd been allowed to spend time with Jane Louise—providing a break from the servitude the little girl was forced to endure.

"She'll come get us when the moon is high. She said, 'Don't go to sleep.'" She nodded to emphasize each word.

"Where are we going?" Suki whispered.

Jane Louise smiled. "Back to her island."

Ix Chel's island, she meant. *Cozumel.*

CHAPTER SIX

Jaguar Temple

Calakmul Biosphere Reserve

January 8

Nervous anticipation wriggled inside Suki's stomach as she waited. Nightfall brought the magical illumination of the ruins. From the windows of the palace, she could see the hidden city spread out beneath her. The jungle surrounding the land was black, but the interior was lit by stelae carved with figures of ancient Maya—warriors, priests, queens, and the various gods and goddesses. Through gaps in the jungle trees overhead, stars twinkled brightly. But the moon hadn't risen above the trees yet.

The interior of the palace was mazelike in design. She'd gotten lost easily at first, but now she knew the layout and could easily get from the patios to the housing structures. There was a pyramid on the northern block of the royal quarters that she wasn't allowed to explore, along with underground tunnels that led to a private cenote. Again, strictly off-limits.

How would they leave?

A servant offered her a drink of *xocolatl,* which she declined as she kept walking the grounds outside the palace, trying to quell her nervous energy. The noises from the jungle were familiar to her now, and she recognized the distinctive screech of howler monkeys in the distance.

Then, finally, she spied the moon high above the courtyard, in the gap between the trees. It was a full moon—or nearly one. It appeared through the gaps in the leaves, a brilliant silver ball. As soon as she saw it, Suki felt the magic stir inside her.

Ix Chel was the moon goddess of the Maya. The moon was a symbol of her power, and now it was also a symbol of escape.

Suki bit her lip and hurried back to her room to find Jane Louise. She parted the bead curtain of the doorway and saw the Beasley girl kneeling on the floor picking up fallen flower petals.

"It's time—" Suki started to say, then cut herself off when she noticed Angélica was in the room.

She and Jacob had been together, off doing who knows what. The two of them were always together now. While Angélica had been his employee at the resort on Cozumel, the two couldn't keep their hands off each other now. It was pretty gross.

Jacob wasn't supposed to come back until tomorrow, though. Had they returned early?

"Time for what?" Angélica asked, cocking her head.

Suki's mind went blank. *Crap.* "We were going to . . . play . . . ," she stammered.

The woman's brow furrowed. "Play what?"

Panic sizzled in Suki's chest. She felt her cheeks flush.

"Hide-and-seek," Jane Louise said, lifting her head and smiling innocently.

Angélica looked from the little girl to Suki and then back again.

"I know I'm a little old for it," Suki offered. "But the palace has so many twists and turns. I promised her we'd play tonight after the sun went down. She's just a little girl, and she works so hard all day."

Angélica stepped forward, shaking her head. "It isn't a good night for that, Suki. I'm sorry. Jacob wishes to meet with you."

Nervous anxiety tightened its hold on her. "Wait . . . tonight?"

"Yes. He wants to see you."

"Oh . . . I guess . . ." Suki's mind raced as she tried to think of a way out of it.

"Are you all right?" Angélica asked, stroking a finger along Suki's cheek.

She didn't like being touched by people she hardly knew, and sometimes even by people she did know. "I worked hard today and got beaten for it. In high school, you just get grades."

"I know. You've learned quickly. Even I am not allowed to be taught what you are learning." There was a twinge of jealousy in her tone. Suki didn't understand why. Angélica was beautiful, smart, and yes—the future dictator of the world had a thing for her.

"Okaaay," Suki said. "Um . . . so he wants to see me now? Can't it be later?"

Suspicion crinkled the other woman's brow. *Crap. Double crap.* "You're acting strange tonight."

"I'm just nervous," Suki said. "I'm still scared of him, that's all. I didn't exactly *choose* to be here. Kidnapped, remember?"

Angélica still looked at Suki as if she were acting pretty sus. But she couldn't know what was going on, right? For all her smarts, she couldn't actually read Suki's mind.

"There is no safer place in all the world than being right here, right now, Suki Roth. You should feel *grateful* to be here. And grateful that Jacob thinks you have potential. But when he asks for you, you *come.* Let's go."

"If you put it that way," Suki said glumly. A little pout would help seal the deal on the surly teenager bit. She sighed. "Sorry, Jane Louise. I guess we'll play another time."

Jane Louise nodded and went back to picking up the fallen petals, and Suki followed Angélica to Jacob's private quarters. She'd gone there a few times to report on her progress. The room was decked out with jaguar pelts; golden statues, vases, and sculptures; wooden masks; and even those wicked-looking swords made from wedges of obsidian. The decor was centuries old, but she was pretty sure he wouldn't react well if she suggested a refresh. As they entered, Jacob emerged from the stone stairway leading to the underground section. He wore Maya clothing, not the Western outfits he donned in the outside world. He was closer to her age now, after whatever he and Angélica had done in the mountains—younger and fitter. But he had the same eyes, the creepy eyes of a man who had lived a long time. Too long. Fear snaked inside her. Just being in the same room as him made her nervous.

"Wait for me in the cenote," Jacob said to Angélica, giving her a nod.

Angélica returned a sly smile and then went down the stone steps. Jacob brushed his hands together, examining Suki.

"You have a difficult decision to make," he said to her, his tone formal and cold.

"I know," Suki said with a shrug. "College, work, join the circus."

His eyes flashed with anger, and she wished she hadn't blurted out that last part.

"Just as I chose to spare Eric Beasley's daughter, I've considered sparing you."

Suki felt her anxiety spiking. "Considered" wasn't very solid.

"Thank you," she whispered.

"I don't need another servant sweeping floors," Jacob said. "You have innate power. You figured out the *kem äm* . . . and you've progressed. I need to decide when you can be put to more important use. You could become one of the Kowinem."

As he said the word, she felt a sickening feeling of darkness pulse within her. The nearest translation in her mind was *traitors*.

"Um . . . what is that?" she asked.

"The Kowinem are an ancient order. The jaguar priests are part of it. There are secrets and magic you haven't learned. The *tzij teojil* are words that draw power into us. Through rings and other jewels, the power can do things beyond your imagining. But in order to become part of the Kowinem, you must do certain things. Swear certain oaths. Blood oaths."

"So if I choose to join you, I'd be stuck," Suki said. "I couldn't leave the club."

"Exactly," Jacob said. "The members of the MS-13 gang are part of the Kowinem. You've seen their power. They too have made oaths. Promises. Because you were raised in a different culture, you do not understand the tremendous opportunity I am offering you, Suki. Other youths here at the compound would *kill* to be offered this chance."

Suki swallowed. "You mean that metaphorically, right?"

He shook his head no.

Her heart began to pound with dread. *Oh crap. Oh crap.* Then she remembered the magic she'd learned. *Nake'ik. Nake'ik. Nake'ik.* Repeating those Mayan words in her mind, grasping on to them, she triggered feelings of peace and calm. The panic immediately started to subside.

"In order to invoke the higher magic," Jacob said, "you need to make a sacrifice. It has always been so. From the beginning. It is an *honor* to be so chosen. When a person is chosen, he or she must kill a family member in secret. A sibling. A cousin. Even a father or a *mother*." He let the word linger in the air.

Suki trembled.

"Your mother has disappeared instead of helping you fulfill your destiny. Your *ch'umilal*." He held up his hand, fingers splayed, the tips pointing toward her. He shook his head. "Life is meaningless when it is cut short for no reason. But when it is offered up as a sacrifice, it can invoke tremendous power. Since your mother is no longer here, you will

43

have to choose another in her place. For the sacrifice to be appropriate, it must be someone you *care* about, not someone you despise. Even a dear friend or a *child*."

Suki stared at him, her jaw hanging open. "Jane Louise?" Was he serious? This was more than gross. It was repulsive.

"Or your father. I plan to kill him anyway, so at least his death would serve your future if *you* did it. I give you three days to make your choice, Suki. Kill one, and the rest will be spared. Otherwise, you all die. The end times are upon us. I will overthrow the United States government first, along with the other major powers in Europe. The plague will take care of the rest of the world as it spreads. The jaguar priests are ready to fulfill *their ch'umilal.* What we've waited centuries for. By killing your president, I will grow in *my* power. You will see. And then you will make your choice."

"So I have to choose in three days?" Suki repeated, dumbfounded.

"The president of the United States will be taken on Friday. We celebrate on Saturday. If you choose not to join us, to claim your birthright, then you will be sacrificed as part of the ceremony. Along with your father and brothers."

Suki couldn't believe what she was hearing. What kind of choice was this?

"My father isn't even here."

"He's in Washington, DC, right now," Jacob said. "And that is where I am going to fulfill my destiny." He lowered his hand. "Three days to decide. You kill someone close to you, or you all die on my altar."

"How could I choose?" Suki demanded. "That's . . . that's just awful."

"Choose or die with them," Jacob said. "There are others who can take your place in this temple. If you do not believe I can achieve my plans, then wait and see. I was *prophesied* to do it."

The look of energy in his eyes was intense.

"Go," he said curtly.

Suki nodded, numb, and walked out of his private chamber, passing through the screen of beads that clicked and clacked as she parted it. Her stomach was sick. Calakmul would force her to make an impossible decision. She'd never thought she'd say so, but this was worse than the death games.

Dizzy, she walked back to her private room.

Her mom was waiting on the mat, sitting cross-legged across from Jane Louise, holding her hands. The moon shone through the window, bathing them both in light. Her mom's silver hair shone in the brilliant glow.

"It's time to go," her mother said in a voice that rang with power.

Filled with relief, Suki dropped down to the mat. "Thank goodness. You figured a way out?"

"Yes, we need to link hands."

Suki didn't hesitate. She took Jane Louise's hand and then the wrinkled hand of her mother.

"Breathe. Feel the moonlight's pull. Listen. Can you hear the sea calling? It's Cozumel. It is a nexus for Ix Chel. Feel it. Hear it call you."

Suki's heart trembled with her burden. But she calmed her mind. She calmed her heart. Holding her mother's hand comforted her, even if it no longer looked like her mother's hand.

In the stillness, she heard a mosquito buzzing near her ear. She hated that annoying sound, but beyond it was something else. Something in the distance.

An ocean crashing on the surf.

Then she could smell it. The salty smell. Feel a cool breeze soothing her neck.

"This is the prayer. This is the word. *Rapinik*. Think it. Pray it."

The word meant *to fly*. She knew that intuitively. But it meant so much more than that.

"*Rapinik,*" they all said in unison.

A tug at the back of her navel.

"Open your eyes, daughters. *Breathe.*"

Suki opened her eyes. The three of them were now sitting on a beach in the sand. The moon was fixed above the horizon, silver— pale—picturesque. A sea turtle rested in the sand right by them. It was huge, beautiful, peaceful. It swung its knobby head to look at them. Weird. Totally weird. Suki turned to look at her mom and saw that the aging had been reversed. She blinked in surprise. It was her mom, just as she'd remembered her when they'd first come to Cozumel.

Relief radiated through her. She'd feared the aging would stick, and she'd have to face losing her mom again after finally being reunited with her.

"You're young again!" she exclaimed.

Her mom flinched, then lifted a hand to her face, touching her own cheek. A slow smile spread across her face, and she looked upward at the moon.

"Thank you, Ix Chel. Thank you."

A car horn beeped nearby.

"*¡Oye! ¡Vámanos pues! ¡Es* okay. *¡Es* okay!"

Suki recognized the man's voice. It was Jorge from Huellas de Pan, the orphanage that had offered them shelter when they were first on the run from Jacob Calakmul.

CHAPTER SEVEN

CHAPARRAL INN

WASHINGTON, DC

January 9

The elevator beeped, and the doors opened. The smell of pancakes and sausage struck Roth first, then the noise of clinking silverware and the murmur of guests. He checked his phone screen again, looking for a follow-up text from Lund, who'd told him Jordan would be meeting them for breakfast—a surprise for the boys. It was time to switch hotels again, which meant they finally got to eat breakfast in the common room. Truthfully, Roth wasn't comfortable eating in a common area right now when any sound made him jumpy. But he knew the boys missed being around other people.

Their stuff would be transferred to another location while they were gone for the day, and they'd transfer to their new hotel that night. The twins were excited to be away from their room for once. The novelty of playing video games and watching TV while they were supposed to be in school had faded fast.

"I'll probably go for the waffles. They're pretty good," Lucas said. "Chocolate chips, syrup—yum-oh."

"I'm so tired of the food being cold," Brillante said. "Reheating it in the microwave just sucks."

It was a short walk to the dining area, which was already crowded. This particular hotel was directly across the street from NASA headquarters, which they could see from the window of their room on the fourth floor.

Roth was tired of moving from place to place like a fugitive. Tired of feeling hunted and on the run. They hadn't brought much with them, having left Bozeman in such a hurry.

When they reached the crowded, open room, the boys were about to hurry to the buffet line, but Roth grabbed their shoulders. "Look who's over there saving us a table."

It was Jordan, his arm in a sling. He lifted a glass of apple juice and nodded to them.

"Jordan!" Lucas bellowed. The twins hurried to the table, Roth trailing behind as he maneuvered through the other patrons.

"When'd you get here?" Brillante asked.

"How's the bullet wound? Can we see it?" Lucas cut in.

"Dudes, it's pretty sick," Jordan said. He grinned at Roth. "No way was I going to stay in that hospital any longer. I was so bored!"

Jordan had a crew cut, not too short, and dishwater-blond hair. He was in his twenties, having left the army for private security. Even with a shoulder injury, he'd managed to take out one of the jaguar priests with his marksmanship skill. He'd saved their lives.

"Have you been to the Spy Museum yet?" Jordan asked. "It's the best!"

"Dad says we can go when this is all over," Lucas replied with a flash of annoyance.

"Go get breakfast," Roth said to the twins. "Grab me one of the packaged muffins." He sank down into an open seat across from Jordan as the boys headed off, positioning himself so he could see them.

"They're good kids," Jordan said. "Any word about Suki?"

Roth shook his head. "Nada."

"That sucks. Lund told me about the ransomware attack." He took a sip from his apple juice. "We're going back to FBI headquarters after breakfast. I'll drive you."

"You can drive with one arm?"

Jordan gave a half shrug. "The sling is just for show and sympathy. I'm not saying I want to arm wrestle Dwayne Johnson today, but it's not that bad. I can even take showers again. Impressive, huh?"

"Why do we need to go back?"

"Lund wouldn't tell me. Just said to drop you off. I'm hoping Monica will be there. Is she still in town?"

Roth arched his eyebrows. "Saw her yesterday."

Jordan nodded his head enthusiastically. "Good to hear."

His interest in Monica, and hers in him, was obvious. Roth always missed Sarina—but sometimes, like now, the loss was a bone-deep ache. He'd figured she was gone forever, but now he wasn't so sure. He'd seen what Calakmul's magic could do. Surely he could have cured her . . .

Even if she had survived the diabetic coma, though, Jacob might have killed her—and Suki—out of vengeance. He didn't know. Couldn't know. Sleep didn't come easily anymore. He was worried sick that his actions would have consequences he wouldn't be able to live with.

When the boys returned with breakfast, they chatted it up with Jordan about video games, sight-seeing in DC, and other small talk. After they were done, they went down to the parking garage and packed into Jordan's Toyota Highlander.

Going up Third Street, they passed the US Capitol building with its huge dome, then turned left on Pennsylvania Avenue. There were so many famous buildings, huge stone structures like Greek temples. So different from the gray limestone of the Maya ruins in the Yucatán and the pyramid shapes of differing sizes and heights. That was the future facing DC. If Calakmul succeeded, the old buildings would be torn down and replaced with new ones. In a few minutes, they were back to the J. Edgar Hoover Building despite the rush-hour traffic. Jordan drove to a car entrance that led underground, and a security guard stopped him at the top and asked to see identification.

Jordan winced as he got out his wallet and showed the man his ID. The man triggered the security obstacles to retract so they could enter the underground parking structure. Monica and Lund and another agent were waiting for them at the bottom of the ramp.

"Wonder if she's dating anyone," Jordan murmured, and the twins snickered in the back seat.

They slowed to a stop, and Jordan rolled down the window. "Miss me?" he asked Monica with a cocky grin.

Monica leaned down and glanced at Roth and the boys. "Welcome back," she said, ignoring the question. "Agent Fields will park the car for you. Come with me."

Jordan got out and tossed the key fob to the other agent, then looked around the gloomy parking garage. The sounds of squealing tires and engines resounded through the echoey space. Roth looked around, feeling tense and exposed.

"This way," Monica said. She brought them back inside, through security, and to a bank of elevators.

"I wasn't expecting to be back so soon," Roth said to Lund as they boarded the elevator. "What's up?"

The doors slid shut and Monica sighed. "The meeting with the director didn't go very well apparently. Everything is business as usual until we get actionable intelligence proving otherwise. We're hoping to get some today."

"How exactly?" Roth asked.

Lund cocked his head. "The student who sent you the translation of the Dresden Codex."

"Did you find her?" Roth asked. She'd proven difficult to track down. She hadn't returned to her apartment since Roth had last contacted her, nor had she responded to any of his texts. The FBI figured she was staying with family somewhere in LA. But where?

Monica nodded. "She works for Dr. Estrada actually. UC San Diego lab, the Qualcomm one."

"No way," Roth said. The only identifying information he'd known about Illari was that she was a grad student somewhere in Southern California. He'd assumed it was UCLA, not San Diego, which was much farther south.

"She and her boss took the red-eye from LAX last night. Lund has someone driving them from Dulles right now."

Roth looked at Monica. "Not the FBI?"

"We couldn't risk it," she confirmed. "It's like we told you, Jonathon. Someone is overhearing our communications. They hacked the servers in San Diego to stop us from finding the data we need. Mr. Lund suggested, and Carter agreed—surprisingly—that it would be best if Lund arranged transportation instead of the FBI. They'll be joining us later."

"Wow," Roth said. "I've never met her before. I don't even know what she looks like."

"It's progress," Lund said. "And totally not surprising that the director won't take this threat credibly right now. We need more information. I think *you* can help us get it."

"Me?" Roth said, surprised.

The elevator chimed when they reached the floor, and Monica led them through the offices to an empty conference room.

"Where is Carter and the other guy?" Roth asked.

Monica gestured for them to sit. The boys looked around and went to the end of the table. They both seemed bored. The first time they'd been to FBI headquarters, they'd been impressed and gazed around constantly. But they'd soon learned that conference rooms weren't very exciting.

"EAD Brower works for the director," she said. "He has a lot of responsibilities. Carter is in an interrogation room with Will Moretti and his attorney."

"Whoa, what a minute," Roth said, holding up his hands, feeling instantly uneasy. Because there could only be one way *he* could be of help. "You want me to talk to Moretti?"

Lund had shut the door and stood with his back to it. "Yes."

"I don't know anything about interrogating someone," Roth said.

Jordan tapped his fingertip on the table. "Give me fifteen minutes with him without his attorney, and I could get him to talk."

Monica rolled her eyes and shook her head no. "It doesn't work that way, Jordan."

"It's worth a try," he said.

Lund frowned at Jordan and gave him a curt nod to shut up. "I know you haven't been trained in interrogation, Jonathon. But I have. So has Agent Sanchez. You're going to have to trust us. We think *you* stand the best chance of getting him to talk. Now, listen. It's all about asking the right questions."

"But I don't know what to—" Roth stopped when he saw Lund fish something from his pocket.

"This is an earpiece. A very small one. Moretti almost certainly won't notice it. You might not know what to say, but *I* do."

———

Roth watched from the other side of a one-way mirror as Carter paced on one side of a table, and Moretti and his lawyer sat on the other. Jordan had stayed behind in the conference room with the boys, but Steve Lund and Monica were both watching the interview with Roth.

It was weird seeing his high school friend, who'd put so many people away over the years, in a blue jumpsuit reminiscent of the scrubs a nurse would wear. Weirder still seeing him with his wrists cuffed. His attorney was a middle-aged woman with a no-nonsense expression.

"So you can imagine our surprise, Mr. Moretti," Carter said, his tone scathing, "to find a man of your pay grade and tenure with overseas accounts worth millions of dollars." He held up a hand and ticked off his fingers. "Cayman Islands, Switzerland, Belize, Montevideo. Just to name a few."

"Agent Carter," said the attorney, "he does not have to recount his finances to you."

"My point, Mrs. Brown, is that there is ample evidence of multiple crimes in addition to the one we've already charged him with: accomplice to kidnapping."

"I am protecting my client's rights, as per—"

"I know, Mrs. Brown. I know." Carter turned to the one-way glass. "Send him in."

Lund motioned for Roth to come forward. He took a deep breath before he started moving, trying to prepare himself for the confrontation. Although he'd have Lund in his ear, he felt completely unprepared. But he had to try. He *had* to.

When Roth entered the room, Moretti's expression instantly changed from stubborn to stricken. He flinched and then looked down at his wrists, unable to meet his gaze. Lund shut the door.

There was a single chair opposite Moretti. Carter gave Roth a disdainful look and then nodded toward it. Roth sat down, feeling awkward and unsuited to the task.

"I guess it's time to roll initiative," Roth said. It was a D&D reference—when a party of characters was about to get into a fight, they'd roll a twenty-sided die to determine the order of combat.

Lund had suggested that he reference their history together, anything to soften Moretti and make him more likely to talk. It hurt to think of the old times, especially since their friend Westfall was dead—killed by Jacob Calakmul. The sting of betrayal hadn't lessened.

Moretti made an involuntary chuckle. He shook his head. "I already rolled a one."

"No, I feel like *I* did," Roth said. He blew out his breath softly, trying to stay focused. "When we got back from Mexico without Sarina . . . I almost told you what was going on. But I knew you were a cop. I figured if I told you she was being held hostage, you'd have to report it. I didn't want to involve you any more than I already had." Roth felt another stab of pain. "But you were already involved."

"You don't have to answer him," Mrs. Brown said. "Anything you say can be used against you."

Roth heard the little voice in his ear. It was so quiet, it felt like it was coming from his own thoughts. *"Remind him of what he said at the hotel. That you pissed off Calakmul."*

"At the Tidwell Hotel, you said I'd pissed off Calakmul."

Moretti lifted his head slightly, meeting Roth's gaze.

"That conversation will not be admissible evidence," Mrs. Brown said. "Anything you say here *will* be."

"He's got your wife and children," Roth said, ignoring the attorney. "He's got my wife and my daughter. He wants to kill me. Because I tried to stop this."

"You can't stop it," Moretti said. "It's too late for that."

"Mr. Moretti, I urge you—"

"Shut up," he said to his attorney, holding Roth's gaze. "I'm just stalling for time, Roth. Just like you did in Bozeman over the last year. It's all going to be over very soon. And then I won't be wearing this jumpsuit or these cuffs."

"Ask him if he knows how Calakmul plans to kill the president."

Roth stared at his friend. "So he's going to win no matter what?"

"There's no stopping it," Moretti said. "If anything, your attempts to stop him is making it all happen faster. I'm sorry, man. I was genuinely trying to help you survive what's coming."

"You didn't know Westfall was going to die."

Moretti shook his head no.

"But you should have expected it. You knew how ruthless Jacob is."

"Ask him about Calakmul and the president."

Roth ignored the instruction. If the question came out of left field, Moretti would realize he was wearing an earpiece. That he was being fed information. It needed to come across more naturally. Friend to friend.

"He doesn't share his plans, Roth. Not with me. Not with anyone. He operates like the cartels do."

Roth shrugged. "I'm not an expert on the drug trade."

"Information is compartmentalized. You catch a street dealer, he can't reveal the inner workings. He knows one person above him and a few below. No one else."

"So you don't know how Jacob is going to kill the president either?"

Moretti shook his head no.

"Good. This is good. Follow your instincts."

"Does Angélica know?"

"Who's that?" Moretti asked.

Was he lying? Or was this an example of Calakmul compartmentalizing information? "She was his personal assistant at the Cozumel resort. Blond hair, glasses."

A blink of recognition flitted through Moretti's eyes.

"You saw her," Roth whispered.

He nodded. "She'd been shot. He was . . . he was really worried about her."

Roth swallowed. So he'd given Jacob another reason to hate him. He was running out of things to say. Questions to ask. Moretti didn't know the specifics of an assassination plot. That knowledge hadn't been entrusted to him.

"Ask him why he betrayed his country. He used to be in the navy. What made him turn?"

Roth rubbed his palm on the metal table. "Remember after high school when you joined the navy? How you tried to get through SEAL school?"

Moretti shrugged.

"If you had, you would have been trying to defend us. What made you change your mind? I don't think you did it just for the money. What was it?"

"Excellent question. Well done."

"The same reason the Aztec took up arms," Moretti said.

"The Aztec?" Roth asked curiously.

"Yes." His eyes flashed with intensity. "They turned against each other to *survive.*"

CHAPTER EIGHT

FBI HEADQUARTERS—J. EDGAR HOOVER BUILDING

WASHINGTON, DC

January 9

"Tell him that a deal might be possible. It's not too late. Immunity if he testifies against Calakmul."

Roth wasn't sure if Lund had the authority to make such an offer, or if Monica or someone else in the room with them had suggested it. He wasn't sure how Carter would react to it either.

"Look," Roth said, leaning forward. He stared into his friend's eyes. His emotions were difficult to process, but there were a lot of years they'd shared. A lot of memories. He hated that his friend had betrayed him. But that didn't erase their years of history. He still cared about Moretti and his family. "What if survival weren't the only outcome? With your help, we might be able to stop him. Do you really want 'Armageddon It' to happen?" He'd dropped a reference to a Def Leppard song they both knew, hoping to soften him.

Moretti gave him a half smile. "There's no stopping it, Roth. All we can do is survive it."

"But what if we could? Isn't it worth trying? What if you had immunity for testifying against Jacob Calakmul?"

Carter chuffed. "It would have to be very helpful information. *Actionable.*"

That was apparently Carter's favorite word.

Moretti glanced at Carter with a look of contempt. "I already have all the immunity I need."

"What kind are you talking about?" Roth questioned.

"The kind that'll come in handy when people start getting sick. Or has it already started?" He glanced at Carter again. "I'm going to be fine. So is my family. Besides, I don't trust any protection the Feds could offer."

"Why not?" Carter demanded, looking insulted.

Moretti leaned back in his chair and folded his arms—at least the best he could manage while wearing handcuffs. "I've worked in law enforcement my whole career. From being an MP in the navy after I washed out of BUD/S to my current job. Do you know how many run-ins I've had with the Feds? The politics of my own department? The power trips? It's pathetic."

"Not *all* cops or agents are bad, surely," Roth said.

"What does it matter? I've seen corruption at every level, Roth. I've had to provide security details for visiting bigwigs. I've busted a state senator's kids for drugs, only to have the case tossed out because of a favor owed. I don't know how many people in this building work for Calakmul directly or indirectly. And neither do *you*." He glared at Carter. "But I'm not the only one."

Roth sighed. He had the same concern. When he went to the death game, he'd seen all the people who'd signed up to be part of the new world that Jacob was bringing. There'd been famous faces among them—the ones Lund had told him not to name yet. So Moretti wasn't wrong to be cynical. Some people felt like they were above the law. And maybe they were right. Jacob Calakmul's reach was vast. He'd proven that over and over.

Then a little thought niggled in Roth's mind. Something he hadn't thought of before. Something that didn't add up.

"Calakmul sent some MS-13 gang members to kidnap my family," Roth said. "They were coming for us the night we got back from Germany."

Moretti's shoulder twitched. "So?"

"We were just sitting at home. Except for Suki. They could have driven up and taken us. No one would have known. No one *should* have known."

Moretti looked down at the table. He said nothing.

Roth scratched the back of his neck. "But someone alerted the FBI they were coming. The FBI came right away to protect us."

"You're lucky," Moretti said, still looking down.

"I know you're the one who arranged it," Roth said. "Agent Sanchez told me. You were trying to help me."

Moretti's attorney looked startled by the news.

Silence hung in the room. Moretti wouldn't look at anybody. Although he was stone-faced, Roth could see his jaw muscles clenching. He was wrestling within himself.

"And Calakmul doesn't know," Roth whispered.

Moretti's eyes shot toward his. He looked frantic. "He does now," he said gruffly. "She works for him." He jerked his head toward the attorney.

The woman rose hastily from the chair, the metal legs of it screeching as she backed away.

Carter walked over to the door. "Oh?" he asked with a cunning smile.

"You cannot keep me here," the attorney snapped. "I have not been charged with a crime. I'm leaving."

"So you can tell your *boss?*" Carter asked. She started toward the door, but he blocked it with his body. "No need to be in such a hurry, Mrs. Brown."

"You cannot hold me against my consent," the attorney repeated, her cheeks flushed. She looked guilty. *Very* guilty.

"Actually, I have probable cause now, thanks to Mr. Moretti implicating you," Carter said. "I think we need to bring you to a separate room and start this conversation all over again from the beginning. Sanchez, can you come in here and remove her, please?"

The attorney's eyes flashed with anger. She backed away from Carter, standing behind Moretti. Then she reached down and quickly traced something on the back of Moretti's neck. Roth had seen Calakmul do that. He'd traced a glyph on Sarina when she was in a coma.

"Don't touch him!" Roth said, scooting back in his chair and coming to his feet.

Moretti twisted his shoulders, having felt her touch, his eyes wide with fear.

Carter drew his gun and pointed it at the attorney. "Hands in the air!"

The attorney complied, hands up. "I did nothing! Nothing!"

Moretti was jerking back and forth and breathing fast. The attorney backed away into the corner.

With a table separating him from the attorney, Roth felt safe looking away from her to study his friend's face. He'd gone pale.

"You okay, bud?" Roth asked him.

Moretti twisted his neck and looked at the attorney with fear. Then he began rubbing his chest with his fist. "I don't . . . something's not right," he muttered. He rubbed his chest again.

Carter kept his pistol aimed at the attorney.

Moretti began to tremble. Sweat popped out on his forehead. "What'd you do to me!" he roared, trying to stand and fumbling. He was becoming increasingly pale.

The attorney stared at him, then a little smile crept across her face. She'd done whatever she'd set out to do.

"*Te maté,*" the attorney whispered.

Roth knew what that meant in Spanish.

I killed you.

———

Lund entered the conference room with a tray of food for lunch. A few sandwiches, bags of chips, and sodas. Monica entered with him. Roth had been pacing the room while Jordan played hangman on a white board with the twins at the far end of the table.

"I'm starving," Jordan announced. "That's all for me, right?"

"It's for *all* of us," Lucas said.

Monica didn't smile. She motioned for Roth to approach her while Lund brought the tray to the far end of the table. He heard them murmuring, but his brain didn't interpret the words because his focus was on Monica. Specifically on the look in her eyes. She had news, and he wasn't going to like it.

"How's Moretti?" he asked with concern when he reached her.

"He's gone," Monica said with a sigh. "They took him to Georgetown, but he went into cardiac arrest in the ambulance. We've got his blood work going to the FBI lab at Quantico to see what toxin killed him."

Roth felt like he'd been punched in the gut. Now his two best friends from high school were dead. The pain in his own chest was searing. He felt tears sting his eyes. Moretti had stabbed him in the back, but he hadn't wanted him to go out like this. He'd wanted him to have a redemption arc, to turn this thing around.

"You won't find any toxins," Roth muttered. "I saw what she did."

"I've reviewed the video footage several times. She touched his back with her forefinger. There's no pinprick, but—"

"She drew a glyph on him," Roth said. "It was her touch that did it. Not poison."

She opened her mouth as if to say, *That's impossible,* then stopped herself. She'd seen a lot of impossible things since they'd met.

"They can . . . do that?" she asked softly.

"I think it's how they started the virus, remember. Glyphs. A sign. A symbol. There are stories in other parts of the world about killing or incapacitating with a touch," Roth said. As an author, he'd studied a variety of topics, including this one. "It's called dim mak. The ancient Chinese knew it. Even ninjas in Japan were supposedly able to do it. It was in *Kung Fu Panda* if you saw the movie."

"Sweet movie," Jordan interjected.

"Vaguely remember it," Monica said. "How would an attorney know it?"

"Who else would have access to people Calakmul would want dead?" Roth said. "From what I've read, death can be instant or delayed. No evidence of foul play. If it could happen here . . ." Roth's chest clenched with dread. "I don't feel safe anywhere."

"I'm sorry about your friend," Monica said, putting her hand on Roth's shoulder. "Lund and I both believed he was on the verge of flipping. Now he can't help us. But hopefully another source can."

"What source?" he asked, his mind a mess.

"Dr. Estrada and Illari Chaska. In light of what just happened, Lund had them taken to a separate location. Grab some lunch and let's get going."

As they left FBI headquarters, using a different exit from the entrance they'd used going in, Roth still felt the paranoid sensation that everyone was staring at them. He kept the twins close, and they were flanked by Jordan on one side and Monica on the other as they pushed their way through the crowds on Pennsylvania Avenue. There were people everywhere, the street full of vehicles and commotion and *noise*. Roth kept looking around, trying to find a source of danger, but the fear was inside his heart. Jacob Calakmul had reached into FBI headquarters and murdered Roth's friend right in front of him. There was no reason someone couldn't do that to Roth or his boys.

Lund summoned an SUV using Uber, and they all crammed inside. It was a short ride, though, only a few blocks. They got out, and Roth stared up at the seven-story building next to them in confusion. "This isn't a hotel."

"Exactly," Lund said. He walked up to the glass doors and held them open for everyone, then closed them. He stared out at the street for a moment before approaching the security guard.

"Can you buzz Talbot Glenn for me?" Lund asked.

"Yes, sir," said the guard. He got on the phone and then spoke briefly. "Yes. Thank you." He hung up and gestured to the elevator. "Elevators are that way." He handed Lund a key card.

"Penthouse is on the top floor?"

They all went to the elevators, Monica shooting Lund a look. "A penthouse?"

He nodded curtly and led them into the elevator. He tapped the key card and then punched the seventh floor. The elevator rocketed up quickly, and they entered a lavish corridor. Monica's cell phone buzzed, and she pulled it out.

"It's Carter," she said and then answered it. "Yes?"

Lund walked down the corridor to the final room and then pushed a doorbell button.

"We're not far," Monica said. "I'll let you know when we've spoken to Dr. Estrada. Thank you." She hung up.

The door opened, and a well-dressed middle-aged man with graying hair opened it. He had on a tweed jacket and plaid shirt and looked like a stereotypical university professor.

"Steve! Come on in!" he greeted them all with a slight Midwestern accent. "Good to see you, old friend." They shook hands, and as Roth entered the penthouse, he was struck by the man's wealth on display. There were antiques everywhere he looked, along with the kind of marble decorations usually displayed in old estates.

"Sorry it was short notice," Lund said. "Where is Dr. Estrada?"

"In the study. This way. Follow me."

Jordan brought up the rear, glancing each way. The boys looked impressed with the furnishings and decorations, and Roth was too, but his mind still felt a million miles away.

Opening the door at the end of a hall, the owner of the penthouse showed them a study that was paneled in dark wood with bookshelves and couches. A young bald man stood by the window—security, presumably, and a man and woman sat on one of the couches. The man looked to be Dr. Estrada. He had long, graying hair, a nervous smile, and salt-and-pepper stubble that suggested he hadn't shaved in days. His companion was a younger woman, heavyset, with dark hair and a distinctly Hispanic look. She had a beanie on her head, a jean jacket over another jacket, leggings, and boots.

"Dr. Estrada?" Monica said, moving to the man and shaking his hand.

"Yes," he said.

"I'm Agent Monica Sanchez. We spoke on the phone."

"Agent Sanchez. Yes. This is my assistant, Illari Chaska." He gestured to the young woman. Monica reached for her hand, but Illari wouldn't accept it. She looked away. She looked very uncomfortable. Worried even.

"This is Jonathon Roth," Monica said, indicating Roth. "And his boys."

As soon as his name was said, Illari started and looked at him with recognition. He gave her a nervous smile.

Lund went to the bald guard and whispered something to him that prompted him to leave.

"Make yourselves comfortable. Do you need any water? Anything to eat?" said Talbot Glenn.

"We're fine," Lund said. "Can we have some privacy, please?"

"Of course. Let me know if you need anything." He left through the study doors and shut them behind him, and Jordan walked over to stand guard.

"Sit on the couch over there," Roth told the boys, indicating the one farthest from the window.

"I thought we were going to FBI headquarters?" Dr. Estrada said. "I wasn't expecting to be brought here."

"Sorry for the confusion," Monica said. "It's for your own protection."

Estrada looked confused and glanced at Illari. "Why my protection?" His gaze shifted back to Roth. "And I take it this is the man the ransomware attackers want in order to decrypt the data?"

Monica nodded. "Yes. The hacker asked for Jonathon Roth. But we're not going to hand him over to them. We need to find that temple in the jungle. The one *you* discovered."

Dr. Estrada frowned. "Do you know how large the jungle is? I couldn't find it again. Not without the data that's been lost."

"The LiDAR data," Monica said. "I know. But you're the only expert who can give us the rough area on a map. Even if you could narrow the search, it would help. This is a matter of national security, Dr. Estrada. We *need* to find that temple."

Roth shifted his gaze to Illari. She was clutching a laptop bag with both hands, practically radiating discomfort.

"You still don't understand," Estrada said. "Even if I could give you a ten-mile radius, you'd never find it. The jungle is impenetrable.

It would take weeks or months to comb through that much land, and that is only if you had the Mexican government's cooperation, which you *won't.*"

"Is there a backup copy of the data?" Lund asked.

"We're trying that route," Dr. Estrada said. "It's taking time to get our supplier to provide it. I told you this on the phone."

Roth watched Illari hug the laptop bag even tighter.

"Illari," he said softly. "Do *you* have a backup copy of the data?"

She wouldn't meet his eyes. Tears pooled in hers.

And he had his answer in her silence.

CHAPTER NINE

Market Square Residences

Washington, DC

January 9

"Will someone tell me what's going on?" Dr. Estrada bellowed. He rose from the stuffed seat and spread his arms. "Do you know Illari, Mr. Roth?"

"I do," he said, not taking his eyes off the young woman. "I'm beginning to wonder if *you* know her."

Illari gave Roth a pleading look. She apparently hadn't told Estrada about her other activities. Roth could understand why. Her involvement in the Mexica—a group that wanted to turn back the clock on history and reinstate old borders, which was how he had contacted her originally— could jeopardize her position at the university. He'd seen some YouTube videos she'd posted where she'd narrated the ancient history of the Mexica and how they'd fared under the conquistadors. She hadn't shown her face in the video, but he recognized her voice. Not to mention Roth had been *paying* her to help him translate things. Although it wasn't illegal for a student to take on freelance work, it would certainly be frowned upon for her to not report both that and her affiliation in a special interest group to her academic advisor.

"Let's all calm down," Monica said, coming up to Dr. Estrada. "There's an investigation underway, and we need your help. No one is in trouble. Let's just try to sort this out, okay?"

Dr. Estrada nodded to Monica and then sat back down, but it was obvious he was still alarmed.

Roth glanced over at the twins. Jordan was showing them a video on his phone. He didn't like that they'd been thrown into the deep end of the adult world, but at least Jordan was helping them find things from their old life—their childhood—to cling to.

"Illari," he said coaxingly.

"You promised," she whispered. Tears trickled down her cheeks.

"I didn't know you were working at UC San Diego," Roth said. "At the lab. But this is a big deal. We're trying to stop something bad from happening. The prophecy you translated for me. We have to stop it."

"What prophecy?" Dr. Estrada said, flinching. "Illari, what's he talking about?"

She clenched her eyes shut and winced. "We can't stop it. We *shouldn't* stop it."

"Are we talking about the doomsday prophecy?" Dr. Estrada asked, bewildered. "It's a myth. The Maya calendar didn't end in 2012. It just started a new long cycle."

"I know," Roth said, facing him. "Look, I get that this is going to sound strange. But in 2012, a death cult run by the Calakmul family down in the Yucatán started up human sacrifices again. Cutting out hearts—the whole nine yards. My family was caught up in the death game the year before last. We had to fight for our lives at a temple in the middle of the jungle. The temple we need *your* help finding."

Dr. Estrada gaped. "You're . . . serious?"

Monica nodded. "Yes. He is serious. Members of our own government are involved in this conspiracy. The servers at the Qualcomm

Institute were hacked by an ex-NSA programmer. We're meeting here because members of the FBI are compromised, and we don't know who yet. The president's life may be in danger. That's why we need to know, Illari, if you have a backup of the data."

"I do," she said, clutching the laptop even tighter.

Monica smiled with relief. "Is it on your computer?"

Illari wiped a tear from her cheek. "No. I wouldn't have enough hard-drive space to hold it."

Why was she holding on to the computer so tightly, then? Roth wondered if she had compromising things on that laptop. Things she was afraid would get out.

"Where is the backup?" he asked.

Illari looked miserable. Her lip quivered. "On an Anasazi account," she said.

Roth didn't know what that meant.

"Anasazi?" Monica asked. "As in Anasazi Web Services?"

"Yes."

That made more sense.

"You're sharing the data with Anasazi?" Dr. Estrada asked.

"So I could do my own research," Illari said, shoulders hunching. "Not just yours."

Roth related to the situation better than others might have. Grad students were at the mercy of their advisors. They had to be loyal. Had to promote their advisor's reputations above their own. One act of disloyalty could potentially wreck a grad student's future if their advisor was so inclined. And this wasn't just any act of disloyalty. It was huge. Roth had never wanted to be a full professor. That part of academia was something he hated, not unlike the politics that drove Carter.

"Let's try working together on this," Monica suggested. "Illari, can you show how you access the AWS servers? And Dr. Estrada, can you pinpoint where you went?"

Illari shook her head. "I can't do it."

"If you have access to the data," Dr. Estrada said tightly, "we have to know."

Roth saw the conflict on her face. "Dr. Estrada, do you know about the Mexica Movement?" he asked gently. He was aware that he'd promised not to seek her out after their business was complete, and he hadn't, but here she was, and here *he* was, and he couldn't keep this to himself. The whole world might depend on it.

"Of course I do," Dr. Estrada snapped. Then he paused and looked at Illari with growing horror.

"That's how I found her," Roth said. "I needed someone who could translate the ancient languages. She's really good, as you already know."

"You're part of that fringe group?" he asked her, grimacing.

"I'm lost," Monica said. "Someone please explain this to me."

It was Lund who offered it. "They want to 'liberate' the Western hemisphere from colonizers."

"Isn't that what Jacob Calakmul wants?" Monica said.

Lund shook his head. "Nonviolently. Through the democratic processes. They basically want to found a new nation. There's a name for it, but I can't remember what it's called."

"Cemanahuac," Dr. Estrada said. "That's the word the Aztec used to describe their world, their empire, before Cortés. And you're part of that movement, Illari? I can't believe it."

"Why not?" she shot back angrily, brushing more tears away. "You, of all people, have seen the evidence of what was stolen from us. Your *own* people. There were millions living in Cemanahuac. Millions. And nearly all of them died." She trembled with emotion. "More than the Holocaust in World War II. More than the Russians under Stalin. Probably more than twenty million."

"That's an exaggeration," Dr. Estrada said. "Smallpox didn't kill that many."

"It wasn't just smallpox," Illari continued. "I'm talking about the *cocoliztli*, the fevers. The fevers that have started up *again*. I told you about the pandemic. It's all over the dark web. People didn't care about how many died then. They just wanted the land and the gold. But they're going to care now when the virus hits *them*. No immunity."

"How can it be the same virus?" Dr. Estrada said. "There would be evidence."

"There *is* a virus spreading around the world right now," Monica said calmly. "The CDC and WHO are studying it. But they need time."

"Why should I help you?" Illari said. "No one helped *my* people. We didn't cause this plague. It's coming from Calakmul. But if it rids this continent of the usurpers—"

"We're talking about over three hundred million people!" Dr. Estrada exploded.

Guilt flashed across her face, chased by defiance and something Roth couldn't interpret. "Jacob Calakmul is wrong," she finally said. "The prophecy isn't even about him."

"Do you know who else it might be about?" Roth asked. "The prophecy specifically names Jacob, but you don't believe it's about him."

"No," Illari said, wiping sweat from her face. "And it makes sense that it's not. Why would Kukulkán make a prophecy about his brother's followers? I think it's about *Kukulkán's* return."

"What are you talking about?" Dr. Estrada said, his brow furrowed.

"A prophecy from the Dresden Codex," Roth said.

"Show him what was on the blank pages," Illari said. "*Show* him."

Roth pulled out his burner phone and went to the photo gallery. He quickly scrolled to the pictures he'd taken at the SLUB in Dresden, then turned the screen and handed the phone to Estrada.

The professor gazed at it, brow wrinkled in confusion, and started to peruse the glyphs. "Kukulkán, foreigners, repent, house of Jacob, jaguars. Flocks of sheep. Torn to pieces."

"Show him the translation," Illari said.

"A few pictures later," Roth suggested.

Dr. Estrada swiped until he saw Illari's handwritten translation. Lund walked to the door, lifting his phone to his ear to make a call, and stepped outside into the corridor.

Dr. Estrada read it out loud. "The god Huracán hath commanded that I, the god Kukulkán, should give unto you this land for your inheritance. I say unto you, that if the aliens . . . or foreigners . . . do not repent after the intercession which they shall receive, after they have scattered my people—then shall ye, who are a remnant of the house of Jacob, go forth among them and shall be in the midst of them who shall be numerous; and shall be among them as jaguars among the beasts of the forest, and as a young jaguar among flocks of sheep, who, if he goes through both treads down and tears in pieces. And none can deliver them."

"And it's a fair translation?" Monica asked the professor.

"If it's Illari's, of course it's fair," he said with a hint of resentment. "She's my *best* grad student."

A flush rose to Illari's cheeks from her mentor's praise.

"Illari," Roth said gently, "I know you want the land back, but I always believed you meant to accomplish it peacefully. You weren't a fan of Huracán. You believed in Kukulkán. My ancestors . . . my family . . . came from Germany. We *endured* the Holocaust. My family in particular came from Karlsruhe. I have relatives who were killed at the concentration camp at Dachau. I can't undo their suffering, but nor would I create new concentration camps for the descendants of the men and women who made them suffer. Repeating the evil that was done to them wouldn't bring them justice. So when I learned what Jacob Calakmul was going to do, I knew I couldn't sleep without at least *trying* to stop him. Even if the prophecy isn't about him, he believes it is."

"But it doesn't make sense," Illari said. "Kukulkán wouldn't waste a prophecy on his enemy. It's a warning, don't you see? The K'iche' word used for 'repent,' the glyph *k'ex k'u'x*. It means 'to change your mind, to change your actions.' To change the way you *breathe*. It's a warning that great destruction will come *if* we don't change. That sounds like Kukulkán. Not a revenge prophecy."

"Do we know how this virus spreads?" Roth asked Monica. "Is it like Ebola?"

Monica shook her head. "Not blood-borne. From what little we know, it's a pathogen that spreads through the respiratory system. Settles in the lungs."

Roth blinked. "Change our *breath*."

Illari looked surprised too. "These are the end times."

"Would Kukulkán want everyone to die without being given a chance to change?" Roth pressed.

Illari screwed up her nose and looked down. "No. No, he wouldn't."

"Please," Roth said to her. "Calakmul took my daughter. My wife. We're trying to get them back. They're in the jungle. We need your help."

Illari sighed, then glanced at her professor.

"I think we should help them," he said. He turned and faced the others. "I've kept secrets too. When I went to the Yucatán over a year ago, something bizarre happened to me. A storm rolled in out of nowhere. We saw a man standing on top of the pyramid we found. He'd summoned the storm, I think. The one that nearly killed us. I've seen tropical storms down there. But nothing like this. It was more violent, more unnatural. There is something about that place that is very, very dangerous. There are secrets there." He shifted and turned to Illari. "If you could help find it, think what it could mean to the world."

Roth felt Lucas's hand grab his. He looked down at his son and realized that the twins and Jordan had come closer. They'd been listening.

"I want my sister back," Lucas said, his chin trembling as he stared at Illari.

"Me too," Brillante said huskily.

Illari closed her eyes and then sat down at the table and pulled out her laptop. Opened it. Roth felt a surge of relief and squeezed Lucas's hand. The screen flickered on, and with the fastest fingers he'd ever seen, she began typing.

"Need Wi-Fi," she said briskly.

Roth was used to making his phone a hotspot, so he took his device back from Dr. Estrada, quickly enabled it, then shared the password with Illari. She logged in through a browser using a VPN, which would hide her trail. In quick succession, she logged into her AWS account and brought up some screen and data files. Dr. Estrada stood behind her shoulder, staring at the screen in disbelief.

"I've mirrored the Qualcomm interface," Illari said. "You drive." She got up out of the chair and backed away, giving him room.

"How did you afford to do this?" Estrada asked as he sat in the chair.

"With some help from a donor," she replied sheepishly.

Roth nearly smiled because he had a feeling *he* was that donor.

Dr. Estrada quickly browsed the data fields that popped up. On the screen was a high-resolution map of the Yucatán Peninsula. There was so much data it was just a blob, but the coastline had been superimposed. Roth recognized it as the east coast of Belize. Data bubbles popped open, and Estrada dived into the feed, zooming across the jungle. Little red and blue icons appeared the closer they got.

Estrada typed some commands. "We started at Xmakabatún," he said aloud. The screen showed the name and some ruins. "Then we went north. The Mexican border is somewhere here," he said, pointing at the screen. "The data doesn't care about borders. Now let's peel the jungle away." He tapped on the keyboard mouse, and suddenly the vegetation was stripped away from the screen, revealing hundreds if not thousands of square shapes. "These are all indigenous. Built by the Maya thousands of years ago. This whole peninsula was heavily occupied. There's some research suggesting the peak of the Classic period was 200 to 500 AD. Some say it might have been as late as 900 AD. There was a big war. A genocide probably. The Postclassic period lasted until the Spanish conquest, so another five hundred years, give or take." He hummed, still zooming across the landscape.

"There!" he said exultantly, pointing. "That's the pyramid I saw! I only got a look at that structure and the courtyard at the base. But see how large this compound is underneath the canopy? It's probably larger than Tikal, which was one of the major kingdoms during the Postclassic period. Larger! See? This is in Mexican territory. This is what I saw."

He clicked on the location and then pulled down a menu. "The coordinates are 18°51'37.5"N 89°31'04.5"W. Precise GPS coordinates. This is it. This is it!"

Illari was smiling as she looked over at Roth and the boys.

"You did it," Monica gasped. "That's the exact location of the ruins?"

The door swung open, and Lund came in, his eyes wide.

Roth felt his stomach drop. More bad news.

"Steve?" Monica asked worriedly.

"Yes," Lund said as he approached. "Yes, of course you can talk to him. The twins are here too."

"Who is it?" Roth demanded.

"It's your daughter. It's Suki."

CHAPTER TEN

Carr Transversal/Quintana Roo C-1

Cozumel, Mexico

January 9

There were few other cars and vans on the highway. The moon was beginning to set, and whenever an occasional oncoming vehicle approached, the headlights were blinding. Suki and Jane Louise hunkered down behind the first-row bench of the van as it moved. It was the same van that the Roth family had escaped in a year ago.

Sarina was crouching behind Jorge's seat, and the two were carrying on a conversation in rapid-fire Spanish. The vibration of the van on the highway was a comforting feeling. But Suki was still shaken. One moment, they'd been in the Jaguar Temple. Another, after whispering a word about the wind, they were sitting on a beach in Cozumel. And, to think, rescue had been waiting for them all along.

"We'll stop by the orphanage for a change of clothes," Sarina said over her shoulder to them, switching to English. "What we're wearing right now will stand out too much."

No kidding. While the traditional Maya garb fit well and was kinda cool, it certainly wasn't something you'd wear sightseeing.

"How did Jorge know we were going to be here tonight?" Suki asked. Jane Louise was looking around with excitement, tugging on the ends of her hair.

"I've been planning the escape," Sarina said. "This island is sacred to Ix Chel, the moon goddess. She's been helping us all along."

"Like how?"

"It's difficult to explain. When I was sick with the DKA, I kept having visions of my grandmother. But it wasn't really her. It was just the way Ix Chel manifested to me. Cozumel is a nexus of her magic. We can come and go to any of her shrines. There was one on the beach, hidden in the bushes. She's been helping you and Jane Louise too."

"Me too?" Jane Louise piped in with awe.

"She's been comforting you," Sarina explained. "With memories of your grandmother. And she helped me conceal myself from Jacob Calakmul."

"By turning you old," Suki said with a shudder.

Her mom laughed. "Yes, by turning me old. Jorge told me that one of the girls who grew up in Huellas de Pan now runs a snorkeling business for tourists. She's got her own boat and will take us to Florida."

"Why can't we fly to Florida from the airport?" Suki asked.

"We don't have any travel ID, credit cards, anything. Once we get back to the United States, we can try to get help. But I'm going to get sick again after we leave Cozumel. We'll need to get to a hospital or urgent care as soon as possible."

The news that her mom's diabetic ketoacidosis still hadn't been cured was alarming, but not necessarily surprising. Magic had saved her, and they'd be leaving a magical place.

Jorge clicked the turn signal, and they slowed to turn off the highway. Suki peeked up through the side window and saw a military truck roar past them with soldiers sitting in the back. She ducked down again, her heart racing.

The van took several turns. Suki was thoroughly lost, but then she heard the roar of a passenger jet and remembered how close Huellas de Pan was to the airport in Cozumel. They drove up to the gate, and Jorge parked and got out to unlock it.

"This feels weird," Suki said, peering through the windshield. "I remember this place."

"Déjà vu," Sarina said. Sighing, she added, "It was a bit like that when I was in the coma. Everything was familiar, but not. My mother was there. My grandmother. My great-grandmother. All my family came from the Yucatán originally. Time is strange in that place. It felt like I was there for an hour at most before I woke up, but I could remember everything I'd seen and done. I learned about Kukulkán and his followers and disciples. About Chichén Itzá and the other ruins. There's so much history that's been lost, but I knew all of it." She rubbed her forehead, her expression a little sad. "It's fading now, though, like it was a dream."

Jorge finished tugging open the gates and then came back. He was wearing a tracksuit and sandals, just like Suki remembered from their previous visit. He had a fluttery gray mustache and graying hair combed back. He drove through the gate and then parked.

"*Vamos,*" he said, getting out again. Sarina went to the sliding door and opened it and then helped Jane Louise climb out. Suki followed, and they all went to the main office building.

Suki's stomach clenched with dread. In her mind's eye, she could see the security people who'd hunted them down. Jacob Calakmul's men. They'd murdered a doctor here. But she was surprised at the changes she saw. There was a playground that hadn't been there before. And new buildings were being constructed where there'd once been a thicket of trees.

"Wow," Suki said. "It's been busy here."

"They're building a dormitory," Sarina said. "So the older kids have somewhere to stay while they attend college." Sarina reached and squeezed Suki's hand. "Your dad made a big donation after you got back."

"He what?"

Sarina nodded. "Jorge told me. It's through a US charity, but the funds have helped Jorge expand. They don't need to depend on the resort food to feed the children and families now. In fact, they've started a shelter in Cancún that feeds low-income families meals twice a day."

"*Es* okay," Jorge said, smiling with embarrassment. "*Es* okay."

He unlocked the door to the main building and flicked on the lights for them. Inside his office were several bags of clothes. "I get food. *Comida*. To eat. You change. Hurry. Brenda is waiting at the boat."

Jorge then shut the door to give them privacy. The clothes looked like the kind you'd get from a thrift store. They had that same smell too. Suki dug through one bag and found a pair of shorts and a black T-shirt with the San Francisco Giants logo on it. It reminded her of living in the Bay Area, so she decided to keep that one. There was also a sweater that was light pink with stains on it, but she figured it would be good to have that too.

"Am I really going to see my mee-maw again?" Jane Louise asked hopefully.

Sarina crouched down and hugged her. "Yes, sweetie. We'll reach her as soon as we can. Then we can all go back home."

Suki swallowed. Calakmul knew where they lived. Home wouldn't be an option unless he was taken down. She also wanted to call Brice really bad. And her dad. Then she realized her mom didn't even *know* she had a boyfriend.

"Yeah," Suki said. It had been about two weeks since she'd been kidnapped, but she didn't know if her family was still in Montana or in DC, like Calakmul had said.

They left the office, and Jorge brought them a tray of tacos.

After they'd changed and eaten, they went back with Jorge to the van. Some children from the orphanage had gathered around it.

"*¡Gracias!*" some of them said with bright smiles. "*¡Gracias por todo!*"

Sarina hugged each and every one of them. A few of the kids came up to hug Suki and Jane Louise too, which was awkward, but Suki permitted it. Then Jorge shooed the children away, and they got back into the van. Once they were through the gate, the kids shut and locked it behind them, and the van went trundling off into the night. This time, they all sat in seats.

Jorge took them to the main part of San Miguel, the prominent city on the west coast of Cozumel. It seemed like a party town. There were tourists everywhere and quite a bit of traffic, even this late at night. Suki recognized the dock where the ferry arrived from the mainland every hour.

Jorge hummed to himself as he drove, moving slowly. People kept crossing the street at weird times, and there were a lot of neon lights and loud Latin music playing. Once they made it past the ferry dock, the traffic lightened up, and they wound their way along the coast. There were so many boats in the various harbors. Then they were heading back toward the jungle again. By the time Jorge turned, they were the only vehicle visible on the road. He entered a marina that had a few streetlamps with bugs swarming in the light.

A woman stood waiting there, black haired, and probably in her early twenties.

"*Es* Brenda," Jorge said, slowing down and then stopping.

Brenda opened the side door of the van.

"Hello, family!" she said brightly. "Come with me. You ready to go home?"

"Yes," Sarina said. She exited first and hugged the other woman. "Thank you for doing this."

"The Calakmuls are evil," Brenda said. "If we can stop them, it's all good. Welcome. You must be Suki and Jane Louise? I'm Brenda."

"Your English is very good," Jane Louise said and gave her a hug. Brenda was about as tall as Suki. She didn't look old enough to own her own boat or run a business.

"Thank you! I work with tourists every day, so I get lots of practice. Do you like ceviche? I have some leftover from the tour earlier."

"What's that?" Suki asked.

"Ooh, I won't spoil it by telling you. It's delicious. We have lots of soda and water to drink and extra gas for the trip. Let's get going, okay?"

Another set of headlights turned into the marina parking lot. Fear fluttered in Suki's stomach. It was a police truck. On the side in big letters was the name of the state Quintana Roo. Had it followed them? They were so close to getting away . . .

There was no way Jacob Calakmul could have alerted authorities. Right? Or did he also have ways of communicating over great distances? She didn't know.

Brenda's smile faded. "Jorge. *Mira.*"

The headlights began to sweep across the parking lot.

Sarina whispered a word under her breath, and Suki felt a prickle of magic go down her arms. Suddenly, the magic of the *kem äm* was swirling around them in golden motes. But she hadn't summoned it. Her mother had.

"They won't see us," Sarina said calmingly. "Let's go."

CHAPTER ELEVEN

GULF OF MEXICO

January 9

The magic of the *kem äm* had helped them escape the police in the parking lot just before moonset. They'd slipped away without being noticed by the officers, and Brenda had ushered them onto the boat and then the boat into the harbor.

It was the first cruise Suki had been on actually. She didn't much like boats, and if it hadn't been necessary for their escape, she would have happily avoided it. But the leftover seafood ceviche—*that* was awesome.

The sun was nice and warm, but the constant wind from the forward motion of the boat and the choppiness of the water made it impossible to get comfortable. They'd passed by Cuba, which Brenda had pointed out to them, and were getting close to the coast of Florida. Brenda had taken tourists to Cuba before, but never so far as Florida. As long as they kept in the direction they were heading, they'd make it to one of the western ports—like Fort Myers, Naples, or Everglades City. From there, they'd try to contact Dad or Uncle Steve to let them know where they were.

Suki felt a lightness she hadn't thought herself capable of anymore. It was so comforting having her mom back. They talked for hours, no longer having to worry about being caught or overheard. Jane Louise had fallen asleep first, and Suki's mom had eventually drifted off too. Suki couldn't sleep. She grabbed a can of Pepsi from the cooler, cracked it open, and took a long drink from it, staring off into the distance. Earlier that morning, some dolphins had started jumping from the waves behind them. That had been pretty sweet. They'd been on the boat for so long, Suki had lost track of time.

"I thought this might happen," Brenda said, her normally cheerful tone sounding more worried. "You the only one awake, Suki?"

"I think so," Suki replied, then glanced over and saw her mom was still asleep, with Jane Louise nestled against her side. "Yup. What's up?"

"A US Coast Guard ship is heading for us," Brenda said. "They're bigger and faster. Wake up your mom."

Suki set down the soda can and then walked crookedly over to Sarina and shook her shoulder.

"Mom, wake up."

Sarina's eyes blinked open. "Are we almost there?"

"There's a coast guard ship heading our way."

Jane Louise sat up, rubbing her eyes.

Sarina looked exhausted still. She squinted at Brenda, who pointed to their right. Suki glanced over and finally took notice of it. It was a large white ship, about five times bigger than theirs, with a red stripe at an angle from the front. A metal tower at the top had radar equipment.

"How far are we from Florida?" Sarina asked.

"Couple of hours still," Brenda answered. "I was hoping we could slip past, but we weren't lucky. They'll reach us in thirty minutes or less."

"That's not a lot of time," Suki said.

"No, it's not," Sarina agreed. "Will you get in trouble?"

"I don't think so. They're going to ask a lot of questions, but the three of you are American, so it's not the same as if you were refugees."

"We don't have any ID," Sarina said. "But it shouldn't be hard to prove our identities. The problem is alerting the wrong people to where we are."

"Yeah," Suki agreed. "Like Dad's friend Moretti." Of course she'd told her mother the whole story about him turning her over to Calakmul.

"Exactly. Brenda, you've done enough. Let's just make the story easy. You found us adrift and picked us up and were taking us to the nearest port, hoping the coast guard would find us."

"Are we going for a *Gilligan's Island* vibe, Mom?" Suki asked with a grin.

"Not really, but that's funny. Hopefully their port is in Florida."

"It has to be," Brenda said. "They patrol the Gulf of Mexico all the time. But they probably won't believe that story."

"Should we say we were kidnapped by a cartel?" Suki suggested. "We managed to escape and convinced Brenda to help us get back home?"

Sarina thought for a moment. "If we admit we were kidnapped, that will trigger a call to the police. Probably the FBI."

"FBI agents raided our house," Suki said. "Dad didn't trust them."

"So we don't want them to get involved yet," Sarina said. "But we also want them to release Brenda. Let's go with the broken ship. We were stranded when the engine failed and just drifted."

"That makes sense," Brenda said. "I found you, but your boat was bigger than mine, so I couldn't tow it."

"Good enough. They'll probably let you go."

"We're *so* good at lying," Suki drawled. "But isn't there a magic we can use to zap us to Florida?"

Sarina shook her head. "It only works in places where Ix Chel has prominence, and then only at night when the moon is strong."

"Bummer," Suki said, scratching her neck. She tried to think of other ways to avoid a confrontation with the boat. "What if we went invisible again?"

"That's not going to trick their radar. And it'd draw even more attention if a boat on their radar turned invisible. Good thinking, though. Once we get to the port, we can use the magic to try and escape."

"I was hoping to get you all the way to safety," Brenda said, discomfort in her tone. "I know your family has done so much for Huellas de Pan. Jorge is grateful. We all are."

"He helped us when we needed it," Sarina said. She sighed. "So have you. Let's see what happens."

In about twenty minutes, the coast guard ship reached them, and someone on a loudspeaker ordered them to stop their boat and kill the engine. The order came in English and Spanish. Brenda complied, and soon they were bobbing up and down in the waves caused by the massive cutter.

"Let me talk to them," Sarina said. "This isn't your fault."

"I know. Good luck," Brenda said under her breath.

Suki's nerves were taut again. But she was grateful her mom was there and that she wasn't alone trying to figure out the adult world. Jane Louise reached for Suki's hand and squeezed it.

The cutter came closer. There were uniformed sailors talking to each other at the bow. Sarina waved her arm at them. "We're American!" she shouted up to them.

"Ma'am, sit tight while we send a vessel to your boat," said the voice from the loudspeaker.

Soon, an inflatable with a motor came from around the other side of the cutter. The two men on board had on life jackets. As they approached the boat, Suki noticed they were armed. That made her nervous.

"Ma'am," said one of the sailors, "you say you're American. Your vessel is registered in Mexico."

"I know," Sarina said. "We were stranded. She found us and agreed to bring us back. We're so glad you came!"

One of the sailors turned to the other before glancing back at her. "Do you have any ID with you?"

"No, it's still back at our hotel. But thank you for finding us. We were really scared. The power was dead. We couldn't call for help. We were gone for a long time."

"There were no reports of a vessel lost in the gulf," the sailor said.

"There wasn't any way we could report it. It was a private boat."

"Are those two girls your children?"

"Yes. The little one is adopted. Can we call my husband? He must be worried sick."

The two sailors looked at each other. Suki's stomach clenched harder. One of them got on the radio. He said a few words, then the radio chirped back.

"Get them on board."

———

The bigger boat made for a much smoother ride. The family was kept in a private room with blankets and plenty of food and things to drink. It was cramped, but at least they could sit down and warm up. Suki could tell that the officer they'd spoken to wasn't buying their story. But the fact that all three of them were fluent in English added to their credibility. They'd allowed Brenda to leave.

The door opened, and the officer returned. His name badge said "Holmes." Suki hoped his first name wasn't Sherlock.

"We're almost to Naples, ma'am," he said. "The captain wants to talk to you."

"Naples?" Suki's mom asked in confusion.

"We're from Key West, but Naples is the closer port. By Fort Myers. We're trying to confirm your story, but it's not adding up. That's why the captain would like to speak with you."

Crap. Crappity crap. Suki looked worriedly at her mom.

"When can I call my husband? When we reach Naples?" her mom asked.

"Yes. There's no cell service out here. But we're going to keep you at our building in Naples while we sort this out. Without ID, I can't release you."

Suki's anxiety spiked to the next level. She began thinking the Mayan word for "peace" over and over again.

"Okay," her mom said, shrugging. "We really appreciate all you've done. We'll sort this out."

"I'm sure we will, ma'am. Thanks for your patience."

"No, thank you. Thank you for everything."

Holmes left and shut the door. And then locked it. Suki frowned.

There was no window to look out from, but they could feel the sensation of the cutter slowing down. After a long wait, it finally stopped, and they felt only the gentle sway of the water. They had no cell phones, no wallets, just some cash Jorge had given them. Suki didn't remember the burner phone number for her dad, and she didn't dare call his regular cell phone because it was probably being monitored. How could they get in touch with him?

"What are you going to tell the captain?" Suki asked.

"Nothing. We're getting out of here as soon as the ship docks." Her mom leaned back, her face looking weary.

"How are you feeling, Mom?"

"I need something other than carbs," she said. She hadn't eaten the provisions the crew had brought because it was the wrong kind of food for a diabetic. "I'm going to need an insulin shot soon."

"Let me help," Suki said. "We need to get away from these guys so we can try to call Dad. Calakmul is monitoring our normal cell phones, I think, so we'll have to find another way to reach him. I know he has a burner phone, but I don't know the number." He'd tried to make her memorize it, in case a situation like this ever arose, but her mind had gone blank.

A few minutes later, Holmes returned. "Leave the blankets here. There's a US Coast Guard auxiliary building here in Naples City Dock. We're there now. The captain is already inside. I'll take you to him."

"Great," Sarina said brightly. "We're ready."

The three of them followed Holmes down the inner corridor of the ship and then up onto the deck. Outside, the smell of dead fish filled the air. It was nasty. It looked like they were in a narrow inlet. Boats and yachts were everywhere. She even saw some painted with signs about dolphin and manatee tours. The part of the city she could see looked busy, full of honking cars and seagulls. It was a noisy situation.

"I'm too tired," Sarina whispered to Suki. "I need you to summon the *kem äm*. You're stronger in it anyway."

"How do I do it? I've never made someone disappear before."

Holmes glanced back at them, motioning for them to approach the gangway. Sailors had gathered there, and a few of them bid them goodbye as they left.

"Thank you so much!" Sarina said brightly, but her voice was strained.

Once they were on the gangway, heading down behind Holmes, Suki felt a prickle of apprehension. She was tired too. "Exhausted" was a better word for it.

"It will work," her mother said. "Hold hands."

They all linked hands together.

"It's the glyph *sach ib*." Her mom whispered the word, and then the glyph appeared in Suki's mind. Thought to thought. *Sach ib*. An ancient Mayan word. It meant *to vanish from sight*.

Suki squeezed their hands. "*Sach ib*," she murmured.

After they got off the gangway and docks, Holmes approached a small T-shaped building right on the north side of the dock. A flagpole was in the middle of the patio with the American flag fluttering in the small breeze. A few palm trees were interspersed in the paving of the parking lot.

Suki's mom tugged on her hand, and Suki pulled on Jane Louise's as they followed the patio toward the parking lot. Holmes walked to the front door of the building with the US Coast Guard emblem on it.

"Captain Baker said you can call—" He stopped suddenly, having turned around to hold the door open for them. He looked confused, searching back and forth.

The three of them walked away from him, heading toward the downtown area. Hopefully it would smell better. They should have been directly within his line of sight, but he shouted, "Captain, Captain! They're gone!"

The tingling prickle of magic danced down Suki's arms, making the gooseflesh come out. So simple. Like breathing out. The magic was powerful.

And that made it frightening. What else could Jacob Calakmul do with it?

CHAPTER TWELVE

Jaguar Temple

Calakmul Biosphere Reserve

January 9

"I have failed you, Great One," Uacmitun groveled. The muscled warrior knelt in submission. It was the act of a man who knew he deserved death. By exposing his neck to Jacob, he'd ensured it would be over in moments.

Rage sizzled through Jacob's chest as he paced in the main hall of his palace. Rage and frustration. His emotions felt more mercurial in his refreshed body. Had it been a mistake to go to Aztlán after all? The Order of the Jaguar Priests had been patient for centuries, biding their time, awaiting the fulfillment of the prophecy so they might enact their revenge, but he felt all out of patience.

No one crossed the jungle unnoticed. Not Sarina Roth. Not Suki. Not the Beasley girl. They must have escaped some other way.

"I'm not going to kill you," Jacob said, his voice throbbing. "I saw Suki last night. Angélica saw the little girl. When did the servants notice they were all gone?"

"This morning. I've had every warrior searching for them. There is no trace of them. None."

It was maddening. Suki was gifted with the *kem äm*, but no one had taught her the kind of advanced magic that would allow her to disappear or cross into the spirit world. Only a skilled sorcerer . . .

Jacob clenched his hand into a fist and slammed it against the stone wall. "It happened after the moon came up," he seethed.

"What?" Uacmitun asked, tentatively lifting his chin. A look of hope filled his eyes.

"Ix Chel," Jacob vented. "She's been helping them all along."

"You think . . . you think it was *her?*"

"I should have seen this before," Jacob snarled. "Ix Chel has three manifestations. The maiden, the mother, and the crone. Once Suki arrived, all three manifestations could be realized. It allowed her to use her full power."

"But where did they go?" Uacmitun asked.

"Where her power is greatest. Cozumel. If Ix Chel thinks she can hinder my plans, I will show her the true might of Huracán. There will be no hindrances. Call off the search. They're not here."

"Are you sure, Great One?"

"Do as I say!" Jacob roared.

Uacmitun scampered away swiftly. Jacob stormed back to his private chambers and found Angélica sitting on a stool with a jaguar-pelt cushion. She was trying on different pieces of jewelry. Seeing the gold flash against her skin made his lust kick in again.

Focus. He was losing his focus!

"What did Uacmitun want?" she asked, turning her head to look at him, her brow furrowed with concern.

"Suki is gone. And Beasley's daughter."

"How?"

"I think Sarina has been here the whole time, disguised as one of the crones. Ix Chel must have helped her. She's been the goddess's pawn this whole time. I want her shrine broken down. Her symbol removed from the ball court. Find every effigy of her and grind it to dust. I will begin searching for the escapees another way."

"Do you want me to go with you?" she asked, rising from the stool.

"No, stay here. Entertain our *guests*." Truthfully, he found the past winners of the death games contemptible. Small. But that also meant they could be controlled, and he'd learned the hard way that a small, controllable mind was much better to deal with than an intellect like Mr. Roth's. "I will let nothing stop us." He approached her, took her hand, and kissed her knuckles. "I desire you *again*. What spell is this that has such power?"

Angélica smiled with gratification. She gave him a coy look. "I will be waiting for you when you return," she said in a sultry tone.

His desire spiked again, but he would wait. He could be patient. Jacob went to his changing room and exchanged his Aztec garb for modern clothing. He strapped an expensive watch around his wrist and looked at the time. It was nearly noon.

"Two of the warrior teams will be playing the ball game this afternoon," Angélica said when he emerged.

"Those games can last all night," Jacob answered. "I will probably be back before it finishes." He approached her, took her in his arms, and kissed her hard. She made a pleased sound in the back of her throat.

He broke the kiss, then left the bedchamber and went down into the depths of the royal residence. The underground tunnels were lit by strands of *kem äm*, gathered in bundles atop metal torches like flames, except the light gave off no smoke. A corridor was blocked by a webbing of *kem äm*, but he waved his hand. His ring deactivated it, and he passed through the opening, restoring the *kem äm* with another wave of his hand. Anyone caught wandering here would be put to death instantly.

Jacob knew the maze trail by memory. It sank lower and lower into the gloom. He crossed the underground tunnel to the adjacent temple. The air was musty. His Western shoes were too noisy as they clipped on the stone floor. After he'd crossed the distance between the royal residence and the temple, the tunnel joined with another, also blocked by the magical webbing. He canceled it, passed through, and brought it back into place.

Jacob maneuvered the tunnels effortlessly. Finally, he reached his destination. It was a stone wall with a carving on it—a stela. The image was of Huracán, the furrows lined with gold. It was a complex image, a profile with one hand holding a cluster of spears and shield, the other making a hand gesture—the symbol of a magical being. One foot was normal, but the other was strangely shaped. Some thought it was a serpent, but Jacob knew better. It was the smoking mirror.

Jacob lifted his hand and drew a glyph in the air. "I salute you, Huracán, enemy of both sides. Lord of the Near and the Nigh. God of the Furious Winds, Possessor of Sky and Earth. *Open.*"

The stela shimmered with magic. Then the stone moved up, revealing another tunnel. Jacob had to crouch to enter it. It was a forced humility. After he passed the stela, the stone closed behind him with a grinding sound. Jacob had entered the chamber of mirrors.

A series of obsidian mirrors was fixed to each of the walls ahead of him, twelve in total. A feeling of doom throbbed within the confined space. This was a place of hallowed magic—a secret guarded almost as closely as the existence of Aztlán. The Jaguar Temple had been abandoned and covered with earth to prevent the Spanish conquerors from finding it. The cenotes had buried the gold. But this chamber, with its mirrors, was worth more than all of that treasure combined. In fact, it was how the jaguar priests of old had moved the treasure from place to place to keep the Spanish from grasping even the smallest amounts of what the Aztec and Maya had.

Jacob walked along the east wall, waving his hand over each mirror as he passed. One mirror led to the Museum of London. Another to Moscow. Each mirror was connected to a sister mirror elsewhere. Only a jaguar priest knew the sign to activate it. Only a few of the elite were trusted with the knowledge.

Jacob walked to the north wall and then stopped. One mirror led to the White House. He waved his hand across it, and the obsidian shimmered darkly. He gazed through it, seeing the corridor with people walking swiftly one way and another. A satisfied smile came to his face. He could walk into the most protected building in the world because of a "gift" that was a relic of long forgotten ways. But today was not the day to seize the president.

Passing the next mirror, which led to Mexico City, he stopped and waited at the third. It was a portal to a mansion on the shore of Lake Chapala in Michoacan. He summoned the magic and looked through the mirror. The mansion was opulent, a drug lord's mansion that was garish in its splendor. The mirror was hung in the private office. No one was there at the moment.

Jacob bowed his head, summoning the power in his ring, then took a step forward. When his hand touched the polished surface of the mirror, he felt a jolt rush through him. Just like that, he stood in Michoacan. The smell of cloves hung in the air. The room was dark, except for a few recessed lights illuminating mountain Aztec and Maya treasures.

Sitting on the stuffed leather office chair, Jacob grimaced at the dish of pistachios on the desk. They weren't to his taste and never had been. Then he opened the desk and retrieved the cell phone he kept there for his infrequent trips through the mirror. It activated with his fingerprint, and he called his chief of security, Victor.

The man answered immediately. "Mr. Calakmul. You're at Lake Chapala?"

"Yes," Jacob said. "Suki is gone."

"What? Where?"

"Ix Chel took her to Cozumel. I think she's with Sarina and Jane Louise. Any news from the men you left behind?"

"Nothing from the resort. But I did get a report from the police in Quintana Roo. A van from Huellas de Pan went to the marina in San Miguel last night."

"The marina?" Jacob sat up instantly.

"The police officer followed it. Just the driver was there, Jorge. Remember him?"

"Yes. The one Mr. Roth has been sending money to. I want him brought in. See to it."

"Of course, sir. There was no one with him. He said he was going to see one of his orphans who worked there. A girl who runs a snorkeling—oh, now I get it."

Jacob's anger stoked hotter. How had Sarina arranged the escape without drawing attention? It was the magic. She was just as much of a threat as Suki.

"Jorge helped them escape. I want them to find his body with the turtles on the beach. Kill him. Today."

"Yes, Mr. Calakmul. Of course. We'll track the boat too."

Suddenly the office door burst open. The heavyset drug lord came in and gaped with astonishment. He had two security guards with him with submachine guns. All three fell to their knees, faces pressed to the marble-tiled floor.

"Any word from DC?" Jacob asked into the phone. He didn't mind if those men knelt for an hour. They knew his power. *He* was the reason they were wealthier than the gods and would soon be ruling throughout the Americas.

"Nothing, sir. All is in readiness for Friday. The other jaguar priests will arrive tonight. The ones you asked for."

"Is there any suspicion?" Jacob asked.

"Our man in the Secret Service said everything is go for Friday. The pandemic meeting is happening on schedule. Every person attending has been cleared. Your contact, the staffer, will be waiting for you by the mirror. Say the code word, and she'll bring you straight to the Situation Room."

"Excellent," Jacob said. "You are sure President Parker will be there? He will lead the meeting himself?"

"Yes, sir. It's all arranged."

"I want you to find where they're hiding Mr. Roth. He's in DC. Do a better job of finding out where."

"I will, Mr. Calakmul. We'll get him. We have spies posted all around Washington, and just this morning there was a spotting of a man with two boys in a Marriott by the NASA building. They didn't totally meet the description, but we're looking into it."

Jacob snorted and ended the call. He set the phone down on the desk and eyed the three men prostrate on the ground. He was feeling vengeful. Petty, even. But the drug dealer had overhead too much. He was now a loose thread.

"I said I don't like pistachios," Jacob murmured. "Kill your boss."

And they obeyed. Without hesitation.

CHAPTER THIRTEEN

MARKET SQUARE RESIDENCES

WASHINGTON, DC

January 9

With trembling fingers, Roth took the phone from Lund. Was it really his daughter, or a trick from Jacob Calakmul? Lucas and Brillante gathered near him, eyes eager, hopeful, and worried.

"Suki, are you okay?" Roth breathed into the phone, turning his back to the others in the room. He couldn't bear to see his sons' disappointment if the hope turned out to be false. He walked to the nearest window and looked out at the wintry sky.

"I'm okay. *We're* okay."

Roth squeezed his eyes shut for a moment and then looked at the caller ID on Lund's phone. It was a number from Naples, Florida. "We?"

"I'm with Mom and Jane Louise. We escaped last night."

Roth's knees gave out. It was too much, too sudden. He found himself on his knees on the floor, Lucas and Brillante holding his arms.

He just sat down right there, pressing his back against the wall. The boys hunkered down next to him.

"You're with *Mom*?" he asked incredulously.

"Yes! She's right here. And Jane Louise too."

"J-Jane Louise?"

"Jacob kept her alive, and Mom's been taking care of her. Now that we've left the Yucatán, Mom's blood sugar is spiking again. I tried to heal her with the magic, but it didn't work. I think it only heals injuries, not illness. Maybe that's why the Maya couldn't stop the smallpox from spreading . . . or maybe I just don't know the right words to use. We got to an urgent care center in Florida, and they rushed us to a hospital to get some insulin."

"What town?"

"Um . . . the town of Naples. I'm borrowing this phone from a nurse."

Monica knelt down in front of Roth, staring at him. He could see she was startled by his reaction.

"How did you get away?" he asked. The relief was so great he could hardly take it. His heart was pounding. His ears were ringing extra loud.

"I'll tell you later. We only have a little bit of cash. No credit cards or ID."

"How did you get Lund's phone number?"

"He made me memorize it after he picked me up from Brice's house that night," Suki said. "While we were sitting in his car for hours. I tried to memorize the number for your burner phone too, but for some reason, his is the one that stuck. It's so good to hear your voice, Dad. Uncle Steve said the twins are there?"

"Yes!" they both shouted simultaneously. They could hear her well enough. Lucas hugged Brillante, and both boys looked so happy—more than they had since they'd left for their vacation in Mexico over a year ago. Roth felt tears in his eyes. He was going to start sobbing.

"What's the name of the urgent care and the hospital? I can pay for any bills. Your mom's with you? Right now? Can I talk to her?"

"She's sleeping. We were on a boat ride all night, and she's really sick. Her body was protected while she was down there. But now . . . it's . . . it's really weird. I'll have to explain it later. But she misses you."

Roth rubbed his forehead, still dazed. He heard another voice from Suki's end of the connection. "Um . . . Jane Louise wants to say hi."

"Okay," Roth said, his voice quavering. Then she passed over the phone, and he heard Jane Louise's voice. It was a little different, but he still recognized it.

"Can you call my mee-maw?" she asked. "Can you tell her I'm okay?"

Tears streamed down Roth's cheeks. "Yes, sweetie. Yes. What's her name?"

"Her name is Barbara. Barbara McKinty. Everyone calls her BJ. But I call her Mee-Maw."

Roth swallowed his tears. "You bet. I'm so . . . I'm so relieved, Jane Louise. I'm sorry I couldn't help you before."

"I know. Tia Sarina said you did everything you could to save me. Here's Suki. She took care of me too."

Roth felt better than he could remember feeling. He felt . . . grateful, so grateful he was almost sick from it, but he was desperate to talk to Sarina. To hear *her* voice.

"I need to give the nurse her phone back. We're at NCH Baker Downtown Hospital on Seventh Street, and the urgent care is Station Medic 1, that's on Eighth Avenue. I need to find us a safe place. I'll call Lund's phone again."

"Okay. That's good. Find a safe place. But here, write down my burner phone number so you can reach me too. Can you grab a pen or something? I'll pay for your mom's treatment with a private credit card. One that Calakmul can't trace. Just . . . be safe."

"I will. Okay, I've got a pen. Give me the number." He did and listened for her to repeat it back to him correctly. "Got it. I love you, Dad. I love you, bros!"

"Love you, Suki!" Lucas chimed in.

"Yeah, me too," Brillante said, a little more bashful.

Roth ended the call and held the phone in his hands like it was a bar of gold.

Monica put her hand on his shoulder and gave him a warm smile. "They escaped?"

Roth nodded, and then the tears came out in a gush. His shoulders trembled, his chest rattled, and he sobbed and sobbed like he hadn't in months. Sarina was *alive*. Jane Louise was *alive*. Suki had somehow managed to get them out of Jacob's lair. How, he had no idea. But the relief and hope were overwhelming. Lucas leaned against him, patting his arm comfortingly.

Steve crouched and took his phone. "We're going to get her back."

"We have FBI offices in Florida. We can pick her up in an hour," Monica said, rising.

"No way," Jordan interrupted. "You know—"

Steve sighed. "Let me handle this. We communicate using any of your channels, and we may as well hand them over to Calakmul again. I'm going to get them. Myself."

"Steve, you can't be everywhere at once," Monica objected.

"It's less than a three-hour flight to Florida from here," Lund said.

Roth felt the tide of tears rushing out again. He wiped his eyes on his sleeve. His family was safe. They would be back together again. They were still in considerable danger—not just from Calakmul's people but from the virus they were spreading—but they'd eluded trouble for this long. There was good reason to believe that they might get back together to face what was coming as a family. And now they knew where to find the Jaguar Temple.

Roth patted Lucas's head and then tried to stand, but his knees were still wobbly. The boys helped him back up. Looking at the others in the room—Dr. Estrada, Illari, Jordan—he felt more emotion welling in his chest. All these people had come together to help. That was a beautiful thing, and he had to believe that if they continued to work together, they could stop Calakmul. Hadn't his family managed to continually elude the man?

"This is under the jurisdiction of the FBI," Monica insisted. "I can go get them myself just as easily as you can. Not every agent is on Calakmul's payroll."

"I know that, but *I* let Moretti take Suki away." Lund's voice had steel in it. "I'm bringing her back."

"If you make it personal, you—"

"Oh, it's *very* personal," Lund cut in. "I've seen what these guys can do. So have you. They took down an FBI chopper and a sniper team. They blew up part of the airport in Bozeman. I'm sorry, Agent Sanchez, but I don't trust anyone else to do this job. I'll coordinate with my guys here in DC to keep the family safe. Now that Jordan's here, he can protect them personally. You now have actionable intelligence about Jacob Calakmul's headquarters. Have the CIA take it out. And cancel the Friday pandemic meeting!"

"The director isn't going to green-light starting another war in Mexico over a set of coordinates. But you're right." She sighed. "I can't trust there won't be a leak."

Lund reached out and took Roth's hand. Shook it. "I'll be back tomorrow with the rest of your family. I promise you."

"I want to talk to Sarina," Roth said. "As soon as she wakes up. Have her call me."

"I will. I need to get to Dulles right now." Lund paused and looked at Monica. "I'm serious. Call the meeting off."

"We've *tried*," Monica said with visible frustration. "The director refuses to do it. It drives me crazy that they're letting politics get in the way of safety. But we'll keep trying."

"There's a reason I retired early," Lund grumbled. "You have the GPS coordinates. Get a Sentinel over that jungle or some UAVs."

Dr. Estrada spoke up. "Remember what happened to us," he said. "The weather changed when we got close."

Lund snorted. "A Sentinel can fly *above* the weather. All we need is to corroborate the location."

"We'll try, Steve. But you know how things work in DC."

"So does Calakmul," Lund countered. "See if you can keep the federal government intact while I'm gone. Give me the car keys, Jordan. We'll get you a replacement vehicle." Jordan tossed him the key fob. Lund nodded to Roth once more and then strode out the door, retrieving his phone to make another call.

Monica watched him go.

"So Steve left the FBI early?" Roth asked her.

"Yeah, I guess you'd call it office politics," she answered.

"That makes it sound like a little snub," Jordan said, shaking his head. "It was more than that." Turning to Roth, he added, "He had a run-in with the attorney general's security detail over a nonincident in Beijing."

"Wait, isn't the attorney general the FBI's boss?" Roth asked. "I don't know that much about the federal government, but I know that much."

"You're right," Monica said. "Lund was in Beijing on assignment, rooting out State Department employees compromised by Chinese intelligence operatives. There was a big to-do about it around ten years ago. Back when *you* were in high school, probably," she said to Jordan with a hint of snark.

"Not my fault you like younger men," Jordan quipped in return. The boys snickered.

Roth shook his head and held up his hands, because this wasn't a time for flirting or for fighting. "Was Lund in the wrong?"

"Of course not," Monica said, her cheeks burning a little. "He's always been a straight shooter. But the higher you go in government jobs, the more political it gets. That run-in with the attorney general's security detail ended Lund's assignment in Beijing. And damaged his reputation in DC. He wasn't fired, but he was put out to pasture. Many believed he was a strong candidate for deputy director before the incident. Might be the reason it happened."

Monica's cell phone rang. She looked at the ID and then went a little pale. "Sanchez," she answered. "Yes, Mr. Brower. Yes, sorry I didn't call you sooner, but we just got the information from Dr. Estrada." She walked over to the table where the professor and Illari were sitting. "What are the coordinates for Calakmul's compound?"

Dr. Estrada turned the laptop screen. "It's right here," he said, pointing. "Not far past the Guatemalan border. There."

Monica squinted and looked closer. "I'll read them to you. The coordinates are 18°51'37.5"N 89°31'04.5"W. Do you want me to say it again? Okay. 18°51'37.5"N 89°31'04.5"W. Yes. That's it." She paused, listening. Then she smiled. "That's good news, sir. Do you think you can convince the director to call off the meeting tomorrow in the Situation Room?"

She looked crestfallen. "Understood. There's more news, sir. Steve Lund just got a call from Suki Roth. She escaped. With Mrs. Roth and the Beasleys' daughter. They're all alive. Yes. Yes, he's here."

Monica approached Roth and handed him the phone. *EAD Brower,* she mouthed.

Roth raised her phone to his ear. "Yes?"

"Mr. Roth, that's wonderful news about your family. I'm happy for you. We just got a call from Senator Coudron, who sits on the Senate Intelligence Committee. The director gave a closed-door briefing on what's happening. Senator Coudron would like to speak to you and Dr. Estrada in the Capitol building."

"Why me?" Roth asked. "I'm just an author. Dr. Estrada is the expert."

Silence hung on the line for a moment, then Brower said, "Mr. Roth, what I'm going to tell you is classified. Please do not repeat it. One of the senators on the intelligence committee is currently in Cancún vacationing with his family. We're sending an SUV to pick you up and bring you to Capitol Hill."

Roth swallowed, and an itching feeling crept over him. Even though his family was safe—for now—this was far from over. In some ways, it was just starting.

CHAPTER FOURTEEN

DIRKSEN SENATE OFFICE BUILDING

WASHINGTON, DC

January 9

Roth had been to several major Comic-Cons during his career as an author, but he'd never been to the US Capitol building. When the SUV drove past it, he glanced at its retreating shape. "Wait, I thought we were going to the Capitol?"

The boys were in the back seat of the SUV with Jordan. Monica sat next to him in a bucket seat in the second row. The windows were tinted dark. One FBI agent drove, another rode shotgun. Dr. Estrada and Illari were in a different vehicle on a different route.

"We are," Monica said.

"How come we just passed it?"

"You don't enter through the front doors, Jonathon. We'll enter through one of the Senate office buildings. The House office buildings are on the other side of the Capitol"—she pointed to the far end of the Capitol—"and the Senate ones are on this side. There are three. Which one are we going through?" she asked, leaning toward the agent riding shotgun.

"Dirksen," replied the agent stiffly.

They were on Constitution Avenue and passed behind the Capitol building. The agent stopped at a stoplight and then continued.

"Boys, that's the Supreme Court," Roth said excitedly. He hadn't realized it was right behind the Capitol.

The Dirksen building looked like many of the structures in downtown DC. It was like the center of the city had been designed after ancient Athens, with temples devoted to politics instead of Greek gods. The building was multiple stories tall, made of gray stone, and had sharp angles, a triangular roof, and square pillars. The entrance was on First Street, but there was a barrier preventing vehicles from entering the street, four retractable metal barricades with the word "Stop" on them, along with some swiveling rails like the kind that blocked a railroad. A few orange cones sat in the street as well. As soon as the SUV began to turn toward the blockade, they were waved ahead by a uniformed police officer. One section of the barrier went down, and the bar came up.

Trees lined the front of the building, where the SUV pulled up to the doors and then stopped in the middle of the street.

The agent in the passenger seat got out first, examining the road both ways. His sunglasses and suit gave him an impressive air. Two more agents strode up from the tree line, looking both ways.

"They have security waiting for us," Jordan said. "Nice touch, Monica."

"Brower arranged it," Monica said. "Let's move." She opened the door and got out first, followed by Roth and then the kids. Jordan shut the door behind him, and the SUV took off. Another SUV drew up behind theirs, and Dr. Estrada and Illari Chaska exited. Roth thought Illari looked very ill at ease. She clutched her laptop bag tightly.

"This way, please," said the agent who had ridden with them. He took them to the large entrance under the triangle roof.

Roth felt a prickle of apprehension. It was disturbing that he felt safe on the streets of DC than he did walking into a secure location like a Senate office building.

The answer was obvious. Because it was more likely Jacob Calakmul had someone waiting for them *inside* than outside.

There were guards at the door, but when the lead FBI agent flashed his badge, the guard waved them in. They had to pass through a metal detector. Jordan had to put his Glock on the tray, along with his ID and carry permit, but he was allowed to retrieve his weapon and holster it again.

A lot of people were walking just past the security checkpoint, all well dressed, and most of them quite young. One of them stood waiting on the other side of the metal detectors, a younger man in his early twenties who was even taller than Jordan and had thick blond hair. He looked like a surfer, except he wore a suit and shiny tan loafers.

"I'm Daniel from Senator Coudron's office," he said. "Agent Sanchez?" He extended his hand to her, ignoring the other agents.

"Yes," Monica answered, gripping his hand and shaking it. "Nice to meet you, Daniel."

He passed out visitor badges to the guests, which they clipped to their shirts. One agent remained to trail them, and the other walked ahead. Monica stayed in the middle with Jordan, the Roths, Dr. Estrada, and Illari.

The twins started up a steady stream of chatter, haranguing Jordan with questions about DC, since he had served there as part of his army service at Arlington. Roth tuned out their conversation and glanced at Illari.

She met his gaze once and then looked away.

"I'm glad you had the data backed up," he told her.

"I wish she'd told *me*," Dr. Estrada sniped.

"This is bigger than you, bigger than me, bigger than any of us," Roth said. "You flew close to the Jaguar Temple. You're lucky to even be here."

Illari looked down, holding her case as if it were her lifeline.

Estrada shrugged. "I know, Mr. Roth. I've spent my whole career exploring the ruins in Guatemala. The preserve in Mexico was always off-limits. Always. No matter how much the university offered. Now I understand why."

Daniel brought them to a steep escalator heading down. The boys craned their necks, trying to soak in the sights. Roth looked back up the escalator, observing the FBI agent who was bringing up the rear, watching for anyone who might approach them from behind.

"Whoa, they have a cafeteria down here!" Brillante said excitedly as they made their way off the escalator.

"They have a Dunkin' Donuts in one of the House office buildings," Jordan told them conspiratorially.

"No way!" Lucas asked. "Are we getting food? I'm hungry again."

"On our way out," Monica said. "We've got a walk ahead of us. Like I said, we're taking the underground tunnels to the Capitol."

"They can't be as cool as the underground tunnels in the jungle," Lucas said. "Remember the one with the boats, Dad?"

How could Roth forget? "The tunnels led to a cenote, and there were dozens of plastic crates next to it full of gold from the Maya," he said. "They used the underground rivers to transport the treasure from one ruin to another, I think."

"You saw the artifacts?" Estrada asked inquisitively.

"For sure. Just a sample. I guess they must have hidden a lot of it away before the Spanish could get it."

"They got a lot," Estrada affirmed.

"We had to escape bad dudes who were chasing us," Lucas continued for Jordan's benefit. "There were inflatable boats in the cenote, so we all got into one, and Dad grabbed an ancient spear to stab the other boats so they'd go flat."

"No way!" Jordan said, looking at Roth, impressed.

"Yeah, well, he almost fell in after he tried jumping into our boat," Brillante said. "Big oof."

Illari snickered at the story and tried to cover it. Her troubled look had softened into a smile. The boys' energy was just infectious.

"Yeah, that was a near miss," Roth agreed. "I'm not a very good swimmer."

Monica hadn't been kidding about the length of the walk. It was a maze under the building that led to some long, slightly inclined tunnels that were painted a pale, flat gray color with a variety of directional signs. When they finally reached the end of the long, narrow tunnel, they arrived at another set of escalators, which brought them into the underbelly of the Capitol building.

Roth found himself geeking out slightly about the historical building. The craftsmanship and statuary were incredible, and the paintings were all originals. They passed a few tour groups, led by staffers, as Daniel led them to the Senate side and then directly to a private conference room. The FBI agent in front went in first and then motioned for the rest to enter.

The room was dimly lit, the walls and furniture a dark mahogany. There were no external windows at all. A short man with salt-and-pepper hair was pacing at the end of the table. A pin on his gray suit proclaimed him a senator. He was no taller than the boys, and he looked overly nervous.

Monica told the final agent and the staffer, Daniel, to wait outside and prevent anyone from coming in.

"Welcome," the senator greeted them with a tight smile. "I'm Senator Coudron."

"Jonathon Roth. These are my twins, Brillante and Lucas."

"And you are Dr. Estrada?" Senator Coudron asked.

"Yes. And my assistant, Illari."

"Thank you for coming on such short notice. I have hearings all afternoon. In fact, I'm already late for one. But this is important to national security. Mr. Roth, or Jonathon, if I may?"

"That's fine, Senator," Roth said.

"I understand that your family had a life-threatening experience down in Mexico a year ago. It was in the news that your wife didn't come back. A coma, I believe?"

"Yes, but as you probably know, she wasn't in Singapore," Roth explained. "We didn't have a lot of choice in the matter. I'm guessing you listened to the recording I made on Agent Sanchez's phone?"

The senator nodded. "Yes, yes I did." He started fidgeting, making Roth more uneasy. "One of my colleagues, a dear friend actually, has taken trips to Cancún for many years, often at the Calakmul resorts. We've known each other a long time. And he . . . he suggested to me that *I* bring my family on a trip with him. He was quite insistent. From what I understand, that trip may have been my last."

Jonathon swallowed. "Who is your friend?" They'd all remained standing, which was growing more awkward by the moment.

Senator Coudron walked to the mahogany table. A folder lay on it, and he flipped it open, removing a photograph of another senator. Roth recognized him instantly. He'd seen the man in the arena at the Jaguar Temple. One of the guests who had come to watch the game.

"He was there," Roth whispered. Both of the twins approached and looked at the picture.

Coudron sighed. "This is very difficult, as you may imagine. My friend has been on the intelligence committee with me for several years. He has access to the highest security briefings imaginable."

Which meant Jacob Calakmul did too.

"Mr. Roth, you were held there against your will. You didn't know why you'd been brought down there?"

"We did not. Some friends of ours in Bozeman invited us at the last minute. They said another family wasn't able to come."

Coudron sighed again. "That family . . . was mine," he said softly. "Mr. Beasley was a significant contributor to my campaign."

"You're not from Montana," Roth said, confused.

"No. Campaign contributions come from everywhere. I was grief stricken when I heard Eric and his family had died. And I've . . . suspected there was more to it than what I read in the news. I followed your story closely, Mr. Roth. Do you know what happened to your wife?"

Roth shook his head no. "Calakmul kept her as a hostage."

"I'm sorry," the senator confessed. "I truly am. Dr. Estrada," Coudron said, turning to the professor, "I understand your research into LiDAR technology may have revealed the location where this conspiracy originated."

"Yes, Senator," Estrada said. "I haven't been inside the temple, not like this family has, but my pilot and I flew near it. We gave the location to the FBI."

Senator Coudron looked queasy. "And you work for UC San Diego. You have no involvement with the government?"

"None. I'm an archaeology professor. We work with Qualcomm."

Senator Coudron pulled out his cell phone. Sighing, he stared at the screen. Then he brought up a contact and dialed it.

"Director Wright. I've spoken to them. I'm convinced they're telling the truth. You may proceed."

Roth startled. The senator was speaking to the director of the FBI.

Coudron ended the call and turned to Monica. "We must do what we can to stop this disaster from unfolding any further. Timing is paramount. Now I must go attend the hearing. I'm sorry, Mr. Roth. Children. I'm sorry your family got dragged into this."

Roth was dumbfounded. He shook Senator Coudron's hand silently and watched as he left. The senator's staffer, Daniel, hung back to escort them to the parking garage.

"Why do I have the feeling that something is going to happen that they didn't tell us about?" Dr. Estrada said with a troubled look.

Monica had a serious expression. "I don't know what operation he was referring to. It's above my pay grade. Now we're going to get you both back to your respective hotels."

"I'll take the Roths," Jordan said.

"I'll have a driver take you."

Jordan shook his head. "We'll catch an Uber. Better if you don't know."

Her brow furrowing, she said, "Lund is on his way to Dulles. You need backup."

"We have backup in DC," Jordan said. "But we're close by. Trust me."

Monica bit her lip with frustration. "I'll take these two to where they're staying. But *call* me when you're safely back to your hotel."

A sly smile lifted Jordan's lips. "If you say so."

"That's not what I meant!"

Roth rubbed his nose. It was horrible watching those two flirt with each other. "Let's go?"

"I know my way back," Monica said. "Daniel, take them out through the Russell Senate Office Building, and I'll take these two through the Hart. Better leave from different buildings than the one we entered through."

Roth understood immediately. If someone had followed them to the Dirksen building, then they might be waiting for them outside.

"Good thinking," Jordan said. "Let's go, Daniel."

"Can we stop by the cafeteria and get something to eat?" Brillante asked.

"No way! The food here sucks. And so do the food trucks and food courts by the museums. Nasty. We'll get take-out from somewhere nice. Somewhere legit."

"Chick-fil-A?" Lucas asked eagerly.

"Decent," Jordan said. "But it's not the Cheesecake Factory. Remember, we gotta stay out of sight and check in to your new hotel."

After they'd walked through the tunnels to the Russell building, Roth glanced at his watch and saw it was 2:30 p.m. His stomach was growling, but hunger wasn't the only thing making his stomach twist.

He and his family were involved in a huge international conspiracy. Lives were at stake. Including the president's.

When they reached security, Jordan pulled out his cell phone and made a call. "This is Jordan. We're leaving now and heading to lunch. Yeah . . . Lund took my car. I'm going to need another one brought to the hotel. Leave the fob at the concierge for me. We'll take an Uber. Thanks, bro."

They headed through security, and then Jordan pulled up his Uber app and ordered a vehicle to take them to lunch.

"Is it good?" Lucas asked.

"You love cheesecake, right?" Jordan responded.

"How many do they have?"

"*So* many." Jordan finished ordering the car. "It'll be here in two minutes. Let's go outside. It'll drop us off nearby, and we'll walk. Then we'll take it back to the hotel to eat."

Jordan led the way, checking both ways before motioning for them to come out. Roth and the boys followed. It was cold and breezy. The nervous pit in Roth's stomach felt more like a black hole. Something felt off. Wrong. The street was empty of traffic, except for a few parked cars in front of the building.

"The Uber will have to pick us up at the corner," Jordan said. "No other vehicles are allowed on this street."

"That's sus," Lucas said, pointing to the wall alongside the sidewalk.

"What's sus?" Roth asked, although he felt it too. Something was . . . wrong.

"That," he said.

Roth looked again. "What?"

"Don't you see it? It's . . . it's glowing."

Brillante turned to look and went pale. "That's a glyph."

Roth couldn't see it. "What does it look like?"

"An eye," Lucas said.

CHAPTER FIFTEEN

Constitution Avenue

Washington, DC

January 9

That meant it *was* a glyph. And Roth had no doubt what it meant. The jaguar priests were watching them.

"I don't see anything," Jordan said, still holding his phone in one hand, the screen tracking the approach of their Uber driver.

"It's right there," Brillante said, walking forward and pointing to the stone wall along the sidewalk. He appeared to be pointing at nothing.

"We need to get out of here," Roth said. If Suki were there, she could blast away the glyph with the wave of her hand, using the bracelet and ring she wore to channel her power.

Jordan nodded to the street ahead. "The driver is meeting us right there. Let's go."

The boys were still staring at the glyph, but they nodded. Roth did too. They all ran for it, Roth's heart hammering. They were still moving toward the intersection when Jordan's phone chirped. He glanced at it and then pointed at the SUV that had just pulled up. It was a Chevy Tahoe, metallic gray.

Jordan reached the vehicle first, just as the driver was rolling down the window. "You Jordan?" he asked. "That your group?"

"Yes. We're late. Need to get somewhere fast or we'll lose our reservation."

Jordan pulled open the car door, and the boys both hurried inside.

Roth glanced to the side and saw someone racing toward them, a man with a leather trench coat and a trim beard. His eyes blazed with anger as he sprinted toward the family.

"Go, go, go!" Roth shouted, climbing into the vehicle.

Jordan noticed the man coming too and hurried into the passenger seat.

"What's wrong, man?" asked the driver in confusion.

"Move! Now!" Jordan barked. He put away the phone and reached for his Glock.

"Dude, I'm just an Uber driver!" exclaimed the stranger, holding up his hands.

"Step on it!" Jordan roared.

The driver looked panicked, but he obeyed the order. He pulled into the street and began to accelerate. A car honked and swerved to avoid hitting them.

"Seat belts," Roth said, scrambling to secure his own. The chase on the autobahn was still fresh in his mind. They could have died. And this time they didn't have Suki to dispel any magic wards that might be summoned against them. Twisting around in his seat, he looked out the back window of the Tahoe. The man was still running. And *gaining* on them.

They'd been accelerating down Constitution Avenue, but the driver hit the brakes.

"Go!" Jordan shouted.

"Red light!" the driver said helplessly.

"Run it!"

"Pedestrians!" the driver wailed.

Some pedestrians had triggered the crosswalk light, and Roth could see them passing right in front of their SUV. As soon as they'd cleared the vehicle, Jordan ordered, "Go! Go!"

The driver gunned the engine, and the Tahoe lurched through the intersection.

"I could get arrested," the driver protested angrily. "This is nuts!"

"Someone's chasing us," Jordan said. "They're back there, going faster than us."

"Who, the cops?" the driver said with some snark.

Roth's heart was beating furiously. Looking back and forth was making him carsick, but he couldn't help himself. Their pursuer was moving faster than he should be able to. He was moving like a jaguar priest. The driver accelerated, gaining distance. Roth put his hand on the back of Jordan's seat to brace himself as they sped toward the next intersection. The Capitol building loomed on their left, its majestic dome an inspiring sight. Usually. Right now, it was just another building. It couldn't save them.

Roth looked out the back window, his stomach lurching again, and didn't see the man anymore. "He's gone," he breathed out in relief.

"No, he's changing!" Jordan shouted with fear.

Roth turned his head and shoulder the other way to see out the side window instead—and immediately wished he hadn't. Their pursuer was running alongside their vehicle, but he was loping like a wolf, using his arms and legs to propel himself. It was a bizarre, disturbing melding of man and beast that reminded him of the ghost stories Moretti's dad used to tell about the Navajo skinwalkers, the *yee naaldlooshii*. The look of hatred on the man's face as he glared at Roth through the window was so intense, so absolute, that Roth feared he would pee himself. He froze in panic, unable to talk.

Jordan reached over and cranked the steering wheel. The driver let out a startled cry as the Tahoe rocked and swerved. Confusion, motion sickness, and terror all slugged it out inside Roth's gut. The half-man, half-beast was struck by the vehicle and sent tumbling away before he collided with a parked car on the side of the road.

"Faster!" Jordan bellowed. "He's . . . he's shaking it off. Faster!" He was looking out the side mirror, eyes wide with panic.

The boys were gripping the seats in front of them in terror. Roth had seen it in their faces before, and it would haunt his dreams forever. He'd put them in harm's way again. Would this nightmare never end?

The driver was trembling with fear. It was good he couldn't see what was behind them. He planted his foot on the gas, and the Tahoe roared ahead. They went through the intersection at full speed. Cars honked. They were lucky they didn't hit any other vehicles.

The road bent hard to the left, then met almost perpendicular with Pennsylvania Avenue, which led away from the Capitol building at an angle. Going straight wasn't even an option because the National Gallery of Art blocked the way. The driver didn't even ask, he just took the right, swerving around another car that had stopped at the red light, and entered the intersection. Car horns blared at them from oncoming vehicles.

Roth nearly lost his lunch all over the seat and floor. He only kept it down by sheer force of will.

"I don't see him," Jordan declared. "Left on Fourth, left on Fourth! Now! It's clear!"

The tires of the SUV screeched. Roth felt dizzy, his ears ringing, his stomach feeling even worse. The Tahoe passed across the lanes of traffic and then turned left in response to Jordan's pointing. Roth shut his eyes, unable to bear the ride. He felt Lucas patting his arm.

"Past Independence," Jordan said.

"You guys are freaking insane," the driver muttered.

"This family is in the witness protection program," Jordan said. "You'll be reimbursed."

"You a Fed?"

"Sort of," Jordan said. "Pull into that parking garage. On the right. Let's get out of sight."

"Are you going to shoot me?" the driver demanded.

"No, bruh. I'm going to *pay* you the biggest tip you've had in your life."

"Really?"

"This family is rich. You just saved their lives. I hope you take crypto."

"I love crypto!" the driver said enthusiastically.

"Pull in here, then call the police to report the accident. I'll call the FBI. It's all good."

Roth felt the SUV slow and turn as they went into an underground parking garage. The tires squeaked on the smooth cement. His stomach was starting to settle, but the aftertaste of bile in his mouth was terrible. The jaguar priest had pursued them instead of attacking. That meant he was determined to catch them. Alive. If Jacob had wanted Roth and the boys dead, he probably would have made their vehicle explode.

He wants revenge, Roth thought with dread. He remembered the sound of Eric Beasley dying in the arena. His anxiety kicked into overdrive.

The Tahoe stopped, and Jordan climbed out and opened the door. Even the stale air of the parking garage was a relief. Jordan helped Roth climb out. The boys got out too, both of them pale with fear.

Jordan pulled out his cell and made a call. "Hey, Monica. You okay? No, we just got attacked by one of Calakmul's goons. We're okay now."

The sound of police sirens could be heard in the distance, echoing strangely in the parking garage.

"The police are probably looking for us since we ran a few red lights. It was weird, like that guy who attacked us at the cabin. He hadn't transformed totally, but he was running on all fours. Seriously, we hit him with the Tahoe." He paused, looking back up the garage ramp. "I don't hear anything. See anything. Maybe he's too injured to make another go at us right now."

Roth looked at the side of the Tahoe. It was dented in as if it had been struck by another vehicle. The driver came around the back, and when he saw the damage, he held up his hands and walked away in disgust.

"We're pretty close to the new hotel. I'll have DoorDash bring us dinner. But I wanted you to know in case the news of the chase reaches you. We're okay. Thanks. I appreciate it." He paused again and smirked at the boys. "Yes, I love you too."

Brillante and Lucas exchanged a look and then rolled their eyes. "She'd already hung up, bruh," Brillante said, unconvinced.

"She's crazy about me," Jordan said, wagging his eyebrows. "That was intense! I loved it! Let me get the driver calmed down, and then we can walk to the new place from here. It's not that far."

Roth nodded again, sitting down against the wall of the parking garage. His sense of hearing was distorted by the thrum of the SUV's engine, the wail of sirens, the echoes of rubber tires squealing as cars left the parking garage. He began to shiver.

After making arrangements with the driver, Jordan returned to their little huddle. "Let's get going. And if you see any more of those invisible warning eyes, let me know, okay?"

"How much did you tip him?" Lucas asked.

"Five big ones."

"Five bucks?" Lucas said with disappointment.

"Five *hundred*, little guy. Like I said, he'll never get an Uber tip like that again. And we have decent collision insurance. He'll be okay. Our office will handle the paperwork."

Jordan reached down to help Roth stand. "You okay, boss?"

"I think so." He felt terrible that he'd put his family in danger by pushing things with Calakmul. He could have done nothing and let the man wreak his vengeance on the world. But he'd felt compelled to try to stop it—by publishing that book, by going to Dresden to see the codex. Even now, he didn't regret that. If he was going to die, he was going to die fighting for a better future.

It was time to relaunch his book with Calakmul's name printed inside it and his own name printed on the outside. To expose him for who he was and what he was doing. He'd hesitated because of Suki and Sarina, but they were safe—or at least safer—and it was time to expose Calakmul to the world. He knew enough about the publishing world to quickly make the changes and attach the independently published book to his own name.

He pledged to himself that there'd be no more waiting. He'd do it tonight.

They walked the rest of the way to the new hotel, which was near the Smithsonian buildings. He had no idea how they'd gotten there, but Jordan knew his way around DC, and the Uber driver would be clueless as to where they'd gone.

With relief, Roth entered the lobby. Jordan went to the main desk and checked to make sure their stuff had arrived at their room. Then he went up first to make sure nothing was wrong. It was a decent suite with two separate bedrooms and a common living room area with a tiny kitchen.

"Still feel like cheesecake for dinner?" Jordan asked the boys.

"Sure, that would be nice," Lucas said, rubbing his stomach. But it looked like he was putting on a front. Brillante was hanging his head, exhausted and worried.

Jordan turned to Roth. "I'm sure Lund will call once he gets to Florida and has the others. Hopefully by tonight, okay?"

"I hope so," Roth said. Naples, Florida, felt very far away, but it was a short flight. Still, how would Lund get them back if they didn't have ID? Surely Calakmul would be watching the airports.

But Lund was a pretty clever guy. Roth was sure he already had a plan in motion.

Jordan gave him a nod and then left. "I'm going to stay in the lobby a while, make sure no one followed us. I'll call in reinforcements too. Stay up here." Roth nodded and used the security deadbolts to block the door, but they felt woefully inadequate. He went to the little bathroom by his master suite and splashed some water on his face.

He heard Brillante ask Lucas if he wanted to play video games.

"No. I just want it to be quiet for a little while. That was pretty scary."

"Totally," Brillante agreed.

Roth listened to the brothers comfort each other. He looked at himself in the mirror, his emotions churning. Sarina and Jane Louise were alive. They'd helped Suki escape. Relief overpowered his feelings of despair. The determination he'd felt in the parking garage hadn't left. Up until that moment, he'd toed the line. It was time to vault across it.

That was good because tears wouldn't stop Calakmul. He thought about the book he'd written of his family's experience in the death game. The trip to Cozumel. He had another version with the correct names and locations, which would expose Jacob Calakmul and his insiders. He had an ad campaign set up with Amazon as well, which if triggered, would cost twenty thousand dollars a month to help boost the signal. There was no chance that Jacob and his henchmen *wouldn't* learn about the book. Even the simplest Google saved query would catch it.

Roth looked himself in the eye. It was time to send it out into the world. He walked over to his computer bag, pulled out his laptop, and powered it on.

CHAPTER SIXTEEN

NCH Baker Downtown Hospital

Naples, Florida

January 9

Most people were grossed out by medical smells, but not Suki. There was a certain smell in hospitals that she found both familiar and comforting. Or maybe it was just nostalgic. When she was a little girl, she'd visit her mom where she worked as a nurse in Fremont. She had asked her mom about that smell, and was told it was antiseptic. And with that smell might come the tangy whiff of rubbing alcohol. These were smells that masked the otherwise nasty aromas common in a hospital—vomit, blood, and various degrees of people's poop.

Being in a hospital was familiar ground to Suki. The distant beep of monitors, the code words the staff used on the speakers. Those weren't fearful sounds. They were comforting ones.

And then the warning feeling came and blew the feeling of safety to bits.

Suki stiffened in her chair. Her mom was asleep on the hospital bed, a blue blanket covering her body. Jane Louise was curled up on another chair, picking at the broken remains of the armrest fabric. A tray with a half-eaten tuna sandwich, an empty juice box, and a cup of pudding sat on the floor by her. A nurse had generously donated her lunch to help ease their hunger.

An IV line was hanging from a chrome pole, dripping fluids into the tubing stuck into her mom's arm. The doctor who'd been helping them was a nice man. Dr. Andrews, a short, stocky older Asian man with buzzed gray hair. He'd stopped by in the last hour to check on them and made sure everyone had enough to eat. They'd caught the low insulin in time, he'd said. There was no sign of DKA.

Suki felt the throb of warning again. She got off the chair and walked to the edge of the curtain. The door on the other side was closed, so she pulled on the latch and opened it a crack. Outside, in the bustle of the emergency main floor, she saw nurses and a variety of patients—some in wheelchairs, one on a gurney, but most standing. It was impossible to tell with her eyes who, if any of them, was the source of warning.

But that warning couldn't be wrong. She'd learned to trust herself because the warnings she felt were tied to her magic. They were in trouble, or about to be. That meant it was time to get out of there.

Suki went back behind the curtain and saw Jane Louise watching her.

"Is Uncle Steve here?" the little girl asked.

That was the code name for Steve Lund, who was coming to help them. Suki looked at the clock on the wall. He was probably still flying down from DC. Her stomach twisted with anxiety, but she began to whisper the Mayan words to calm herself. She walked to the bed and shook her mom's shoulder.

Her mom's eyes fluttered open. "Sorry I fell asleep. Is everything okay?"

Suki shook her head. "We have to get out of here."

Jane Louise startled.

Suki bit her lip, glancing at the little girl. She hated the fear in her eyes—hated even more that she'd put it there, but fear made sense. This was all *wrong*.

Her mom's brow wrinkled. "Did something happen while I was asleep?"

Suki shook her head again. "No. The vibe changed. Like what happened when we went to Calakmul's resort. I get these feelings sometimes. Warnings. We need to go. Now."

Her mother didn't hesitate. She didn't second-guess or question. "Okay, *mija*. I trust you." Sarina rubbed her eyes and then swung her legs off the edge of the bed. She looked at the drip line in her arm and, thankfully, knew exactly how to stop it. She undid the tape holding the needle to the crook of her arm and then pulled it out.

"Get me a Band-Aid and a cotton ball. Over there," she ordered.

Suki did so, and her mom had her put the cotton ball on the injection site and then covered it with the Band-Aid. Jane Louise hopped off the chair. The feeling of fear was growing rapidly in Suki's chest—turning into an urgent beat that matched the pounding of her heart.

"I'll need more insulin," her mom said. Then she looked at the table and searched around. They found some packages of syringes and a partial bottle of insulin in the trash can that the nurse had used earlier.

"We have to *go*," Suki said, her voice rising in panic.

The look of fatigue on her mom's face was telling. Ix Chel might have restored her age, but she hadn't restored her health.

"They don't have any extra vials here," her mom said after a few moments of more searching.

"I'll check the hallway again," Suki said. Jane Louise took Sarina's hand and squeezed it. Lund had the phone number for the hospital. He'd call as soon as he landed, but they would be gone. She had his phone number memorized, though. Maybe she should use the phone in the room to leave him a—?

The next throb of warning hit her hard.

No time. She'd have to find another way.

Suki went to the door, cracked it open again. There were even more people in the corridor now. Someone was crying. The rust-like smell of blood overwhelmed the scent of antiseptic.

There was an abandoned wheelchair just a few feet away. Suki hurried to it and then unlocked the wheels and pushed it back to the room just as her mom and Jane Louise emerged.

"Sit down," Suki ordered. Her mom did so, and Suki began to push her away from the crowded end of the hall. Her neck hairs were tingling with anticipation.

They passed a few other rooms, hearing the murmuring of nurses and patients. At the end of the corridor was an emergency exit door. There would be an alarm attached to it. That would bring orderlies running, right? And her mom was in no condition to take off at a run. They also passed a supply closet, but how long could they stay hidden before a staff member found them?

Glancing over her shoulder, she didn't see the source of her warning, but she still felt it throbbing inside her. Then, amid the crowd, she saw a police officer talking to Dr. Andrews, who had helped them.

There was no more time. Suki pushed the wheelchair to the exit door. Immediately, the Mayan word *Silanik* came to her mind, unbidden. *To quiet or silence something.*

Suki summoned the magic of her bracelet and ring. Both started to glow. She repeated the word in her mind and passed her hand in front of their group.

"Push the door, Jane Louise," Suki instructed.

The little girl jogged ahead and pushed on the handle. The blue strobe light didn't activate. She stared at the bulb. Nothing happened.

Suki pushed the wheelchair out the back door.

Darkness settled over the park. It wasn't even 6:30 p.m., and it was already pretty dark. They'd ditched the wheelchair behind the hospital and then walked down the street about a mile before finding a community park that held a playground, a baseball diamond, and a ton of tennis courts. The sign said "Cambier Park."

There were lots of trees and, interestingly, iguanas all over the place. They sat down at an empty park bench, and Suki told Jane Louise to play on the playground for a little while. There weren't a lot of kids but enough that the Beasley girl didn't totally stand out. Suki then asked a stranger—a mom—if she could borrow her cell phone. She left a message for "Uncle Steve," telling him where they were and saying they'd need a ride home before it got dark.

As the twilight vanished, the tennis court lights stayed on. Maybe a third of them were in use with players whacking at the rubber balls over and over, which gave Suki a nasty flashback to the death games. She paced. She sat down by her mom. Then paced again, wondering how long it would take for Lund to arrive. What if he didn't show up? Would they stay all night in the park? That wouldn't be fun. And they'd become more noticeable with every passing hour as everyone else left the park.

"Suki," her mother said, hands on her stomach. "I need protein. Or whole grains. No sugar."

"I don't want to leave you all alone," Suki said.

"You aren't. Jane Louise will be here. It's okay."

Suki bit her lip. There wasn't a warning feeling. "I'll be quick." She went to the playground and told Jane Louise to keep an eye on her mom, saying she'd be right back with some food. She remembered seeing a restaurant next to a cigar shop across the street. It was called Captain & Krewe, and it sat next to a vacant lot with the footings of a demolished building at the base. Suki jaywalked to cross the street and ordered food for takeout, including a cheeseburger for Jane Louise, a crab BLT for herself, some fish tacos for her mom, and three bottles of water. With some of the money that Jorge had given them, she paid in cash and then walked out and nearly jumped out of her skin when she saw a police car had pulled up.

The driver door opened, and a hefty officer came out. He saw her. *Crap. Crap. Crap.*

"Hey," the officer said to get her attention.

Suki swallowed and gave him a blank look. "Me?"

"Yeah. I need to talk to you."

Could she outrun this guy? Carrying dinner? He looked out of shape, so maybe? But if she gave away their location, he could call in backup. She had to bluff her way through this.

"Okay," Suki said, shrugging. She walked up to him and looked up, keeping her face as blank as a piece of . . . blank as a . . . her brain just wasn't working.

"You from around here?" he asked her.

"Uh-huh," she said. "My mom asked me to pick up dinner from Cap'n Krewe. Live over there," she added, hefting the bag and pointing it vaguely down the street.

"Looking for a teenage girl, a woman, and a little blond girl. Seen anyone like that around?" The officer's shoulder radio crackled, emitting some police chatter.

Suki thought about her drama teacher. Some of the lessons she'd learned about acting. *Play the part. Get into the role.* Sometimes, a scene went haywire, and you had to ad-lib something.

"What?" Suki asked as if she didn't hear him.

"I'm looking for three people," he repeated. "A woman, a teenage girl, and a little blond girl. Seen anyone like that?"

"Nope," Suki said, shaking her head.

A car honked on the street. The police officer turned around to look at a minivan stopped in the road. Relief nearly made Suki weak. Uncle Steve was at the wheel.

"Officer!" Lund yelled. "That's my daughter. What's the problem?"

"Dad!" Suki yelled with relief. She hurried to the passenger door.

"You see anyone like that, you call the police, okay?" the officer said.

"Okay!" Suki agreed. She opened the door and got inside.

Sarina and Jane Louise were already in the back. The windows were tinted, so she hadn't noticed them.

"Have a nice day, Officer!" Lund said with a kindly wave. As soon as the door was shut, the window up, and they were rolling away, he snorted under his breath. "Idiot."

Suki started to gulp in air. "I've got dinner."

"Yes, please," Jane Louise said patiently.

"We can't go back to the airport," Lund said, checking his lane and turning immediately down a side street. "There's news about the three of you going through Florida right now. Not your names, just your descriptions. We need to find another way back."

Suki's sigh of relief stopped midbreath.

CHAPTER SEVENTEEN

The Villas

Naples, Florida

January 9

It was so good hearing Dad's voice through Lund's iPhone speaker. They'd filled each other in on what they'd been through, the twins piping in every so often. It felt so awesome being together as a family again—tethered by cell phone towers up and down the East Coast. Suki wanted so badly for them to be together again. Jane Louise had fallen asleep on the double bed, a peaceful smile on her face, and Suki and her mom sat on the other bed with the phone. Before Jane Louise had lain down, Dad had promised her they'd get in touch with her mee-maw.

Lund sat on the gray fabric couch by the window. The blinds were drawn, and the lamp was off, adding to the darkness of the room. It was nine o'clock, and they all needed to go to bed, but this time was precious. It meant the world to her.

"Can I talk to Lund for a minute?" Roth asked. "Is he still there?"

"He's here," Sarina said. "I miss hearing your voice, Jonny."

That was her pet name for him. It made a warm feeling wriggle inside Suki when she heard them talk like that. Teenagers weren't supposed to like it when their parents showed affection for each other. But Suki secretly did. Especially now, after all this time apart.

Lund rose from the couch and approached the bed. Sarina handed him the phone.

Other than the two beds and the couch, there wasn't much to the room. Just a work desk with a rolling chair. They'd already discussed the sleeping arrangements—Suki and Jane Louise would share one bed, and Suki's mom would keep the other by herself. Lund had said he was going to get more coffee and stay awake all night to help protect them. He'd rented the room and then brought the family in through the side door of the hotel. They had no luggage, no clothes to change into, but that was okay. Even the strange hotel smell didn't bother Suki so much.

"You guys at the new hotel?" Lund asked, holding the phone out so they could all hear.

"Yeah. Monica called earlier. She said the pandemic meeting is still happening tomorrow with the president's cabinet."

Lund chuffed. "I heard the same. It's beyond irrational. A bomb threat at a high school during finals week is taken more seriously than this. I'm appalled. I thought Director Wright would be more sensible."

"I don't know what else we could have said to convince them. Not even the visit with the senator seemed to work. The jaguar priests are *here* in DC. Well, at least one is. She said the FBI director isn't convinced it should be canceled. They're not even boosting security."

Lund sighed and shook his head. "Brower's not an idiot. And neither is Director Wright. But that's the thing about the executive branch, Mr. Roth. It maneuvers about as fast as a Winnebago in the sand. Without a *credible* threat, they won't take action."

"What about an *in*-credible threat?" Roth said, snorting. "Maybe nothing will happen tomorrow. Maybe that's not Calakmul's plan. But Moretti confirmed there's a threat to the president, and Senator

Coudron verified that the corruption is deep inside. What about the attorney? Has she talked yet?"

"We've gotten nothing out of her. And no grounds to hold her because we can't prove she caused the heart attack. Personally, I'm holding out hope that the CIA will learn something tonight during their operation down in the jungle. If a drone can confirm the location of that temple—and that there are people there—then the story will be legitimized. I just hope it's not too late."

"Me too. Thank you so much for getting my family back, Steve. Seriously. You have my eternal gratitude. If things get weird here in DC tomorrow, I'll let you know."

"Well, Jordan better let me know first," Lund said with a chuckle.

"I will, boss!" It was Jordan's voice, distant but clear. Suki smiled.

"Good night, Mr. Roth," Lund said.

"Hey, can I talk to Suki real quick?"

"Sure."

Lund switched the speaker off and handed the phone to Suki.

"Hi, Dad."

"Hey. I just . . . I wanted to say how proud I am of you. You saved us in the arena. And you're saving the family again. Keep listening to your instincts, okay? The warnings you keep getting. You were right to leave the hospital."

"Thanks," Suki said, her throat suddenly clenching with emotion. Her dad didn't dole out praise all that often, so it felt more meaningful when he did.

"Keep your eye on Mom. She has insulin in her, which is good. But she doesn't have much more, so she may allow her sugar to run high to make it last longer. I'll work with Monica to get her a new pump and supplies for when you arrive, but make sure she's drinking enough and eating healthy. No waffles and syrup from the hotel for breakfast, okay?"

"Got it," Suki said. She was hoping there would be waffles, although she suspected Lund would be choosing their breakfast and wearing a disguise when he picked it up. They certainly couldn't go down there as a group. "Take care of the twins, okay? Don't let them watch too many gamers on YouTube."

Her dad's laughter made her smile. "I think they're watching *SpongeBob* with Jordan right now. We're good. I love you, Suki. Can I say good night to Mom?"

"Sure. Love you too, Dad."

Suki wasn't that keen on showing her emotions. But after all they'd been through, she realized how important it was to say the words. You never knew when another chance would come—or not.

Her mom had fallen asleep, so Suki gently shook her shoulder to wake her. She smiled and took the phone back. "Jonny."

As her parents spoke, Suki sat on the bed and wrapped her arms around her knees. Her gaze kept returning to her mom. She still couldn't believe she had her back, that she was herself again, really and truly. Ix Chel had a power greater even than Aztlán, which had made Jacob Calakmul younger. They didn't know much about the magic that had made this work, but they were all grateful for it.

"I love you," Sarina whispered. "So much. I hope you understand why I stayed. Ix Chel needed me, and I knew the kids had you. Jane Louise had no one. I felt . . . I couldn't bear to leave her. And I sensed that Suki was coming. I knew I had to be there to get them both out."

Suki felt tears prick her eyes. She loved her mom. Her selflessness, her willingness to sacrifice herself to help others. She respected her mom's decision not to try to escape.

"I love you too, Jonny. Good night. We'll see you tomorrow."

——

The hotel door beeped and unlocked, and Lund entered carrying a tray of food from the breakfast buffet. Scrambled eggs, sketchy bacon, some waffles and syrup cartons, fresh fruit. The TV was blaring the morning news and traffic report as he set the tray down on the worktable.

"I'm going to get the drinks," Lund said. "Apple juice, orange juice, milk? What do you want?"

"Apple juice," Jane Louise said.

"Milk is good," Suki said.

"I'll have water," her mom said. She looked tired but rested. Lund looked like he had indeed been up all night. It was eight o'clock in the morning.

"You going to get some sleep before we go?" Suki asked him.

"I've had some coffee," Lund answered. "It'll kick in soon. And I need to make some phone calls. I'll be back."

He left, and the door clicked shut. They all shared the breakfast food, but Jane Louise didn't have much of an appetite and went over to the couch by the window.

Suki watched TV for a while, thinking about how awkward it would be to be a weather forecaster. Then she noticed motion from the corner of her eye. Turning her head, she saw Jane Louise had opened the curtain and was waving to someone outside.

Suki's stomach did an uncomfortable twist. She got off the bed, set her plate down, and went to the window. There was a car parked out there, and a family was getting into a GMC Yukon that had bug guts splattered on the grille and hood and windshield. There was a little girl outside, waving back to Jane Louise. The dad was staring through the window with a concerned look. Suki met his gaze, and his eyebrows lifted. Suki gently pulled Jane Louise away from the window and let the gauzy curtain fall back into place.

"Go sit on the bed," Suki suggested. The door beeped again, and Lund returned with a tray of glasses with different drinks, as well as another mug of coffee.

Suki gestured for Lund to come to the window. He set the tray down by the breakfast spread. Sarina reached for the water, and Jane Louise took the apple juice.

Lund gave Suki a questioning look when he reached her.

"Jane Louise was waving at a kid outside," Suki whispered. "The dad saw her. Then he saw me. I think he might have recognized us."

Lund went to the edge of the curtain and parted it to peer outside. "The GMC?"

"Yeah."

Lund frowned. "Most people ignore Good Samaritan opportunities. He's on his cell phone. Sitting there. The whole family is in the vehicle."

The warning feeling was throbbing hard now. "We'd better go."

"Agreed," Lund said. "Let's get moving."

Sarina nodded and hurried off the bed. Taking Jane Louise by the hand, she moved to turn the TV off, but Lund told her to keep it on. It would help convince the hotel staff they were still there.

"Out the side door," Lund said. "Like the way we came in."

As they left, the nervous feeling continued to build inside Suki. She was so tired of feeling it, so she started to repeat the calming mantra. They walked down the corridor swiftly and exited through the side door. Even though it was morning, it was still humid, although the temperature was only in the fifties. Suki rubbed her arms.

Lund unlocked the car, and they got inside the minivan. The Yukon appeared around the side of the hotel, creeping slowly. Suki saw the dad in the driver's seat, still on the phone.

"Buckle up," Lund said. He fired up the engine and then did a quick reverse. The Yukon stopped.

Lund put it in gear and started out of the parking lot. The Yukon began following them. How long before the police were dispatched?

Suki clicked her seat belt, remembering the morning after Christmas when they'd escaped another Yukon, full of MS-13 members. No snow on the roads this time, at least.

Lund clicked the side of his phone. "Driving directions to Everglades City," he said to it.

The CarPlay app on the rental put up driving directions from Naples to Everglades City. It was southeast of Naples, deeper into Florida.

"What's in Everglades City?" Suki asked.

"A way out where no one can follow us," Lund said with tightness in his voice. He sped out of the parking lot toward the highway. Palm trees stood in thick walls around the edges of the parking lot. The Yukon started after them.

"Let's see how well you can drive, Mr. Hero," Lund grunted, accelerating toward the intersection instead of slowing down.

"Turn left on US Highway 41, Tamiami Trail," said the robotically female voice on his phone.

Suki gripped the safety handle and grimaced as the minivan sped into the intersection in the middle of the slow-going morning commute without stopping. She closed her eyes.

Honks, brakes screeching. Her stomach was flooded with butterflies as the van accelerated.

CHAPTER EIGHTEEN

Jaguar Temple

Calakmul Biosphere Reserve

January 10

"I salute you, Huracán, enemy of both sides. Lord of the Near and the Nigh. God of the Furious Winds, Possessor of Sky and Earth. Open."

The stela ground opened again, and once more Jacob lowered himself to pass beneath it into the sacred chamber with the obsidian mirrors. He wore a casual business suit, open-collared shirt—no tie. In one pocket, he carried a blowgun and a brace of poison darts. In the other, a Glock with hollow-point bullets. He wasn't sure he'd need either, but it was good to be prepared.

The other jaguar priests had already gathered within the close space and were waiting for him. The thrill of anticipation was dulled by the disappointment that he hadn't yet achieved all of his aims. Roth continued to defy him. So did Suki.

The other jaguar priests took a knee as soon as he was with them. Each bowed his head. Each man had been chosen for his dedication and skill. This would be the ultimate test.

"Welcome, my brothers," Jacob said. "Today we are one in purpose. Each of us must do his part to fulfill the Jaguar Prophecies. If all goes well, this night will be a special celebration, a special sacrifice. On the altar of the temple, I will cut out the heart of the president of the United States. If I should fall or fail, one of you will step into my place. Angélica will announce who I have chosen. This is the moment we have trained our whole lives for."

"What of the little girl? The sorceress?" asked Rinaldo. Jacob recognized the anger in his voice. He felt the same burn in his own chest.

"She escaped with her mother and the Beasley girl," Jacob said, controlling his own reaction. "They were taken by the US Coast Guard in Florida and then escaped. We will find them and bring them back. Ix Chel cannot thwart our designs, no matter how she meddles. And they have no immunity to the disease."

"What will stop her from meddling in this?" asked Mataré in a vindictive tone. He was the most ruthless killer of them all.

"She is the moon goddess, not the Lord of the Near and the Nigh," Jacob shot back. "The believers in the FBI have said they do nothing. They see nothing. We are the masters of the obsidian mirrors. They know not how we are coming."

Jacob flexed his thoughts and invoked the magic of his ring. The power of the *kem äm* began to churn within the chamber. The obsidian mirrors were instantly wreathed in gray smoke, not toxic but a residue of the power connecting the mirrors together, allowing someone to pass from one to the other.

"The Americans sent drones against us last night," Jacob said haughtily. "But they could not penetrate our defenses. They were scattered like bats. Their bullets cannot harm us. The cartels await my orders with their brave foot soldiers. They wait with great anxiety for the word to destroy the Americans. And so they wait in London. And so they wait in Berlin. And so they wait in Madrid."

He saw these men tense with pleasure. Some were quivering with anticipation.

Jacob clenched his hand into a fist. "Tonight will be another Night of Sorrows. When Cortés was driven from Tenochtitlán following the murder of Moctezuma. This time, he and all of his modern-day spawn will be driven away, hunted down, and killed. We will build temples in the north. We will uncover the secret temples hidden beneath so many cities. The death games will be the new sport of the people. And it begins tonight. It begins *now*."

"*Ajwäch,*" they began to chant. "*Ajwäch. Ajwäch. Ajwäch!*"

The one who knows secrets. The master of them.

Jacob looked at Mataré once more. He had nearly caught Mr. Roth and the boys the previous day in Washington, DC. He was still furious at his failure, at their escape. After being knocked aside by the vehicle, he'd used the magic to heal himself and had nearly gone on a rampage and killed everyone in his path. But prudence had prevailed. He'd backed off, but his vendetta against Mr. Roth was now personal. He hated the bitter taste of disappointment. He wanted to resume the hunt, believing the quarry was close. There'd been a report of a group of four arriving at a hotel near a Smithsonian building shortly after the chase. It wasn't much, but it was something to go on.

"Remain here and wait for news from Victor about the hotel," Jacob said. "When I return with the American, I will unleash you on the rest of our victims. Just as Moctezuma's body was thrown down the temple steps to the violent mob, so will we do with the president's corpse here tonight. Their world will be baptized anew . . . baptized in blood."

He could sense their hunger for the image he painted, their willingness to pursue this goal to the end. Jacob held up his fist and brought the magic of the *kem äm* to his eyes so they glowed. A little growl came from his mouth, but he did not transform. He would not show any vulnerability to these men, any one of whom might seek to take his place so as to *be* the *Ajwäch* himself.

Jacob strode to the obsidian mirror connected to the White House and passed through it, cloaking himself in invisibility as he stepped through.

———

The smell of coffee, old carpet, and oak wood flooded Jacob's senses, along with artificial warmth from the heating system. His nerves were taut. He'd been preparing for this moment his whole life. The greatest outcome of having a secret team of gifted people was that it gave him the ability to get into the most secure places. During the height of the Maya and Aztec empires, key members of the Kowinem had infiltrated every kingdom, every tribe. Their friendly smiles and regular acts of kindness had belied the murder in their hearts. When it came time to depose a king, a single member of the order could literally walk past any sentinels and protections, proving that no one was safe. An obsidian blade to the heart. A pinprick from a poison dart. A dusting of powder on a spoon handle. There were many ways to kill an enemy.

Jacob stood in the slim corridor within the White House. He saw an office, door open, with a woman behind a computer screen. Another office door was farther ahead. A younger man in a white shirt and dark tie leaned against the jamb, talking to a female staffer in a flirtatious way. A fake plant sat on the right-side wall. Several framed photos of famous Americans hung on the walls—and so did the obsidian mirror.

The female staffer was the one who was waiting for him. She had walked him there before during their practices, so he knew the way without her, but she had the badge that would open the door.

"Any plans for the weekend?" the male staffer asked her.

"I've got so much on my plate this weekend," she answered.

Jacob walked up behind her and blew a breath against her ear, followed by the password, whispered so faintly the amorous young man wouldn't hear it over the ambient noise in the hall. She shuddered when she felt it.

"They're talking about doing a shutdown," the young man said. "Better go for drinks while we still can. Want to meet somewhere?"

"Maybe another time," she said and turned and began walking away. Jacob followed her.

"Do you want my phone number?" he called after her.

She ignored the question and quickly turned the corner.

"Are they all like that?" Jacob whispered to her from behind, keeping pace.

"Oh yes," she said with an edge to her voice. "They think they're gods for working here."

"They will soon learn their place," Jacob said. "Onward."

The White House was a labyrinth of sorts. The construction had started in 1792, and in 1800 it had been occupied by the second US president. The only damage it had sustained was during the war of 1812. That would change. It was a symbol of the power of the nation. And such symbols needed to be destroyed. Or repurposed. The Spanish had torn down a pyramid in Izamal to create a cathedral to their religion, and Jacob intended to do the same with the Greek-style structures in DC.

The Situation Room, where this particular cabinet meeting was happening, was underground. Uniformed marines guarded the entrance in their ceremonial garb. There was so much protection outside the White House that the defenses *inside* were relatively sparse. The young woman's badge, with her name—Christina Reyes—showed she belonged, but her bag was checked, her identity confirmed. And then she was through the doors, Jacob slipping in behind her. The doors shut.

They went down the stairs to the underground lair. The Situation Room was where the president held important meetings. He'd seen images of it only on Angélica's tablet—a large conference table encircled by thick chairs. The president always sat at the head of the table with the crest of his office hanging on the wall behind him. It was a glyph of sorts, a symbol of his power and authority. There were large monitors attached to the walls. Jacob tilted his neck back and forth, loosening the gathering tension. His heart rate was accelerating with anticipation.

At the bottom of the steps stretched another corridor, and voices from staffers filtered to them. Not everyone was allowed in the room, usually just the cabinet and key support people. The faces looked at her as she approached.

"The meeting is underway, Christina," one of them said.

"Secretary Owens wanted a copy of this," she said, reaching into her bag and pulling out a stack of papers clipped together.

"You can't go in there," said another.

"I don't want to interrupt. Can you bring it to the chief of staff?"

"I'll hand them over," offered a young man. "But you can't go in there. None of us can." He took the stack of papers from Christina and then thumbed through them before nodding.

"Thank you," she said, turning to walk away. Jacob remained. He'd memorized the path back to the mirror, so he no longer needed her.

First he'd invoke a silence glyph so that cries of alarm or pain wouldn't reach this corridor.

The man with the stack of papers went to the door and pulled on the handle, opening it slightly. Jacob stepped up close behind him, staying just far enough away to avoid a collision. As he watched, the young man motioned to another young man, just inside the door, who hurried over to him.

"This just arrived for Secretary Owens," he whispered, handing over the stack of papers.

He was blocking the doorway, and there wasn't enough room to slip past him. Jacob transformed into a small harvest mouse, maintaining the web of invisibility. He slipped through the door and entered the room silently. It wasn't full, the way he'd been expecting. Some of the attendees were speaking from TV screens. The big screen showed an image from a slide deck with European cities and numbers of infected people.

The president sat at the head of the table, leaning back and looking stern. The crest was behind him on the wall.

After accepting the papers, the staffer shut the door, walked over to one of the men seated in the big chairs, and bent low to whisper in his ear before setting the papers in front of him.

Secretary Owens nodded curtly.

Jacob transformed back into a man, still invisible, and stared at those assembled. Some looked bored. Others anxious. They were discussing the pandemic's exponential growth in Europe. There were already a lot of cases breeding in New York. A handful had recently been reported in DC. It would only grow faster and faster as the victims spread it to family and friends.

They were discussing possible solutions, but there was no solution. Not for them. Only those with the immunity glyph would be protected from it. No modern medicine could stop this ancient disease.

He listened to the conversation for a moment, savoring the opportunity that was before him. He drew a glyph on the door, which created a barrier of *kem äm* to keep everyone else out. Next to it, he added a glyph of silence. He didn't disguise the glyph with invisibility, like the glyphs on the Dresden Codex and the secret signs his people had used elsewhere. This was prominent.

Immediately, someone noticed. "Look at the door!" shouted a man across the table, pointing at the glowing strands of magic that had suddenly appeared.

Jacob noticed several of the people at the table were in dress uniform. Generals in the US military, with stern faces and grizzled hair. Some women as well. But it was the president he was here for. The leader.

Jacob sloughed off the invisibility, standing alone at the foot of the table.

Several gasped in surprise at his sudden appearance.

Jacob touched the tabletop with his fingertips. "My name is Jacob Calakmul," he announced, looking directly at the man at the head of the table. The most powerful and protected man in America. Who was now helpless.

"I know who you are," the president answered. But it was not the president's voice. Jacob had heard recordings of his speeches. He knew the way the man talked. It wasn't him.

The man *pretending* to be the president leaned forward. "We've been expecting you."

CHAPTER NINETEEN

Situation Room

The White House

Washington, DC

January 10

Shock was an emotion Jacob rarely felt. Fear—not since his father had tried to murder him. He'd learned how to control his weaker emotions. But standing at the table, realizing he'd been duped by Mr. Roth once again, caused such a mixture of fear and distress that he was stunned silent for a moment. Stunned enough that the man at the head of the table continued talking.

"You are under arrest," said the pretend president. "There are many crimes you are guilty of, including the murder of federal agents, military officers, and the terrorist bombing of the airport in Bozeman, Montana. But the fact that you are here with the intent to harm the sitting president of the United States is a serious enough charge that we'll stop right there before tallying up any further charges, Mr. Calakmul."

This was not how Jacob had expected it would go. He'd walked into a trap. He took a deep breath, regaining some composure. The agitation inside his body was troubling. It was fear, the weakest emotion. But he would not succumb to it. Fate had brought him here for a reason. The prophecy would be fulfilled.

"Once again, Mr. Roth has proven an adept opponent," Jacob said, his throat dry. He tried to master his tone, struggling for a moment, but it became stronger. He looked at the others—probably FBI agents disguised as the cabinet—gathered to apprehend him. It was an elaborate ruse. He'd known the FBI and CIA had impressive disguise capabilities. He'd seen what he was expecting to see—what he'd been meant to see.

"My name is Mr. Brower. In order to complete the ruse, only the president and vice president and select members of Congress knew about the real threat. The real cabinet is being briefed at this moment in a secure location. The Department of Defense has sent a strike force to the Yucatán. Your little vendetta is over, Mr. Calakmul."

Jacob nearly laughed in his face. "Is that what you think this is?"

"I know you *think* this is about a prophecy scrawled on a bit of bark centuries ago," Brower said with just enough disdain to be mocking. "The German authorities would like to interrogate you for your people's involvement in their country as well. But we get you first."

Jacob held his hands out palms up, in a gesture of submission. "Very well, Mr. Brower. You've won, clearly. I am in your custody. Does that satisfy you?" Jacob wanted to rip the synthetic mask off the man's face. He glanced at the other agents who were beginning to push away from the table. None of them were holding firearms. They'd learned how ineffective bullets were from their people's previous experience with jaguar priests. They were prepared to take him down by hand.

Brower pushed back from the table and rose. He was a tall man, taller than Jacob. "Put your hands behind your head and get down on the floor."

"You want another act of submission?" Jacob said, chuckling. "I think I will keep you *alive*, Brower. Until I carve out your heart on an altar dedicated to my god Huracán!"

"You talk a brave game, Calakmul," Brower said flatly. "But you are just a man."

"Am I?" Jacob countered. He summoned the magic of his ring, which started to glow.

"You are leaving here in handcuffs," Brower warned, "or zipped in a body bag. I don't care which."

"We'll see," Jacob said. With the magic, he shorted the power in the fluorescent lights, plunging the room into darkness. With a thought and the silent command *k'äjirik*, he shattered every monitor, every tube of glass in the ceilings, even the glasses of water on the serving table.

Dropping into a low squat, Jacob used the table as a shield and transformed into a jaguar. The transformation was his most vulnerable moment. He wouldn't have dared it if any of them had drawn weapons.

In the chaos that ensued, some reached for cell phones to create light. In his jaguar form, Jacob snarled, shrieked, and leaped at the nearest agent, raking claws against his chest. Chairs were thrown aside, shoved back. People stumbled. They shrieked in terror.

Some had guns and finally drew them as the flickering cell phone light revealed the huge jaguar in their midst. Foolishly, someone fired at him, but Jacob had already summoned his shield. The bullet turned back on the agent shooting it, striking him in the chest and slamming him back. He coughed in surprise, but the sound of the bullet slamming home suggested a bulletproof vest.

Jacob killed a woman next, then another man. The man who'd been seated on the left side of the table ran to the door to try to escape, but the *kem äm* hurled him across the room. Glass was everywhere, crunching, crackling.

"Don't shoot!" Brower yelled. "Box him in with chairs!"

Chairs! Jacob wanted to laugh but could only let out another ferocious scream. He jumped up on the table and roared against the agents on the other side. He slashed at them, his claws ripping through their costumes. The smell of ozone was strong in the air.

"Agent Buzz! Agent Buzz!" Brower shouted.

With his heightened senses, Jacob realized they'd unleashed a chemical into the room. It was probably something that would make him— or all of them—fall asleep or become disoriented.

Jacob invoked another bit of Maya magic—*uxlabinik*—which allowed him to hold his breath for longer than a mortal person could. An agent tried to smash a chair into him, but he caught it with his powerful jaws, wrenched it from the man's grasp, and flung it across the room. He leaped at his attacker, going for the jugular, and killed him. Agents were scrambling to put on gas masks, which they'd concealed beneath the table.

It was pandemonium. Someone was crying in fear. Literally weeping. At least twelve federal agents, all heavily trained, against one jaguar priest, but they were terrified, disoriented by the dark, and tripping over themselves in the maelstrom. There was no escaping the killing room. Jacob ravaged them all, except for Brower, who had backed into the corner of the room, barricading himself with discarded chairs, trying to hide. He cowered like the coward he was.

Jacob transformed back into his human form, and with a boost of energy given by the magic, he flung aside the chairs one by one, puncturing the plaster and drywall. Motes of *kem äm* illuminated his arms and made his eyes glow.

As he hurled aside the final barrier, he saw the terror in Brower's eyes. Jacob grabbed him by the necktie and hoisted him up before slamming him into the wall, pinning him there. With his other hand, Jacob tore the gas mask off his face. With it came bits of the disguise mask he wore, but most of it remained. Good enough. He would fool some witnesses at the Jaguar Temple before he died.

Jacob held him there, savoring the feeling of helplessness in the man's eyes. His agents were all dead or unconscious from the incapacitating agent. A few, perhaps, feigned death.

"You, I keep," Jacob muttered.

Brower was gasping involuntarily and kept breathing in the drug until his eyes rolled back in his head. Just to be sure, Jacob removed a needle from his pocket and jammed it into Brower's thigh. It was a far more potent dose. No matter that he'd intended it for a different man. Brower looked passably like the president, and it was only the show that mattered. The pomp and ceremony.

Now that Brower had gone totally limp, Jacob hoisted him onto his shoulder and carried him to the door. The cameras in the room would reveal little of what had happened in the dark, but they would, of course, find the destruction left in Jacob's wake. And they'd realize that no matter how they prepared, they were no match for the magic and power of the jaguar priests. He'd been like a young jaguar going through sheep. None would deliver them.

He released the webbing on the door and invoked another word to cause it to fly off its hinges and smash into the far wall. Then he covered himself and Brower with invisibility and a protective web and started down the corridor.

Marines had gathered in the corridor. They had assault rifles, but Jacob didn't even hesitate. He kept walking toward them.

"No targets! Even on infrared!"

"Hold your fire!" shouted an officer.

"Mr. Brower! Mr. Brower!" someone shouted.

Jacob, feeling the weight of the man on his shoulder, reached into his other pocket and withdrew the Glock. He pointed at one of the marines crouching in the corridor. They all looked intense, ready for a fight. Ready to start shooting. It would only take one little push . . .

He shot a single round into the lead soldier's helmet, dropping him.

Training took over. A hail of bullets came at Jacob, and the *kem äm* deflected them all right back at the men who'd shot them. Shouts of pain rang out, followed by more rapid-fire bullets.

"Hold fire! Hold fi—!" His order was silenced by his own men's bullets hitting him.

Jacob kept walking. Confusion, cries for medics.

A stun grenade rolled down the corridor, striking the *kem äm* barrier in front of Jacob. He invoked a glyph of darkness so that when it exploded in brightness and noise, he could neither see nor hear it. The blast resounded back into the corridor where it had originated. He drew another glyph, inflicting a plague of weakness and debilitating sores on the soldiers.

Jacob left, seeing the smoke in the air, the pock marks on the walls. He walked to the stairs, opened the door, and started up the steps. He felt the strain of the agent's weight, but the magic supported him. When he reached the top of the stairs, he kicked open a door and saw more marines waiting there. Among them was another man in dress uniform, with the insignia of a general.

"We're evacuating. Answer me! What's going on down there?" the gray-haired general barked, his gaze on the open doorway. Confusion wrinkled his brow when no one emerged.

Jacob raised his arm and shot him at point-blank range. The soldiers, confused, trained their guns on the opening of the stairwell. Jacob walked right at them, and the *kem äm* shoved them backward.

Strobe lights were flashing from the emergency lamps. In his mind, Jacob retraced his steps back to the corridor. This time, the hallways were full of panicked people who were fleeing their offices, carrying laptops and coats. Some were crying in terror.

Jacob reached the obsidian mirror and saw the assistant standing there, frightened, wondering what to do.

Jacob invoked the magic of the mirror, and it began to shed gray smoke again.

"I'm here," Jacob whispered to her. "Go inside. You will be safe."

The young woman immediately stepped toward the mirror. It swallowed her, bringing her instantly back to the underground chamber. Jacob drew a glyph to make the mirror invisible, then adjusted the man's weight on his shoulder, limp as a sack, and stepped through the mirror behind her.

As he emerged into the sacred chamber, he saw the jaguar priests awaiting them. They saw him toting a man in a suit, gray hair, one who looked like the American president but roughed up. Jacob dropped him at their feet.

"The Americans are coming for us," he told them grimly. "Awaken the jungle to receive them."

CHAPTER TWENTY

Providence Inn

Washington, DC

January 10

Roth tried Lund's phone for the third time that hour, and again it went to voice mail. There'd been no response to his previous texts either. He'd wanted to hear from Suki and Sarina that morning. But they were offline. It probably meant that they were on a flight back to DC. But what if something had happened? He'd been thinking about everything they'd talked about the night before. Including the magical place Suki had visited that could de-age someone—he knew the legends of Aztlán from his research, but it was in Utah of all places? Too weird. That kind of power, that magic, would be a carefully guarded secret. And possibly another impetus for Calakmul's determination to overthrow the US.

The boys were watching the hotel TV from the couch. Jordan was in another room in the hotel, sleeping. Another one of Lund's security guys was on duty, but not in the room with them. Neither of them had heard from Lund about his plans.

"Can we watch a cooking show?" Lucas complained to Brillante. "I'm sick of this cartoon. I'm sick of staying in hotels!"

"Bruh, it's almost over."

"I think we're going to be stuck in hotels for weeks!"

"No, I meant the show."

"Fine. Then can we switch it?"

Living out of a hotel was getting intolerable, but so was the stress of their lives. It had taken a toll on all of them. Roth wanted to reassure his sons, but he had no idea when they'd be able to go back to Bozeman. He suspected it wouldn't be safe until the situation was dealt with, one way or another. Now that he'd launched the new version of his book about the death games, attached it to his author profile online, and amped up the ad spend, their lives could be disrupted for a long time. He went into the little kitchenette and pushed aside a plate of half-eaten breakfast. Then he switched to his e-mail app and saw dozens of new messages had just arrived. The subject line of one grabbed his attention.

I KNEW IT WAS YOU.

Roth felt another twist of unease as he opened the e-mail and read the message.

Dear Ryan Anglesey,

Or should I say, the fabulous Jonathon Roth. I guessed that you were the author of *The Jaguar Games*. Then you confirmed it. I was going to reach out before but doubted myself. There were certain turns of phrase that gave you away. I love the Merwyn Chronicles. *The Jaguar Games* makes for an interesting read, too, but I know it's not fiction. It can't be. I think the story you told is about your family, including the coma your wife is supposedly in. I work for a humanitarian organization in Manhattan. We've seen a lot of people sending money down to Mexico, especially the Yucatán. Large-sum donations. You didn't specify where the location in the book was, but I think I know. I have a degree in accounting and have learned a few tips and tricks about "following the money." This money isn't going to charity. It's going to shell companies owned by a family called Calakmul. In the book, you called them the Mulak family. Pretty close. These shell companies are very big and very much off the radar of the Treasury Dept. I've pieced together a lot of the "what" and the "who" but wasn't able to figure out the "why" until I read your new book. I have a suspicion that what's in your book is a trail to understanding this highly illegal operation. Please tell me I'm wrong. Please. This is nuts.

OP

Roth read through it again, a smile spreading on his mouth. Not many people had read his secret book. By changing his name on the book from the pseudonym to his own, it would get sucked into the Amazon algorithms that would expose thousands of the readers of his fantasy books to this new book. This guy had figured it out already before he'd even noticed the change in author.

"Dad, look at this," Brillante called.

"Just a minute," Roth said, wondering whether he should respond. Was it a trap by Calakmul's goons? Were they phishing him by e-mail to see if he'd respond?

"Dad!"

He looked up from the table. The kids weren't watching a cooking show. They were watching the news. The chyron on the screen said *Drama at the West Wing—Bomb Threat Clears White House.*

The video footage, taken from outside the White House fence, showed people being evacuated. A man in a dark suit, probably a secret service agent, had a rifle with a shoulder strap and was directing the camera crew away from the fence.

"That's pretty sus," Lucas said, staring at the screen.

Roth listened to the coverage for a little while. According to the news, the building had been evacuated because a bomb threat had been called in during a cabinet meeting. The president and vice president had already been removed by Marine One, the executive helicopter.

Something bad had happened. Something he'd tried hard to prevent. They'd attempted to call off the meeting, but no one had listened.

He hefted his phone and called Monica.

She picked up quickly. "Can't talk right now, Jonathon. Emergency going on."

"I'm watching the news," he said. "So the cabinet meeting happened? How many were hurt?"

"I'll call you soon. It's bigger than that. Stay where you are. Bye."

It's bigger than that?

"Dad, do you know what's happening?" Lucas asked.

"I don't. Monica said she was in the middle of it."

"This is crazy. Did Calakmul try to bomb the White House?"

"I'm not sure. But I'm going to try to find out."

He went back to the bedroom and pulled out his laptop, the one he'd been using at Starbucks to write his new book and research the ancient Maya.

Bringing it back to the desk in the other room, he told the kids to turn the volume up so they could all hear the broadcast. He typed in his log-in information, and after the computer connected to his burner phone's data, he opened up a browser using a VPN and looked at some of the chat rooms he followed on the dark web, where conspiracy theorists liked to hang out and speculate. The comment streams were exploding.

My sister works for the Pentagon. It's not a bomb scare.

Someone tried to assassinate the president.

I saw smoke coming from the west wing.

Roth combed through the different threads, torn between agitation and fear. He'd been living in the Bay Area when the Twin Towers were hit. The airport had shut down. What would happen if Lund, Suki, Sarina, and Jane Louise were prevented from landing in Dulles or Reagan?

Waiting for a cell phone to ring was maddening. He kept it on the table beside him, and every few seconds he'd glance at the blank screen, waiting for it to light up.

The news anchors were talking in circles now, repeating the limited information they had about the event, over and over, and then interviewing talking heads who made pointless speculations. Roth had a feeling none of them were even remotely close to the likely truth. It was the beginning of the end times.

The phone lit up, and Monica's name came up on the screen.

Roth grabbed for it so fast it shot out of his hand and slid off the table, but he caught it.

"Nice save, klutzy papa," Brillante said, giving him a thumbs-up.

Roth shook his head and answered the call. "Monica!"

"The director wants to speak with you at headquarters. Now."

Roth swallowed. "Me?"

"Yes. You were right. Get an Uber and get over here. Come to the east entrance. I'll meet you there."

"What about the twins?" Roth said. "Is it dangerous over there?"

"I think it would be prudent if they stayed at the hotel. I can send an agent to pick you up if you want Jordan to stay with them."

Roth scratched his forehead. "I don't want to leave them alone. I haven't heard back from Lund this morning, and I'm starting to freak out."

"What's happening right now is bigger than just your family, Jonathon. Calakmul showed up in person. There are bodies in the Situation Room that were clawed to death."

"Oh no," Roth groaned.

"I need you to come in. Right now. Leave the boys with Jordan. I'll send—"

"No, Lund left a second guy. I'll come with him. I don't want to be separated from my boys for long. I can't, Monica. Not after all we've been through. Not with what might be coming."

"I understand. But the director needs to talk to you now. You're the only one who's personally dealt with Jacob Calakmul. We need to know what he could do *next*. You're our only asset on that front."

"I'm an asset?" Roth said incredulously.

"Sorry, I didn't mean it like that. It's FBI lingo. You're important. Very important. Come to headquarters right now, okay?"

"I will."

"Call me when you're en route."

"Okay. Thanks, Monica."

"For what?"

Roth sighed. "For caring about my family. And our country. This can't be easy on you."

"Protect and serve," she answered. "I'll do everything I can to keep your family safe and get you back together."

That gave him a small swell of relief. "Bye."

———

Jordan called in the young bald man who'd escorted Dr. Estrada and Illari from the airport the previous day to bring Roth to the J. Edgar

Hoover Building. Jordan was awake and would personally stay with the boys to make sure they were okay, giving the second guard a chance to catch some sleep.

Their Uber pulled up alongside the building, and they got out, the guard first, examining the area. Roth had texted Monica as they were circling the building, and when he got out, she emerged from the privacy-glass doors and gestured for them both to come forward. They did, and found several agents waiting for them, including Carter.

"Mr. Roth," he said, nodding to him respectfully.

Roth suspected it was because he was suddenly *important* to Carter.

They passed through the security checkpoint and went to the elevators. The other agents accompanied them, forming a veritable human wall around them.

"East elevators. On the way," one of them said quietly through his earpiece.

When they reached the floor, the office space was noisy and charged with energy, completely unlike their previous visit. Whatever had happened at the White House had stirred up the hornet nest.

"Director Wright is a blunt-speaking man," Monica said, walking alongside Roth on his right. "Just be crisp and clear. Answer his questions. Don't embellish anything. He might cross-examine you, but just tell the truth. You're not in trouble. In fact, you're our best hope right now."

That assuaged his feelings a little . . . but only a little. He'd still received no messages from Lund. He continued to hope that they were all en route to DC.

He was taken to an executive conference room in the middle of the floor, away from the windows. The old-building smell was mixed with coffee. Roth felt his anxiety surge as an agent opened the door for him. A voice issued through a phone speaker mounted on the table. It was older technology, but probably very secure.

"Mr. Roth has just arrived," said a stern voice. "I will call you later, sir."

"Thanks, Bill. I'll be with the president."

Roth had seen pictures of the FBI director on the wall. He was ginger, which was striking, with thinning hair and broad shoulders. He wore square-rimmed glasses, a striped tie, and had a politician's smile—one that seemed disarming and friendly but didn't quite reach his eyes.

He rose from the conference room chair and reached for Roth's hand, giving him a firm handshake. Roth took in the rest of the room—a woman and two older men sat around the table, along with a security guard with a Kevlar vest over his white shirt and a large rifle slung over his shoulder from a strap. Where was EAD Brower? He was one of the director's top deputies.

"I'm Director Wright," the director said, releasing his hand.

Obviously, he already knew who Roth was, but Roth introduced himself nonetheless.

Monica and Agent Carter joined them, but the others stayed outside.

"Have a seat, Mr. Roth," Wright said. "I have some images to show you of a crime scene at the White House. I hope you can stand the sight of blood. There's a lot of it." He pushed a laptop toward Roth and lifted the screen. "I need to know if a man did this. Or an animal."

CHAPTER TWENTY-ONE

FBI HEADQUARTERS—J. EDGAR HOOVER BUILDING

WASHINGTON, DC

January 10

The images triggered memories Roth would rather have forgotten. The helpless fear that had consumed him when his family was trapped in that arena. When he'd watched Jacob Calakmul transform into a jaguar and then pad slowly and deliberately toward Eric Beasley. He'd tried to protect his kids from the sight and sounds of the man's brutal death, but there'd been no escaping it for any of them, and the memories had woken him up in a cold sweat on many nights.

"I've seen enough," Roth said after scanning the images briefly. He closed the laptop screen, and the carnage winked out. His stomach was sour. He felt his body processing the surge of adrenaline spiked by his fear and disgust. It was a primal fear deep in the heart of every man.

In a natural struggle against a true predator, humans were the inferior species.

Director Wright pulled out a printed photograph of a man wearing nice clothes standing at the foot of the table. It was Calakmul in the Situation Room.

"This him?" the director asked.

"Yes," Roth answered, trying to quell a shudder and failing. He was sweating profusely now. Calakmul was in DC. Not the jungles. Or at least he had been hours ago.

"Look at this one," Wright said, pulling out another photo. "This was the last image before the power went out. We have no footage of what happened down there. Take a look."

Roth breathed in through his nose. He felt Monica's hand on his shoulder.

It was another photo of Calakmul. Roth knew immediately why the director was showing him.

"The glow?" Roth asked, pointing to the halo around Jacob's hand. Around, more specifically, the ring on his finger.

"What is it?"

"I've already explained this to you guys. You didn't believe me."

"Explain it again. To me."

"When we were at the Jaguar Temple, they called it the power of the *kem äm*, the Mayan word for 'spiderweb.'"

"And it is . . . magic?" Wright prodded.

"I don't know," Roth said honestly. "I can't explain the physics of it. Maybe they can't either. A science-fiction author coined the phrase 'Any sufficiently advanced technology is indistinguishable from magic.'" He tapped the photo. "The *kem äm* can be woven into a shield and used as a barrier. It repulses force used against it, repulses it *harder* than the initial force. Like a baseball."

Wright wrinkled his brow. "Say more."

"A baseball pitcher can throw a ball around eighty-five miles per hour. A typical baseball bat speed is around seventy miles per hour. The energy of the swing combined with the energy of the pitch results in the ball traveling around a hundred miles per hour. So a bullet hitting the *kem äm* comes back faster than what was shot at it. It may be uncanny, but it follows the laws of physics. We can't explain why yet, but my daughter can control it. And maybe my wife."

Wright cocked his head slightly and smiled, that same smile that didn't reach his eyes. "I thought you were a history professor, Mr. Roth."

"I settled on history," Roth said. "I've been interested in many different subjects. Like the fact that modern engineers can't figure out how the pyramids of Giza were actually built, or how precisely they were measured and configured. Same with the pyramids down in the Yucatán. Same with ancient ruins built on other continents as well. The structures align to the zodiac stars, to planetary orbits, to the sun and moon, even to the jiggle in the earth's rotation."

"Jiggle?" the director asked.

"The technical term is 'obliquity,' but most people don't know that word. The Maya measured it accurately. And they were far more accurate than they *should* have been able to be thousands of years ago. Sorry for the digression. I can't help myself sometimes. Now, there was no footage of Calakmul at the Bozeman airport, was there? These are your first photographs of him?"

"Indeed. We have the NSA scanning world databases to match it, but that will take time. Time we don't have." He paused and looked down at the photo, then back at Roth. "Everyone in that room was an FBI agent that I personally selected for this dangerous assignment. They *knew* that shooting him would be ineffective. Agent Sanchez has always been clear on that. But someone fired a weapon anyway out of sheer terror. Others tried using chairs as weapons, it appears, judging by the haphazard clutter in the room. Our backup detail couldn't get in. My agents couldn't get out. Except for one."

Roth felt confused. "Who?"

"Every other agent I put in there is dead. But EAD Brower is missing. After the smoke cleared and the Situation Room was secured again, although I hesitate to say it will *ever* be secure again, we found the remains of everyone else."

Roth met his gaze. "Why would Calakmul show up to a room full of FBI agents when he was expecting to find the president?"

"Every agent was wearing a disguise. They were impersonating the cabinet. It was a trap."

That was a plot twist that Roth wasn't expecting. Senator Coudron had made the call approving this mission.

"Brilliant," Roth murmured. "You saved the president's life."

"Yet we continue to suffer enormous casualties every time we face even one of these people. The sniper unit in the helicopter. My section chief from Salt Lake and his team. The agents who went to your house, Mr. Roth. Agent Garcia will reveal *nothing* about how the *kem äm* works. I'm tempted to send him to Guantanamo for some unorthodox interrogation methods. I will admit to you that I've been very skeptical up until now. The bodies of the agents killed in the hangar at Bozeman . . . I thought it possible that a sufficiently twisted killer could make a body seem to be eviscerated by an animal. But there was no time to arrange for such a thing in the Situation Room. And from your account, added to what we've seen, I have to suspend my disbelief and assume everything you've told us is true. I lost my friend today, as well as a team of highly trained special agents, all experts in hand-to-hand combat and situational creativity. How can we take these people down if we cannot touch them?"

Roth was pleased the director wasn't doubting anymore. Getting past a person's natural cynicism was always the hardest part in pushing new ideas.

"As I said, my daughter can get past it," Roth advised.

"How?" Wright asked, leaning forward intently. The smile was gone.

"When we escaped Calakmul's resort that first day, we were lost in the jungle for a while. We stumbled onto a pyramid temple, the kind the Maya built, and when we went inside, we found crates of gold. The crates were the big black plastic ones, the kind you can get from Walmart. But they were full of treasures. My daughter grabbed a bracelet because she'd seen it glowing. I couldn't see it. There's a genetic component to all this, I believe. My wife's family was originally from the Yucatán Peninsula."

The director looked at Monica. "Where's Suki right now?"

"We don't know, Director. Steve Lund went to get her."

A frown. That was the immediate reaction on hearing Lund's name. There was more bad blood here. Personal enmity could derail any hope of cooperation.

"I hired Lund to be my—"

"I know," Wright said, cutting him off. "So you're telling me a seventeen-year-old girl and your wife are our biggest hope of stopping a terrorist who wants to destroy Western civilization?"

"Calakmul was impressed by her ability to use the magic," Roth said. "So yes, that's pretty accurate." His insides twisted with worry, but he felt he had to mention something else. "My boys also have some sensitivity to it."

"Oh?"

"Just yesterday, when we left the Dirksen building after meeting Senator Coudron, they saw a glyph on the exterior wall. I couldn't see it. But they could."

"Tell me what they saw."

"The Maya didn't draw letters. They drew pictures or symbols that meant certain things when combined. For example, the glyph *utchi* is made of three symbols: *ut*, *ch*, and *i*. It means 'It happened' or 'It came to pass,' which is a phrase found over six hundred times in ancient texts like the Bible. Don't get me started on the similarities between the Maya creation myth and the Book of Genesis. The glyph for *utchi* looks like the profile of a smiling man with pointed teeth."

"Pointed teeth?"

"The Maya were big on cosmetic dentistry. It would blow your mind what they knew about tooth anatomy. So yeah, a glyph with a guy with pointed teeth wouldn't be weird to them at all."

"Are you saying Calakmul bit the people in the Situation Room with his teeth?"

Roth shook his head. "No. I told you. He can literally transform into a jaguar. That's probably his favorite form, which is a huge symbol of power to the Maya. But from my readings, a Maya sorcerer can transform into almost any animal. Birds, fish, crocodiles."

"Really?" The question was asked innocuously but with an undertone of disbelief.

"I know this sounds like the *X-Files*. I get that. But historians for centuries have found evidence of shape-shifting in almost every culture. Werewolves in medieval France. The skinwalkers of the Navajo. Dracula. It's there. I don't know how it happens. I can't explain it. But yesterday, my boys saw a glyph on the wall, and then a jaguar priest started chasing us. He ran *faster* than our Uber. On all fours."

Director Wright leaned forward, resting his head on his thumb and forefinger. "You saw this happen?"

"We hit him and put a dent in the car."

"Sir, if I may?" Monica spoke up.

He looked at her and nodded curtly.

"There's a weakness that happens when these people transform," she explained.

"I read your report, Agent Sanchez."

"Do you believe it now? Jordan Scott was able to kill the jaguar priest at the cabin because he was just starting to transform. Calakmul would have been vulnerable in the Situation Room if he transformed into a jaguar."

"The power went out," Wright said thoughtfully. "It was totally dark."

"We can't afford to rest on our old assumptions," Monica insisted. "I didn't know about the plan to impersonate the president."

"You weren't supposed to know," Carter said icily.

Wright held up his hand. "That was *my* decision."

Carter looked smug.

"And it was *wrong*," Wright finished. Roth bit off the chuckle before it escaped his mouth. He rubbed his lips, trying not to laugh.

"That's why you're *here*, Mr. Roth. Agent Sanchez. What is Calakmul's next move? He did not abduct or kill the president. Clearly, he realized they were all imposters, so why take Brower instead of killing him like the others?"

Roth thought about it. "If they were all in disguise, who was Brower playing?"

"President Parker. He has a similar build, and he was determined to take the highest risk himself."

"That's why Calakmul took him," Roth said.

"But he *knew* he was an imposter?"

"That wouldn't matter to Calakmul," Roth said, leaning forward. He pointed to the picture of Jacob on the table. "If he only *looked* like the president, it would be enough. He's going to bring him to the Jaguar Temple in the Yucatán and sacrifice him on an altar. He'll do it in front of everyone who has gathered down there, including Senator Coudron's 'friend.' The one who went to Cancún for the holidays."

Wright rubbed his temples. "So you're telling me that my friend is about to be murdered in a gruesome and horrific way?"

"I'm sorry, yes. I'm guessing Calakmul will continue his plan as though nothing happened. He's going to attack at the Mexican border using cartels and paramilitary types. And he'll let his plague wreak havoc on us until we start a civil war against each other because some will be so desperate to survive that they'll do anything to join him.

Calakmul wants revenge against Europe too, because . . . you know . . . the Spanish."

"Europe?" Wright exclaimed.

"Because of how many Aztec and Maya were decimated as a result of war and disease. And plundered. Much of the gold that was stolen from them was shipped to Spain and then, to put it bluntly, money-laundered across the European powers. But the jaguar priests kept the majority of it. So why did you flinch when I mentioned Europe?"

"London. Berlin. Madrid. Ground zero of the global pandemic that's underway," Agent Carter said emphatically.

"These people," Roth said, tapping the table, "the Order of the Jaguar, are part of the Kowinem. That's a Maya secret society, a group that propped up and undermined the royalty. They were the kingmakers. They're going to hit us financially, politically, medically, and even . . . to quote the Disney movie, *ecumenically*."

Wright looked confused again. "Your thoughts jump from one thing to another so fast, Mr. Roth."

"Ecumenically . . . from Pirates of the Caribbean? Anyway, it means going against Christianity in general, as a whole religion, not a particular denomination. The Spanish forced the Indigenous people of Mesoamerica to convert to Catholicism. We're going to see a reverse of that. Maybe a mark, or a glyph, that will separate the believers from infidels."

Director Wright frowned with anger. "If I understand you, Mr. Roth, other world leaders could also be targets. They'll attack the financial markets, which no longer operate on a gold standard— because they have more gold than we think—they'll use bioweapons and *kem äm* to make us sick and scared, and then they'll come through the border cities and use the gangs like MS-13 to cause chaos and confusion and overwhelm our law enforcement agencies. Does that sound about right?"

"And it's already started," Roth said. "Because they believed they were fulfilling a five-hundred-year-old prophecy made by Kukulkán, the Maya god."

"How did they get inside the White House, though?" Wright demanded. "The security cameras show nothing. Even the ones unaffected by the power outage. There was no sign of him entering the Situation Room. He just appeared out of nowhere like a magician."

"He was probably invisible," Roth said. "The Maya talk about that in their legends. Was anyone allowed in during the meeting? He could also have been in disguise himself."

Wright turned to one of the agents seated by him. "Do you remember, Alex?"

"A staffer from Secretary Owens came to deliver a file," replied the agent. "But she didn't enter the room."

"Have you found her yet?" Roth asked.

Alex shook his head. "The White House has been evacuated. They're looking for her, but she's probably traveling back to her home."

Roth shook his head. "No. She's probably with Jacob Calakmul."

"How did he escape? Or do you think he's still at the White House . . . invisible?"

"He could be," Roth said. "Or he had another escape path."

Director Wright grabbed his cell phone and made a call. "Buck, this is Bill. The White House is not secure. Keep the president away." He went pale. "What? When did you . . . just now? I agree. Get him back in the air right now."

He ended the call. Everyone was silent.

"The prime minister of Great Britain has vanished."

CHAPTER TWENTY-TWO

CAPTAIN MITCHELL'S AIRBOAT TOURS

EVERGLADES CITY, FLORIDA

January 10

"Well, we appreciate the last-minute accommodation," Lund said, sliding several hundred-dollar bills across the windowsill.

"It's a little colder than normal this morning. Do you want some ponchos or something?"

"Sure. We'll take them."

The manager handed some ponchos wrapped in plastic to Lund, who distributed them to Jane Louise, Suki, and Sarina, keeping one for himself.

"Captain Tom Channell is your pilot today. He's prepping the airboat right now, and you'll be on your way."

"We're really excited to go," Lund said, feigning enthusiasm. Suki could see him glancing nervously at the highway. Captain Mitchell's Airboat Tours was right off the Tamiami highway, about forty-five minutes from Naples. With the traffic accident Lund had caused, there hadn't been many cars coming up behind them.

After pulling on her own poncho, she helped Jane Louise with hers and then helped Sarina. A little drizzle had started.

Suki felt a sudden warning prickle down her spine. She tugged on Lund's sleeve. He looked at her, then glanced toward the parking lot where their van was parked with only two other vehicles.

"Do any of your girls want to hold an alligator? They're small." The manager smiled in a friendly way.

"Maybe when we get back," Lund said. "Is Captain Tom ready yet?"

"He'll be here soon."

It was a risk being here. But as Lund had explained, it would be an even bigger risk to stay on the highway to Miami. Local sheriffs had probably put together a roadblock farther ahead. The Tamiami ran east-west through southern Florida, connecting Naples to Miami through the Everglades. There were few towns along the way. Lund had handed Suki his phone and asked her what kind of shops or hotels might be on the route, but all she could really find were airboat and jungle tours.

That had given Lund the idea to get off the highway and bribe an airboat captain to take them off the grid for a while. The Everglades wove between the trees like a maze, he'd said. Only the local boat captains knew them.

A police car zoomed past on the highway going about a hundred miles per hour. Her stomach lurched with dread. At least the car hadn't stopped.

A tall older man with thick graying hair and cargo shorts came up to them. He had big dimples in his cheeks and looked close to seventy.

"I'm Cap'n Tom, welcome!" he said with a cheerful voice. "So glad to take you guys on an airboat tour. Have you been on one before?"

"I have," Lund said. "But this is their first time."

"You're in for a treat. I have a copilot, a cantankerous cat named Madge. She's in quite the mood today, but if any crocs or piranhas try to attack us, she's our best course for staying alive. I'm just kidding! It's perfectly safe! Unless we run out of gas."

Another patrol car zoomed past.

"Wow, they're in a hurry," Captain Tom observed. "Why don't you follow me, and we'll get going. January isn't exactly peak tourist season, as you can see, but the Everglades is a beautiful place."

Suki followed him to the short, squat dock by the small office building they'd been waiting in. The airboat had three rows of blue benches in front and then a pilot's seat mounted in front of the cage with the propeller. Lund was furiously texting someone, glancing back at the parking lot surreptitiously.

"Watch your step, there's an alligator right there," Captain Tom said, pointing off the dock. Sure enough, Suki saw the ridged back of the reptile and half its snout protruding from the brackish waters.

"Can it climb up here?" Jane Louise asked nervously.

"Alligators are pretty lazy, so no. It's easier for them to climb up the bank. So when we get back, there may be four or five blocking the way back to your car. Hopefully, that's not a problem. Just kidding!"

His constant, unfunny joking was starting to get on Suki's nerves.

They reached the only running airboat. "Take these headsets," Captain Tom said, handing them out. "It'll help you hear my stories and jokes better. Once we're all on board, we'll get going. This tour will be two hours long unless we get stranded in a low spot. No, we'll be all right. I know these waters pretty well. Most of the time."

They all put on the headsets, and then Captain Tom spoke through the microphone on his. "If you can hear me, jump off the dock into the water. Kidding! Don't do that. This is Madge. Wave to her but don't pet her. She doesn't even like it when I pet her."

Madge was sitting on a stool lashed to the captain's chair. She was black with dashes of white on her paws and belly, had bright yellow eyes, and looked like she'd just been woken up abruptly.

Jane Louise waved at the cat.

"The engine is really loud once it gets going, so these headsets will provide ear protection as well. They're not equipped with Spotify. Sorry about that. Why don't you get settled on the bench? You can sit two to a bench, or all together if you want to squish. Makes no difference to me."

Suki and Jane Louise took the front row and Lund and Suki's mom, the second. Captain Tom then seated himself in the pilot's chair and fastened his seat belt. He cranked up the throttle, and the engine began to roar.

That was a good thing, because he didn't hear the patrol car pull into the parking lot.

"Off we go!" he said, and the airboat left the dock, heading away. The nervous feeling in the pit of Suki's stomach began to grow. The police car stopped right next to their van. That meant there'd be officers waiting for them when they got back. Unless Uncle Steve had another play to make. Knowing him, he probably did.

"The best view is ahead of us," Captain Tom said, "not behind. Once we're farther out, we'll enter the mangrove forest. I'll stop now and then to point out some curious sights. Do you have any questions?"

"How fast can an airboat go?" Lund asked, an edge to his voice.

"We normally go at thirty-five miles per hour but can crank it up to fifty. A modified one can go over a hundred miles per hour. This one can't. Madge won't allow it. She's my GPS system and regulator. She'll start clawing my leg if I go too fast. Just kidding! Look, there's a pair of gators right off to the side. Looks like a papa wants to get frisky with a mama, and she's running away."

Suki sighed with relief as the airboat continued to pick up speed.

"The Everglades is one of the rarest sights in North America. You'll find several species of trees here, but the most interesting is the mangrove. I have one mangrove joke but I'm too *swamped* to tell it . . . ha ha!"

Suki rolled her eyes. Jane Louise smiled. She held Suki's hand as the airboat cut through the water.

"Right now, the water you see is pretty shallow, about four to five feet deep. In the peak season, it's even shallower, sometimes only a foot deep. But we're still faster in an airboat than walking. Not kidding!"

The airboat continued to accelerate, and Suki felt the wind and spray on her face. It was fun, but she was too distracted by the problem of the police to enjoy it.

"Okay, see the trees coming up on the left? Those are mangroves. The Native Americans called them 'walking trees.' The roots dangle from the branches and then form new units. The most popular are the red mangroves, but there are also black and white. Like chess pieces. They can survive in salty water, unlike most trees. They shed the salt through their leaves. In fact, those leaves can get pretty salty, along with some of my jokes."

He turned the airboat into the mangrove forest, which consisted of a series of tunnels. The trees grew up overhead but left enough room for the airboat to pass in between, like a twisty highway on the water. Captain Tom began to show them the maneuverability of the airboat. It could easily pull off a 360 or a hairpin turn. He was a skilled pilot and continued to adjust the throttle to build up speed and take the turns. Other times, he'd stop and explain the wildlife, both the reptilian and mammals, before continuing to zoom through the maze again.

Suki looked back at Lund and saw that her mom's head was dipping. Alarm coursed through her. Her mom looked tired and weak. How much longer would she last like this?

Lund tapped his wristwatch for her to see, indicating he was keeping track of time. Suki wasn't sure how long they'd been gone, probably about an hour, when they reached a little lagoon. Captain Tom talked about piranha in the waters and, of course, asked if anyone wanted to go swimming.

"Well, it's about time to head back to the shack," he said. "We need to navigate the mangroves again. I hope I don't get lost this time!"

Lund spoke up through the headset. "How close are we to Ochopee?"

"What?"

"How close are we do Ochopee?"

"We're going back to Everglades City."

"How much to drop us off at Ochopee instead?"

"Why do you need to go there?" His brow wrinkled in confusion.

"How much to drop us off there?"

"Oh. I see." He was getting it now. He rubbed his nose. "So . . . I know this area pretty well. We're only fifteen minutes from there."

"That's what I figured," Lund said. "How much?"

"Two hundred? Call it a tip?"

"I'll give you a thousand in crypto if you keep your mouth shut about where you dropped us off."

Suki almost added, *And if you can keep your mouth shut for the rest of the trip too.*

"A thousand in crypto. That's . . . that could be worth a lot more if I hold on to it."

"Exactly. Just drop us off at another airboat dock. An out-of-the-way one."

"Donna's Wildlife check station is on the east side of Ochopee. It's pretty small."

"Works for us. Take us there now."

He squinted at Uncle Steve. "You got it, sir."

The rest of the tour wasn't full of banter or jokes. True to his word, in about fifteen minutes, Captain Tom was navigating up a channel toward an old dock with two airboats tied up. No cars in the parking lot. When they got there, a woman in shorts came out and greeted Captain Tom. They obviously knew each other.

"This is Donna," Tom said.

"What's your e-mail address?" Lund said. "I'm sending the payment now. You'll have to register to get it."

"Of course!" He shared his e-mail address, and Lund showed him the screen from his crypto account. Suki saw the sum of one thousand on it before he clicked send.

"What you doing this way, Tom?" Donna asked.

"Had to drop these folks off. They're getting picked up here, right?"

"Exactly," Lund said. He motioned for them to follow him.

"That was pretty slick, Uncle Steve," Suki said under her breath once they were out of earshot.

"The police will be swarming the other place. My people are sending a driver from Miami to take us to the airport. Should be here in . . ." He paused to check his watch. "Five minutes. Timed it pretty good. Haven't lost my touch." He checked his phone. "Still out of cell service. Wait until we're back on the highway."

"I'm really thirsty," Sarina said. "And I need to eat again."

"They're bringing food and drinks too," Lund said. His brow wrinkled when he checked a text message. His phone rung a second later.

"Lund," he said, answering it. He kept walking and then stopped in his tracks. "When?" He paused, listening intently, his eyes narrowing with worry. "Brower? Are you sure? We're an hour outside Miami. State police are looking for us, and that means the jaguar priests are on our tail too. I need that private plane ready to take off in an hour. We're on our way."

He ended the call and stared at the phone. Then he looked at Suki and her mom. "It's started. Calakmul tried kidnapping the president this morning."

CHAPTER TWENTY-THREE

Tamiami Trail/US Highway 41

The Everglades, Florida

January 10

"We'll be at Miami Executive Airport in about . . . thirty minutes," Lund said from the passenger seat of the SUV, talking to Suki's dad on his cell phone. The driver had picked them up from the airboat dock and was now hurrying down the highway toward Miami. Suki was watching the canal from the window while Jane Louise rested against her shoulder. There were miles of fencing alongside the road to keep crocodiles and alligators from becoming speed bumps.

"Yes, here she is. Switch to FaceTime so you can see each other." From her peripheral vision, Suki could see him handing the phone to her mom.

"Hi, Jonny," her mom said with relief. "Oh, it's so good to see you. What did you do to your beard? And your hair?"

"It's part of my disguise," he said with a grin. "I'm not a scruffy-looking nerf herder anymore."

"I like you scruffy looking better. But you're wonderful. We're doing fine. How are the boys? I want to see them too."

Suki listened in on the video call, thinking about her brothers. She missed those little derps, only they weren't so little anymore. Would they ever be able to go back home to Bozeman? The commotion at the White House was chilling. The news was only reporting that the White House was evacuated because of a bomb threat. Not that a maniac had decided to launch an invasion against the United States. If Jacob Calakmul was in DC, then she didn't feel safe going there. But she also wanted to be reunited with her family. The end of the world would feel less daunting if they could face it together.

The Everglades were very different from Cozumel and the Yucatán. The trees weren't as tall, and it was much flatter. In Cozumel, it had felt like they were driving through a tunnel of trees, but the openness of Florida had a way different vibe. There were a few palm trees on the left side, with little businesses every few miles, and big billboards, most of them featuring airboat tours. Some had buildings with thatched roofs like they were entrances to the Tiki Room show at Disneyland. Not a lot of cars were parked there since it was the off season. Occasionally they'd pass rickety wooden bridges that crossed the canal on the right-hand side.

They passed a billboard featuring a Native American village next to Shark Valley. That sounded pretty sus. Then open fields and standing water for miles ahead of them.

"Sure, here she is." Her mom handed the cell phone to her.

"Hi, Dad."

"I'm so glad you got out of Naples all right," he said.

"It was pretty chill," Suki said. She didn't like talking on the phone. Texting was way better. But it was a relief to hear his voice. "Where are the twins?"

"They're with Jordan at one of the Smithsonians. The Natural History one . . . it has the rock collection and dinosaurs. I think they were all going a little crazy being stuck in that hotel room."

"Being stuck in a hotel room sounds like paradise right now," Suki said wistfully.

"How about I get you a Frosty from Wendy's and some fries when you get in town?"

"That sounds pretty chill. The driver brought us food, so Mom has energy. She's looking pretty good."

"We'll get her a pump when she gets to DC. Oh, I miss you. The FBI wants to see you and how you use the *kem äm*."

"They don't believe you after everything that's happened?"

"No, they need to learn how to get through the *kem äm*. There's a special forces team heading into the jungle, I think. Yeah, Monica said the president authorized it. They know bullets won't work that great, so they're going to be testing the defenses of the temple in other ways. The drones haven't been able to get close. They keep short-circuiting and falling out of the sky. I think an aircraft carrier is already over there."

"Wow," Suki said, impressed. "I hope they figure something out."

"The FBI director has asked me to bring the twins to the White House."

"Really? I thought the president was evacuated?" Suki noticed a sign showing Miami was the next exit.

"He was. But the boys can see the glyphs now. There were some glowing ones along the walls of the Senate office buildings. They wonder if there are some in the White House and that's how Calakmul was able to get in undetected. I'm not sure I want to put them at risk. They've been going from room to room, using dogs to sniff. They've already tried different kinds of tech as well, like goggles that can see different light spectrums. They didn't find anything."

"That's legit," Suki said. "It would be cool if dogs were able to sniff them. I'll help if I can. If he tried to hurt us, I could just pull down his shield, and then the army dudes could blow him away."

"Yeah, you could! But I'd rather not risk any of my kids. I'm okay with you talking to the FBI folks, though. They have a research team at Quantico. I think they're going to take us all there when you get up here."

"Sweet. We're getting close to the airport, I think. Do you want to talk to Mom again?"

"Sure. Love you!"

"Love you," Suki said, feeling awkward. She handed the phone back, and her mom and dad started talking again.

"So are we going to a big airport or a little one?" she asked Lund.

"A smaller one on the west side of Miami. I have a buddy with an executive jet who sent his pilot down to help us. We can bypass all the security stuff and the police this way."

"That's awesome."

Suki watched the sign with the exit and heard the clicking of the turn signal as the driver slowed to turn right at the upcoming intersection. The turn had lots of trees, and it didn't look like Miami at all. There were no skyscrapers or hotels, except for a dinky one they'd just passed. Her stomach began to twist with worry.

"This the right way?" she asked.

"The airport is south of here, so, yes—we're going the right way," Lund said. He turned around in his seat. "You got a funny feeling about this?"

"*I* do," Jane Louise said, her expression somber.

Suki jolted in her seat. "So do I."

Lund frowned. He tapped Suki's mom on her knee and gestured to the phone.

"I've got to go. Love you, Jonny. I can't wait to see you. We'll be there in just a few hours. Bye." She hung up and gave the phone back to Lund.

He quickly made another call. "Jenson. This is Steve Lund. Are you at the executive airport? Good. Anything strange over there? Is the pilot ready with the jet?" He listened for a moment, then nodded. "Okay. Go sweep the area for me. Keep an eye out for anything suspicious, okay? We're almost there."

He hung up. "They haven't noticed anything. But now you've got me nervous."

"Can they track your phone?" Suki asked.

"I don't think so. They'd need to get a hold of it to plant spyware, and I don't let it out of my sight. It's also encrypted with some pretty strong firmware. But that doesn't mean they haven't been watching the airports and paying attention to who's chartering unexpected flights."

As soon as he said it, Suki's stomach did a little double flip. "I think that's it."

"How long would it take if we drove to DC from here?" Sarina asked, sounding worried too.

"Sixteen hours, give or take," Lund said. "I've thought about it. Flying's faster."

"What if we changed airports?" Suki suggested. "Have the pilot meet us at another one?"

"Expensive but prudent," Lund agreed. "Let's change the venue. Fort Lauderdale isn't that far north. They'll have an executive airport too. I'll call Jenson and reroute."

———

It was another hour drive from Miami to Fort Lauderdale. She couldn't see the beach, but she knew they were close to it because of all of the hotels and resorts. It reminded her a little of Cancún.

As they pulled off the freeway to the exit, Lund turned around again.

"How do you feel?"

"I'm nervous, but now I can't tell if there's an external reason for it. I just want to get back to Dad and my brothers."

Lund's phone rang. "Jenson. You beat us to Fort Lauderdale? Good. We're almost there. Is the pilot ready to go? We want to pull in, get on, and take off. Is air traffic control okay with that?" He listened, nodding. "Well done. We should be there in five minutes. See you soon."

When they passed a Wendy's, Suki's stomach growled. She reached for Jane Louise's hand. "Excited to see your mee-maw?"

"Uh-huh," Jane Louise said. "I still feel nervous, though."

"Me too. There's a word in Mayan that helps me, though. Let me teach it to you. *Nake'ik.* You try it."

Jane Louise blinked. "I know that one! *Nake'ik.*"

"Nake'ik. Nake'ik. Nake'ik," Suki said soothingly, invoking the power of the *kem äm.* A peaceful feeling settled in the SUV. Their fear melted away.

They reached the executive airport shortly after getting off the freeway and drove to an access gate with a security guard. The driver rolled down the window, and the guard looked in at them.

"You Mr. Lund? Can I see some ID?"

Lund held out his wallet with a picture. The guard nodded, not looking in the back seat at all, and then made a gesture. The gate was electronic, and it opened with a clacking noise.

Lund called Jenson again. "We just came in. Where's the plane?" He listened for a response. There was an executive jet—not a Pegasus, thank heaven!—out on the tarmac already. A small set of portable stairs had been rolled up to the open door. "See it. Where are you?"

A man in a windbreaker and Dockers slacks stepped out of the plane and waved to the driver. The driver, who hadn't said a word the whole time, parked by the ramp and nodded to them.

"Everyone get out from Suki's door," Lund instructed. "The SUV will help shield us from sight. Let's be quick."

Lund drew his gun and stepped out of the SUV. Suki swallowed nervously and opened her door. The screech of the airplane engines was loud but not earsplitting. Lund gestured for her to head toward the stairs. As she started, she could see the pilot waving to her from inside the window. He was trying to get her attention.

Her gaze shifted to the man in sunglasses waiting at the top of the steps. She sensed the magic of the *kem äm* instantly. He raised something to his mouth, a flute? No, a blowgun—

She reacted instantly, invoking the power of the ring and bracelet, and put up a shield that wrapped backward like a hemisphere around her and the vehicle. The dart shot at her, then ricocheted back at her attacker, who also used the *kem äm* to deflect it. The dart pinged harmlessly against the hull of the jet.

"He's here for us!" Suki shouted, pointing. It wasn't Jenson. It was a jaguar priest in disguise.

Lund whipped his handgun around and put himself in front of her. "Get back in the car!"

Suki felt Jane Louise squeeze her hand. She'd already gotten out of the car. The intruder leaped over the rail of the stairs and landed gracefully on the tarmac. From his jacket, he drew an obsidian dagger and started toward them.

The driver took off with the passenger door still open, stranding them on the tarmac. Suki felt her mom grab her other hand. The three of them stood there, and suddenly the magic of the *kem äm* exploded around them. It sucked away the jaguar priest's disguise *and* his shield. It sucked the dagger out of his hand and sent it spinning. Suki had never felt the magic this strongly. The three of them, standing hand in hand, had become a vortex of power.

The man's face transformed from Jenson's to that of a stranger with glowing eyes, a furious scowl, and a look of panic twitching on his face as he realized his hold on the magic had been ripped from him.

"Shoot him!" Suki said.

Lund fired three quick shots, all clustered into the man's chest. There was no shield. No protection. He jerked in pain, then collapsed on the tarmac, his glowing eyes fading to brown.

Just like that—he was dead.

The power continued to churn around them. Suki felt it, feared it, understood deep in her bones that if it continued to grow stronger, they would summon a hurricane that would strike the coast of Florida. She'd never felt such a strong surge of power before—a flood of energy that dwarfed her previous uses of the *kem äm*. Intuitively, she knew it was because she was holding hands with Jane Louise and her mother. Together, the three of them were embodying the power of Ix Chel.

And the goddess was angry.

CHAPTER
TWENTY-FOUR

Jaguar Temple

Calakmul Biosphere Reserve

January 10

Jacob sat at the president of Mexico's ornate desk in the National Palace. The president, Señor Chaboya, was pacing nervously, surreptitiously glancing at the imposter US president, forced to kneel between two jaguar priests.

Victor was on the phone.

"Mr. Calakmul, we have the German chancellor."

"Excellent," Jacob said, feeling a surge of delight. "Another success. Have him brought to the Jaguar Temple. La Noche Triste begins this evening. One by one, they will fall."

"Yes, sir. The cartels are preparing to launch raids against checkpoints in California, Arizona, and Texas. The Department of Homeland Security is still unaware of the impending attacks. They're focused on the confusion in Washington, DC, right now."

"The confusion will make them blind," Jacob agreed. "Excellent. What news from the Pentagon?"

"Special Forces are deploying quick-strike units to Mexico. They have one aircraft carrier, the USS *Botany Bay*, in international waters. The satellites are in position to track our land."

"Good," Jacob said. "I want them to watch the carnage. I'll have Uacmitun hunt the Special Forces in the jungle. He'll make quick work of them."

"Sir, there is one piece of troubling news."

"Oh?"

As silence fell, Jacob glared back at Mr. Brower. Did the man speak Spanish? Did he understand what was being said? Jacob decided he didn't care. Soon the fake president would be dead, another prop used in the drama of conquest.

"Barcenas is dead."

Jacob leaned forward in the chair, resting his elbow on the polished table. "What?"

"He was killed at an executive airport in Florida by Steve Lund."

Anger sizzled inside Jacob's bones. He squeezed the handset. "Suki did this," he said in a low voice quavering with wrath.

"I believe so. The FBI was called in. Lund, Sarina, Suki, and Jane Louise took off thirty minutes ago, bound for the Marine Corps airfield at Quantico, Virginia."

Another wave of blistering heat sizzled inside Jacob's chest. The Order of the Jaguar Priests had not successfully infiltrated the marines. Quantico was off-limits. Lund had chosen that destination because he'd guessed they would be safe there.

"Where is Mr. Roth?" Jacob growled.

"He's still at FBI headquarters with the director. We have eyes on the floor, but they're heavily guarded."

"And you still don't know where they're staying?"

"The best lead we have is the Providence Inn. The databases show nothing certain. We're trying to hack into the surveillance cameras, but that's taking time, and we still won't be able to see into the rooms. It may be premature, but I'd like to send some men to the hotel to make inquiries in person."

"I'll send Mataré. He has a score to settle."

"If you wish. Is that all?"

"That is all. Good work, Victor. The end times are here."

"Let them come," Victor said, and Jacob ended the call.

He set the phone down in the cradle and pressed his fingers together over his mouth. He gave Brower another look, meeting the man's fierce glare with an expression of unconcern.

"Do you speak Spanish, Mr. Brower?"

"Un poquito," Brower said huskily.

"Then I will say this in English, just in case," Jacob continued. "Tonight, you will die in a ceremony nearly as ancient as the world. A little dart with a special toxin will prick your flesh, rendering you conscious but immobile. It will increase your heart rate. Awaken your senses. You will feel . . . everything. I will stand over you with a dagger made of obsidian. Sharper than any surgeon's scalpel. At midnight, in front of a cheering crowd of the elite, I will unbutton your shirt, cut open your chest just below your nipple, and extract your heart. You will be alive when this happens, Mr. Brower. Your bleeding body will be thrown down the steep steps of the temple. But it is the *heart* that Kukulkán desires as a proper sacrifice." Jacob said this last part with a mocking tone. The god of creation had always spoken symbolically. He wanted his followers' devotion, their desire to serve, their willingness to help one another. His devious brother had hungered for more literal sacrifices.

"I swore an oath to defend the Constitution, not a single man," Brower said. "You'll have to root through a lot of rib cages to get *that* out."

"Bravely spoken," Jacob said, impressed. "But I'm no fool. I know your country's people better than its protectors do. Precious few of your fellow citizens would *not* betray that bit of paper for a swallow of carbonated soda or the momentary thrill of a tiny pill."

Jacob nodded to the two jaguar priests with him. "Take him to the temple dungeon with the others."

"Yes, Great One," said one of the priests. They hoisted Brower to his feet and walked to the obsidian mirror decorating the wall of the office. A wreath of black smoke exuded from it, and they stepped into the mist and disappeared.

Jacob looked at Señor Chaboya, who had sweat dripping down the sides of his face. He looked terrified. He swallowed noticeably. Was he expecting to die?

"Do not let the American military act within your borders with such impunity," Jacob said. "Send the marines against them. The army. They cannot win. And when I rebuild Tenochtitlán—here, where it once stood—I will make you ruler over it, Señor Chaboya. In my house, there are many mansions. You will get yours if you remain faithful."

"Y-yes, Great One," Señor Chaboya said, looking relieved. He sank to his knees and began murmuring incoherently.

Jacob sat at the desk, savoring the feeling of strength and power it gave him. As in any war, there was no controlling all circumstances. The surprise in the Situation Room had proven that to be true. Power was a game. The jaguar priests were immune to the bullets and missiles that the US government could unleash against them. Even the most expensive and complex fighter jet was powerless against the fury of a tornado. *Battleships* could be sunk by tsunamis. But there was a teenage girl with a stolen bracelet who could pierce the defenses provided by the *kem äm*. And so could any other who knew its secrets.

Suki would die and with her, her power and knowledge. Especially her knowledge of Aztlán. He'd right the mistake he'd made in letting her live. Indeed, the whole family would die. He should have killed them a year ago when he had the chance.

Jacob rose from the seat and walked to the obsidian mirror, invoking its power. He shielded himself with *kem äm*, just in case someone was waiting for him on the other side.

He was greeted by the other guardians posted there. It was his own "situation room." A place where the jaguar priests of the past had spun their webs of deceit and murder in order to topple kingdoms and corrupt high priests. The mirrors gave them the ability to spy on their enemies. And to reach those who were thought to be unreachable.

After exiting the portal, he walked briskly through the winding tunnels. He felt young, alive. The master of the moment. Hundreds of the wealthiest, most corrupt people in the world were assembled here to see the dawning of a new age. People who had deceived their neighbors, friends, and even family members to achieve a position of rank in the old world become new again. Instead of skyscrapers, there would be pyramids built throughout North and South America. Instead of football and soccer, the death games would provide entertainment. Instead of cheering for Britain's Premier League, there would be cheering for the warriors in the arena.

Then he entered his private chamber and found Angélica prostrate on the bed with Uacmitun standing over her.

His warrior chief looked startled by his sudden arrival.

For an instant, the world slowed. Betrayal, seduction, revenge, murder. The explosion within his heart made his eyes start to glow, made the promised taste of blood tingle in his mouth. He would shred them both to pieces. He would . . .

No.

The selfish part of his mind stopped abruptly. This was not as it seemed. If he transformed into a jaguar, he'd be vulnerable. Uacmitun knew this.

"Atin ri ik," Jacob gasped, invoking the word that would dispel all illusions.

A warrior who had been invisible stood in the corner, a blowgun pressed to his lips, ready to shoot. It was Bajibal, one of Uacmitun's young protégés. The young man's eyes widened with shock when he realized he was visible.

Jacob leaped at him. The dart hissed from the tube, deflecting off his shield of *kem äm*. The young man's neck was broken in a fluid action as soon as Jacob landed.

Uacmitun had staged this scene. He came at Jacob with a *macuahuitl* sword that must have been concealed in the sheets. Channeling the power through his bracelet, he sucked the web of *kem äm* away from Jacob to make him vulnerable.

Angélica didn't scream. Didn't move at all. She was paralyzed, he realized. Victim to the same toxin used on the sacrificial victims.

The sword had jagged teeth of obsidian. Uacmitun swung it deftly, powerfully, trying to saw Jacob in half.

K'awex. Speed.

Chuq'ab. Strength. Muscle.

Jacob invoked these words, his ring granting him special power over those who also had magic items or only knew the words. He dodged the first sweeps of the blade, nimbly evading the deadly edges that would have killed him. Then he lunged forward, smashing the heel of his hand against Uacmitun's nose. It would have been a killing blow, but the hardened warrior had turned his head just in time, so the blow landed on his cheek instead, cracking the bone. Uacmitun roared in pain and tried again to slice through his master.

Jacob spun around behind him and kicked the back of Uacmitun's knee, forcing him to kneel. The warrior swept the sword around behind him, trying to catch any part of his nimble prey.

"Tuqar!" Jacob seethed, invoking a word that would send ripples of weakness through Uacmitun's body. The man's muscles began to quiver

with the exertion, and when he tried to get up, Jacob kicked him in the face, knocking him back down. The *macuahuitl* sword struck the ground and slid away. The warrior scrabbled for it on the ground.

"*Moyirik!*" Jacob shouted at him, and Uacmitun's eyes went milky white with blindness. Kukulkán healed infirmities. His brother caused them.

Uacmitun's prime physique was trembling with weakness. The sword seemed too heavy for him. He was gasping for breath, turning one way, then another, confused by his sudden inability to see.

"*Salabataj!*" Jacob invoked the word that would dislocate his enemy's shoulder. The pain made Uacmitun shriek in agony, and the blade landed on the stone floor with a thud.

"Kill me!" Uacmitun pleaded in despair. "Kill me, Great One! You are invincible!"

"*Memarik,*" Jacob shot back, depriving the man of his ability to speak. Uacmitun began to choke until he gasped. He sank to his knees, head bent low, exposing his neck for the killing blow.

It did not come. Jacob called out for his servants, and they hurried in. "Take him to the arena," he ordered in their tongue. "Chain him there for all to see."

The feelings of rage and power had begun to shrink. This was not a fight to the death like the one he'd had with his own father. A fight between equals. Uacmitun wasn't a worthy foe. But making an example of him would instill fear in the others.

After the servants had dragged the two bodies away, Jacob turned to the bed. Angélica was starting to twitch. He knelt near her, stroking the hair from her face.

Tears were in her eyes.

He kissed her mouth and tasted a salty drop on his tongue.

Her body continued to convulse as the toxin wore off. There were so many plants within the jungles of the Yucatán. Some with healing properties that could cure cancer. Some that would remove fevers and sicknesses. The ancient Maya knew their efficacy from Kukulkán, but that knowledge had mostly been lost, burned by the Spanish priests out of fear and superstition. But the Order of the Jaguar Priests had their own records. Their own ways of remembering the past.

"I was . . . so afraid," Angélica whispered when she finally regained the ability to speak.

"That I would kill you in a blind rage?" he asked, smiling. He kissed the tip of her nose.

She nodded, shuddering, her arms coming up and wrapping around him. She was trembling still. The violence of their plan had never sat well with her on a personal level. In theory, she agreed with him, but her heart was soft. And now violence had been visited on her directly.

He comforted her with kisses.

"He . . . he . . ."

"Hush," Jacob said soothingly. "When we returned from Montana, he saw that we were both younger. He realized you knew the secret of Aztlán. The secret of eternal youth. He lost his mind with the lust for that knowledge. And for *you*."

Lust was a powerful seducer. It could make the wisest into fools. Jacob had seen it growing inside his warrior chief. He was used to getting his pick of the servants. He'd wanted Angélica from the beginning because she was forbidden.

Hadn't Saint Augustine said it so well? "Lord, give me chastity. But not yet."

Angélica swallowed, then said, "He . . . he always looked at me . . ."

"I know. One cannot help but gaze at the beauty of the sun. But you are mine. My Malintzin. You taught me how to defeat the West. How to twist their pride and greed against them. And you will bear me a son, one we will teach in our ways. One who will rule the world after us."

CHAPTER TWENTY-FIVE

Smithsonian National Museum of Natural History

Washington, DC

January 10

Roth leaned back in the chair, rubbing his forehead. He'd decided to fully cooperate with the authorities, no further incentives or guarantees needed. They'd been shocked to learn about his secret book—and that it was no longer such a secret—but their annoyance was blunted by the flood of e-mails he received, some of which contained further information about Calakmul's operation. His editor was pretty upset too, and not just about the right of first offer clause he'd violated by publishing. He hadn't been able to talk to her about what had happened to his family yet, and she was just learning about it. All this had also accelerated the FBI's timetable for reaching out to the McKintys about Jane Louise and what had really happened to her family.

Since nothing could be gained by staying silent, Roth had also given the authorities the names of every person he'd seen watching the death game. The FBI were now opening investigations into all of them. The information had been so vital, so shocking, that when Director Wright had communicated some of it to the president, he'd asked to meet with Roth and his family in person. That meant it was time to reunite with the boys and get to a better safe haven, a military base like Quantico. His burner phone buzzed in his pocket, and he reached for it, expecting to see Lund or Suki calling.

It was Jordan.

"Hey, where are you and the boys?" Roth asked. "I was just about to—"

From the receiver, he could hear traffic and wind. "He found us."

Roth's heart skipped a beat. "Where are you?"

"It's the guy who pursued us in the Tahoe. He came to the hotel. I got the boys, and we ran down the back stairwell. We need backup!"

Monica hurried over to him, asking him something. He barely noticed her, his entire focus on his phone, but he had enough presence of mind to switch the phone to speaker.

"Where are you?" he shouted.

"We're crossing the gardens at the Smithsonian Castle. We're a couple of blocks from FBI headquarters."

"Why didn't you grab a car?" Roth demanded.

"No time to wait for one."

Roth's pulse was racing.

Monica put her hand on his shoulder, jolting him to attention. "I can send SUVs to pick them up. Is this guy following you?"

"I don't see him," Jordan said, not at all thrown off by her interjection. "But he could be anywhere."

"He can probably smell them," Roth muttered. "Animals track by scent."

Monica nodded. "The National Museum of Natural History is just past the Castle."

"I know it," Jordan said. "There's usually a lot of people there. Are crowds a good thing right now or a bad thing?"

Roth wasn't sure. But he didn't want his boys hurt. "Are you sure you're not being followed?" he asked.

"I don't know how they found our hotel, so I can't be sure of anything. I can see the building."

Monica looked at Roth. "Jordan, listen. Take the boys to the museum. It'll be harder to find you in a crowd. If he can track you by scent, the more bodies, the better. We're coming for you right now."

"Roger. You worried about me?"

"Don't do anything stupid. Keep us posted. We're only two blocks away. We're taking you all to Quantico."

Within minutes of Jordan hanging up, Roth and Monica were under armed escort, taking the elevators down to the parking garage. Roth noticed some of them were carrying canisters of bear spray. He didn't know if that would work any better than guns, but at least bear spray was less likely to kill anyone it rebounded on. Once they were situated inside the SUV, Roth noticed his hands were shaking with nervousness.

Monica gripped his arm. "It's going to be okay. We'll get to them in time. You've been an enormous help, Jonathon. Thanks for sharing everything today."

But he couldn't help it. It felt like the other shoe was about to drop—again. Sarina and Suki were okay, Jane Louise was alive, so of course something was happening with the boys. But he couldn't let himself think like that—that line of thinking would drive anyone crazy. Rubbing his forehead, he said, "I still can't believe Jane Louise is alive. I could never bring myself to sell her home, so maybe part of me . . . hoped. It's hers. Her grandparents can help her."

"The McKintys will be overjoyed to learn their granddaughter's okay," Monica said. "The director wants all the legal ducks in a row first before we call, but—" She paused, pulling out her phone. Carter's name was on the screen. She answered it on speaker. "Yes?"

"News from Mexico. I'm with Director Wright. Is Roth with you?"

Monica looked worriedly at Roth. "Yes. Can I put this call on speaker?"

"Yes, it's important."

Monica switched to speaker.

"Thanks," Wright said on the other end, accepting the phone from Carter. "I'll see you in Quantico, Mr. Roth, but I didn't want to wait to mention this. Satellites are picking up activity throughout the Yucatán Peninsula. It started last night."

"What sort of activity?" Roth asked.

"Other Maya ruins have started glowing," Wright answered. "I'm going to butcher the pronunciation here, but Izamal, Dzibanche, Xpuhil, Uxmal. That's just four. Tourists are also being kept out of Chichén Itzá and Tulum because *they* started glowing this morning. The others I mentioned are also normal tourist spots. Any idea why all the temples are glowing, Jonathon?"

Roth wasn't sure. "No, but Calakmul owns resorts all over Mexico."

"It could be a distraction," Carter suggested, his voice slightly muffled.

"We need more boots on the ground," Wright added, "but this is the CIA's turf. Thought I'd mention it. Homeland Security is reporting more activity along the border-crossing areas. Higher rates of traffic than usual. The Pentagon is also intercepting comms from the Mexican army. Things are heating up fast."

That wasn't a good sign. Something told Roth that was precisely why it was being shared with him—the director was revealing the urgency of the situation to him, showing him how badly help was needed.

"Understood. We're going to get my sons."

"I know. Godspeed. See you in Quantico," Wright said, and then Carter ended the call.

They exited the SUV as another one pulled up behind them, and four more special agents got out.

"Agents Benson and Sullivan," Monica said, introducing the first two. "Agents Donaldson and Stoker. We're getting your family out."

There was no sign of trouble. They walked directly to the doors and entered. Monica flashed her badge to the security guard, and they bypassed the metal detector.

"Welcome to the Smithsonian," the guard said with a courteous nod.

After passing that station, they entered the vast rotunda. Roth gazed up at the huge room, which sectioned several floors above the one where they stood. There were forty or fifty other people milling about, including classroom students on field trips. It was noisy. A huge elephant statue on a pedestal seemed to oversee the chaos.

Roth withdrew his phone and called Jordan again.

"You here?" Jordan asked breathlessly.

"Yup. Where are you guys?" Roth asked, looking around.

"Hall of Fossils, west side of the building," Jordan said.

"Meet you there," Roth said. He motioned for Monica to follow and headed toward the Hall of Fossils, which had a spiral decoration on the entrance that said "Journey through Deep Time." They passed a bench with a bronze statue of Darwin sitting on it. Two of the agents waited at the opening. Another two went inside with them and fanned out immediately.

It took him a frantic moment to find Jordan and the twins, but he finally spotted them by a display of the extinction meteor that had killed off the dinosaurs. The boys were wearing hats instead of their usual hoodies, and he'd hardly recognized them. Relief flooded his chest, even though the danger was far from over. When he got to them, he hugged them both tightly.

"It's okay, Dad!" Lucas said. "Jordan's a pro. He kept us safe."

"Let's get out of here," Roth said urgently. Monica nodded in stern agreement. They all started walking together back to the entrance of the exhibit.

"We're heading your way," Monica said through her communications device.

"Do I get to come to Quantico too?" Jordan asked hopefully.

She nodded. "I know army guys aren't as tough as marines, but you'll play nice, right?"

"Oh, I'll play nice," Jordan said, jutting out his chin.

Roth put his arms around his boys. "Let's get to the SUV . . ."

There was a man standing at the entrance to the exhibit. He was six and half feet tall, dark haired, dark complexioned, and thick with muscle. The two agents who'd stayed at the entrance both lay on the ground, incapacitated or worse.

The last time Roth had seen this man, he'd been racing after their Uber.

CHAPTER TWENTY-SIX

January 10

Monica tapped her comms. "Backup, engage now! Hostile, repeat, hostile!"

The jaguar priest tilted his head back and forth, his frown turning to a malicious smile as he advanced.

Jordan drew his weapon.

"That won't work here!" Monica said to him. They were all backing up.

Roth felt a surge of panic. He had to protect his boys. They had to get out of there. A slight diversion. Maybe that's all they needed to escape.

"Federal agent!" Monica shouted, alerting everyone to the danger. "Get to the nearest exit. Now!"

Some bystanders looked confused, but the ones who saw Jordan's weapon started to scream and run. Confusion and panic ensued. Children scattered. Some started to cry.

"Stay back, bro!" Jordan warned, aiming the gun at the man's face.

"I'll stall him. Get the Roths out of here," Monica said.

"No way," Jordan countered. "Four against one are better odds. The other two guys I saw are yours, right?"

"Right. Jonathon, run!" Monica said.

The jaguar priest rushed them.

Roth grabbed the boys by their shirts and pulled them away. Both of them resisted at first, their faces taut with fear—they cared about Jordan, and they all knew the jaguar priests to be ruthless and efficient at killing. It pained Roth too. They didn't know how to use the *kem äm*, so they wouldn't be able to withstand his power. Still, both Jordan and Monica had been trained for combat situations. Roth hadn't. The boys certainly hadn't. And despite Jordan's shoulder injury, he wouldn't give up without a fight.

"Hurry!" Roth urged, hastening the boys deeper into the exhibit, which he hoped would loop around to another exit. There were openings leading to other parts of the hall to the right and left and another one farther ahead with fossils on display.

"What about Jordan?" Lucas said, his voice catching with worry.

Roth heard the crack of multiple gunshots. He looked back and saw Jordan firing into the ceiling lights above them. Glass from the shattered bulbs came crashing down.

The jaguar priest leaped forward in the hail of glass, aiming a kick at Jordan's leg. A loud snap could be heard. Jordan let out a howl of pain. Worry twisted in Roth's gut, but he had to focus on the boys. Had to. He dragged them to the first opening on the right and went through it. He could see part of the action through the glass walls as he pushed the boys lower down and crouched to get out of sight.

"That way!" he murmured, pointing to the left. He wanted to get out into the main hall where the crowds would be larger.

He saw the jaguar priest grab Jordan around the neck, but Monica attacked him fearlessly. She wrapped her arm around the jaguar priest's neck, trying to leverage him across her hip and choke him.

The priest let go of Jordan and pivoted, wrenching Monica's arm away from his neck effortlessly. He headbutted her in the face with his forehead and then waved his hand in a glyph. Monica flew away from him, hitting a glass display and shattering it. She groaned in pain and slumped to the floor.

"Monica!" Jordan raged. Even with a broken leg, he attacked, hoisting himself up on his arm and grabbing the priest by the belt. He dragged him down and started punching him in the face, blow after blow.

"Go, go, go!" Roth urged, pushing the boys toward the exit. For a moment, he thought Jordan might actually win the fight.

A powerful fist struck Jordan in the throat. His eyes bulged with pain, but still he fought. He tried grappling the man in a jujitsu maneuver, but the priest was bigger and stronger and broke his hold. He broke some of Jordan's fingers too, wrenching them back hard. Another bark of pain before the priest grabbed Jordan by the back of the neck and slammed him face-first into the ground with all its glass shards.

An FBI agent ran up, knocking the jaguar priest back with a scissor kick. The other agent hurried into the fray, spraying the bear spray at the jaguar priest. Two against one again.

Roth and the boys reached the entrance to the *Deep Time* exhibit, but there were so many people struggling to get out that there wasn't room for them.

"Police!" roared a voice, trying to clear a path through the crowd. Screams filled the audience hall beyond. People were running toward the exits on both sides.

Gunshots. The two agents were taken down by the jaguar priest. Monica was also lying on the ground, bleeding profusely. It pained Roth's heart to see the devastation.

A single officer entered the fray, holding a Taser. He aimed it at the jaguar priest. "Hands in the air! Hands in the air!"

The jaguar priest snorted and started toward him. The officer didn't hesitate to pull the trigger. The leads shot out of the Taser but ricocheted off an invisible barrier. The jaguar priest raised a pistol and shot the officer.

An opening had appeared in the crowd, so Roth maneuvered his boys and started running again. They made it into the large rotunda, which echoed with shrieks and the wail of sirens. Police and security were directing the crowd toward the exits. There were so many people, it would be hard for the jaguar priest to find—

A sting of pain struck Roth's neck. Reflexively, he reached back and felt the dart sticking out of his skin. He yanked it out, realizing with horror what had happened. He'd seen how fast Eric Beasley had been brought down by a similar dart. He only had seconds.

He reached into his pocket and pulled out his cell phone, thrusting it at Brillante. Roth's legs lost their strength, and he couldn't run. He couldn't even stand.

"Dad!" Lucas shouted. "Run!"

"Hide!" Roth urged his boys. "Hide! Don't let him catch you!"

His body was overcome with spasms.

"Dad!" Brillante roared, staring at the phone that had been shoved into his hand.

Roth tried to speak, but he couldn't say anything. The drug had immobilized him, but he was fully alert. He could hear the screams of his boys and the crowd. Could feel the twins trying to drag him away.

He tried to warn them again, but no sound came through his lips. He slumped down on the marble floor of the rotunda, unable to scratch the itch that was radiating from the back of his neck where the needle had struck. Helpless. He was totally helpless.

Brillante looked back and then grabbed Lucas, who was sobbing, and the twins raced away. Roth watched them go, relieved when they joined the crowd of students because surely, they'd blend in. He felt the shuddering of the stone floor from the stampede of people. But vibrations, heavy ones, were coming toward him. A very strong man heaved Roth up onto his shoulder without even a grunt of effort.

"FBI! Freeze!"

The jaguar priest turned, and Roth, dangling from the man's back, saw their FBI jackets. At least a dozen agents were there. They were all unarmed but in fighting stances, encircling Roth and his abductor.

The jaguar priest pivoted again, looking at the officers. Then he swung Roth off his shoulder and set him down on the floor.

"You sure bullets don't work against this guy?" one of the agents said.

"You know what happened the last time someone tried," said another. "Take him down."

Roth could hear the sounds of fighting, the groans of pain, but he could only see what was in front of him—the elephant statue. A body skidded past Roth and struck the base, the man's eyes still open even in death. Roth stared at him, unable to move, to speak, to scream for help. He hoped his boys were outside by now. He hoped they were tucked into the crowd and would keep their heads down and keep running.

"Backup! We need more backup!"

A shot was fired. Out of frustration or some other reason. But it didn't matter. None of it mattered. It only took a few minutes before they were all down, dead or incapacitated. Roth thought about Jordan and Monica. Were they dead? He hoped not. The last he'd seen, Monica was bleeding, and Jordan had been incapacitated. Had the priest broken his neck too? Roth didn't know.

His heart clenched with dread as the jaguar priest hoisted him up again over his shoulder. He heard a word whispered in ancient Mayan, and then his captor began to walk. Bouncing against his back, Roth saw a SWAT team storm into the rotunda with assault rifles. What good were they against such a man? Even knowing that weapons were useless, they couldn't quell the learned instinct to use them. It would be the same way with the military too.

Roth saw more SWAT teams rush in from the other direction. In fact, the jaguar priest must have walked right past them. They were converging in the rotunda.

"Where is he? Where's the target?"

The jaguar priest kept walking, moving past escalators and the café entrance, and Roth couldn't do anything as he bounced against the man's muscled back like dead weight. They entered another exhibit. One marked "Hall of Human Origins."

There was no one left inside. No, Roth saw a mom with two kids and a stroller, huddled against the wall in the corner, shivering in fear. The jaguar priest either didn't see them or didn't care. He just kept walking. Roth heard echoes from the SWAT team as they continued their search of the building. They wouldn't find him. He was invisible to them. Cloaked in a magic that was thousands of years old.

Roth didn't know what happened next. One moment, he could see the floor bouncing, and then suddenly they were engulfed in odorless black smoke. He felt a tugging inside him, a premonition of dread, and then they were in a darkened room. It was humid and smelled of stone.

Roth saw an arrangement of black obsidian mounted on the walls. The pieces were circular, rough cut, and gilded in gold embedded with jade.

Other men were gathered in the room, and they began to chant in Spanish, almost gleefully. *"Mataré. Mataré. ¡Mataré!"*

Roth knew the word. It meant something about killing.

The jaguar priest carried Roth out of the chamber. There was a grinding of stone, and then the priest had to crouch to get past a barrier of some sort. Roth saw a final glimpse of the room with the obsidian mirrors. His mind shot to the legends of Kukulkán's brother. How images of him showed an obsidian mirror for a foot. Now Roth understood. The followers of Huracán, the wicked brother, could travel between the mirrors. That was how Jacob had reached Washington, DC, and other capitals around the world. It wasn't just a random teleportation, but a connection from mirror to mirror, bound through the magic.

That meant they were back in the Yucatán. Roth was so disoriented from being carried on the man's back that he couldn't tell which way they'd gone, only that they were in a maze, perhaps within the great pyramid of the Jaguar Temple itself. He was in enemy territory. And the US military was about to attack.

Roth realized that he was going to die. And not just any death. He'd be sacrificed on an ancient altar in front of a crowd.

Jacob Calakmul would have his revenge at last.

CHAPTER TWENTY-SEVEN

Marine Corps Base Quantico

Washington, DC

January 10

Suki gazed out the window of the private jet at the murky river water beneath her. They'd left Fort Lauderdale a few hours before and were now arriving at a heavily guarded military base in Virginia. That should have made her feel safe, but it didn't. The squirming, negative feeling was still there. Not about Quantico, she didn't think, but something was wrong.

"What river is that? The Potomac?" she asked Lund, who was seated across from her, a glossy wooden table in between them. Her mom sat next to her, across the aisle, with Jane Louise across from her. It was much more comfy than a regular airplane. Private planes, admittedly, were pretty sweet.

Lund glanced out the window. "No, that's Chopawamsic Creek. It feeds into the Potomac."

"Got it. So this military base is where the FBI is trained?"

"It's on the same property, but farther west. We're going to the Marine Corps base. That's where the airport is. And the hospital for your mom." Lund tilted his head as he gazed out the window. "Interesting."

Suki looked out again and then craned her neck. A fighter jet was farther back, following their plane as it descended.

"Whoa," Suki said. "Does that mean we're important or dangerous?"

"Maybe a little of both," Lund answered with a smirk. Then he shifted his attention to Suki's mom. "How are you feeling, Mrs. Roth?"

"Tired but coping." She had a bottle of water, half-empty, and a tray of food that she'd been eating to maintain her blood sugar. She'd given herself another shot of insulin, but they needed a blood test to check her glucose levels.

Suki's stomach fluttered as the plane dipped lower. She gripped the armrests. Each chair was equipped with a private monitor on a swivel screen, but the flight was short enough that none of them had bothered to turn theirs on. They were exhausted from their ordeal.

"How far is DC from here?" Suki asked, trying to get rid of the oppressive feeling by distracting herself.

"About an hour, depending on traffic."

Suki watched through the window as they were about to meet the ground and then felt the bump and jerk of the tires hitting. The jet began to rapidly slow down.

Lund pulled out his phone and switched it off airplane mode before making a call. It must have been unsuccessful because he immediately dialed another number.

"Hi, Carly. Jordan didn't answer. Where are Mr. Roth and the boys?"

The change in his expression made Suki's stomach drop. She looked over at her mom and saw her eyes fixed on Lund's face, her brow wrinkled with worry.

"No," Lund whispered in shock, grimacing. Suki had never seen him look this way. He was always in control. This was bad news.

"Got another call coming in from the FBI director. I'll call you back."

Suki swallowed and watched as Lund ended the call and accepted another. "This is Lund. We just landed at Quantico. What happened in DC?" He sat silently, his lips twitching as he listened. He looked disturbed. Angry. Disappointed.

Not knowing was torture for Suki. Something had happened to her dad. Maybe to the boys too. She looked at Lund, silently pleading with him to tell her.

He listened dumbly to his phone, then squeezed his eyes shut for a second. "Okay. Okay. Where's the president? I see. This is bad. This is really bad. What about the units down in Mexico? Have they made contact yet? Hmm. Understood." He listened some more. "Understood. Sorry about Brower. It's . . . it feels like the beginning of Armageddon. See you soon."

He ended the call.

"Where's Jonny?" Suki's mom asked firmly. "Where are my sons?"

The jet was taxiing across the runway to a side aisle. There were several black SUVs parked there. They seemed to be waiting for them.

Lund gave her mom a sorrowful look. "A jaguar priest just went on a rampage at one of the Smithsonians in DC. Your husband and boys were there. The security team was slaughtered. Video footage shows your husband was hit by a trank dart and collapsed. The man—we're presuming he's a jaguar priest—carried him off and turned invisible. The boys . . . no one knows where they are."

He might as well have just gut punched Suki. She looked at Lund accusingly. "I . . . I thought Agent Sanchez was protecting them. And Jordan. Your guy."

"Agent Sanchez was thrown into a wall hard enough that it broke her spine," Lund said tightly. He was trying hard to control his emotions. "Jordan is in critical condition. They're both in an emergency room in DC."

Another blow. Suki knew it wasn't Lund's fault. Fear overwhelmed her. Her dad would be taken to Jacob Calakmul, who'd made it clear what he wanted to do. Her father would be sacrificed on a Maya altar. She closed her eyes, feeling tears burning hotly. She shook her head, trying to stop them, trying to blot out her imagination, but it didn't work.

She started sobbing.

It wasn't fair! Ever since they'd gone to Mexico with the Beasleys, their life had blown up. Now the world was blowing up.

Before the jet stopped, Suki felt her mom's arms embracing her. Suki quivered, her nose dripping, and held on to her mom, clinging to her.

These feelings writhing in her chest. These terrible emotions of loss, of grief, of anger, of hatred. These were emotions that the world would soon be feeling. Set loose by a *jerk* because of what had happened to his ancestors five centuries ago. What a mess.

Her mother held her, stroking her hair and murmuring softly. Suki knew that her mom was hurting too. Her husband had been abducted. Her boys were missing. Then she felt a small hand stroking hers, and when she opened her wet eyes, she saw Jane Louise kneeling in front of her. This little girl who had watched her family die was trying to comfort her. They were both trying to make her feel better despite their own pain.

There was something weirdly awesome about that.

Suki sniffled, wiping her eyes. The pilot had emerged from the cockpit and was opening the door. The roar of a jet engine could be heard outside as another jet took off.

Suki felt embarrassed for crying so hard. She'd unwittingly wiped her snot on her mom's shirt. But moms didn't care about gross stuff like that. Moms were incredible.

Suki looked at Lund. He seemed defeated. Grief stricken. He was staring out the window, tears in his own eyes, and by some incredible flex of self-will, they hadn't fallen.

There was a shrinking part of Suki that wanted to blame him for this unfortunate twist of events. But Lund had tried everything in his power to protect her family. He'd done the same in Bozeman. In fact, he'd been grazed by a bullet protecting Suki's life from an MS-13 gang. It wasn't his fault.

"Hey," Suki said.

Lund continued to gaze absently out the window.

"Hey," she said again.

He turned to look at her, his expression suggesting he was bracing himself for a rebuke.

"Thanks, Uncle Steve," she said to him, choking on the words. "It's not your fault. You got us out of Florida okay. You can't be everywhere at once."

She didn't know what had inspired her to say those things. But she saw the wrinkle in his forehead, the relaxing of his tense shoulders.

"Calakmul . . . he's pretty intense. No joke. He's . . . he's a boss. That's why we're so afraid of him."

Lund frowned and nodded. He didn't offer any platitudes. Any fake promises that they'd get her dad back or the boys were okay. He was real. He wouldn't fill her with false hope.

"Thanks, kiddo," he said gruffly, wiping his eyes.

Suki reached out her palm to him. He knew what it meant. He placed his palm on hers, and their thumbs embraced. An introvert's hug.

Lund sighed as they pulled their hands back. "I do have a tracker on your dad's burner phone," he said. "If they've taken him out of cell phone range, it won't show up. But we can try that at least."

He pulled out his phone again and switched apps. His brow furrowed. "That's weird."

"What?" Suki asked.

"The phone is still on. And working."

Suki felt a gush of hope. "Did dad escape? Or can you find the guy who kidnapped him?"

Lund looked perplexed. "I don't think so . . . it's at the Lincoln Memorial."

Suki and her mom exchanged a look.

"Call the phone," her mom said.

"It's the boys," Jane Louise said with a smile.

Lund tapped on the number and called. He held the phone to his ear. Suki could hear Brillante's voice. "Uh. Hello?"

"This is Uncle Steve," Lund said. "I'm with your mom and Suki. We just landed. Are you safe?"

"Is it really him?" whispered another voice. Lucas's.

"It says it's him on caller ID," Brillante said. "Um, we're hiding at the Lincoln Memorial. We didn't know what to do."

"They took our dad," Lucas added, sniffling.

"I know," Lund said firmly. He shifted his gaze to Suki. "And we're going to do everything we can to get him back."

CHAPTER
TWENTY-EIGHT

Jaguar Temple

Calakmul Biosphere Reserve

January 10

Uacmitun's betrayal at such a pivotal moment cast a shadow on Jacob's mood. If someone so loyal had been tempted to turn against him, what did that mean for the rest of the warrior clan? Had the man simply seized on an opportunistic moment? Or were there more seeds of discontent spreading roots beneath the surface?

He could not let such insidious thoughts distract him tonight. He stood before the obsidian mirror, watching as Angélica helped arrange his ceremonial attire. A large crowd had already gathered at the arena, waiting for him to arrive.

Angélica took a leather bracer with several poison darts and added it to his belt. The darts were to paralyze the sacrificial victims for the ceremony. At such close range, he wouldn't need a blowgun to shoot them. Just a little prick. Then Angélica brought out the sacrificial blade, a dagger made of sharpened obsidian. The serrations would make it easy to cut through flesh and bone. She sheathed the weapon and wrapped its belt around his waist before cinching it tight.

"Are you ready for the ceremony?" she asked. Her own face and arms were decorated in Maya ink. "You don't want to delay it?"

"This moment has been underway for centuries," he said. "Why would I hesitate now?"

"The Americans," she said. "I've heard their jets passing overhead."

Jacob reached out and stroked her cheek. "There is nothing to fear. The protections surrounding the Jaguar Temple will not fail. Their drones have dropped like cicadas from the trees. The jungle will continue to protect us. And if they somehow come close enough to the stelae guarding the grounds, the *kem äm* will repel them. Even if they know about the underground rivers, I have put shields there as well. Soon the war will be at their gates. Not ours."

She smiled, but he saw the worry in her eyes.

The bead strands rattled, and a servant came rushing in, falling to his knees and pressing his forehead against the ground.

"Great One!" he gasped.

Jacob lowered his hand and looked at the servant who'd intruded. Another problem? Another distraction?

"Yes?" Jacob asked tonelessly.

"Mataré is coming! He carries a man. Your foe!"

"Who?"

"The father of the family who won the death game last year!"

"Jonathon Roth?" Jacob said incredulously. He turned to Angélica in surprise. Her face showed the same reaction.

"They come to the throne room now!" the servant said urgently.

Jacob gripped Angélica's hand, and they marched out of the private room. The throne room of the palace was very close, and when they got there, they found Mataré standing proudly, arms folded. Jonathon

Roth was on his hands and knees. Other servants had gathered, and they whispered among themselves, commenting on the sudden arrival.

Jacob was impressed. No, he was *delighted*. It was Mr. Roth at last.

"Attend to our guests!" Jacob commanded the servant, who instantly dispersed to fetch the jugs of *xocolatl* and trays of meats and fruits. Mataré was breathing heavily, sweat dripping down his face. Mr. Roth was a heavy man. Even with the strength of a jaguar priest, he'd undergone a test of endurance.

"You found him," Jacob said in the old tongue, knowing Mr. Roth was passable in Spanish.

"And I killed in order to claim him," Mataré said proudly. "They could not stop me."

"You will be rewarded," Jacob said. "A kingdom to rule. A grand one."

"Thank you, Master of Secrets," Mataré said. "I must prepare for the ceremony."

"Go. You are highly favored."

Mataré smiled, bowed to Jacob, and then departed, leaving Jacob and Angélica alone with Mr. Roth in the now empty throne room.

Jacob switched to English.

"Once again you return to the Jaguar Temple, Mr. Roth. A fitting night, of course, to return. We are reenacting La Noche Triste. I'm glad you will be here to participate in it."

Roth lifted his head, looking defeated and frightened. He glanced around the chamber, taking in the elaborate stonework.

"So you're going to kill me?" he said with a sigh.

"You knew that was the only acceptable outcome when you chose to defy me. Surely it cannot be a surprise to you. Did you honestly believe I would not enforce my threats?"

Roth scratched his neck but still remained in a subservient posture. "When you didn't let Sarina go, I thought she was already dead. I didn't know you'd spared Jane Louise."

"I was using them both as security for your good faith. Now we both see that it was prudent for me to do so."

"Indeed. You won."

"Do not try to flatter me, Mr. Roth. You survived longer than most who have roused my displeasure. Your cooperation with the government has unleashed mighty enemies against me too soon. Confronting the military was always part of my plan. They are a powerful crocodile. But even a jaguar can seize a crocodile by the neck and drag it out of the river. There are many of us. We are enough."

Roth sighed and shook his head. "I know that I cannot plead for my life. But I ask that you spare my family."

Jacob took a step forward. "If they were here, I would make them watch you die," he said coldly. "There was a time of war among the ancient Maya when the captives were fed on the flesh and blood of their own fathers and husbands. And then they were starved to death. That is what I would do to your family, Mr. Roth. In a dungeon at the gates of Xibalba where no one could hear them scream. Consider it a mercy from Ix Chel that they're *not* here. After I've cut out your heart, your flesh will be fed to the jungle. Prepare for midnight, Mr. Roth. It comes swiftly."

Roth lifted his head and glared at him defiantly.

"I wasn't expecting to survive as long as I did. I've had another year with my kids. I outsmarted you in Germany and Bozeman. I'm the one who tricked you in DC too. The Situation Room trap. That was *my* idea."

Jacob's blood began to boil with rage. Was Roth trying to provoke a harsh reaction? Did he wish to be killed quickly, mauled by a jaguar, instead of facing the ceremonial dagger?

"Am I supposed to be impressed?" Jacob countered.

"No. You're supposed to be worried," Roth said, rising to his feet. Jacob didn't like his look of defiance. It was intolerable.

"I'm not," Jacob answered simply.

"We both know what's on the blank pages of the Dresden Codex. The prophecy isn't about you. That's why I know you're going to lose. Whether or not I die is inconsequential in the end. As long as you . . . lose."

Mr. Roth was trying to play mind games. But Jacob found himself thinking of that look on his father's face, all those years ago, when he'd brought him to Aztlán. He'd seen something in a vision. Something that had prompted him to try to kill Jacob. No one else knew about that. No one else *would* know about it.

"Kukulkán is coming," Roth said. "The prophecy is about *him*. Not you."

"Your posturing is insufferable," Jacob said angrily.

"I have nothing to lose," Roth said, holding up his hands. "I already know I'm a dead man. And so are you. You've persuaded everyone you're the 'chosen one.' But you're just like Cortés, making decisions based on a myth you don't even understand."

Jacob was furious now, but he didn't want Roth to know how much he'd unsettled him. If it was a ploy to win an early death, it was close to working.

"Take him to the dungeon with the others," Jacob said tightly to Angélica. He pointed his finger at Roth. "I am the master of the Great Secret. Not *you*."

"Said Nero before his own centurions killed him. I'm the only one who can help you survive this. Think about it."

"If you speak another word, I'll cut out your tongue," Jacob threatened.

And he meant it.

CHAPTER TWENTY-NINE

JAGUAR TEMPLE

CALAKMUL BIOSPHERE RESERVE

January 10

There was a pit in Roth's stomach. He had a feeling he wasn't going to survive the Jaguar Temple a second time. Ever since he'd been captured by that enormously strong man whose name literally meant killing people, he'd shoved his worry and sense of dread as deep inside himself as he could. He needed his mind more than anything. Still, he could feel it lurking there. It didn't help that he was faced with the visual evidence of the powerful magic Calakmul had on his side—it was there in his unlined face and his physique, which was even more like that of a jaguar now that he'd been de-aged in Aztlán.

"So . . . are you considering my offer?" Roth asked Angélica in a low voice after she'd led him away from a seething Jacob Calakmul.

"What?" Angélica said with a false laugh. They passed a servant who bowed meekly to her and continued on his way. Angélica was wearing the ceremonial garb he'd seen her in during the death game. Like she was a Maya princess. Gold jewelry decorated her throat, arms, and ankles.

"Everything I told Jacob was intended for you," Roth said. "I didn't know if we'd get the chance to speak privately."

"You're serious?"

"I don't have time to joke around. The prophecy isn't about Jacob."

"And how do you know that?" She sounded incredulous. Of course she would be.

"I texted the pictures from the Dresden Codex to Suki's phone, as demanded, so I presume you've seen them. But I didn't text the translation."

"We already know it," she said dismissively.

"Are you sure you've interpreted it correctly? I have a grad student from UC San Diego who's been helping me. She works with the Qualcomm Institute. Heard of it?"

"Yes," she said, giving him a sidelong look.

"A professor there has pinpointed the location of this compound. Satellites have been repositioned to watch this place twenty-four seven. We know about the other temples lighting up."

Angélica stopped midstride and looked at him in confusion. "Other temples?"

That surprised him. She didn't know about them? Roth had assumed it meant that Jacob had more than one stronghold in the Yucatán. Was that not so?

Roth stopped and turned to look at her. "Chichén Itzá started glowing this morning. So did Uxmal and a few others I can't pronounce. You didn't know?"

There was something in her eyes now. Fear? Worry? This was new information to her. Did that mean Calakmul hadn't told her? Or was it possible he didn't know himself?

"Help get me out of here," Roth said in a low, urgent voice. "It's not too late to switch sides. You helped Lucas when that warrior wanted to murder him. I just don't think you're the kind of person who'd want to be responsible for so much carnage."

"It doesn't matter what I want," she whispered. "It's too late. The end times have already started. If I'm by his side, I might at least be able to influence him."

"The end times aren't what you believe they are. I saw the room with the obsidian mirrors. That's how they got into the White House. To DC and other places. Help me get the other leaders out of here the same way."

She shook her head firmly. "I've never been in that chamber. I don't know how the magic works."

"But they *are* the 'smoking mirrors' from the legends of Huracán, Kukulkán's brother. The one who tricked him."

"Yes," she said tightly. "Mr. Roth, I'm risking my life by even speaking to you in this way. Jacob is not . . . he's not a man who forgives." She directed him toward another corridor.

"No, and you know too much." He'd noticed that she looked younger now, which matched what Suki had told him about their visit to Aztlán. "You know where Aztlán is. From what my daughter says, he was the only one who knew."

She flinched.

"Someone will try to kill him now. Because they know *you* have that knowledge. You're a liability to him."

She made a face. "Someone tried already. His warrior chief. Earlier today. He'll be executed publicly. I would be too if I helped you."

Roth hadn't been off the mark. He stopped in his tracks to buy more time. Calakmul's plan was already crumbling from within. That's what happened when a tyrant seized power—sometimes immediately, and sometimes not for years. The pattern could be seen throughout history, from Nero to Caligula. But how could he take advantage of that? How could he convince her to help?

"We need to keep walking, before someone sees us," Angélica said. She motioned for him to follow, and he fell in step alongside her.

"The next guy isn't going to be as *nice* to you as Jacob is," Roth pointed out. "And anything Jacob gave you can be taken away by someone else. Besides, I'm guessing Jacob's not the trusting type. You probably have to prove your loyalty every day."

"Please, Jonathon," she said, shaking her head. But her voice quavered a little, and he knew he'd struck a nerve.

"You can't fault me for trying. I've told the US government everything I know. And they believe me. We tried to capture Jacob in the Situation Room. We know about the jaguar priests' greatest weakness. How they are vulnerable when they begin to transform."

She made a face and shook her head again.

"Look, you didn't know about the other temples. I'm assuming he doesn't know either? He would have told you."

"Yes. But he's been distracted. He's been . . ." She pressed her lips together.

"As hot-blooded as a twenty-year-old?" Roth surmised. "That's the thing about Aztlán. I'm guessing it literally rewound your age, which means it also unwound the brain's development."

She looked at him in confusion. "What are you talking about?"

"Sorry. I have a tendency to talk as fast as I think. I was in college for a long time because I'm fascinated by everything, including the field of neuroscience. The prefrontal cortex is in charge of executive functioning. Long-range thinking. Strategic planning. It doesn't fully form in men until around age twenty-five. But it happens earlier for women. It's always been that way. You must have noticed it, Angélica. His rashness. His temper. His emotional instability. You've been dealing with an earlier version of him. His hard drive has all the files. But his brain is using old code."

He'd hit the mark with the technology metaphor. He saw her wrinkled brow, her guilty expression.

"You're in the same position that Malintzin was in," Roth said after they'd turned the next corner. There were stairs leading downward. Malintzin had partnered with Cortés during his invasion of the

Americas. She'd even borne him children. Her name had come to mean *traitor* among the Mexican people. If she hadn't helped Cortés, he never would have succeeded in deposing Moctezuma.

"He calls me that sometimes," she said. "I hate it. She was a puppet to the Order of the Jaguar Priests."

"And you aren't?"

"Why do you think I hate it?" she asked sadly. "I know what I am."

"So help me! We can both escape. You can start a new life. Leave this behind."

"There isn't enough time! The sacrifices start at midnight. The plague is already spreading. It's not that I relish so much suffering, but a price should be paid for the centuries of injustice visited on our people. Still, I plan to soften Jacob's fury after he's won." She looked away. "I don't think the children deserve their fate. I begged him to spare them, but he says that our people's children weren't spared."

"He's not going to win. You know the man you have isn't the president of the United States, right?"

"Yes," Angélica said. "But it doesn't matter to him. Anyone will do. As long as there is someone to kill."

"You helped us before," Roth said. "I can help you once we get away. I did a pretty good job of staying under the radar with your boyfriend."

She gave him a half smile. "You did. Until Dresden. And your actions spurred him to expose himself to the world too soon."

They started down the steps into the lower levels of the palace. Rods of stone topped with swirling orbs of *kem äm* illuminated the way down.

Partway down, she stopped. She reached into her waistband and withdrew a small leather packet. It looked a little like a wallet with a pointed covering and a jade stone embedded in it.

"There are three darts in here," she said. "The toxin works very fast. Paralyzation lasts for about ten minutes. After what Uacmitun did to me, I decided I need to carry my own protection. If someone is shielded by *kem äm*, it won't work. This is all I can do for you. You'll have to find a way to get yourself out of that cell." She handed the pouch to him, and Roth took it gratefully and stuffed it into his pocket.

She touched his wrist. "I didn't agree with what Jacob wanted to do to your daughter. To subvert her against you. But I don't think he could help himself. She showed too much promise, and he likes a challenge."

"Thanks for this," he said, patting his pocket. It was something.

Angélica motioned for him to continue down the stone steps. When they reached the bottom, they passed through a curtain of beads and entered a corridor. It was a dungeon of sorts, but instead of doors with iron bars, there were just open gaps shielded by webs of *kem äm*.

Several warriors were standing guard. They addressed Angélica in Mayan, and she responded curtly and motioned for them to take Roth away.

He looked at her dispassionate face, her mask of indifference. She truly was Malintzin reincarnated. And Roth would do anything he could to help her make it out alive as well.

A warrior grabbed Roth by the arm, squeezing hard, and jerked him toward one of the doorways. He waved his hand over it, and the magic of his bracelet summoned the *kem äm* to it. Then he shoved Roth into the dark, small room. The *kem äm* filled in the gap, illuminating the man in a dirty suit who sat in the corner. A man who looked like the president.

"Mr. Roth?"

"Mr. Brower."

Roth slumped down against the wall across from him. The cell was pretty narrow, about seven feet across and ten feet long. Roth watched as the warrior walked away, but he knew they were patrolling the main corridor.

"I'm sorry they caught you," Brower said. "Did they bring you in through the White House too?"

"No, one of the Smithsonians. The one by FBI headquarters," Roth said. "There's an obsidian mirror in the White House?"

"Been there for years," Brower said with a resigned sigh. "No one I know remembers where it came from. They took my watch, so I don't know what time it is. *And* we're underground."

"It was late afternoon when I was caught. It's probably five or six o'clock? I don't know the time zone differences between the East Coast and Mexico."

"DC is two hours ahead, but that doesn't really matter right now. They're killing us at midnight," Brower said. "These barriers are like a force field. I flicked a little pebble at it, and it shot back at me just like you said it would. Not that I needed more convincing after what happened in the Situation Room."

"Who else is down here?"

"British prime minister. German chancellor. Oh, and the king of Spain."

"Wow," Roth said, shaking his head. He gestured to Brower. "And you, Mr. President."

"Our government, like others, has redundancy built in. I wish I'd taken your warnings more . . . urgently. I'd convinced myself that a room full of trained special agents would be more than enough to take down *one* terrorist. We even used a nerve agent. Nothing worked."

Roth draped an arm across his knee and gazed at the shimmering wall of *kem äm*. Suki would have been able to wave it away with a flick of her hand, but the magic had never worked for him.

"The director showed me the photos from the Situation Room. Guess you've seen Jacob in jaguar form?"

"I don't think I've ever been more terrified," Brower said. "I'm sorry you're here. I wish I were the only one."

"I'm glad you're here," Roth said.

Brower cocked his head.

"Because I'm going to need help getting the others out of here." He fished in his pocket and removed the special pouch. "Got three poison darts. We'd better make them count."

CHAPTER THIRTY

The White House

Washington, DC

January 10

There's a first time for everything. As the military helicopter passed over the rooftop of the White House, Suki gripped the armrests, gazed out the window, and watched the lawn approaching. She wore a headset and microphone, as did her mom, Jane Louise, and the others in the helicopter.

"Is this the president's helicopter?" Suki asked, looking at Lund, seated across from her.

He shook his head. "It looks similar, but this one's a VH-60N White Hawk. His is a Sea King. It has some special mods."

"You'd think so," Suki said. Her stomach twittered as the helicopter started its descent. She glanced at her mom, taking in Sarina's improved color. She had a new insulin pump attached, and her blood sugar was under control and being monitored real-time. The doctor at the Marine Corps hospital in Quantico had given her lots of IV fluids too. Her mom nodded out the window with a small smile.

It was normal for uniformed marines to be the honor guard for the president's comings and goings. But the marines who'd come out to greet the helicopter were dressed in camo, faces painted, and were loaded for bear.

When the door to the helicopter was opened, the noise of the rotors became deafening. They left their headsets behind, and the marines helped them disembark. They were on the south lawn, close to the rounded part of the building's facade with its distinctive columns. As they walked quickly away from the furious winds caused by the helicopter, Suki shielded her eyes to survey the portico. Her brothers came running out at full tilt.

Seeing them, Suki grinned with relief and motioned for her mom to look. Walking after the boys was a tall guy in a suit with ginger hair and glasses, flanked by men in FBI jackets.

"Mom! Suki!" Lucas shrieked in relief. They met midway across the lawn, and the boys nearly tackled their mom in a double hug. They looked so freaked out and worried that Suki's heart hurt for them. They'd been through a lot.

"I hardly recognized you two," Sarina said, her voice catching. She ran her fingers through Lucas's dyed locks, while peeking underneath Brillante's hoodie. "You're both taller! And more handsome. Look at you!"

"I'm glad you're feeling better," Lucas said. "And I'm *really* glad you're not as old as Abuelita! Oh, Mom!"

The twins went for Suki next and nearly bowled her over.

"Whoa, it's okay! It's gonna be okay," Suki said. She accepted the hugs, though, and tousled Lucas's hair. Brillante gave her a hug.

Jane Louise smiled at the twins, and when they both stood awkwardly in front of her, unsure of what to say, she hugged them both. Lucas had an extra big smile on his face when she did.

"This is Director Wright, the head of the FBI," Lund explained, introducing him to the rest of the family. "He personally picked up the boys from the Lincoln Memorial."

"We've been hiding out from that bad dude who got Dad," Brillante said with a trembling voice. "Man, this sucks."

"And they brought us here, to the White House!" Lucas said. "Like, the actual one!"

"I thought it was evacuated?" Suki asked.

Director Wright nodded. "It has been, except for the military. They've swept the entire building with K-9 squads. No sign of Calakmul. We were hoping, Suki, that you'd take a look as well?"

They'd already asked that, of course, and she nodded. "I'm ready." Calakmul had taken her dad. She would do anything she could to help rescue him.

Director Wright turned to one of the soldiers. "Keep the White Hawk here. If we need to leave quickly, I want it available."

"Yes, sir," said the marine.

"Where's the president?" Lund asked.

"A secure location, but he's itching to come back. The UN Security Council is calling a meeting to talk about the abductions. We need intel going into it."

Suki and the others walked across the stiff grass, and then they entered through the portico doors.

"We got to go to the Capitol yesterday," Brillante said. "And now we're in the White House. This is nuts! But I'd rather be back home as a family."

"We're going to do everything we can to get your father back. But we need your help too. We're going to walk through every hallway, every room," Director Wright said. "Starting with the ground floor. If you see anything unusual, let us know. As I understand it, not just anyone can see the *kem äm*. Is that how it's pronounced?"

"You said it right," Suki replied. She looked both ways as they walked down the entrance, but nothing stood out.

"Let's hold hands," Sarina suggested. "That boosted our ability before." She took Jane Louise's with her left and Suki's with her right.

With the three of them linked, Suki felt the power of the magic begin to race through her.

Instantly, she sensed a brooding power within the building.

She stopped and looked at her mom. "Feel that?"

"I do," Sarina said.

"It's that way," said Jane Louise, reaching out and pointing.

"All three of you feel it?" Director Wright asked with a surprised tone.

"We have a special connection to the magic of Ix Chel," Suki explained. "The three of us together. But what's here is powerful. It gives off a strong . . . vibe. Sorry, that's the best word I know to describe it."

"Whoa," Lucas whispered.

"Show us," Director Wright said.

The three of them walked in lockstep with each other. It didn't take long to reach the right corridor. The presence of dark magic gave off a strong, intense feeling. As soon as Suki saw the obsidian mirror on the wall, she felt fear snaking through her.

"It's bad magic," Jane Louise whispered.

Sarina nodded. "It's evil."

"What's evil?" Director Wright said. "I don't understand."

"*That,*" Suki said, pointing to an obsidian mirror mounted to a wooden frame on the wall. Then she noticed the glyph in the corner, glowing with *kem äm*. It was an invisibility glyph, like the one she'd seen on the Dresden Codex. "Oh, you can't see it." The frame looked really old, like it had been hanging there a long time. Maybe Calakmul had added the glyph before departing through it so his trail would be hidden.

"I see it," Brillante said. "That's pretty sus."

Suki invoked the magic of her ring and the bracelet, and the glyph vanished. "Now can you see it?"

Director Wright stared in surprise. The mirror on the wall had been invisible to him before, but he could obviously see it now. "That's been

225

hanging in this corridor for years. Didn't think about it being missing until now."

"That's how Jacob Calakmul got in here," Sarina explained. "It's called a smoking mirror, and it's part of the magic of the god Huracán. He's the founder of the Order of the Jaguar Priests."

Suki's stomach churned with fear. The obsidian mirror was issuing plumes of black smoke. Its magic had been activated. But not by them.

"They're coming," Suki warned.

"Who's coming?" Director Wright asked.

Lund drew his weapon. "You can take down their shields?"

Suki felt her mom squeeze her hand. She, her mom, and Jane Louise exchanged looks and then shifted their attention to the obsidian disk. The power of Ix Chel rose within Suki, and the image of a glyph came to her mind.

"*Raqinik,*" she said forcefully.

At the command, she felt a surge inside her chest, amplified by the combined strength of her mom and Jane Louise. A loud cracking noise filled the air, and the obsidian mirror and its wooden frame broke into pieces and fell onto the carpet. The noise was earsplitting and frightening.

The plumes of dark smoke wafted away and vanished.

Director Wright had his hands over his ears but let them fall away as the noise stopped.

"That's how he got in," Suki said. "It's a portal. Someone was about to come through to our side. They were probably watching us."

"Whoa," Brillante murmured. "You stopped them!"

"The mirror is broken. They can't use it again," Sarina said.

"Could we have used the portal to get inside their hideout?" Lund asked. He edged forward, looking at the obsidian shards on the carpet.

"Only the followers of Huracán can use them," Sarina said. "Not even Ix Chel knows their secret."

"Are there any more in the building?" Director Wright asked. "Or was this the only one?"

Suki could no longer feel the dark magic. "That was it."

"Dark magic or not," Lund said angrily, "I wish I could've used it to get Mr. Roth back. We're clearly at a disadvantage here."

"I'll let the CIA director know about the mirrors," Wright said. "I'm presuming there are mirrors like this in London and Berlin."

Lund shook his head, frowning in frustration.

An idea came to Suki's mind. She looked at her mom. "There *is* another way to get in and out of the temple. The same way you used."

Lund turned around, his eyebrows lifting. "Wait . . . you can get back *in*?"

Sarina nodded. "But only from Cozumel," she said. "That island is a conduit of Ix Chel's power. When we're there, we can travel from one shrine to another in moonlight. It only works at night. That's how we escaped. The grounds are extensive, and there are hidden shrines to Ix Chel that I'm sure Calakmul doesn't know about. He'll probably have the main shrine guarded if he hasn't already destroyed it."

"But can you bring people with you?" Lund asked emphatically.

"What are you suggesting?" Sarina asked. "That we go *back*?"

"Are there any Special Forces teams already down there?" Lund asked Wright hopefully.

"We have a SEAL team on an aircraft carrier in the area and the 82nd Airborne is ready to deploy," Wright said. He looked at Suki's mom. "Mrs. Roth, our soldiers can't do anything against Calakmul's priests without help. But if we can take down their magic shields, our bullets would work, right? It might be the only way to save the hostages before Calakmul sacrifices them. Including your husband."

Sarina lowered her head. "As long as my children are safe, I'll do it. I'll take you there."

"Mom!" Lucas gasped, eyes wide with fear. "You can't go!"

Suki felt a knot of pain in her heart at the thought of her mom going. Even though she had been given fluids and was on regulated insulin again, it would take a day or so for her to bounce back from her weakened state. And even if Jane Louise hadn't been too young, Suki suspected the girl was only a conduit for Ix Chel's power, not able to use the *kem äm* by herself. It was a terrifying thought, but Suki was the best choice for this mission.

A realization struck her hard. *She* was the one Ix Chel had chosen to help. And if there was any way she could stop her dad from dying, she was going to do it.

"No, I'll go," Suki volunteered.

CHAPTER THIRTY-ONE

THE WHITE HOUSE

WASHINGTON, DC

January 10

"No!" Sarina said adamantly. "If anyone is going back down there, it's me. He's my *husband*. And I know the compound. I've lived there for the past year."

"Mrs. Roth," Director Wright said, "I think we should discuss all possibilities before discounting any."

"It has to be me," Suki said to her mom.

"I'm not going to let you," Sarina said. She still looked fatigued from their journey. Suki could see that her mom was still recovering from the ordeal her diabetes had put her through, and any more physical stresses at this point would set her back.

"Mom, you're too sick. You've been through so much. And so have I. You need to be here for the boys, for Jane Louise. I know the compound enough. I could find my way to Dad. And the longer we waste time, the greater chance he's going to die." She felt her throat start to catch. "I can't let that happen. Not if I can stop it."

"She knows how to take down their shields," Lund said to Director Wright. "That gives us a chance to use weapons we couldn't before."

Sarina shook her head, but Suki could sense her resolve wilting. She was too much a nurse to ignore her own symptoms. They hugged each other. "It'll be okay," Suki whispered. "Ix Chel has been preparing me for this. I trained with that horrible lady, remember? The one who liked to whip my legs? I can use the *kem äm* better than you can."

"Maybe so," her mom said, "but I can use it well enough."

"It's supposed to be this way, Mom. Can't you feel that it's supposed to be this way?"

It wasn't just talk. The rightness of it filled her like moonlight. The shimmer of tears in her mother's eyes told her she was right.

"I can tell you feel it too," she pressed. In her peripheral vision, she saw Jane Louise's shallow nod.

"You're not a little girl anymore," her mom said, lifting a hand to her cheek. She allowed it, because right now she needed the bolstering of her mother's touch, if only for a second. "But you're still my daughter."

"I'll always be your daughter. I need to do this, Mom."

"You need to be safe. If anything—"

Her voice broke, but Suki was already shaking her head.

"Nothing bad will happen to me. She's on our side, and I have the power to do this. I know I do."

"You're strong enough," her mom said, her voice still shaking. "You've always been strong."

"I just need some people who can go with me." She looked hopefully at Uncle Steve and Director Wright.

To Suki's surprise, the US government wasn't keen on trusting a seventeen-year-old girl with the nation's future. So she had to give them a taste of the power of *kem äm*.

She blocked both ends of the corridor with shields so the marines could try—and fail—to get past it. One of them had been repelled a dozen feet. She levitated paperweights and knickknacks from office desks and sent them in orbit around the FBI director just like she had with the rubber balls in the arena. Her brothers thought that was pretty sick. Her mom looked nervous but accepting. Director Wright, standing in the hallway among floating staplers and snow globes, looked bewildered.

Suki put the items back where she'd found them and released the barriers in the corridor. Tilting her head, she looked at the director. "It can do other stuff too," she said. "I know healing glyphs that can mend injuries. I healed Calakmul's assistant while we were flying back from—"

"W-wait," Lund interrupted, holding up his hand. "You can *heal* injuries? Like what kind?"

"All kinds," she said. "An FBI agent shot Calakmul's girlfriend in Bozeman. He was pretty upset. The bullet went through her and nearly killed her, but the magic helped her." She thought about telling them about Aztlán and how the magic could even reverse someone's age but thought better of it. The government might be interested in learning more about that one—but to what end? The magic was uncanny, unnatural, and everything within her revolted against the idea of it being used recreationally. Besides, she was far from sure she could find it again. She didn't know where it was beyond that it was in a canyon in southern Utah.

"Monica and Jordan," Lund said to Director Wright. "Can I bring her to the hospital?"

"Monica's the FBI agent who was helping Dad and the twins, right?" Suki asked.

"Yeah, she's really nice," Lucas said.

"The jaguar priest threw her into a wall," Brillante said darkly. "He hurt Jordan too."

"I can help them," Suki said. "I can't raise anyone from the dead, but the magic can heal injuries. I'm the person who should go rescue Dad too."

Sarina shook her head. "Suki, it would be *very* dangerous. The warriors are very skilled. And the jaguar priests—you've already seen what *one* can do. Not to mention Jacob himself. He could undermine your ability to use the magic just as you could with him."

"Hold on, I'm not suggesting we start a suicide squad, Mom. We go in, rescue Dad and the other hostages, then get out."

"We could only bring up to thirteen people total," Sarina said. "That's the limit of the magic for that spell. You can't move an army. That limits the size of the team."

"Why thirteen?" Suki asked.

"Thirteen is a sacred number to the Maya. And that spell only works while the moon is visible. You'd have a limited chance to get in and out."

"A limited chance is better than no chance, Mrs. Roth," Lund said. "I was thinking a SEAL team, a small group, just to protect her and the hostages. But I'm more familiar with the 82nd Airborne. They're trained to get in and get out and fulfill a mission no matter what."

Director Wright pursed his lips. "This is incredibly dangerous. I'm not sure the president will authorize a mission involving a teenager."

"You heard Uncle Steve," Suki said. "A limited chance is as good as you're going to get right now."

"You can get through their shields," Wright said thoughtfully. "That means bullets would kill them. But if they ganged up on you, then everyone would die."

Suki had already realized that part. "As long as we do it at night, I can get us out of there too. I don't think they have that power. They have to use the mirrors to get around. And I don't care if the president doesn't authorize it. If I can save Dad, then that's all the reason I need. I mean, I just need Aragorn, Gimli, and Legolas, and I'll be good."

Lund chuckled. "My employee Jordan Scott was in the 82nd Airborne. He won best warrior for the state of Maryland *after* he left the army. If you can heal him, he'll go with you."

"I can try," Suki said. "Why don't we start there?"

Wright put his hands on his hips and sighed. "Let's get you to the hospital. I'll call the chairman of the Joint Chiefs of Staff. We already have authority to strike the temple in the Yucatán. Maybe that's all the permission we need to get."

"What about the attorney general?" Lund asked. "Don't you think your boss would want to know?"

Wright smirked. "I already know what he'd say. That's why I can't tell him."

———

An armored SUV brought them to the hospital where Jordan and Monica were being treated. Even though the traffic was heavy in downtown DC, they bypassed all the red lights and drove at ambulance speed.

Sarina squeezed Suki's hand. She looked fearful. "I don't want you doing this, *mija*," she whispered.

Suki bit her lip. "You know I have to save Dad," she answered. "It's Ix Chel's plan." The boys and Jane Louise were in the back seat, and Lund was riding shotgun, with another FBI agent behind the wheel. Director Wright had stayed back at the White House to make some calls and see what he could manage on short notice.

"Can I go too?" Lucas asked. "We can see the glyphs now."

Suki looked back at him. "Sorry, bro. You don't meet the height requirement for this ride."

"That's not fair."

"I know. None of this is fair."

When they reached the hospital, Lund got out first. He checked the sides and then opened the door for Sarina and Suki to get out. The other kids climbed out too, and they all walked into the hospital.

The smell reminded Suki of their time in Naples, but she didn't sense danger this time. Still, the urgency of the situation was weighing on her. The sun had already gone down. How soon before Calakmul would start the human sacrifices? Would he wait until midnight?

Lund secured the elevator, and they all went inside. He pushed the button for the third floor, and a little thrill shot up her spine as they started up. Elevators had always made her feel giddy. Once inside the ward, they went down a corridor crowded with doctors and nurses and the chirping and beeping of equipment. The smell of sanitizer was strong.

They reached the first room, and Lund knocked before entering. Jordan was propped up on a hospital bed. His leg was wrapped in bandages, and he had a bruise and lacerations on his cheek. His arm and hand were also wrapped up. He looked like he'd fallen off a building and survived.

"Hey," Jordan said in a scratchy voice, sounding dejected but trying to be cheerful.

Suki had never met him, but her brothers had told her about him—that he was funny and brave and had a serious crush on Monica Sanchez. The twins looked devastated to see him like this. They inched closer, looking fearful, unsure of what to say.

"You're pretty messed up," Brillante said.

"I can't exactly play video games on my phone anymore," Jordan answered, his expression at odds with the tone he was trying to convey. He knew about Monica, no doubt. "But yeah. Pretty messed up. The swelling needs to go down before they can fix me up."

"Are you in a lot of pain?" Lucas asked.

"Not really. That's a positive. Sorry I let you guys down."

"You didn't," Lucas said, shaking his head. "Don't think that."

"We wanted to see you," Lund said, stepping around to the other side of the bed. "But we also came to help."

"Did you bring a Mountain Dew? That would really help," he groaned, shifting on the bed.

Lund looked at the girls. "Suki? Sarina? Want to give it a try?"

Her mom looked at her. "Let's hold hands as we did before." Then she glanced down at Jane Louise, who'd come in with them. "With all three of us, the magic is stronger."

Jane Louise held Sarina's hand, and Sarina held Suki's. Suki reached out tentatively. Jordan looked at her like she was acting a little weird.

"I don't get it . . ."

"Just . . . wait," Lund said. "They're going to give you a Maya blessing."

He settled back against the pillows and closed his eyes.

Suki's hand hovered over his leg. Should she try to heal that first? He was broken in many places. The idea came to hold her hand above his head and touch him there, so she pressed her hand against his stubby hair. She felt the power well up before she even uttered the word. Strength flowed into her, coming from Jane Louise and her mom, but *she* was the outlet.

"Kunaj," Suki whispered. Back on the Pegasus jet, when Jacob was trying to keep Angélica alive, he'd whispered a healing word—*utzirisaj*—over and over. The Mayan word for healing, *to make whole*. He'd taught it to Suki and told her to use it. But his power came from death, not life. When Suki had tried to heal Angélica, another word had come to mind. A whisper from Ix Chel: *kunaj*. It was a stronger word, and it had immediate effect in reviving Angélica.

This time, saying that word with her mom and Jane Louise, the power manifested even more quickly. More powerfully. Suki felt a rush from the magic and a peaceful feeling.

Jordan stiffened in surprise.

"Whoa," he said, opening his eyes as she pulled her hand away. He looked at Suki in wonderment. Then at Lund.

"I'm better," he whispered in shock.

"You feel better?" Lund asked hopefully.

"No, I'm better. Like . . . completely better. Like . . . I haven't felt this good since . . . well, better not say that here." He swung his legs off the edge of the bed. Then he started ripping off the IV tape and pulled the needles out of his arms. The alarms went off.

Suki backed away, smiling in surprise.

Then he got off the bed and dropped to a low squat, holding both his arms out. His leg had had a compound fracture. It shouldn't have been able to support his weight at all.

"Dude!" Lucas and Brillante gasped simultaneously.

Jane Louise grinned.

Lund watched, seemingly stunned into silence, as Jordan began ripping the bandages off his hand. "Seriously, I could do the Tough Mudder, like, right now," he exclaimed. He was partway through his leg bandage when a nurse came in and gaped.

"What are you doing out of bed?" she said. "How are you even standing!"

Jordan stopped, looked pleadingly at Suki. "Can you . . . can you heal Monica too?"

Suki still felt pretty fresh. With the three of them working together, it had been easy. "I'm pretty sure we can."

"Better put on your clothes first," Lucas suggested. "Your butt's hanging out."

CHAPTER THIRTY-TWO

JAGUAR TEMPLE

CALAKMUL BIOSPHERE RESERVE

January 10

He should have just let Angélica die in Bozeman. Instead, he'd given her power over him, and she'd betrayed him.

Jacob paced in a circle on the stone platform in the middle of the sacred cenote beneath the palace. The waters were a deep turquoise color, made so by their purity and the thousands of jade stones that covered the floor beneath the water. Larger pieces, some as big as a dish, had been stacked around a stone circle in the middle of the cenote. A bridge made of stone and mortar connected to the staircase leading back to his private chamber. The walls were irregular and thick with hanging stalactites. A shaft of light came from above, a series of glyphs carved in the ceiling so that it was light night and day. It was his private bathing chamber. He'd only recently begun to allow Angélica to meet him there.

He heard the scuff of her bare feet on the steps. His feelings of anger and disappointment were too powerful to endure. She'd hurt him, badly, and not just with her own betrayal. Uacmitun had revolted against Jacob because of her. Others might be tempted to do the same, knowing she'd been to Aztlán. He could not rule his new world if he was always wondering who might stab him in the back with a jagged obsidian dagger.

He paused in the center of the circular platform, his back to the bridge and the stairs, then squatted down low, as if observing something on the ground. He didn't want her to see the look on his face. Not yet.

He flexed his hands and then closed them into fists, tensing his muscles until they quivered before relaxing them. One deep breath. Then another.

"Jacob?"

It was her voice. There was a note of caution in it. He was supposed to be mingling with the guests at the temple, preparing them for the sacrifices that would begin later. He straightened, wearing the ceremonial garb of his office, master of the Kowinem. He would preside over the sacrifices as he had before. But there was one sacrifice he had to make first.

"Come to me," he said, trying to keep his voice composed so as not to reveal himself or his intentions.

He heard the tread of her bare feet against the stones of the bridge. The turquoise waters lapped against the stones. It was only eighteen inches or so deep. Similar to the Roman baths of old. Thoughts of Nero had been on his mind because of Mr. Roth. He wanted to smash the author in the face.

Angélica touched his shoulder, and he turned his head. Her revealing Maya dress was provocative, and so was the colorful golden jewelry she wore. Gifts from him. The ink on her cheeks and arms was expertly done. She stroked the curve of his shoulder with her finger.

"Do you want me . . . again?" she asked huskily.

That was the torment of it. He *did* want her. Even after she'd betrayed him. His pulse quickened, and the throb of desire struck him forcibly. She had power over him, and she *knew* it. It was time to break that power.

"No," he said, shaking his head.

She lowered her hand, her brow pinched with confusion. "What, then?"

"Nero wasn't stabbed by his guard," Jacob said. "Some say he committed suicide after the senate declared him a public enemy."

Her brow pinched further.

"Mr. Roth knows history. He taught it in college. Why would he get it wrong?" he asked her, but he already knew the answer.

"I . . . I don't know," Angélica answered in a confused tone.

"So unlike him to be wrong about such a detail. Then I realized his speech wasn't meant for me. It was meant for *you.*"

He turned completely around to face her, his emotions conflicted still. She was beautiful. Intelligent. She knew him better than anyone. And that made her betrayal sting all the more. She'd been his Malintzin, his interpreter of American culture, technology, and corruption. He'd turned her into his most capable ally and confidante. They were lovers. He'd given her a gift he'd shared with no one else. The gift of eternal youth. And it still hadn't been enough to secure her loyalty.

"Jacob, you're frightening me."

"Am I? Is it fear or guilt that you feel, Angélica?"

She winced.

"I ordered you to take Mr. Roth to the dungeon with the other prisoners. I was curious what he would say to you when the two of you were alone. So I used a glyph and turned myself invisible and followed you. *I followed you.*" He held up his hands, as if to take her face between his palms.

Angélica dropped to her knees in front of him. "Forgive me! I beg you! Forgive me!"

He grabbed her head between his palms, pressing against her temples, trying to tame the vengeful wrath that scorched inside his chest. "What have I not given you? You've had treasures beyond counting! I gave you your own island, your own resorts, your own power! Was it because I held back my magic? Because I didn't want you to pay the price that I had to in order to learn it? Was that why you betrayed me?"

She was sobbing uncontrollably now, tears rushing down her cheeks. He released her and stepped back, struggling against the dueling desires to comfort her and kill her.

"Please! Please! Spare me!"

"I cannot spare you!" he shouted at her. "Not after this betrayal. Not with what you know. You doubt that I will win? Even now? Because . . . because Mr. Roth somehow convinced you that I have the brain of a young man?"

She slumped down onto her hands and knees on the circular platform. She choked and sobbed, her entire body trembling with fear.

"And you gave him darts," Jacob said incredulously. "You gave him . . . darts." He shook his head, grunting with the absurdity of it. Had she really thought that it would help Mr. Roth escape? Such a pitiful weapon against all the vast resources and power he controlled.

"Pleeease," she groaned, her head shaking back and forth.

He looked at her, trying to harden himself and regain his feelings of contempt. If he did not destroy her, then he would lose all respect among the jaguar priests.

"You knew that I was not a merciful man. If you wanted mercy, you should have worshipped Kukulkán instead. Not the god of the night sky. The god of divination. The god of temptation. You were going to be my *queen*. Now I must find another."

"Make me your servant, then," Angélica pleaded, gazing up at him with tear-streaked eyes. "Make me the lowest of your creatures. I will do anything . . ."

He was tempted. All the years he'd invested in her . . .

He'd be throwing away a great treasure. Could he cling on to Angélica still? But why should he? She was a cursed treasure.

It felt like his world was unraveling in front of him. Mr. Roth could have been lying about the lights blinking on at the monuments, but if it were true . . .

What if Mr. Roth was right about the prophecy too? What if the Dresden Codex really did herald the return of Kukulkán? No, he wouldn't think like that. He couldn't let himself. He had to break the past to create his own future.

Breaking her *neck* would be too easy. Her torment would be over too quickly. No, he wanted her to suffer, just as he was suffering. Why not give her some false hope before she died?

"I will let the gods of death decide your fate," Jacob said ruthlessly. "If you leave this cenote alive, then that means even *they* do not want you. The gods of Xibalba are known for their cunning and treachery, after all. This is your chance, Angélica. Run."

"Is there nothing I can—?"

"Run!" His voice echoed across the curved stone walls of the cenote. The waters rippled.

With fear shining amid the tears, she bolted away from him down the length of the bridge.

Jacob invoked the magic of his ring and turned himself into an alligator. She was terrified of crocodiles and alligators. She'd told him as much. Reptiles gave her nightmares.

He had no doubt he'd catch her before she reached the steps leading out of the cenote. Alligators were faster on land than they were in the water.

And faster than any human.

CHAPTER THIRTY-THREE

Jaguar Temple

Calakmul Biosphere Reserve

January 10

In their confined cell, Roth and Brower could do no more than talk while they waited for someone to come for them. Three darts wasn't much, but it was something. Enough to incapacitate a guard after the *kem äm* was removed. Roth sat by the opening, crammed in the corner. Brower was against the far wall, within sight. The plan was that Roth would use one dart to prick the guard in the ankle after the barrier was removed. Brower would lunge out of the room and attack anyone else in the hallway in the hope his FBI training in hand-to-hand combat would be enough to take out their foes. They'd try to save the remaining two darts but would use them if necessary. Then they'd free the other prisoners, somehow, and make their way to the jungle. Not a great plan, but the only one they had.

"Let me ask you this, Jonathon. Do you believe the Maya gods are real? That this Kukulkán deity is going to return like the prophecy said he would?"

"I don't know," Roth said slowly. "I've spent the last year researching it."

"I know you have. Which is why I'm asking you. These two factions have been enemies for a very long time, I gather."

"It's been a stumbling block that so many historical documents were destroyed by the Spanish in the 1500s. The priests who interviewed the native Maya and Aztec interpreted what they were told through their own lens."

"Give me an example."

"Take Kukulkán or his Aztec version, Quetzalcóatl. A bearded god who appeared from the east, taught the people construction, to live harmoniously with each other, and to stop performing human sacrifices. Sounds a little like Christianity. Some of those priests, back in the 1500s, wondered if one of the twelve apostles had come to Mesoamerica as a missionary. Some reports even said Quetzalcóatl had holes in his hands. There was a statue found in the Yucatán, for example, that depicted him that way. There's another statue in Oaxaca that also had holes in the hands. So was it an apostle . . . or was it Christ himself? We only know a fraction of what they knew five centuries ago."

"It could mean all sorts of things," Brower suggested. "A religious person would see evidence of what he or she believed. It's the Baader-Meinhof phenomenon."

Roth smiled. He was liking Brower more and more. A smart guy. "Yeah, I know. It's also called the recency bias or the frequency illusion. I'm glad you mentioned it because I had the same thought too at first. But here's the weird part. Farther south, in Peru, where the Inca built Cusco and had a completely different culture and belief system, there is the legend of Viracocha. It's strikingly similar to the legend of Kukulkán and Quetzalcóatl. A bearded man who showed up and taught the people to live in harmony and instructed them in advanced technology—oh, and Viracocha could walk on water. That was a detail the Aztec and Maya didn't have in their legend, but a familiar tradition in Christianity, right? From what archaeologists have told us, those two civilizations didn't interact with each other. Both have legends that talk about a great flood too, just like myths in other parts of the world."

"I've never heard of Viracocha before."

"Neither had I before I started studying this stuff. And the Inca also had a legend that Viracocha would return. Just like Quetzalcóatl in Aztec lore and Kukulkán for the Maya. Modern scholars say it's just the Spanish influence weaving Christian myths into local culture, but I'm not convinced. I can't explain it. And guess what—a Cherokee tribe had similar myths, and they lived much farther north. No connection with the Aztec and Maya at all."

"How do you explain it, then?"

"I don't know that I can," Roth said with a sigh. "But all of these legends mean something. There's an author who wrote a book called *Fingerprints of the Gods*. He tried to tie all of these legends together, from Mesoamerica and the Mediterranean. His theory is that there's a common origin story. We can't know that for sure, of course. What we do know is that these ancient Mesoamerican civilizations all knew the planets. That they were incredibly educated on the cosmos, even more so than European scientists back in the day, and that they left prophecies and predictions about what would happen in the future."

"And you think Calakmul has misinterpreted those predictions?"

"I do. I think they were about Kukulkán. Or Viracocha. I think it heralds a return of this more enlightened people. The ones who didn't want human sacrifice. The Aztec, you see, believed human sacrifices kept the universe in balance. The two sides have been at war for a long time. What if the prophecy is about the end of the Calakmul family? The end of the line?"

"I wouldn't be opposed to that," Brower chuckled. "I've never felt so helpless before. Whether it's technology or magic, it's more advanced than what we have."

"I know," Roth agreed. "It's stumped archaeologists for decades."

"How so?"

"How did a primitive people manage to move such huge pieces of stone, each one weighing tons, in order to build these huge temples? The wall at Saksaywaman in Peru, for example, has pieces that weigh two hundred tons. They fit so precisely and without mortar that they've stood for centuries, or even millennia. But there is no evidence of where this engineering know-how came from to *lift* such a stone, let alone slide it perfectly into place. Even in our modern cities, you can see cranes as evidence of how buildings so tall could be built. Nothing like that here, though. Some of the pyramids here in Mexico are even bigger in circumference than the pyramids of Giza."

"Truly?"

Roth held up his hands. "There's more that we don't know than what we do know. And I've only been researching this for the last year. I realized in the arena during the death game that we were playing the game the wrong way. Instead of whacking the rubber balls, the ancients had used their kind of magic to levitate them and send them into orbit. Wouldn't it also be possible for them to have used the *kem äm* in a similar way with construction? A force that amplifies force to lift the stones?"

"Just like that force field blocking the door bounces back harder than something thrown against it?"

"Exactly. That's why I kind of hope Kukulkán does return. He could teach us knowledge that has been lost for centuries. For *millennia*. We always assume the present is controlling the future. That our inventions are going to change everything. Futurists have been predicting for years that we should look more closely at the past."

"Futurists like Ray Kurzweil?" Brower said.

"Yeah. Didn't he say something about exponential curves? I don't remember the quote, but it reminds me of what you said back at FBI headquarters."

"I've followed his work. We think the future is linear. With technology, it's exponential. If you take thirty steps, you don't get to thirty. You get to a billion."

"Yes!" Roth agreed emphatically. "Have you read Alvin Toffler's work?"

"I love Toffler. He said that the illiterate of this century will be those who cannot learn, unlearn, and learn again."

"Yes! Oh, I wish we weren't about to die. I could hang out with you. We keep looking to the future for the answers. But what if the Maya already had a cure for cancer? Or diabetes?"

"It would put a lot of pharma companies out of business," Brower said.

"It might even put the Defense Department out of business. Isn't that another reason why the Spanish might have burned the knowledge they'd found? What if they learned something they weren't ready to accept? That established history wasn't accurate. Better to burn the codices and keep the world in ignorance. Rather than learn, unlearn, and relearn."

"We can't undo what the Spanish did when Cortés came. Or what the other immigrants did when they came to the Americas after that. I don't think anyone is going to just go back to Europe and start over again. Despite what Illari and her faction want."

"Agreed. What Illari and her ilk want isn't going to happen. But that doesn't mean the status quo can't change in other ways. There was a Hungarian doctor who figured out germs were killing mothers in a maternity ward in Vienna. No one believed him, even though he was *right*, and he was eventually put into an insane asylum. It took Pasteur's backing of the same idea to convince people of the truth. Knowing something isn't enough. Being a good communicator is essential."

Brower gave an amused grunt. "When you first arrived in DC, I wasn't open to the idea that people could transform into jaguars. Or that shields could repel bullets. It wasn't until I saw it happen with my own eyes that my skepticism collapsed. Now that I know what's *possible*, I think I can help persuade others to consider another perspective."

"I get what you're saying. My mind was pretty closed too until we were put in a life-and-death situation. I knew we couldn't beat the Beasleys physically. It forced me to consider other options."

"When they come for us, we're not going to have a lot of time," Brower said. "So let's think outside the box once more. If the *kem äm* amplifies force and repels matter, then if I shoved a guard into another web, it would amplify the force of my shove. Do more damage to him."

"Yes," Roth said, sitting up straighter.

"I studied aikido in college," Brower said. "It was all about using momentum and small applications of force to have an outsized reaction."

They both heard the door at the end of the corridor open on its noisy hinges. Roth's heart rate began to intensify.

"I think this is it," he whispered.

Brower nodded and rose to a crouch, arms folded around his knees. His suit was already torn in a few places. Roth picked up the poison dart and squeezed it tightly between his fingers.

"Bring the German chancellor first," Jacob Calakmul said, his voice echoing down the stone corridor. "Then the British PM."

Roth and Brower exchanged glances. They'd both assumed that *they* would be first. And why was Jacob down here in person? Roth's confidence began to quiver.

From beyond the web of *kem äm*, several warriors marched past their cell. In a few moments, they returned, dragging a man in a suit with gray hair back toward the stairs. Then another was fetched.

"Why is Calakmul speaking English?" Brower whispered.

"The king of Spain next," Calakmul directed. He came to stand just outside their cell, his back to them. Roth saw he was wearing his ceremonial attire, so his calf muscles were visible, just beyond the *kem äm*. The temptation to stab him was hard to control, but he knew better.

More commotion, and another man was hauled away. The king of Spain was gibbering in Spanish. He looked terrified.

"Take them to the temple and bring them to the altar," Jacob said. Then he turned and faced their cell. There was something wild in his eyes. He looked unhinged.

"Are you ready to die, Mr. Roth?" Jacob said. "It is time to climb the temple."

Roth realized why Jacob was speaking in English. It was for their benefit. He was saving Roth and Brower for last to show them they had failed.

Jacob waved his hand over the doorway and the *kem äm* disappeared. He stood outside the entrance, his gaze mocking.

"Aren't you going to try and stab me?" he taunted. "You think I am easy prey? I don't need any guards to handle you both. It insults me for you to presume I haven't considered your every move. Or do you believe my brain is still *underdeveloped?*" He said the last words with bitterness.

Roth knew several things in that moment—Jacob had somehow heard his entire conversation with Angélica. Now Angélica was dead, and he would die next.

And Jacob would enjoy every moment of it.

CHAPTER THIRTY-FOUR

Jaguar Temple

Calakmul Biosphere Reserve

January 10

Pressing his back against the stone wall of the cell, Roth came to his feet slowly. He gripped the dart tightly in his hand. He couldn't see a whorl of *kem äm* swirling around Jacob. Was Jacob so confident he'd win? Was it just hubris, or was it earned? He kept his eyes focused on his enemy's. In his peripheral vision, he saw Brower slowly rise as well. It was two against one. The other warriors had already taken their captives away.

Roth was a bigger man than Calakmul. Force was a function of weight and speed. If he moved fast, he might be able to knock Jacob down. And he had Brower, who obviously had much better training than he did. It might work.

"Well?" Jacob challenged. "Will you die without resisting? I thought you better men than this."

Brower attacked first. He lunged across the small gap of the cell, hand reaching for Jacob's wrist.

Jacob sidestepped the attack, which put Brower in between Roth and himself. He drew a symbol in the air with his hand—the one with the glowing ring—and Brower slammed into the wall.

"I can't see!" Brower gasped.

"But you're an FBI agent," Calakmul quipped. "You've trained for this moment!" He struck a blow to the side of Brower's head.

Roth took a quick breath and charged. He just needed to nick Calakmul's skin with the dart. One little nick, and the man would be paralyzed in seconds. With his forearm raised in front of him like a battering ram, Roth tried to collide with Jacob, but the jaguar priest was impossibly fast. He didn't evade the attack—he came right at Roth with his own body, and it felt like slamming into one of the stone stela statues throughout the temple grounds. Roth's teeth rattled. He tried to jab the needle into Jacob's exposed arm but found his own momentum blunted when Jacob seized his wrist with his other hand. Roth tried to lever him backward, but he couldn't move the other man, not even an inch.

Brower kicked backward, trying to catch Jacob unaware.

But again, the jaguar priest anticipated the attack and swiveled just slightly, drawing Roth into the path of the kick. The shoe struck Roth in his hip painfully, and he grunted.

Jacob squeezed Roth's wrist and torqued it. Involuntarily, Roth's fingers opened, and the dart dropped to the ground. His heart sank.

"You thought you could best me?" Jacob hissed in Roth's face. *"You?"* He slammed his knee into Roth's groin, knocking the wind out of him and causing a stomachache that was debilitating. Roth groaned again, unable to breathe, unable to even stand.

Brower attacked again. He was fighting blind, but he lunged at Jacob, who dodged his various blows and kicks, returning punches to ribs, kidneys, kneecaps, and other sensitive spots. Roth hugged his own body, struggling to breathe, watching the one-sided fight continue until it ended abruptly. Then he saw the dart on the ground by his hand. His whole body ached with agony, but he grabbed it.

"Fight me!" Jacob roared. "Have you nothing left in you? I will kill *millions* in your country. I will burn your precious Constitution like the Spanish burned the codices. *Fight!* This is your only chance to win!"

Roth was going to throw up. The kick to the groin had ruined him, and now that he had an injured hand, he felt utterly helpless. He was on his knees. And that's exactly what Calakmul *wanted* him to feel. This was part of his revenge.

Brower slumped against the far wall, breathing heavily. He was in pain too.

They were not fighting a normal, mortal man. The quickness, the strength—these were all augmented by Maya magic. There was no *way* they could beat him. Roth doubted even someone from the elite Special Forces could, despite their years of training. Hadn't they seen the proof at the White House?

Roth swallowed, trying not to throw up. It took every bit of will-power not to. The dizziness, the pain was the worst he'd ever felt. But he kept himself from vomiting. A small victory.

Lifting his head, he looked up at Jacob's angered face.

"We can't beat you," Roth said, stifling a groan. "I knew we couldn't. You wanted it this way."

"It didn't have to end this way, Mr. Roth. I gave you a chance to protect your family. You would have had power and riches beyond belief. But you chose to rise against me. To spite me. You will be *very* alive when I wrench your heart out. Your family will suffer too. Because of you."

Roth had made his choice, and he couldn't undo it. He wouldn't, even if he could. He glared at Calakmul. "I knew I couldn't win. But I also know that neither can you."

"I've *already* won," Jacob snarled.

"Huracán won the last round. But he's losing this one. The Jaguar Prophecies weren't about you, Calakmul. Kukulkán is coming. And you can't stop *him*."

"You pretend to know our history. You know *nothing*," Jacob seethed.

"What is history?" Roth shot back, cradling his injured arm. His body throbbed with pain. "It's more than a set of lies agreed upon. Napoléon had it *wrong*. He may have won battle after battle, but in the end he *lost*. And so will you. When the story of this world is told, your name won't even make a footnote."

Roth couldn't hurt Calakmul with his fists. Or a dart. But he *could* hurt him with words. He saw the rage in the man's face, and then he felt the blows rain down on him. He slumped to the ground, twitching as the blows came, but there was no pain. He realized, startlingly, that Jacob could no longer hurt him. A thought memory flickered in his mind before he fell unconscious, of how the human brain released certain chemicals before death to ease someone's suffering. He'd heard it in a talk a long time ago, a talk about a zebra dragged into a lion's den. There was something innate in a living body that tried to protect it before that last moment. Had evolution and nature instilled that particular pharmaceutical? Or was something else at work? He'd always wondered if it was true.

And he wondered, as the blackness enfolded him, if he would ever wake up again.

———

He did.

The sound of arguing voices roused him from the stupor. Spoken in English. That was confusing. Roth's entire body ached. His hand was sore, possibly broken. He sensed that immediately. He felt like he'd been walloped with a baseball bat. If there weren't bruises now, there would be, all over his back, his arms, his hip.

Of course, he likely wouldn't survive long enough to see them form.

Roth couldn't open his eyes, so he just listened, trying to understand the voices rattling through his skull. It didn't smell like the dungeon. The air hung with the scents of incense, cooked meat—even *xocolatl*, which made him crave a sip of the drink for its restorative powers.

"What else have you lied to me about? I've heard fighter planes flying over the jungle. Why haven't you summoned a storm to drive them off?" It was a man's voice that Roth didn't recognize.

"I will in due time!" Jacob answered angrily. "They cannot get through our shield. And I *want* them to watch what happens. I want the satellites to see it!"

"But it isn't President Parker!" yelled the other man. "That's one of Wright's deputies. You have the wrong man!"

Roth suspected the fellow was American. He might even be Senator Coudron's friend, the one who had come to Cancún to escape the end times.

"What matters is the ceremony," Jacob countered. "The message that despite their technology, their bombs, their missiles, they cannot reach us. They cannot stop us. He's just a man in a suit. That's all I need."

"You promised me—"

Roth heard the smack of a fist against flesh. He struggled to open his eyes, managing it to some extent, but the images were foggy. He saw someone go down on his knees, holding his mouth and a cut lip.

"Your pitiful rank means nothing here!" Jacob shouted at the man cowering before him. "You are nothing more than one of the pitiful Aztec nobility who suffered baptism by a Catholic priest after switching sides. I honor my promises, but you disgust me, Senator. And you try my patience too far. Leave before I decide to sacrifice *you* as well."

Roth's vision cleared, and he saw a man wearing the ceremonial cedar armor and feathers, like the kind Roth had been dressed in for the death game. He barely recognized the senator from Texas, oiled and tanned and looking very out of place in a Maya outfit, with golden wrist bands and necklaces. The fake tan looked awful. Had it been sprayed on?

Roth blinked up at Jacob. He wore his ceremonial attire as well, looking as he had during the death game. Brower was gone. Roth twisted his neck, trying to get a view and felt his lower back stab in agony.

"Get out!" Jacob shouted, gesturing to what was presumably a door.

The senator skulked away. They were in the throne room of the palace. Servants were standing aside, exchanging worried glances. They didn't know English. But they'd seen enough to realize their guest was now in disgrace.

Jacob turned and looked at Roth with repugnance. He said something in Mayan and gestured at Roth.

He heard the soft padding of feet approach him.

"They will carry you to the top of the pyramid, Mr. Roth. You are in no condition to climb it yourself. I want you to watch the first execution before it is your turn. I want there to be no clouds to block the scene from the satellites. I *want* them to see you die, Mr. Roth. And feel the helplessness of what is coming for *them*."

Roth wheezed in pain as they hoisted him from beneath his arms. Was his back broken too? He didn't know, but his legs hurt terribly. They didn't care about his discomfort.

Roth folded into the fetal position as they carried him, arms tight against his sides, muscles clenched, his knees bent toward his chest. His leg spasmed, and he reached down to knuckle the muscle as he groaned.

It hurt to move, but he wanted to see if his plan had worked. If he'd angered Jacob sufficiently to cause him to forget to search for the other darts in Roth's clothes.

He felt a single dart still in his pocket.

If he could disable Jacob, just for a moment, the tables might turn. He had enemies who would leap at a sign of weakness.

Roth hoped he still had a chance to turn the tide.

CHAPTER THIRTY-FIVE

San Gervasio Archaeological Zone

Cozumel, Mexico

January 10

Suki felt like she was in an action movie. The helicopter flew low across the ocean, the rotors loud and constant. She was surrounded by the toughest-looking dudes she'd ever met, dressed for war, their faces smeared with camo paint, wearing jungle fatigues with assault rifles strapped to their shoulders. Each had a patch on their left arm with a double-A insignia. They were part of the 82nd Airborne division. But all that firepower would be worse than useless if she didn't bring the *kem äm* shields down.

Jordan lifted the microphone part of the headset away from his face and leaned forward.

"Want a Pop-Tart?" Jordan asked her, offering her a package in a metallic foil wrapper.

"Not really hungry, to be honest," she replied, copying him by moving the microphone away.

"Ever flown in a jet before?" he asked her. "That was a pretty sweet ride."

"Yeah, all the time," Suki drawled. She also wore military-style fatigues—in her own size—and camo paint. She had a canteen of water, night vision goggles, and boots that were surprisingly comfortable.

"Five minutes from target," came a voice over the headset.

The other soldiers began to prepare for their exit.

"You used to be part of these guys, right?" Suki asked Jordan.

"Yup. I was with the Old Guard in DC for a few years and then joined the 82nd. We trained to be deployed anywhere in the world within eighteen hours."

"Ever been to Mexico?" she asked him.

"Does Tijuana count?"

"I'm not sure where that is." They were going to San Gervasio, to the shrine of Ix Chel. From there, she would have to attempt to use her power to move them. "I just hope I can do this alone. Last time, my mom and Jane Louise helped."

"I believe in you," Jordan reminded her. "And so does Monica. You saved us."

The memory of her healing in the hospital was still fresh for all of them. She'd been on the cusp of death, her recovery nothing short of miraculous. When Suki had watched Jordan sweep Monica off her feet and whirl her around, she'd gotten a lump in her throat. Moments before, Monica had been alive only by the grace of machines. There was power in the Maya magic that would change the world. Power Suki somehow had access to.

"I'm glad you're both okay. You were pretty messed up."

"What you did? That was pretty dope. And without you, we won't be able to win this fight. Did I mention I've already killed a jaguar priest? And smashed into another with a car? I'm practically a pro."

"About five times already." She twisted the ring around her finger nervously.

"Good. I wouldn't mind taking out a few more. Your dad is pretty awesome. Our job is to keep you safe and get the hostages out of there."

Suki nodded, feeling her stomach lurch as the helicopter began to descend. Her dad would have *hated* this ride. Some of the 82nd Airborne team had parachuted into the San Gervasio ruins earlier to secure the location for the helicopter to land. They were going to use the parking lot next to the ruins since it was a more open space, and the tourists were already gone. The park shut down after sunset. Suki had memories of sneaking on board the van from Huellas de Pan in that very parking lot. Looking out of the helicopter, she saw complete darkness, except for the moon. A team would wait for them at the ruins to extract them, presuming they were successful, and bring them back to the aircraft carrier off the coast of Mexico.

The helicopter went down fast and hard, and Suki felt her spine jolt as the aircraft met the pavement of the parking lot.

Jordan helped unbuckle Suki from the protective straps, removed the head gear, and then assisted her out of the helicopter. The other soldiers had already jumped out. Once they were clear, the helicopter lifted up and took off again.

"Welcome back to the unit, Scott," said one of the soldiers who'd secured the site as he came up and gave Jordan a fist bump. "Miss us?"

"As much as I miss diarrhea," Jordan shot back. "How long have you guys been here?"

"Four hours. A long time. Area is secure."

"Awesome. Suki, this is Captain Mike Rose, winner of the Best Ranger competition two years back-to-back. He's a good friend of mine. This is Suki Roth. Captain Rose is going to protect our back door and get us out of there."

"How's civilian life?" Captain Rose asked.

"The pay is better," Jordan said.

Another soldier came up and saluted Captain Rose. "You coming with us, sir?"

"Not this time, Stackpole. We're going in if you guys get stuck. Heard the SEALs are having a rough go of it down there. Let's show them who's boss."

The soldiers grunted, and Suki rolled her eyes at the rivalry.

"There's no one here," Captain Rose told Jordan, knifing his hand to point across the parking lot. "Only one road leading to the highway, and I've got it blocked. We've patrolled the ruins. Empty. Park opens at 8 a.m., so we better be gone long before then, or there's going to be trouble." He looked at his watch. "That doesn't give you a long time, soldier. How exactly are you getting down to the Yucatán and back?"

"She's our ride," Jordan said, pointing his thumb at Suki. "Gather the team."

The soldiers they'd flown in with came around in a circle. Captain Rose looked skeptical, but he stood there and listened in.

"You were given a pretty pathetic briefing by the brass, so let me fill you in on a few things," Jordan said. "What they said about shooting is true. Do not open fire unless I give the order, and I'm not giving it until this girl tells me it's clear. Where we're going, the laws of physics work differently. They have invisible shields that can deflect bullets. Back at us. I know that's hard to believe, but I've seen it. One of these dudes took out a SWAT team in DC this afternoon. But we have *her* on our side. She can hack their shields and bring them down. Just like in *Independence Day*."

"These aliens?" one of the soldiers asked.

"However you want to think about it, I don't care," Jordan said. "These guys can also turn into jaguars and other animals. They are at their most vulnerable during the transition. If you see a man grow fangs, shoot him then, not after. If they charge, pull a knife and go for the throat before they bite you. We're probably going to see some stuff you've never encountered before. Your instinct will be to pull the trigger.

Don't. Not until I give the order. We're going in quiet, and we're going to improvise. Got it?"

Suki saw heads nodding in acceptance, but a few of them had incredulous looks. They'd heard this before, at least in part, but some things you just had to see.

"But how are we getting there, Scott?" one of them asked.

Jordan turned to Suki. "Tell us what to do and where you're taking us."

Suki swallowed when all their eyes came to her. She'd never liked being the center of attention, and that hadn't magically changed now. They looked mean. They looked dangerous. She was glad for both things because *they were on her side.*

"Everyone hold hands," she said, then smiled at the shocked looks on their faces.

She'd given it some thought. Her dad and the prisoners were probably being kept in the dungeon beneath Jacob Calakmul's palace. The palace had many servants, most of whom were helpless and nonviolent but loyal to Calakmul. They'd run and warn him if soldiers suddenly appeared. However, most servants weren't allowed to enter Jacob's inner sanctum. No one was. If they started there, she could lead them to the dungeon and fight the warriors who were guarding it. That was the quickest and most direct way.

It was just herself, Jordan, and three other soldiers going in. Jordan had explained a team was four soldiers. That would give Suki the chance to bring others out, since she could only teleport thirteen people total.

It was a small group. Very small. But their job was to go in and get out quickly.

She grabbed Jordan's hand and then the hand of another member of the team. Captain Rose pursed his lips like it was the lamest thing ever, but he watched as the soldiers formed a small circle.

Once they were all connected, Suki spoke again. "It'll be fast. Where we're going in the jungle, there are a series of temples that look like pyramids. I'm not exactly sure where we'll land, but we're going to the royal building where Jacob Calakmul lives. He's in charge, and he's the most dangerous person there. Everyone else defers to him. The warriors were pretty sketch. They have these weapons like swords, except the blades are jagged obsidian instead of steel. And they carry blowguns. You get hit by a dart, and you're helpless but conscious. Those are their obvious weapons. Their most dangerous weapon is the Maya magic, the *kem äm*. It's pretty cool. I've been trained to use it, but I'm just a beginner. I don't want to fight Jacob Calakmul because he'd win. If he comes at us, just grab hands again, and I'll teleport us out. Okay?"

"I know it sounds weird," Jordan said, "but trust me. It's legit."

"I've heard only a little about what happened in the Sit Room at the White House. Any chance we could get a little demo?" Captain Rose asked, looking at Suki.

"It threw a Marine about twelve feet," Suki answered. "Want to try that?"

"I would *love* to try that," the captain said, smirking.

Suki used the ring, summoned the magic, and put a circular shield up in front of her. The soldiers blinked in surprise at the glowing motes of magic.

"Give it a punch," Suki suggested.

He did and was instantly knocked back about five feet.

"Any other questions?" Jordan asked. "Bullets ricochet off it and come straight back at you too, only faster. Before we go, I want to put dibs. I'd like a shot at Calakmul, or that guy who kicked my butt at the Smithsonian. And there are some people down there who have betrayed our country. They're betting on Calakmul winning. Let's prove them all wrong."

He squeezed Suki's hand. "Let's do this thing."

Suki steadied her breath. The moonlight was bathing them all. She glanced from soldier to soldier. She was grateful they had their names on their fatigues because she wouldn't have remembered any of their names except for Jordan's.

"And so . . . you all start singing 'Kumbaya'?" Captain Rose asked with amusement.

Suki ignored him. She lowered her head and closed her eyes. Her mom had said it was like a prayer. The Mayan word was *rapinik, to fly*. She felt the magic tingling inside her. She was at Ix Chel's most sacred ground, a place where the nobility and the populace throughout the Yucatán had come to make marriage alliances and conceive children. It was the place Cortés had first come to. That thought struck her mind forcibly. It was knowledge that shouldn't have belonged to her, because she'd never read it in any book.

"*Rapinik,*" she whispered, smelling the hint of salt on the air.

The magic thrummed inside her, then through her, and they were instantly in a different location. The smell was familiar. They stood in a corridor of the palace, in a shaft of moonlight coming in through a window. She released the hands of the others and glanced both ways. It was a corridor connecting Jacob's private rooms to the throne room. A few torches were fixed in the walls, but instead of flame, they swirled with motes of *kem äm*.

A feeling tugged in her heart. The feeling bid her to go to Jacob's room. Fear spiked inside her mind. He was the *last* person she hoped to run into.

Jordan signaled two of the soldiers to face one way, while he and the other faced back toward Jacob's room. The soldiers looked stunned by the transition, but they promptly obeyed and raised their weapons. It was muggy. Sweat began to gather on Suki's brow.

"Which way?" Jordan whispered to her.

She'd intended to head toward the throne room and slip down the other passage toward the dungeon. But the nagging feelings grew stronger. She'd learned not to deny them.

"This way," she said, pointing toward Jacob's private chamber. Her stomach twisted with worry.

Jordan motioned for the others to follow. He was in a combat stance, weapon up, leading the way. The soldiers fell in around him, Suki boxed between them. She was sweating heavily now and not just from the humidity.

They reached the beaded screen leading into Jacob's chamber. Suki listened but she didn't hear anything. But she *felt* someone . . . or something . . . was there. She swallowed, trying to calm her nerves with the mantra she'd learned.

Jordan parted the curtain with his fingers and glanced inside. He looked at her and shook his head. No one was in there.

She nodded for him to enter. Jordan barged in quickly, sweeping the chamber with his weapon. The beads clicked and rattled against one another. Suki entered, remembering when she'd come in here last, when Jacob had said she would have to kill someone she loved in order to gain her full powers.

The room was decorated with ancient artifacts—gold, silver, jade. There were chests made of wood, carved by master craftsmen. There were changing screens and a variety of clothing, some modern, some ancient. Suki glanced around the room, but the feeling wasn't coming from the room. It was coming from another doorway. She'd never gone that way before—she hadn't been allowed, so she didn't know where it went.

The blackness called to her.

This is so sus, she told herself. Her mind screamed for her to go back the other way and head in the direction where she knew the prisoners were being kept. But her heart beckoned her down.

She clenched her fists and then started toward the opening.

The soldiers were looking around, scanning the room and the different antechambers connected to it. When she reached the portal, she smelled wet stone. It led to a cenote.

"Down there?" Jordan asked, joining her.

She nodded. She didn't trust herself to speak.

At any moment, Jacob could return. She didn't even want to think about that. Best not to. Ix Chel was leading her toward something in the cenote. She didn't know what or why. Maybe it would help them. Maybe it was a dead end, and they'd be trapped. Either way, she was following her gut on this one.

Jordan put on the night vision goggles and then started down the steps. His partner, Friedlein, went next, followed by Suki, who was followed by Killian and Mercado. The tunnel was carved into solid rock and angled sharply down. It was tall enough they didn't need to crouch. The smell of wet stone got stronger. The sound of their boots echoed as they went down. That wasn't good.

As they turned the final bend, the smell of the cenote grew strong, and Suki could hear the lapping of the waters. But the beckoning feeling was stronger.

Jordan froze, bringing his weapon up to aim. "There's a dead body," he whispered. "A woman."

Suki peered around him and saw Angélica lying on the stone ramp. She'd been savaged by a wild animal. Blood stained the jade-colored water at the edge of the cenote.

"She's not dead," Suki said, feeling the truth strike her forcibly.

Angélica was still alive. And so was her baby.

CHAPTER THIRTY-SIX

CIA HEADQUARTERS

LANGLEY, VIRGINIA

January 10

Dr. Estrada gazed in awe at the marble floors in an offset checker-board pattern—dark gray and light gray. The round sigil of the Central Intelligence Agency was emblazoned with a compass rose in the center. This was like a scene from the movies, but it was really happening. He glanced over at Illari, wonderstruck.

She walked alongside him, next to Director Wright. They'd flown in a helicopter to Langley, riding over the crush of traffic on the beltway. It was dizzying how many places they'd been to over the last couple of days.

A CIA operative greeted them at the front of the building. "Director, I'm Agent O'Keefe. Director Kershaw is waiting in the ops room. Dr. Estrada, Miss Chaska—welcome to Langley."

Dr. Estrada nodded, and they were given security badges and taken through the security turnstiles. Even though it was after seven p.m., the agency was thrumming with people. It looked like an all-hands-on-deck moment. The smell of stale coffee wafted on the air.

"This is a big facility," Dr. Estrada commented to Director Wright as they walked.

"Used to be the largest intelligence base in the world. But now Germany's BND holds that honor. Don't tell Director Kershaw I mentioned it." He gave him a sardonic grin.

"I won't," Dr. Estrada said. He was an archaeologist, not a spy. This was all way out of his league.

"This way," said the agent guiding them. They were brought to a secure room accessed by badge. When the door opened, Dr. Estrada had to remind himself not to stare. It was the quintessential war room of a spy agency—monitors bracketed to the walls, desks covered in computers and monitors, each one showing a different scene. It was pandemonium, as information was relayed in real time. Men and women with headsets were talking simultaneously.

There was a series of ever-shifting satellite images on the main monitors. Dr. Estrada recognized them as video feeds of the jungle compound in the Yucatán that he'd flown over all those months ago.

"Is that from satellites?" Dr. Estrada asked over the commotion.

"No, those are from infrared cameras on the drones we have positioned over the compound," replied the agent. "We've switched over now that we have a web of drones overhead. Here's Director Kershaw." He indicated a serious-looking woman with brown-rimmed glasses, hair just past her shoulders, and a frown. She had on a business suit, black, with a tan blouse beneath. He guessed her to be in her sixties.

When she got close enough, Director Wright shook her hand. "Gina."

"Bill," she replied sternly. Then she reached for Dr. Estrada's hand and shook it with a firm grip. "Doctor. Welcome. Is this Miss Chaska?"

"Yes," he replied, and introduced Illari. Although he'd been shocked to learn about her affiliation with the Mexica, not to mention the work she'd been doing for Mr. Roth, he didn't think less of her for it. He'd been keeping a secret himself, after all, and these were unprecedented times. Moreover, her decision to store the information had been helpful to all of them, and he'd be a fool to blame the means for the end they all desired. Calakmul was unleashing madness and violence on the world, and they needed people like Illari to stand against him. For all she might agree with some of his arguments, she would never stoop to violence to achieve her desired goal.

"Miss Chaska, can you work with Agent O'Keefe?" She nodded to their escort. "He'll connect your laptop to our network so you can access the data set. There's something of particular importance going on right now, and you are both uniquely suited to lend assistance to the government."

"What do you mean?" Dr. Estrada asked.

"I'll show you. O'Keefe—now."

Agent O'Keefe led Illari to a nearby desk, which had a spot cleared away, and they began to set up her laptop.

"How's it going hunting down the NSA moles, Bill?" Director Kershaw asked Wright. "Need any help?"

"We're doing our job. You do yours. Gina, why don't you tell Dr. Estrada about the lights?"

There was obviously a bit of rivalry between the two, but Dr. Estrada imagined there would be, given they worked for competing agencies. He needed a shower and a cup of *xocolatl*, but he had a feeling neither would be coming soon. "Lights?" he asked in confusion.

"Have you ever been to Cholula, Mexico, before?" Kershaw asked him.

"I have," he answered. "The largest pyramid in the world is there."

Wright frowned. "I thought it was in Giza? I've been to that one."

266

Dr. Estrada shook his head. "Cholula is four times larger than Giza and twice the volume. You don't know about it because it's buried. It looks like a hill."

Wright glanced at Kershaw in confusion.

"He's right," she said. "There's a little Catholic church on top, built by Cortés. The pyramid wasn't rediscovered until 1910."

"You know your history," Dr. Estrada said, impressed.

"Actually, I learned it from Wikipedia on my phone about an hour ago," she said with a chuckle. "That's why you're here. Let's sit down, and I'll explain what we know while they set up your assistant's laptop."

She brought them to a small briefing table, just the three of them so they could face one another. The layout of the room made him think longingly of the Qualcomm Institute in San Diego. They all lowered into their chairs.

"Dr. Estrada," Director Kershaw said, leaning forward so he could hear her better, "the jungles of the Yucatán have continued to light up beyond the original locations. We're seeing residual photonic evidence from hundreds if not thousands of structures beneath the jungle canopy. The epicenter was Chichén Itzá. It's spreading up and down from there. These are large swaths of jungle that are typically dark after sunset, except for a few scattered locations that have power."

"Director Kershaw, the majority of my research is in Guatemala, not the Yucatán. I don't know how I can help you."

"This is bigger than Guatemala or even Mexico, and you're an expert in Maya history and culture. I don't have time to read a hundred books. Neither do my agents. So . . . a few questions. Let's start with Cholula. What is its significance other than being the largest pyramid in the world?"

"It was dedicated to Quetzalcóatl by the Aztec."

"And Quetzalcóatl is Kukulkán?" she probed.

"Yes. Same god, different language and culture but similar enough. Both names mean 'feathered serpent' or 'precious serpent.' You know, it's a common belief that Montezuma thought Cortés was the return of Kukulkán, which is why he didn't attack the Spanish at first."

"Is that what scholars believe today?"

"They have been debating it for years. And not just scholars. Some religions believe that Christianity existed in Mesoamerica during, after, or even *before* the Nativity story even happened."

"We'll address the metaphysical later," Kershaw said. "O'Keefe, is her laptop set up?"

"Yes. We're logged into the AWS account," Agent O'Keefe answered.

"Okay. Switch the main screens back to satellite imagery, please."

Dr. Estrada gazed at the large screens along the far end of the wall. The screens flickered and then showed a global satellite array of North and South America. He could see the terminus of where night had fallen across Brazil and the East Coast, though lights from major population centers provided dots and clusters of illumination.

"Isolate the light spectrum that Wachowski discovered," she said next.

"Which light spectrum?" Wright asked. "Infrared? Ultraviolet?"

"Man-made ranges. Streetlights. Neon signs. Halogen tubes. Stadiums. We're matching the light signature we found down in the Yucatán."

The screen shifted again. Dr. Estrada stared in confusion for a moment, but then he saw it—a serpentine pattern of light going from Arizona, down through Mexico, through the Central American countries, and ending in Peru.

"This is all the same light spectrum?" Director Wright asked, his voice betraying awe and fear.

"Yes. Satellites don't lie."

"Have you told the president?"

"I don't know *what* to tell the president," Kershaw said. "Dr. Estrada, Miss Chaska—what do you make of it?"

Dr. Estrada rose from his chair, dumb with wonder, and walked to the front of the room where the screens displayed the images. Illari joined him, her face full of awe. The pattern formed an unmistakable image of the feathered serpent.

"The head of the snake is here," Dr. Estrada said, pointing to the band in Arizona . . . no—southern Utah. He traced it down its circuitous path, long and slender.

"Tlachihualtepetl is here," Illari said, pointing to a spot just east of Mexico City. It was glowing in a concentrated way. "In a snake's biology, this would be the . . . heart . . . I think."

"What is that?" Kershaw asked. She and Director Wright had joined them up front.

Dr. Estrada looked at Illari. "That makes sense. Tlachihualtepetl is the Nahuatl name for Cholula. It means 'made-by-hand mountain' . . . or 'temple.' The ancients all built temples on higher ground."

"And it goes down here to the Yucatán. There's El Castillo. Tulum. Tikal. So many lights."

"All the way down to Peru," Wright said. "I've been to Machu Picchu. So you're saying that the Aztec and Maya built this pattern? It's man-made?"

"This is incredible," Dr. Estrada said in awe. "Yes. This is all man-made. But no one civilization made it. The different parts of the design must have been built independently of each other."

"How is that possible?" Kershaw asked. "They had no GPS. We're talking thousands of miles."

"We don't know," Dr. Estrada said. "Just like we don't know who built the Serpent Mound in Ohio."

"The Serpent Mound?" Wright asked, perplexed. "There's another one?"

"The largest effigy of a serpent, until now, was in Ohio. That one was four hundred meters long. Archaeologists haven't been able to pinpoint when it was built, but it's probably over two thousand years old. Evidence suggests that multiple civilizations constructed it."

"This is a sign," Illari said in awe, pointing to the satellite imagery. "Look at the distance. This is the area of Cemanahuac."

"What does that term mean?" Kershaw asked.

Wright spoke up. "Agent Sanchez mentioned it. You brought it up in your meeting with Lund. It's the Aztec empire reborn, correct?"

"Not exactly," Dr. Estrada said, feeling piqued. "It is what the Aztec empire may have called itself. It comes from the Nahuatl words meaning 'to be surrounded by water.'" He pointed out the geography on the map as he spoke. "The Atlantic Ocean, the Pacific Ocean. There is even a belief that this area up in Arizona and Utah used to be under water—that Aztlán . . . where the Aztec came from . . . was somewhere there. The origin you see." He gestured to the board. "Of the snake."

"This is Cemanahuac," Illari insisted, her eyes glowing with hope. *"Finally."*

"The Aztec never reached or conquered Peru," Dr. Estrada objected.

"I'm not saying they did," she shot back. "The Maya, the Aztec, the Olmec, the Inca—they all worshipped the serpent god. Like you said, they were building this independently of each other. Each of these civilizations had a prophecy about his return. It's happening."

"You mean Calakmul is claiming to be the return of the Aztec god?" Kershaw asked in bafflement.

Illari shook her head. "No! He believes the Jaguar Prophecies are about him. But this is so much bigger than him. This is the land Kukulkán is reclaiming. This will be Cemanahuac. United at last. It was never united before. There was always war. Conflict. Betrayal. But he's coming back to change all of that."

"Cemanahuac is an Aztec myth!" Dr. Estrada said.

Illari turned on him. "Myths come from somewhere. What if there is a common origin?"

"There is no *evidence* of that!" Dr. Estrada shot back. "It's just a theory."

"I'd like to hear it," Director Kershaw said. "Whatever is happening is happening quickly. Our assets in the Mexican government have said that they're preparing to attack our ships and our jets and our borders. There was an order given from the presidential palace to mobilize the military."

That was news to Dr. Estrada. He gazed at her in bafflement.

"That is not the way of Kukulkán," Illari said. "It will be a peaceful conquest. He will bring healing, peace, and new technology, all through a principle of nonviolence."

"Director Kershaw," said an agent breathlessly, rushing to the front. "There's something you need to see. Switch the screens!"

They flickered back to the drone footage of the temple. The lens had zoomed in to the base of the temple, where a crowd of men had gathered.

"Identity confirmed," said another agent. "EAD Brower, the German chancellor, the British prime minister, and the king of Spain. They are all at the base of the pyramid, surrounded by warriors of some sort. Now they are being pulled up the steps."

"Nonviolence? That's not how it looks to me," said Kershaw adamantly. "I need to speak to the BND director and MI6 before their leaders are executed. Where is the insertion team?"

A woman agent spoke up. "They just landed in Cozumel."

Kershaw grimaced. "We're too late."

CHAPTER
THIRTY-SEVEN

Jaguar Temple

Calakmul Biosphere Reserve

January 10

Suki felt a strong instinct to heal Angélica and rushed to where she lay sprawled out. Why, she didn't know. This woman had assisted Jacob Calakmul in trapping them in the Yucatán a year ago. But she'd also convinced a warrior to spare Lucas's life after he'd climbed out a window and onto the roof. Maybe she'd done something to upset Jacob. Or maybe it was Ix Chel's very nature to protect the lives of a mother and child.

"Know her?" Jordan asked, crouching next to the body. The other soldiers were gazing around the chamber, taking in the splendor of the cenote.

"Her name is Angélica," Suki said. "She's Calakmul's girlfriend."

"Not anymore, clearly," he answered. "She's lost a lot of blood."

Suki lowered her head and placed her hand on Angélica's shoulder. Her life was just a dim little spark. Suki could sense two heartbeats, timid little throbs that clung to life. Focusing, she drew on the power of the ring and bracelet.

"*Kunaj,*" Suki uttered, invoking the magic. She'd healed Jordan and Monica a few hours ago. With her mom and Jane Louise's help. These wounds were even worse. Immediately, the power began to swell. It spread from Suki's hand across Angélica's body, mending broken bones, fixing punctures. It didn't pull the blood back into her body, but it created fresh blood cells. Gashes and rips were repaired. It all happened within moments, just as it had for Jordan and Monica.

Angélica gasped and lifted her head. She wore jewelry from Jacob's collection, bright necklaces, earrings, and bracelets, along with a traditional Maya outfit similar to the ones she'd worn during the death games.

"Suki?" Her voice quavered.

"Where's my dad?" Suki asked.

"How did you . . . ? What are you doing here?" She looked past Suki at the soldiers and shrank from them in fear. "How did you get past the barrier?"

"The same way I got out with my mom and Jane Louise. Did Jacob . . . do that to you?"

Angélica shuddered and nodded. "I tried to help your father escape."

Gratitude swelled inside Suki's heart. "Thank you. Where is he?"

Angélica shook her head. "It didn't work. Jacob saw what I did. He brought me down here to kill me. He'll kill me again if he finds me."

"Help me get my dad, and I'll help you get out of here," Suki promised. She looked around at the cenote, at the strange-colored water. It was pretty poggers. "What is this place?"

"It's a sacred cenote," Angélica said. "A place where they stored the treasures of jade. How did you know I was here?"

"Ix Chel led me here." Suki bit her lip, wondering if she should tell Angélica she was pregnant. Considering the father of the child had just tried to murder her, it probably wasn't a good idea to spring the news on her just yet. "Can you stand up?"

Angélica rubbed her arms and rose without wincing. "I'm healed."

Suki nodded and smiled. "So you'll help us?"

Angélica nodded firmly. "I can. I will. But if we don't destroy the smoking mirrors, they'll be able to escape."

"You mean the mirrors made of obsidian? Like the ones in the White House?"

"Yes, and there are others. The Order of the Jaguar Priests uses them to maintain their influence throughout the world."

"My priority is getting my dad and the other kidnapped leaders out of here alive," Suki said.

"I know. But there's a tunnel connecting this palace to the pyramid where they're going to sacrifice the leaders. They've already been taken there by now. We can use the same tunnel and get there faster. The chamber with the smoking mirrors is on the way."

Suki turned to Jordan.

"Secret tunnel?" he asked.

"Through the mountain?" she replied. It was a reference to the *Avatar* TV show. She had a feeling he knew it too.

"I like this place," Jordan said, nodding. "Let's block the mirrors, then. That makes a ton of sense."

"I think we need to take the secret tunnel," Suki agreed. "Especially if it's a shortcut."

"The servants are forbidden to use it," Angélica said. "Let's hurry before it's too late."

Suki glanced at the cool-looking cenote once more and saw the large chunks of jade in the shallow water. There was a stone ramp leading to a circular platform in the middle of the cenote. His own sacred indoor swimming pool. Suki shook her head, and they hurried back to the steps. Two of the army soldiers went ahead, weapons raised, to clear the path. Suki's heart was pounding from the effort by the time they made it back up to Jacob's room.

Angélica had a haunted look on her face as she surveyed the room. "That way," she said, pointing to one of the passages leading out.

Suki knew the palace compound pretty well, but she'd never been to this part before. That was probably another reason Ix Chel had given Suki the idea to help Angélica. As they went down the corridor, Angélica summoned *kem äm* to light the torches along the walls.

Suki was nervous to go somewhere so shielded from moonlight, knowing they'd need to fight their way out, but surely Ix Chel was steering them in the right direction.

"There's something you should know," Angélica said as they walked quickly.

"What?"

"I can help remove the shields protecting the jaguar priests and the warriors, but they will still be faster and stronger than your soldiers. In addition to physical strength, they can also injure you in other ways. Like with disease and blindness."

Suki hadn't thought of that. She'd assumed that removing the shields would be enough, and kapow, a bullet would kill them.

"That's a problem," Jordan said. "Unless we hit them first."

"Your weapons are noisy," Angélica said. "Once you start shooting, they'll hear and prepare other ways to defend themselves. Like speed and quickness. Invisibility. You won't even know they are there until it's too late. I know the Kowinem. They have powerful dark magic."

"So how do we protect ourselves?" Suki wondered.

"By being as quiet as possible. Follow me."

After traveling down many steps, they reached the tunnel heading from the palace compound outward. As they moved through the darkness, Suki sensed the other smoking mirrors, just as she had sensed the one at the White House. It had an intense feeling of evil. Of wrongness.

"Whoa, I can feel them," Suki said.

"Feel what?"

"The mirror things."

The tunnels were pitch-black, except for the *kem äm* torches. They couldn't see far ahead, and there were also various side tunnels branching off, perfect places for someone to hide. Suki's nerves were twanging with the danger.

"This main tunnel leads to the pyramid where the sacrifices happen," Angélica said. "I don't know where the mirrors are, but they're off this main path somewhere."

"Keep going," Suki instructed. Her instincts were starting to warn her again. Was it just the magic of the mirrors or something else? She felt like she had in Florida when they were driving to the airport. It was a nervous, sick-to-her-stomach kind of feeling.

Angélica didn't seem to sense anything at all. She looked serious but not frightened.

Farther on, they reached a side tunnel, and Suki could feel the wrongness emanating from it. "That's it," she said, pointing. "They're there."

"If we don't break the mirrors," Angélica warned, "they will *all* be able to slip away."

Jordan nodded firmly. "Side mission. Let's knock it out and then go back this way."

"Our job is to rescue people," said another soldier worriedly.

"This is how they kidnapped the leaders," Angélica said. "And there are more to be abducted later. This was just the first round. Without strong leaders, when the border attacks start, there will be confusion about what to do. That will increase instability."

Jordan nodded. "We go for it."

Suki tried to choke down her fear. "Let's hurry. I've got a bad feeling about this."

Jordan led the way with his partner, followed by Angélica and Suki. The final two looked reluctant, but they followed them.

Deeper in, Suki sensed magic down one side shaft, and then another. It was like a maze, but she could sense a path through it.

They reached a stela with a glowing symbol carved into it. It radiated a feeling of darkness.

"Huracán," Angélica whispered fearfully.

Suki sensed the mirrors beyond the stela. "The mirrors are behind this rock, but I don't know how to move it. There is probably a password or rite that needs to be performed."

"Anyone have any C-4 explosives?" Jordan asked.

"Pretty sure that would cause this tunnel to cave in, Scott," said Friedlein, his partner, doubtfully. "And we'd be announcing ourselves. It's not our mission."

"We could rig it with explosives and a trip wire," suggested Mercado.

"Quiet," Suki said. There was something approaching them from behind. Her insides shriveled with worry. "Someone's coming."

"Infrared," Jordan said. The soldiers all switched to night vision.

"Nothing," said another, dropping to a knee and aiming his rifle into the corridor.

The stone behind them grew brighter and began to grind and lift.

"Uh-oh," Jordan muttered, turning as the stone began to rise.

A jaguar shrieked as it bounded out at them. One of the soldiers pulled his trigger on reflex, sending bullets spraying down the corridor.

Suki brought up a web of *kem äm* in front of them just before the ricocheted shots killed them all.

CHAPTER THIRTY-EIGHT

Jaguar Temple

Calakmul Biosphere Reserve

January 10

Jacob soared over the temple compound in the form of a native pere-grine falcon. Its speed and fierceness suited him. Beneath his wings, he saw the glowing structures of the pyramids and buildings of Calakmul. In the past, the city of Calakmul had been a dominating force for the ancient Maya. Jacob's family had deposed the original rulers and taken over the kingdom—renaming it in their image—and made it even grander, more prosperous. It would be so again.

The whir of a drone came from above. Jacob banked sharply and focused his attention on the military weapon used for spying and surprise attacks. It hovered above the protective strings of *kem äm*, which formed a semispherical shell around the compound. The military had tested the aerial borders of Calakmul, and each time, the magic had repulsed the drones. But more had been sent, and now Jacob and his people were being monitored with their cameras. With an angry thought, he sent a pulse of magic and fried the circuitry of the drone as he passed it. He saw sparks lash out from its hull, and the drone plummeted until it hit the shell of *kem äm* and ricocheted off it into the blackness. He wanted an audience. He just didn't want to make it too easy for them. Games were no fun when the other side presented no challenge.

Jacob did another circuit around the compound. As he passed over the arena, he gazed down at the crowd assembled there. These were the faithful, awaiting the victory that would put them into prominent positions in the new order. They'd gathered from around the world to protect themselves and their families from the devastation about to be unleashed on the population of the planet. They'd received the glyph that would protect them from the disease ravaging Europe and, soon, the rest of the world. Each had invested time and their winnings from the death games to furnish protective compounds where they'd live while death ravaged the world and depleted the population. There would be tens of thousands of homes left vacant by the plague. And the faithful would inherit them. Gangs schooled in the *kem äm* would be Jacob's enforcers. Already they were preparing to cross the borders and wreak havoc on America. And after that conquest, they'd turn their vision on other countries, which would be destabilized and vulnerable.

Jacob had thought he'd be feeling a sense of triumph. But his victory would feel bittersweet because he'd had to kill Angélica. With her dead, the only other person who knew the general location of Aztlán was Suki Roth. He'd offered her the chance to be someone powerful in his new world, and she'd spurned him. She'd be dealt with. He'd see to it she died too.

Banking sharply, he used his magically enhanced senses to locate Victor, his chief of security. He sensed him down in the plaza near the main temple at Calakmul. Tucking in his wings, Jacob sped down like a bullet and transformed back into a man as he landed.

Victor, walking at a fast pace along a *sacbe* path, was so startled by his sudden appearance he nearly dropped the satellite phone he was holding. "I need to go," he said into the phone. "Mr. Calakmul just arrived." Then he ended the call.

"Who was that?" Jacob pressed, walking alongside his longtime servant. The Maya had made this network of plaster and limestone roads that literally glowed in moonlight.

"Arturo in Cozumel. American paratroopers landed at the ruins in San Gervasio."

"How does he know they're American?"

"The patches on their uniforms are from the 82nd Airborne. It's a quick-strike team."

It was concerning news, but Cozumel had little strategic interest for Jacob at the moment. His resort on the island was where he'd lured the wealthy into the death games. It had been abandoned, temporarily, and would be returned to after victory was achieved.

"Does Arturo know what they want?"

"He has no idea. I was going to send the Mexican military in to deal with them. I tried to reach Angélica to report this to her, but no one knows where she is."

Just the mention of her name made Jacob wince.

Victor knew his master's moods and noticed the reaction. "Is there . . . trouble?"

"She's dead," he answered flatly, trying to be unemotional about it. He'd invested so much in her. Had cared for her deeply. He felt himself losing control of his composure, his face muscles twitching.

"What did she do?" Victor asked angrily.

"She betrayed me, but I had my vengeance. I left her bleeding to death in my private cenote."

Victor sighed and shook his head. "First Uacmitun, then her. I'm sorry, sir."

"You've been faithful and will be rewarded," Jacob promised. "How is the perimeter?"

"The warriors have been ambushing the Americans sent into the jungle. They are blind to all we do, reliant on night vision and radios. The jungle provides our sense of hearing, sight, and smell. We kill them and then listen to the radios request information. One team at a time, they will fall."

"Excellent," Jacob said. That made him feel better. The warriors could leave the protection of the barrier, and through the magic emblems they wore, they were protected from bullets. The jaguar priest Petlacalco was leading them, adding his power to theirs to take out the invaders one by one.

"Are you ready for the sacrifices, sir? Who will be killed first?"

"The Americans, of course," Jacob responded. "While the satellites watch helplessly. We've waited five centuries for this. We wait no longer."

Victor grinned. "Your father would be proud," he said.

The words caused a stab of pain in Jacob's chest. No one else knew what had happened that day in Aztlán. Again, he thought about the look in his father's eyes before he'd tried to murder Jacob. He must have seen a vision of some kind. Must have. Now, all these years later, he felt a twinge of doubt, stirred by that memory and what that infernal Mr. Roth had told him.

It didn't matter. He would be firm in his purpose.

They were standing at the base of the temple now. The grooves and edges of the carvings were glowing with *kem äm*, revealing the pattern of a jaguar pelt up and down the pyramid. In Chichén Itzá and other structures built to honor Kukulkán, serpents were used as decoration, but this temple had been built to honor a different god. A superior one.

"What about that man who helped Suki escape?" Jacob asked. "The one with the orphanage in Cozumel. Is he dead?"

It would make him feel better to know he'd struck back where it hurt. That he'd bested Jonathon Roth in more ways than one.

Victor's brow quirked with concern. "I was going to tell you later, sir. It was strange. The orphanage was abandoned. Everyone was gone."

"Gone? Where?"

"We don't know. They're hiding somewhere on the island. Or maybe they took the ferry. I have someone looking into it, but there were more important things."

That was strange. How had that little man evacuated the entire orphanage without drawing attention? Someone would have reported it.

"I want him dead," Jacob insisted. "If I must, I'll send a jaguar priest to do it."

"No need, Mr. Calakmul. We'll find them." His satellite phone chirped again, and he answered it. "What is it, Arturo?"

It was time to climb the temple and start the sacrifices. The crowds had gathered in the arena, which faced the east side of the pyramid. They would be able to witness the carnage that was coming, would literally be able to see the blood flowing down the temple steps. In the days of the Aztec, sacrifices could last for days at a time, making rivers of blood as tens of thousands offered up their hearts. That would happen again, except in pyramids built inside the territories farther north. The first would be built in Washington, DC, made out of the rubble from the US Capitol building. The people would come to witness the executions. Just as they had in olden times.

"What?" Victor looked stunned.

Jacob turned and gave his security chief a sharp look.

"Get the marines there at once. Drive them out! Do you hear me? Send in five hundred men. I don't care how many. Get it done, now!" He ended the call with a furious shout.

"San Gervasio?"

Victor nodded. "A military helicopter landed in the parking lot with another team about a half hour ago."

Jacob flinched internally. Why was he just finding out about this? Cozumel was sacred to Ix Chel. Was it really a coincidence that the Americans had chosen it? Or was something else going on that Jacob was blind to?

"That's *my* island now," he said forcefully. "Drive them off. See to it. I'm going to send one of the jaguar priests there to assist and interrogate."

"Yes, sir. Smart move."

"We're starting the sacrifices. Nothing will stop us. And find out if the stelae at the other ruins are starting to glow. I heard a rumor that troubles me."

Victor nodded and then headed off toward the arena. Jacob summoned his magic and drew a glyph in the air with his hand.

"Cazador."

"Yes, Great One." The voice came through the glyph as if the other man were standing right beside him.

"Go to the chamber of the smoking mirrors. Make your way to the ruins of San Gervasio. There are American soldiers there. Kill all but a few. Find out why they are there. Victor is ordering soldiers to drive them out. See it done and then return."

"Yes, Great One. It will be done."

There was no doubt in Jacob's mind that Cazador would be successful. Surely the jaguar priest would want to be present when the Jaguar Prophecies were fulfilled. But he was obedient. He would obey unswervingly. The obsidian mirror would bring him to Jacob's resort in Cozumel, and from there he'd travel the jungle in jaguar form to reach the ruins. The Americans would not be allowed to linger on Cozumel.

Jacob gazed up at the pyramid and then began climbing it. He'd sent the victims ahead of time to be made ready for the sacrifice. They'd be afraid. They'd be helpless. That was the point.

His only regret was that he hadn't killed Mr. Roth sooner.

CHAPTER THIRTY-NINE

Jaguar Temple

Calakmul Biosphere Reserve

January 10

Roth gazed up at the massive Jaguar Temple glowing with the illumination of the *kem äm*. Two warriors gripped him by the arms, which were still sore from the beating Jacob had given him. The temple was larger than the famous Chichén Itzá, a hundred and fifty feet to the other pyramid's hundred, and more complex in design and structure than the tourist trap.

Turning his head to the left, he saw Brower also being held by two warriors. There were five stelae at the base of the temple, each one carved with images of Maya kings, the grooves and glyphs radiating the now familiar magic as well, and servants carried torches with globes of it, to further light the scene. A crowd was gathered beneath, the nobles of the new kingdom about to be born, come to witness the event, their faces highlighted by the glowing stelae and glyphs in the vicinity. Roth scanned the faces, recognizing some from his time in the arena. They wore feathered headdresses and had runes painted on their arms and legs. Gold and jade and obsidian jewelry decorated their bodies as well. It looked like a glimpse into history.

There were several sets of stairs built into the front of the massive temple, and the base had stairs leading to a lower level as wide as the entire front. In the center of the temple, there was a main center aisle of steps going steeply to the top, with a single stela glowing from the center. At the top of the plateau, Roth saw three shining structures. He couldn't tell what they were, but they were rectangular, unlike the obelisks of the stelae below.

A horn blared from somewhere above, and the crowd fell silent. It was the same sound that had initiated the death game. Roth's stomach clenched with dread. The other leaders had been brought out, along with their warrior escorts, but the two Americans were going up first because they would be the first sacrifices. Roth saw a look of sheer terror in the German chancellor's eyes as he glanced back.

Once the fatal tone from the horn subsided, the warriors gripped Roth's arms and led him to the lower stairs. He'd recovered slightly from the beating and moved on his own power. The steps were narrow, and he'd learned in his studies that they were best traversed by angling the body perpendicular to the steps. Those who climbed the temple in an attitude of humility, not facing it directly, found it easier to make the climb. Roth watched as the warriors did this and then mimicked their footwork. Brower did the same, and they climbed up to the plateau that was level with the height of the stelae planted in front. The enormity of the edifice just stunned his mind. He'd visited medieval castles before, but this was so much bigger, more like the pyramids of Giza.

Another short set of stairs flanked each side of that level, and they were brought up to the next one, which was where the main stairs were located. Roth craned his neck. He couldn't see the three structures on top of the pyramid anymore—the angle of the ascent was too steep.

"They're making us climb to our deaths?" Brower said.

"It's part of the ritual," Roth explained.

"What if we refuse?"

"Do you think it would be fun to get dragged up there?"

Brower sighed. "Probably not."

Helicopters thundered over the jungle canopy, but Roth couldn't see them. The sound reminded him of being chased on Cozumel, but he didn't think these were Calakmul's aircraft. Still, they wouldn't help them. They were too late, and the *kem äm* would prevent anyone from getting in.

The warriors barked a command in Mayan, and although Roth didn't understand it, the implication was clear. Time to keep climbing. They walked to the wide center staircase and then started up the steep incline. After about a dozen steps, they reached a landing where the single stela was erected. It was in the exact middle and highlighted the staircase going up. The platform was about twenty feet in diameter and maybe five feet wide. Roth turned his neck and looked down at the crowd that had gathered closer to the base of the pyramid. They wanted to watch the human sacrifices, no doubt. Roth clenched his teeth and felt the warriors tug on his arms.

The center stairs were the tallest and the most narrow. Roth's pulse was racing from the effort of climbing them, but he'd always liked hiking, and under less life-threatening circumstances, it would have thrilled him to climb such an ancient structure. The steepness of the angle and the relentless spacing of the steps soon had him gasping for breath, his leg muscles throbbing with the exertion. When they were halfway up, he made the mistake of looking back and felt a sudden rush of vertigo when he saw how steep it was.

He saw the Spanish ruler being dragged up the steps, struggling against the warriors holding him. He looked frantic, like he wanted to fling himself down the steps and commit suicide rather than face what was coming. There would be no compassion shown to him. Roth knew that. He turned away from the awful scene, looked up, and kept climbing.

By the time they reached the top, he was panting and out of breath. The warriors weren't winded at all. The humidity in the air was stifling, despite it being January. It was probably seventy degrees. The three structures he'd seen from below were revealed now, all arranged on the plateau of the upper level. They were three smaller temples with front-facing openings, a sacrificial altar arranged on each one. To Roth's surprise, he saw another part of the temple rising even higher behind the three buildings with another pyramid-shaped temple atop it. From the ground level, that temple was totally invisible.

The three structures were glowing with the *kem äm*. From the center one emerged another warrior. He surveyed the captives and then walked to the edge of the pyramid steps to look down. He nodded and turned back. A few minutes later, Jacob appeared up the steps. Roth's face throbbed with pain from the memory of being beaten by the man.

"Are you ready to die, Mr. Roth?" Jacob asked smoothly, his eyes flashing with the desire for vengeance.

Roth wondered if he yanked an arm loose if he'd be able to shove one of his escorts off the stairs. It was a long way down. But he had the feeling that both warriors were expecting him to make a last-ditch effort to free himself. He'd save his effort.

"We're all going to die . . . sooner or later," Roth panted.

The noise of the helicopters got louder. Jacob's eyes flashed with annoyance.

"Not your helicopter?" Roth asked.

Jacob frowned. "How typical of the Americans. They've wasted so many drones trying to penetrate our shield. Why not waste something even more expensive? They cannot get through, Mr. Roth. Thwarted by an ancient technology."

"How did the Spanish get past it?"

Calakmul gave him a withering look. "Are you stalling your death, Mr. Roth?"

"Maybe," Roth shot back. "Does it hurt to tell me, though?"

"It took time to adapt to the weapons the Spanish brought. The cannons. The muskets. We've continued to adapt the *kem äm* for the times we live in. All creatures must adapt, Mr. Roth. Adapt or die. A lesson that you Americans continually forget."

Several attack helicopters appeared over the tree line. Roth wasn't familiar with the type they were, but banks of missiles protruded from each side of the crafts, and the noise of the rotors prompted shrieks from the jungle birds and howler monkeys.

Jacob lifted his hand and then clenched his fist, his ring glowing in a pulse of magic.

He uttered a word in Mayan, and the stela built into the staircase shot streaks of lightning into the approaching helicopters. Roth watched in horror as the helicopters exploded, sending shrapnel cascading through the air. When it hit the shield of *kem äm*, the burning bits of metal scattered and shot back up into the sky in arcs, like fireworks.

Jacob lowered his hand, smiling vindictively. "They cannot touch us. And it frustrates them. They are helpless. *Powerless.* Just like you."

Then he switched languages and uttered a command.

The warriors holding Brower dragged him to the center altar, which was round and made of dimpled stone. There were grooves and bloodstains, and Roth stared in dread as Brower struggled against his captors.

Roth strained against the two holding him, but they increased the pressure against his sore arms, keeping him put.

Jacob pulled a dart from a leather pouch at his waist and then quickly jabbed it into Brower's neck. The toxin's effect was practically immediate. Brower quit struggling, and they deposited his body on the round altar. The warriors backed away, murmuring in their ancient language.

Jacob slipped the needle back into the pouch and then drew an obsidian dagger.

He stood next to Brower's head, brandishing the knife in the air, the light from the building illuminating him for all below to see.

Jacob shouted to those below, speaking in Mayan, his words amplified by the stelae as if they were speakers. A feeling of darkness engulfed Roth's heart—this was wrong. It was *evil*. He watched Brower's eyes twitch with fear, his mouth paralyzed in a grimace he couldn't relax.

Then Jacob turned and ripped open the buttons of Brower's shirt, exposing his pale skin and thatch of chest hair. With his palm, Jacob smoothed open the shirt and traced his finger along Brower's ribs, right by his heart.

Roth's gorge began to rise in his throat. He closed his eyes, unable to witness what was about to happen. His knees started shaking, and he felt like he was going to faint.

It was a nightmare he couldn't wake up from.

He heard a gasp, the sound of something wet dribbling, and then a choking noise.

A cheer sounded from the multitude gathered below. A cry of victory, of power. Of triumph. They'd come to watch an execution. They'd come to take part in it. Just like in medieval times.

Roth's ears began ringing. He was going into shock. He was going to vomit.

EAD Brower was dead. And he hadn't even been able to scream.

CHAPTER FORTY

Jaguar Temple

Calakmul Biosphere Reserve

January 10

Suki's heart thumped with the sound of the bullets deflecting off the web of *kem äm*. Her powers were strong when certain planets or the moon was in sight. The times she'd practiced in the ball court, she'd been able to do more, lift heavy things, control multiple items all at once. In the tomb-like corridors beneath the temple, her connection with the magic was more limited. And it didn't help that they were near the source of a totally evil magic.

The jaguar priest was also protected from their bullets, which were still ricocheting like burning coals through the corridor. Suki watched the jaguar, trying to see him through the hail of ammunition. The stone door that had blocked the mirror room continued to grind open.

Suki glanced at Jordan, his rifle raised but not firing. He looked deadly serious as he glanced back and forth between the jaguar and the mirror room.

"We're in between," he said in a low voice to her. "Not a good spot to be in."

She noticed two hand grenades poking out from the front pockets on his vest. She knew the basics. Pull the pin. Boom. The jaguar priests inside the room wouldn't be expecting it.

"Roll a grenade in there when I tell you," she said, hooking her thumb and pointing underneath the stone door. "I'd rather collapse their room than ours."

Jordan grinned and let go of his rifle, which was hanging from his shoulder by a strap. He yanked the grenade out of his pocket and pulled the pin, holding on to the safety lever.

"Four seconds," he told her.

Suki nodded and held up her hand to count. *One, two, three.* "Now!"

Jordan released the safety lever, and Suki used the bracelet to draw any *kem äm* from the other side of the stone door into it. Motes of golden dust swarmed her hand.

There was no protection on the other side, but it could be reinstated if they didn't act quickly enough.

"Roll it!" she urged to Jordan.

He counted silently in his head and then did a softball underhand throw and rolled the grenade beneath the stone door. Suki put up a shield in the gap to protect them from the explosion.

The blast rocked the corridor, just a dull tremor. The tunnel was made of solid stone. Suki's shield defending them from the jaguar priest came down. Their attacker, a man once more, rushed forward. He jammed a dagger into the neck of one of the soldiers before she could raise another one.

Suki saw the motes swirling around him, drawn to her hand, and ripped the magic away from him.

"Now!" she shouted.

"Fire!" Jordan ordered. Before he could lift his own rifle, one of the other soldiers with a handgun shot the jaguar priest point blank in the chest with three rounds. The popping noises from the gun weren't what Suki had been expecting, but the results were instant. The priest's face gaped with shock and pain, and then he fell on his back, writhing, struggling to breathe, blood blooming from his chest wounds.

The army guy who'd been stabbed fell to his knees, blood dripping through his fingers. Suki rushed to him and put her hands on him, invoking the healing magic. *This* was her strength, not fighting. She closed her eyes so she wouldn't see the blood. Tapping into the magic thrumming inside her, she filled the soldier with healing energy.

When she opened her eyes again, he was healed. He stared at her, dumbfounded, patting his neck above his body armor where the blade had gotten through.

Then he grinned. "You . . . you healed me!"

Suki smiled back and turned to look at the stone maw leading to the room where the mirrors had been. All she could see was stone dust swirling against the *kem äm*. The feeling of dark magic was gone. The grenade had broken all the obsidian mirrors in the room. It had killed whichever jaguar priests were in there too.

"We did it," she gasped.

"Did what?" Jordan wanted to know.

"The mirrors are broken. They can't get out."

One of the other soldiers, Killian, was standing over the jaguar priest. The man wasn't breathing anymore, his face gone slack. He was dead.

"If Suki hadn't put up a shield, we'd all have died," Jordan said, panning his glance across the group of soldiers. "Got that?"

"We need to leave," Angélica insisted. "More will come."

"Lead the way," Suki said.

They went back down the corridor they had come from, and Suki released the *kem äm* at the stone door. The tunnel was narrow and confined, and then it hit a fork. Angélica led them through the twisting tunnels, going up as soon as they encountered stairs. They were climbing higher now. Did that mean they were near the surface of the pyramid?

"Where does this corridor exit?" Suki asked Angélica.

"On the front face of the pyramid, near the bottom of the main stairs. We'll be above the crowd. The sacrificial victims will be brought to the altar at the top of the main stairs."

More stairs to climb. Suki swallowed and steadied herself.

"I'll go up with Suki," Jordan said. "You three keep up cover fire to slow them coming after us but come up the steps too." Looking at Suki, he added, "Once we get to the top, you can teleport us back to Cozumel, right?"

"That's the plan," Suki said. "I think I'll be able to see the moon from the top of the pyramid."

"That's the plan," he repeated. "Up and away. Got it?"

"Roger," said a soldier. "Lock and load."

"Lock and load, rock and roll, create and improvise," Jordan said. "Let's do it."

When they reached the top of the stone steps, there was a corroded metal door blocking their path. A square piece of it was open, like a spyhole—about eight inches tall and six inches wide. The door was discolored with rust and moss and looked like it had been a recent addition, not by the original Maya who had built Calakmul.

Jordan reached it first and gazed outside. He held up two fingers and then pointed to the right and left. The other soldiers nodded.

Angélica pressed her fingers to her lips. The noise of a crowd outside could be heard through the open partition embedded in the door. Suki saw the moonlight outside, which was a comforting sign.

Jordan examined the doorframe and then pointed at the latch. The door would swing outward, which meant they'd likely be spotted immediately. Suki's heart was racing. None of the people out there had *kem äm* shields activated. She sensed the power, but it was more like a force field over the entire area. No one was individually protected. Of course, that could change in the space of a moment. They had to hurry.

"No one is shielded," she whispered to Jordan.

Then she heard a cry of exultation coming from the crowd. Jacob's voice radiated as if from a loudspeaker. He was speaking Mayan, but she understood the words.

"To thee, god of the night sky, god of the hurricane, of hostility, discord, and rulership. To the god of jaguars and sorcery, of beauty and war, I offer this next sacrifice! Your enemy Jonathon Roth!"

Jordan's head turned.

"Dad!" Suki groaned. They were too late.

Jordan frowned with determination and shoved the latch up. Slamming his body into the door, he threw it open, knocking down one of the warriors guarding it. Another soldier shot down the other with his rifle.

"Move, move, move!" Jordan screamed as they all spilled out into the night sky.

Suki didn't wait for the others. She rushed past them, to the narrow steps in the center of the pyramid. A huge glowing stela was planted on the base of it, shimmering with magic. It was taller than her, a formidable obelisk. She ran toward it, knowing it was in front of the stairs she needed to climb. The army guys would follow. She had to get to her dad. Her mind connected with the stela instantly, like a Wi-Fi signal infused in her DNA. She saw the glowing symbol of a king and queen embedded in its design. It looked . . . strangely familiar. As if she recognized it, and it recognized her.

Her bracelet started to glow, awakened by the magic of the place. She'd never stood there before, hadn't been allowed to climb the temple when she was a prisoner. Now she knew why.

Her ancestors had been from this place. Their magic was in her blood. The bracelet she wore belonged to her family. The stelae throughout the temple grounds would obey her. She was part of the royal house.

Welcome, Daughter. Welcome home.

CHAPTER FORTY-ONE

Jaguar Temple

Calakmul Biosphere Reserve

January 10

Jacob stared down at the corpse sprawled halfway down the pyramid steps. Blood dripped from the obsidian blade clenched in his hand. Gazing down from the crest of the pyramid, before the temple, he felt a surge of vindication. Although his victim hadn't been the true president of the United States, for the crowd assembled below, this was a sign of his triumph. None could stay the jaguar priests. They would trample through the sheep unopposed. Helicopters and drones and military inventions had failed against the ancient technology of the Maya. The pharmaceutical companies would fail against the plague spreading faster and faster across the world. Blood sacrifices would be performed throughout North and South America, Europe, and Asia.

In a few years, every knee would bend to Huracán through the power of the Calakmul family. Just as the Jaguar Prophecies had said they would.

Jacob motioned for the warriors to bring Mr. Roth to the bloody altar. He faced the crowd gathered below and lifted his voice, using the magic of his ring to amplify it throughout the stelae. He wanted every soul to hear it proclaimed as he brandished the blade once again.

"To thee, god of the night sky, god of the hurricane, of hostility, discord, and rulership. To the god of jaguars and sorcery, of beauty and war, I offer this next sacrifice! Your enemy Jonathon Roth!"

The warriors didn't have to wrestle the author onto the slab of stone. He went willingly. The Spanish king was blubbering like a babe, gripped tightly by his captors. The British PM looked stoic. Of course he would be. They'd always faced impossible odds with equanimity. The German chancellor looked outraged and more than a little terrified.

Jacob pointed at the three men. "You're next," he growled.

Jacob turned away from the crowd and walked to the altar. The warriors stood back, watching Mr. Roth as he held his own arms out, exposing his chest to the knife. His fists were clenched, but he looked determined to face his death without cowering. He looked strangely . . . peaceful.

"You won't plead with me again to spare your family?" Jacob said mockingly.

"What good would it do?" Mr. Roth answered. "You always win."

"I'm glad you've finally realized that," Jacob said. "You could have been in the crowd below tonight instead of up here as an offering. I will take pleasure in cutting out your heart, Mr. Roth."

"That's because you're a psychopath. Get it over with. I know how this is going to end."

Jacob withdrew a dart from his pouch and walked to Mr. Roth's side. No matter how brave the author proclaimed to be, Jacob wasn't going to cut into him unless he was truly helpless.

"You won't be parted from your family for long," Jacob said. "You will all be together in torment in Xibalba."

And that's when the gunfire erupted. The rattle of automatic weapons echoed through the acoustically perfect space of the pyramid courtyard. Screams of terror sounded from the crowd below.

Jacob had already summoned a shield of *kem äm* to protect himself before mounting the steps to the pyramid. He was taking no chances tonight. But the disturbance had caught him completely unaware.

He strode to the edge of the steps and looked down. Men—soldiers from the American military—were running up the steps. There were only four of them and a young woman. No—*two* women. One was Angélica. His nostrils flared with shock and fury. The soldiers were shooting down his warriors as they rushed down to intercept them.

"Dad!"

It was Suki's voice. He hadn't recognized her in the military clothing she wore, but he knew her voice. She had used her magic to penetrate the defenses of the temple grounds. And she'd healed or revived Angélica from the dead.

Warriors were using blowguns to try to hit the soldiers, but Suki had put up a shield to defend them as they vaulted up the narrow steps.

"Mataré!" Jacob shouted to the other jaguar priest who was with him on the heights. He pointed down the steps. "Kill them!"

He saw the look of hatred on the other man's face as he beheld the intruders. He didn't need to be told twice and transformed into a jaguar. The jaguar priest bounded down the steps, emitting a frightening shriek as he lunged toward them.

Jacob turned around, glaring at Mr. Roth. More gunfire blasted at Mataré, the bullets deflected by the jaguar's shield as he charged.

Mr. Roth lifted his head. He'd heard his daughter's voice. The look of anguish on his face suggested he hadn't known his daughter would be coming. He didn't want her to die. He certainly wouldn't want to be killed right in front of her. Good.

"We end this now, Jonathon Roth!" Jacob said firmly. He rushed to the edge of the altar and pressed a hand on Mr. Roth's chest to hold him down. He lifted the obsidian knife, determined to plunge it in and end his enemy's life.

There was a sound like the rushing of wind. Like the violence of an impending storm. The jungle trees swayed. Birds began to cry and took off in a panic.

And then the *kem äm* shield fell away. All of it. The stelae went dark. The sacrificial torches plunged into blackness. All the magic vanished, and only the light of the moon was left. Jacob felt exposed. He stared at the ring on his finger, the one holding Mr. Roth down. That stone had gone dark too.

Suki had extinguished all magic. How? How had she . . . ?

Jacob felt a prick of pain on his forearm. It took him no more than an instant to understand. Jonathon Roth had stabbed him with a dart he'd hidden in his closed fist.

Jacob stared in shock as a drop of blood welled up from the puncture spot. Mr. Roth pulled the dart out, his face grimacing with anger.

"*Sic semper tyrannis,*" Mr. Roth breathed and then kicked Jacob hard in the groin.

Already the toxin was working. Jacob felt the numbness spreading through his body along with the anguish of bodily pain. The blow knocked him backward. His leg muscles wilted. His arms dropped helplessly to his sides. He staggered back, knowing he would be completely immobilized in another second. Immobilized and then captured. The thought of this horrified him beyond words. Trapped by the Americans. Held in awful cells in shackles and chains. His wealth and power muted by a precocious teenager whom he'd taught enough to destroy him. *No!*

Jacob turned, gazing down at the fleeing crowd drenched in moonlight. He swayed. His body was now almost totally useless. He only had strength enough for one more act.

Chin drooping, he tottered to the edge of the steps. And then he let himself fall down them. He would rather die than face that future.

And he realized as he collided with the first stones of the steps that *this* was the vision his father had seen—his failure.

Jacob's neck broke halfway down.

CHAPTER FORTY-TWO

Jaguar Temple

Calakmul Biosphere Reserve

January 10

Roth watched Calakmul totter over the edge of the pyramid. He knew he'd been more than lucky so far. He'd heard Suki scream his name, though, and all that he could think of was getting to his daughter. Had she been recaptured by the jaguar priests? Who was firing the rifles down below? How was he going to escape the warriors who remained atop the pyramid with the other hostages? The *kem äm* was gone—somehow—but they were still stronger and more adept. Armed too, in all likelihood.

He and Suki weren't safe—far from it—but at least Jacob Calakmul was dead. The man who'd orchestrated this nightmare was gone.

Roth rolled off the edge of the round sacrificial altar, landing on his hands and knees. A warrior was already springing toward him, gripping the wooden handle of a deadly Maya sword. Roth couldn't remember the name of the weapon, but he knew it was powerful enough to saw a horse in half. The conquistadors had learned that the hard way. They were made of wooden paddles, about the size of a cricket bat, but with shards of obsidian along both edges.

"Help us!" one of the hostages shouted.

If Roth had been more like the Rock, he could have punched his way out of the situation. Fight scenes were fun to write in novels, but fiction couldn't save him here—if it came down to a physical fight, the odds were not stacked in his favor. He had to be smart. He needed a weapon of his own.

As he backed away from the altar, his foot bumped into the obsidian dagger. Had Calakmul dropped it? The warrior vaulted at him, swinging the obsidian sword in an arc that could decapitate him in a single swipe.

Roth dropped fast, feeling the wind through his hair as the weapon was swung above his head. He grabbed for the dagger, feeling for the edge, and then discovered the handle. He picked it up by the sharp edge, then backpedaled away while the warrior rushed him again, shouting angrily, with rage in his eyes.

The *kem äm* had all been sloughed away. Only the moonlight helped him see. He was afraid he'd stumble off the side of the pyramid if he went too far backward without looking, but he couldn't take his eyes off the warrior. He evaded another slashing motion, but he knew he'd only get lucky for so long.

He brought his hand around and whipped the dagger at the warrior. In high school, he'd gone to Scout camp several years in a row. He'd even been a merit badge counselor his last summer of his senior year. Knife throwing was something all the boys had learned. And Roth had been pretty good.

The obsidian dagger sailed from his hand and embedded in the warrior's chest. The man had wooden shoulder pads as part of his armor, but his chest was open. He'd always had the *kem äm* to protect him. Not this time.

A look of shock and pain came over his face. He stopped his advance, staring down at the hilt protruding from his chest.

Roth didn't hesitate. He rushed forward and wrenched the Maya sword from his hand. The warrior gasped and then fell down. Dead.

There was no time for him to process what had happened before another scream of challenge deafened him. At least the space was too narrow for their guards to rush them. Each prisoner had had two warriors guarding him. One of Roth's guys was down, and now the other came sailing at him. Roth wished he had a Glock. He could have ended the fight in an instant.

Roth stepped forward, using his own blade to counter the first. The two weapons cracked into each other, and Roth felt a jolt of pain shoot up his arm. The warrior shifted, reversing the thrust, and pivoted on his heel, shifting the attack to his other side. Roth deflected the blow and then rushed forward, pressing his other palm against the flat of the paddle, and struck the other man in the chest. He wasn't trying to slice him—the weapon would have cut off his own hand if he'd gripped it by the edge. No, Roth wanted to apply leverage and force. And when he collided with the warrior, he shoved him back until he hit the sacrificial altar, which tripped him.

The warrior fell backward, grunting in surprise. Roth swung his blade over his own head, driving the sharp edge down to finish the man. But the warrior was too quick and rolled to the side to escape.

Instead, Roth cut off his arm. The arm that held his sword.

Roth stared in surprise at the severed limb, hearing the warrior's shriek of pain as he rolled aside and left it behind.

A foot struck Roth in the back of his knee. He hadn't heard or seen anyone else. He felt his leg spasm with pain. Someone grabbed him by the hair from behind and torqued his neck back, exposing his throat.

Roth swung his sword up over his head and felt the obsidian hit wood and stick there. He tried to wrench it free, but it was stuck. The man behind him flailed, his grip on Roth's hair loosening.

Then Roth saw another warrior, one opposite the altar, plant his foot and level a javelin at him. It was the same kind of javelin that Roth had used to puncture the inflatable boats all those months ago. He tried to shift, but the javelin came too fast. He felt it pierce his chest, just within his lower ribs. Pain and shock struck him simultaneously. He couldn't breathe. He'd just been skewered.

The man grappling him from behind dug his fingers into Roth's hair again and hoisted him by the roots. Roth groaned, his leg muscles turning to mush. He couldn't stand up anymore and felt blood flowing down his shirt. The warrior brandished a Maya sword. Was this the same man who'd threatened Lucas's life when he'd climbed up on the roof? Images of the twins flashed through his mind.

More gunfire echoed through the night sky. Whatever was happening, they were too late for Roth. He tried to lift his sword again, but his fingers were numb. He felt the hilt slip away from his hand and heard the blade clatter noisily on the stone.

Light exploded like a supernova.

It blinded Roth. Had his head just been cut off? Was this what it felt like after a visit with a guillotine?

Except . . . he felt his heart beating still. He tasted the coppery flavor of blood in his mouth. The brightness was beyond anything he'd experienced, like a dozen floodlights all aimed at him at once. This wasn't the *kem äm*. This was something else.

A gurgled cry sounded from behind Roth, and the grip on his hair went slack. Roth sagged to his knees, still feeling the javelin protruding from his chest. He couldn't breathe, each moment making the pain constrict more tightly.

As he slumped forward, one hand pressing against the stone floor, the other pressing the wound beneath the javelin, he tried to see through the blinding light. What he saw inside the light stunned him.

CHAPTER FORTY-THREE

Jaguar Temple

Calakmul Biosphere Reserve

January 10

Welcome, Daughter. Welcome home.

Suki reached out and placed her palm against the glowing stela. The glyphs carved into it glowed more intensely, like weak batteries suddenly fed energy. Thoughts swirled in her mind as her consciousness expanded. This stela was connected to all the others within the Calakmul compound, which was much more vast than the buildings and pyramids nearby. The compound went on for acres and acres, mostly buried under the jungle's growth. She could sense the other stelae, *feel* them, and her mind swelled with the knowledge they contained. This one was carved into the likeness of two rulers, a king and queen, the last to rule Calakmul. They'd been deceived by the jaguar priests, ensnared by their cunning. They'd wanted to fight the Spanish conquistadors and protect the lives of their people, but instead they'd succumbed to the manipulations of the Kowinem, who had used the Spaniards' arrival to try to overthrow their Aztec overlords ruled by Moctezuma. The Maya had hated their subjugation to both groups and yearned for freedom. The Order of the Jaguar Priests had taken advantage of it.

The shriek of a jaguar filled the air. Looking up, Suki saw one of the monsters charging down the pyramid steps, coming right for her.

Suki wasn't afraid of it. She stood there, feeling connected to the rulers. Their blood flowed in her veins. She didn't understand the relationship, but it went through Grandma Suki's line. She was a rightful descendent. That meant the stelae and *kem äm* would obey her. With this insight, she looked up through the eyes of a glyph already positioned at the top of the pyramid and saw her dad lying on a sacrificial altar. Jacob Calakmul stood above him with a dagger. He was protected by a shield of *kem äm*.

No! No, no, no, no!

But the solution came to her as if Ix Chel herself had presented it—she could shut down the defenses completely. She could draw all the *kem äm*'s power into the single stela she was touching.

Do it, she thought forcefully.

It felt like she'd triggered a vortex. All the *kem äm* around them—from the torches to the shields to the echoing magic used to amplify voices—*all of it* was sucked into the stela she touched. The sigils glowed and sizzled with power as the swarm of *kem äm* reached it.

The rest of the compound went dark.

Suki cast her gaze upward. The moon was still shining, and strangely, parts of the walls were shining. And the streets were shining. Knowledge flooded her. The stucco in the walls and streets were made of limestone powder, which reflected light. The streets of the Maya had always been intended to glow in the dark.

Jordan put his hand on her shoulder. "Suki! Get behind me!"

She turned and looked at him. "The shields are all down. No one is protected."

"Fire at will!" Jordan yelled. "Repeat, fire at will!"

The 82nd Airborne needed no further encouragement. Warriors were already charging up the lower pyramid steps to get to them, and the bullets sliced through them. Jordan raised his rifle and aimed at the jaguar priest coming down from the top, about to reach them. He'd been a jaguar but not anymore. Suki's power had stripped his away.

Bullets blasted against the stone, causing puffs of dust. The jaguar priest was quick, though, and came down the last steps altering his movements in a zigzag pattern to confuse Jordan. He kicked the barrel of the assault rifle away and then came down at Jordan with his fists.

Suki, still touching the stela, held out her hand and sent a blast of lightning into the jaguar priest. It threw him back against the steep steps, and he yelled in pain.

Jordan swung the weapon around again and shot him with a quick burst of bullets. Blood bloomed from his chest. Suki watched in horror as he tried to rise, gasping for breath, despite his injuries. Something animated him, even though he should have been dead. A sickening feeling hung in the air. Fear seeped into Suki's bones.

Jordan stared in disbelief and then emptied his magazine into the jaguar priest, the bullets literally tearing him to pieces. He collapsed in the shadows, still twitching but unable to move.

Jordan detached the magazine and shoved another one in.

"He's dead," Angélica said, coming to stand near Suki and Jordan. "He was the worst of them."

"Let's save my dad," Suki said, gazing up at the steps. She removed her hand from the stela at last, and it too went dark.

The other three soldiers followed her up, spraying bullets at anyone who came after them. A few javelins were hurled at them, but they clattered uselessly against the stone steps. The soldiers had their night vision goggles on, ensuring they could see, where others could not, and the muzzles of their rifles flashed with light as they shot their attackers. Suki started up the steps, Jordan jogging next to her.

The steps were so steep and tight that Suki ambled up them sideways. She felt the strain of the climb and was panting in moments, hurrying up the steps. Then she heard a noise and gazed up. Someone was falling down the steps, crashing violently against the stones.

"Look out!" Jordan warned.

Suki moved to the side, and the body came sprawling, stopping just by her, upside down. In the moonlight, she recognized Jacob Calakmul's face. His eyes were wide open, his mouth gaping. She saw his chest move up and down, but he didn't move. Not even his body twitched. He was helpless.

Angélica gasped.

"It's him," Suki said in surprise. She gazed up the steps of the pyramid. How had he fallen?

Angélica grabbed a knife from Jordan's flak vest. With a wild look in her eyes, she plunged it into Jacob's chest before anyone could stop her.

"They're still coming!" shouted one of the army guys. "Too many!"

Suki looked down and saw warriors climbing toward them from all over the pyramid. They fearlessly came onward, leaping from stone to stone to get up faster.

Suki looked at the knife buried in Calakmul's chest and didn't begrudge Angélica's choice. Whatever had passed between them before, he'd left her for dead, and she didn't want him surviving to come after her later.

Suki charged up the steps again, clambering up row after row. Jordan was right next to her, followed by Angélica and the three army dudes. Her heart was pounding in her chest as she gasped to breathe and keep up her momentum. *Almost there!*

Something blew up in front of her. The light was so blinding that covering her face wasn't enough. She stumbled and almost lost her footing. It was like going from a dark house into the noonday sun. It hurt her eyes, but she blinked them open anyway, trying to see. What had caused it? All she knew was she was blinded by it. Regardless of the pain, she dropped onto her hands and clawed her way up the final steps.

It was like staring into the sun. A glyph came to her mind, and she traced her finger through the air, invoking the magic of the *kem äm*. The stabbing pain of the light subdued, or maybe it was her ability to endure it that had changed. She felt strangely calm.

And then she saw the Maya dude with a glowing sword and feathered wings. She watched as he took out the warriors atop the pyramid, one by one.

She saw a few men dressed in modern clothing cowering in fear. Where was her dad?

Jordan reached her next, but he was shielding his face with one hand and trying to aim the rifle with the other. Angélica joined them and then the other soldiers.

"No, he's on our side," Suki mumbled, pushing Jordan's arm down.

The Maya warrior-god turned and faced them. He had a white goatee, white hair, and bronze skin.

Suki dropped to her knees, overwhelmed by her awe and fear.

"Put down your weapons," he said in perfect English.

There was a compulsion to follow the words. If Suki had been holding one, she would have slammed it to the ground. The soldiers did so instantly. Then, one by one, they all went down on their knees.

"It's Kukulkán," Angélica murmured with awe.

"I am not," said the angelic Maya in perfect English. "I am His follower. My name is Ezequiel Cumenon. Tend to your father, Socorro."

She looked to the left and saw her dad with a javelin sticking through him, kneeling on the stones. "Dad!"

She scurried to him, shocked by the blood on his shirt. He slumped down, and she caught him before he collapsed. With one hand, she yanked the javelin from his chest and began murmuring the words of healing over and over.

Her dad shuddered, his body quivering as the magic swept through him. She kept repeating it over and over. *"Kunaj, kunaj, kunaj."*

"So . . . who are you?" she heard Jordan ask the angel.

"I am a *tioxalaj winaq*, a divine servant," he said, and Suki looked up briefly as she continued to pour out the words and her magic. His glow was fading, but it still radiated from him, as if he were standing amid a shaft of lightning. "I came to punish the jaguar priests. I've been waiting a long time for the Jaguar Prophecies to come to pass and the wards that had been blocking us from coming to finally fail. I will hunt down the rest of the jaguar priests so that none can escape. Their time is ending. There will be no more death games. No more torture."

Suki felt her dad's shuddering breath on her cheek. Her attention jolted back to him. He was winded, in a lot of pain, his clothes dirty, bloodstained, and scuffed up. But he looked so surprised and relieved to see her.

"Suki?"

She smiled at her dad. "Hey. I think you're going to make it."

He wrapped his arms around her, and she hugged him back hard, feeling tears dripping from her eyes. She was so grateful she'd come in time.

"I can't believe you're here," he whispered to her.

"I couldn't just let you die," she said, grinning as she wiped away tears. "You need someone to look after you."

"Where are the others? Are they safe?"

Suki nodded vigorously. "With Mom. Jane Louise is too."

Her dad lowered his head and sighed in relief. "I kicked Jacob, and he fell off the pyramid. I don't know if he's still alive."

"Oh, he's dead," Suki assured him.

"Are you sure?"

"Um. Yeah. I saved Angélica, and she stabbed him in the heart."

"Return to Cozumel," Ezequiel said, his voice booming. "This land must be purged for the awful murders it has done. We must prepare for His coming. It is nigh."

Suki helped her dad to his feet.

Jordan motioned for the other men to gather around them. Some were leaders—she had no idea who they were, but they looked disturbed by the angel's presence.

The angel looked sternly at them. "Prepare for His coming. Your worldly kingdoms are soon to end."

Angélica looked fearful, but the angel didn't object when she joined them. The crowds below had begun to trample each other in their haste to escape the light-shrouded figure. He strode to the edge of the pyramid, looking down.

"Let the purging begin," he declared. Light exploded from his body.

"Rapinik," Suki breathed. The magic of the Maya whisked them away, back to Cozumel.

CHAPTER FORTY-FOUR

SAN GERVASIO ARCHAEOLOGICAL ZONE

COZUMEL, MEXICO

January 10

It was a gut-wrenching feeling, like the Avatar ride at Disney World meeting Highway 17 through the Santa Cruz Mountains. When the motion suddenly stopped, Roth dropped to his knees and promptly began turning his body inside out once again. He smelled the jungle still, but there was a different odor here, a more tropical one.

"Whoa, whoa, whoa!" Jordan shouted in alarm. "What's going on here?"

"*Es* okay, *es* okay," said a comforting, familiar voice. Roth recognized it instantly. It was Jorge from Huellas de Pan.

"Captain! Captain! Where are you?" Jordan called out.

Roth wiped spittle from his lips on the back of his hand and looked up, still too dizzy to stand. He was kneeling in a parking lot, near a gift shop with a thatched roof. He recognized it as the parking lot of the ruins of San Gervasio in Cozumel.

Jordan had his rifle up and was aiming it at Jorge, who approached with his hands up in a soothing gesture. No one else was in the area.

"No hurt," Jorge said. "No hurt."

"Who is this guy? Where is everyone?" Jordan asked, his voice trembling with emotion. He'd just been in the middle of an intense situation and was still in soldier mode.

Suki stepped in front of the barrel of Jordan's gun, and Roth almost swallowed his tongue. "Drop it, Jordan!"

"I don't know who this is, friendly or not," Jordan said. "Suki, step aside."

"He's our friend," Suki explained. "Please . . . just lower your weapon. I'll talk to him."

Jordan lowered his weapon and pulled his radio out. "Command, this is Eagle. Over."

Jorge shook his head. "No work. It no work here."

"Can someone tell me what in blazes is going on and what just happened?" asked a man with a strong British accent, rubbing the sleeve of his dirty shirt.

Roth struggled to stand and nearly dropped. The people around him had also been there on the pyramid top. The prisoners and rescuers had been teleported as a group. One of the army soldiers helped steady him. "Prime Minister, my name is Jonathon Roth. I was abducted too. This is my daughter, Suki. And this man is Jorge, who runs an orphanage here on the island of Cozumel."

"Cozumel? *Vat?*" asked another man, this one with a German accent.

Roth took a deep breath. "Just . . . give us a minute. If you please." He turned to Suki. "I don't speak Spanish very well, and Jorge doesn't speak English very well. How are we going to talk to him?"

"Let me help," Angélica offered. "I can translate."

Suki turned to her. "A group of army people were supposed to be waiting for us. Find out what happened."

Angélica looked out of place now in her bloody Maya dress, but if she felt self-conscious, it didn't show. She spoke clearly and gently to Jorge, and Roth knew enough Spanish to recognize she was asking about the soldiers.

Jorge answered rapidly but with a smile and made several hand gestures to articulate his points.

"This place is sacred ground," Angélica said. "Soldiers from the Mexican army were coming to attack the Americans." She paused. "He said . . . he said he told them all to leave."

"That doesn't sound right," Jordan answered brusquely. "I know Captain Rose. He never would have abandoned us without a fight."

Jorge shook his head and rattled off more Spanish.

"There was no fight," Angélica explained. "He told them to leave and wait for you at the beach. He will bring you all to them so you can return home."

"What sort of nonsense is this?" the British PM demanded. "Who are you? Why would they strand us here voluntarily?"

Jorge's face became stern. A blast of white-hot light exploded around them, just as it had on the pyramid in Calakmul. It was so bright it burned the eyes. Roth heard a strong, powerful voice utter a command in Spanish.

"*¡Iros!*" It was Jorge. But it no longer sounded like him. It no longer looked like him either.

Just as they had atop the pyramid, they cowered before a being sheathed in lightning.

Then the light coalesced, just as it had with Ezequiel, until it was gathered around Jorge in a pillar. He looked dangerous—*powerful*—his eyes piercing to the soul.

"*¿Ahora me crees?*" he asked with a tone of impatience.

"Now do you believe me?" Angélica gasped, translating for them.

Roth's mind was still blown. Jorge was some powerful Maya demi-god? When they were captured by Calakmul's men at the orphanage, one of the security officers had held a gun to Jorge's head. Why hadn't he shown his power then?

"Yes, we believe," Suki answered. She bowed her head to him.

Jorge frowned and motioned for her. "Up. Up. *Es* okay. *Es* okay." The light dimmed, and then it was gone.

He began to speak quickly, gesturing as he did. He'd paused for Angélica to translate his words.

"This island is dedicated to Ix Chel. It is a place of healing. A place of rebirth. It will be a spiritual center of Kukulkán's kingdom when he returns. No soldiers are permitted here. I was here the day that . . ." She stopped, her eyes growing wide. Jorge gestured for her to repeat what he had said. "I-I was here the day that Cortés came with his soldiers. I have lived on this island for many, many years awaiting the fulfillment of Kukulkán's promise. It is near. He is coming."

Jorge tapped his chest. *"Me llamo* Jeremiah. *Mi apodo es Jorge."*

"He said his name is Jeremy. No, Jeremiah. His nickname is Jorge."

Jorge spoke again, slowly and deliberately.

"He and his two . . . companions . . . Ezequiel Cumenon, who we have met, and one other named Isaiah. These three have been the guardians of the prophecy. They have served the people of this land for . . . for thousands of years. They will prepare the kingdom of Cemanahuac for Kukulkán's return."

Roth knew that word. Illari Chaska believed that someday all the people of Mesoamerica would be united under one government. A peaceful one. She'd called it Cemanahuac.

Roth nodded and then turned to the leaders. "The CIA told us that many of the ancient pyramids were glowing again. All through Mexico and down to Peru."

"¡Sí! ¡Sí!" Jorge exclaimed. Then he pointed. *"¡Mira!"*

Beyond the tiki hut and the souvenir shops, Roth saw that the jungle was glowing brightly. It wasn't the moon. Jorge spoke again with great emphasis.

"The time is coming soon," Angélica translated. "Great plagues are coming. Wars among nations. Those who come to Cemanahuac will be healed and protected. Ours will be the only people not at war one with another. The good and the meek from all nations will gather here. Tell your people this. The jaguar priests are no more. Their cartels and their secret covenants are being purged. This will happen until the . . . plague . . . the . . . consumption will end all nations."

Headlights and the sound of an approaching car came up the road from the highway. Roth turned and looked and slowly, once again, made it to his feet. It was the van from Huellas de Pan that they'd ridden in before. He recognized the dad at the steering wheel.

Jorge waved them over to it.

"It will take us to the beach where the soldiers are waiting for us," Angélica said.

Jordan looked questioningly at Roth. "Did you understand any of that?"

"They're letting us go," Roth said. "That's what matters." He looked at Angélica and touched her arm. "Thank you. I'm grateful you're still alive."

"It was Suki," she answered. "She destroyed the obsidian mirrors. None of the jaguar priests can escape."

Roth could imagine Ezequiel Cumenon chasing them down with his jagged sword. It made him smile. He squeezed her arm. "What about the people who gathered down there? Will they all be . . . purged?" He thought of Moretti's family. Did they even know what was going on? The thought of innocent kids dying made his stomach shrivel.

The van door opened, and the leaders climbed in. The British PM took the passenger seat.

Angélica turned to Jorge and asked Roth's question.

Jorge looked at him with compassion and answered simply. "Only those who will not renounce the jaguar priests and their ways will be judged worthy of death."

"That's legit," Suki said, nodding her head. "I think we should go. I'm sure Mom is pretty worried."

Jorge took Suki by the hand and began to speak to her in Mayan. Suki listened intently, her eyes bulging with surprise. Then Jorge patted her hand and motioned for them to get into the van. Jordan was standing by the open door, waiting for them.

Angélica paused, then turned to Jorge and asked one short question. "*¿Me puedo quedar?*"

Roth knew what she'd asked. *Can I stay?*

He looked at her knowingly. "*Si. Para el niño.*"

Angélica put her hands in her face and started to weep. What did that mean—"for the child"? Then he got it. Roth put his hand on Angélica's shoulder as she wept.

"Your child will have a different future because of you. A better world. This is a real second chance."

She raised her tear-stricken face to him, nodding mutely. There were a lot of emotions to unpack. Roth was grateful she'd switched sides in the end.

Suki tugged on his arm.

It was crowded in the van and frankly smelled pretty bad. But as the vehicle turned around and bumped down the road, Roth put his arm around his daughter and held her close.

"Thanks for saving me," he whispered huskily and kissed her hair. "I . . . I didn't think I'd get to see you again. Any of you."

Suki smiled with relief, rubbed her nose, then her eyes, which were beginning to tear up. "Mom can't wait to see you."

CHAPTER FORTY-FIVE

GUANTANAMO BAY NAVAL BASE

CUBA

January 11

A gentle knock sounded on the door. Suki was already awake. Awake and exhausted. The base doctor had given her a sleeping pill the previous night. She'd waited too long to take it and then woken up after just a few hours of rest.

Another tap at the door. Suki sighed, rolled off the bed, and walked to the door, scrunching her nose and rubbing her eyes. When she opened it, she saw Jordan Scott standing in the opening. His military clothes were gone, replaced by civilian attire—light brown Levi's and a blue denim shirt with sleeves rolled up to his elbows, revealing tattoos down his right arm. He had on a white T-shirt underneath, and she saw a necklace with dog tags.

He leaned against the doorway. "I do a lot for your family, Suki, but waking up a teenager isn't part of my job description."

"I was awake. Chill."

"You look like crap."

"Thanks, I guess. Where'd you get the new clothes?"

"They have a NEX here at Gitmo."

"Was that even in English?"

"A NEX is like Costco for the military. Your dad asked me to see if you were awake. They're going to call FBI headquarters soon, and it'll be your first chance to talk to your mom and the twins. I miss those guys."

"I'm coming. Do I get a change of clothes too?"

Jordan shrugged. "Your dad is wearing nurse scrubs. You can have some of those if you want."

"I'm good," Suki said. "I need a shower really bad, but I'd rather talk to my mom."

"Follow me, then."

She reached into her pocket and felt the flat piece of quartz still there. It was about half the size of her cell phone and just as slim. Jorge had told her it worked best when it was totally dark, so she'd tried it out after getting to the base. With it, she could see other places. It was a temporary gift, and she'd have to return it when asked for it. She'd used it to see Brice, her boyfriend. He'd been watching a Studio Ghibli movie on his couch in his theater room, squeezing a plush plague doctor pillow she'd given him for Christmas. He'd looked . . . pretty simp.

She'd also used the crystal to try to find Jacob Calakmul. She was pretty sure Angélica's dagger had killed him, but she'd needed confirmation. She'd found him in a mass grave with Maya warriors who'd been shot up by Jordan and the other soldiers. That was pretty gruesome, so she'd moved past it. She'd looked up her mom and brothers and Jane Louise—and found them asleep in a hotel room.

Her dad was in a conference room with some military woman. He wore teal-colored scrubs, and his hair was freshly washed. When she hugged him tight, she smelled bodywash. No more introvert hugs. She was so glad he was alive.

"You look like you just came off a movie set after kicking some alien's butt," he teased her.

"I think it was the alien that was kicking everyone's butts," Suki said.

"I took out the jaguar priest who hurt me earlier," Jordan cut in. "That was my kill."

"I tranked Jacob Calakmul," Roth said. "Do I get points for that?"

"That was pretty epic, Dad," Suki said. "Almost as much as defeating Sans in the boss fight in the genocide run."

"I have no idea what that means," Roth said, chuckling.

"Wait. You've beaten Sans?" Jordan asked Suki, impressed.

"Wait, you've played *Undertale*? I took you for more of a *Super Smash Bros.* kind of guy."

"Game on, girl. Whenever you dare."

"Okay, you two," Roth interrupted. "Let's talk to Mom and the boys. This is Petty Officer Brown, she's our liaison officer working with Quantico. Thanks for doing this."

"Are we just talking to Mom and the boys, or do we have to talk to the big people?" Suki asked.

"Jordan and I talked to them last night when we got here. Along with Captain Rose. We talked for, what . . . two hours?"

"Yeah," Jordan said. "At least. This is just family time."

"Are you all ready?" Officer Brown asked politely.

Suki nodded. The officer used a touchscreen sitting on the conference room table to complete the setup. The video conference screen at the head of the table flickered, and then Suki saw the twins hogging the screen, arguing with each other.

"It was your turn last time, let me talk to her first!" Lucas complained.

"Dude, she's right there!"

"What? Where? You made me miss it!"

"Uh, hi Suki," Brillante said, giving her a little salute.

Her heart clenched with relief when she saw their faces.

"Boys, you're too close to the camera," someone said. "Back up a little."

"Hi, Monica," Jordan said, wagging his eyebrows.

The FBI agent appeared as the boys backed away from the camera. Suki saw her mom, looking healthy, and it made her throat catch. Jane Louise was sitting at the table too, grinning brightly.

"Dad! Do you know what we had for breakfast?" one of the boys said. "French toast with crushed Cap'n Crunch! It was awesome!"

Suki started to laugh even as she felt the tears sting her eyes. She wanted to reach through the screen and touch them. Then she saw Lund standing against the wall, watching the scene. He'd done so much to try to save their family.

"Hi, Uncle Steve," Suki choked out, rubbing tears from her eyes.

He gave her a proud look. "Hey, kiddo."

———

Flying back to the United States in a military cargo plane wasn't nearly as comfortable as if it were a private jet or a commercial airline. It was noisy, bumpy, and they were strapped into jump seats along the sides, with tons of military gear crammed in the middle. At least they were all wearing some new clothes. The liaison officer had taken them shopping at the base exchange where they'd picked up some new apparel.

Roth had taken two showers, which had felt amazing, and managed to get all the pomade residue out of his hair. His beard was still nothing but a bristle of whiskers on his face, but he was beginning to feel more like himself. He'd need to, with what lay ahead.

Once more he was a world-famous author—but for different reasons from before. His e-mail and social media were exploding. Everyone wanted to know more about his novel about the death games and what had inspired it. Even more so because he'd taken the new book down—the FBI and CIA had ordered him to pull it now that the situation was resolved and no further information was needed from the public. He'd listened, of course, but pirated copies were circulating through the dark web and other places faster than the NSA could take them down.

The notoriety was something he would need to adjust to. He hadn't sought it and didn't want it. All he wanted was a chance to see his wife again. To hold her hand. And hopefully not blubber like an idiot.

There wasn't really anything to do on the plane other than endure the sickening bouts of turbulence, although Jordan was hamming it up with the army guys from the 82nd they'd come with. So Roth had plenty of time to stew on his thoughts. He'd asked about what had happened to the world leaders who'd been captured by the jaguar priests and learned they'd been hustled back to Europe with State Department officials the previous night. The news outlets didn't even know about it. Their reports focused on the global pandemic, the unknown occurrence at the White House, and Mexico's political posturing. One report he'd seen in his little bedroom in the military base had theorized that a biolab in Mexico had inadvertently unleashed a genetically engineered form of the plague that was spreading through Europe and making everyone sick.

There was no way the truth was going to stay out of the press for much longer, however, not with so many notable people involved, and especially not with his book blowing up across the globe. He knew some social media sites were already talking about it, tagging his profile, pleading for more information. This wasn't the time to respond. Nor did he have the leave to do so. He'd made an agreement with Director Wright that the Roths could go home for a little while so Suki could do the school play. Then they'd be back in DC to "consult" with the government about a few things. Like all the glowing structures in Mesoamerica. Others might have the natural ability to tap into the *kem äm*, but in the meantime Suki, Sarina, and the boys had the corner on that talent.

Suki wouldn't be going to college anytime soon.

The pilot announced some military jargon, and the sudden plunging of the plane brought the realization they were preparing for landing. He gripped the harness straps, feeling his stomach roil with nerves. Not just from the bucking plane but the uncertain future.

"Dad?" Suki asked.

He glanced at her, trying to smile despite his sweating face. Another ripple of turbulence shook the cargo plane.

Suki gave him a knowing grin. "The pilot just said all the engines failed. We're going to be stuck up here forever now."

It was similar to the punchline of a joke he'd told her and the boys when they were flying to Cancún that first time.

"Ha ha," he said, then grinned. "Good one."

"I thought so."

He gritted his teeth until after the plane landed. It took forever for it to taxi to the hangar, and his patience was wearing thin by the time the pilot said they could unhook from the harness straps. He released his fine, but Suki couldn't figure it out, so Jordan came by and helped her.

Suddenly the back of the jet let out some noises, and the entire back section began to lower. Since they were near the rear of the plane, they saw the hangar and could see the military jeeps and people who had gathered. He saw the twins bouncing up and down.

"It's *Ausfahrt*ing," Brillante said to Lucas, pointing to the rear of the jet.

Roth grunted at their juvenile humor. Suki shook her head. But they both grinned as they made their descent because *everyone* was there. Sarina, Jane Louise, Lund, and even Monica, looking whole and healthy again. It hadn't seemed possible that they'd get here—that they'd all survive. But Jacob Calakmul had been defeated. They'd . . .

Well, they hadn't won, exactly. But they'd come out ahead, for now. That was something. That was everything. To Roth's surprise, Jordan raced down the ramp ahead of everyone, more accustomed to the tricky descent than Roth and Suki. When he got to the bottom, he lifted Monica off her feet and twirled her around. The twins began hooting as he kissed her, but Suki looked away, mumbling something about PDA. Roth barely noticed because his gaze was fixed on his wife. His beautiful wife. Weeks ago, he'd thought she was lost to him forever, but here she was, healthy and whole, and he couldn't be happier than he was in this moment. It wasn't possible.

Sarina met him at the bottom of the ramp. "You," she said, shaking her head at him. "You made it."

"I was just thinking the same about you." He tried to laugh, sort of cried, and then they were hugging so tightly it almost hurt. It felt so impossibly wonderful that they were back together, that she was in his arms again, her hair tickling his bare chin, an unfamiliar sensation because he hadn't been beardless in decades.

"This is . . . this is unbelievable," he whispered, choking. "I can't. I wasn't sure this was going to happen."

She sniffled, rubbed her eyes, and then they kissed, and he didn't care that everyone was looking at them. The pain and worry in his chest ebbed. Their lives wouldn't be the same. But as long as they were together, they'd figure things out. After the kiss ended, they held each other for a long moment, Roth reassuring himself this was really happening—that his family had finally been reunited.

Sarina broke his grip and went to Suki and hugged her tenderly, kissing her cheeks, her hair. The boys were laughing and crying and talking over each other. Suki's eyes were *leaking*, not full-on sobbing, and then Jane Louise came up and wrapped her little arms around Suki's waist.

"Ready to see your mee-maw?" Suki said, choking up.

"I did," the little girl said sweetly. "They arrived this morning."

Roth tried not to lose it again when she hugged him next.

EPILOGUE

GALLATIN HIGH SCHOOL

BOZEMAN, MONTANA

January 21

The audience clapped vigorously at the end of the performance during the bows, and then everyone got to their feet to make it a standing ovation. Roth rose, his hands sore from the applause, but he smiled and then did a finger whistle when the cast parted to have the technical crew come forward and Suki took her bow.

Two weeks ago, Roth had been at Ford's Theatre with the boys, listening to how Lincoln had been assassinated while attending a comedy. So sitting in this theater, watching this comedy, had him on edge. Even though Lund had assured Roth the high school was safe, and every entrance and exit was being monitored, there was still the nagging worry that something *bad* could happen. He glanced over at Jordan and Monica, who were talking to each other, pointing to the stage. An FBI agent was present, for pity's sake, and still Roth was restless.

PTSD sucked.

"That was *so* good," Lucas yelled.

"It was amazing," Roth agreed.

Brillante was still clapping. "Brice was awesome. I loved that one character . . . what was her name?"

"Lady Hyacinth!" Lucas said. "The best!"

Suki's boyfriend had played nearly all the D'Ysquith characters and done a fantastic job of it.

Roth pulled out his wallet and grabbed a ten-dollar bill. Handing it to Lucas, he said, "Run to concessions and get me another cup of caramel Bugles."

Brice's mom had made them, and they were simply the best.

"I wants me another Mountain Dew," Brillante said. "I'll go with him."

People were already starting to leave the high school theater, so the twins dodged through the crowd and disappeared. Roth turned and looked up at the lighting booth, and Lund gave him a courtesy nod and a thumbs-up.

He felt tiny arms wrap around his waist and looked down, finding Jane Louise there. He tousled her hair and smiled at James and BJ McKinty, who had brought her to the performance. James wore a leather newsboy cap and had a goatee and polo shirt. BJ, who had adopted the entire Roth family after they'd brought her precious granddaughter back to Bozeman, had spiky hair and wore the most colorful clothes. She'd brought them treats constantly since they'd been back— everything from cake pops to homemade cookies to chocolate-dipped strawberries.

Monica had facilitated the introduction, and she'd been there when the Roths met the McKintys. There was no acrimony, no anger. They knew Sarina had been held against her will and that the death of their daughter's family hadn't been the Roths' fault. It was because of the Roths that Jane Louise had survived.

Roth had worked with a new estate attorney to transfer the Beasleys' assets back to Jane Louise through a family trust that her grandparents would be the custodians of until she was old enough.

"Did you like the play, sweetie?" Sarina asked, squeezing Jane Louise's shoulder. The little girl hugged her next.

"It was funny," she said.

"We enjoyed it too," BJ said. "Thanks for inviting us."

"A pleasant evening," James said simply. Not a man of many words. He worked in air traffic control at Bozeman Yellowstone International, so he'd been involved with the ruckus after Jacob Calakmul had blown up a hangar.

"Glad you could make it. How's work, James?" Roth asked, trying to draw him out.

"We've heard that the FAA might be shutting down international travel soon. The plague is spreading through Europe so fast."

Roth glanced at Monica. She and Jordan were holding hands. That was sweet to see. He'd have to ask her what the federal government was going to do about the plague. Would they admit where it had really come from? Or would there be a more believable cover story?

Roth had refused multiple interview requests from the media, who were trying to match what his book said with current events. The official story about the near attack from Mexico was that the Mexican government was undergoing a coup and political unrest in every state, but there were plenty of smaller stories that dissented from that version of events. There were also accounts from those who'd witnessed humans shifting to animals and dozens if not hundreds of conspiracy theories about everything from what had really happened in the White House to what was causing the plague. Air traffic to Europe had come to a halt due to the spreading illness, and from what Roth had been told, things would only get worse unless a cure was found.

They needed a glyph to stop what a glyph had started. Illari Chaska was researching that, and Suki and Sarina would be able to test her findings using the *kem äm*. The possible ramifications were staggering. Already, Suki could use glyphs to heal injuries, and the government was seeking out other individuals who might also be able to channel the power. Officials had demanded more of the jewelry that could be used to control the *kem äm*, but so far none had been forthcoming with the collapse of the Mexican government.

In the meantime, Roth had stopped reading his e-mail, overwhelmed by all the demands on his time and attention. Things were *far* from normal.

"Sarina," BJ said, "before we came here, Jane Louise asked when she could see your family again. The mansion is too big for us, so we're staying in our house for now. She's not ready to start school yet. Not with so many rumors out there. Agent Sanchez said we should probably home school her for a while. I don't mean to intrude on your lives, but . . . ?"

Sarina hugged Jane Louise again. "The twins would love to watch movies with her, and I think Suki considers her a little sister. She's . . . she's part of our family now. We'll be heading to DC next week but come over every day until then."

BJ smiled and gave Roth a hug. "And you're my baby boy now," she crooned to Roth. Then she squeezed past him and hugged Sarina. "And you're my baby girl." Then she tapped Jane Louise on the shoulder. "Want to get a sundae from McDonald's on the way home?"

"Yes!" Jane Louise said. She waved goodbye and left with the McKintys. Roth felt his heart clench. He didn't like to see her go. When she wasn't around, he worried about her. He'd asked Lund to make sure the McKintys had a decent security system, but even so, it didn't feel like enough. Not after he'd had to walk away from her at the death game. There were news vans parked at the edge of the Beasley property night and day, waiting for someone to show up to talk to. Thankfully, they didn't know about the McKintys yet. Lund's crew was keeping them away from the Roths' home.

"I miss that little girl every time she leaves," Roth admitted, feeling that painful ache.

Sarina leaned against him. He put his arm around her and pulled her in. With a new insulin pump regulating her blood sugar, she had the flush of good health again. As a family, they'd decided to keep their knowledge of Aztlán a secret for now. At least until they saw how the government handled the information they'd already been given. They'd see what demands were made of them too—Suki, Sarina, and the boys wanted to help, and they had the ability to make a real difference with their knowledge of the *kem äm*, but they also wanted to maintain some control over their lives.

Roth saw the twins coming, Brillante with his Mountain Dew and Lucas with *two* cups of homemade caramel Bugles.

"Let's congratulate Suki," Roth said to Jordan and Monica over the commotion. The cast and crew usually lined up in the corridor outside the theater to greet the audience. Jordan nodded, and the couple joined them. They had to shuffle along with the crowd to join the line to see the theater members. It was so noisy that Roth's ears were ringing. He felt his heart racing, his body start to sweat. A feeling of panic made him want to tear through the crowd and run for his truck. But he took some calming breaths, held on to Sarina, and suffered through the noise.

When they got to Suki, she was standing next to Brice, her arm around him. Her face was flushed, and Roth could see the crowd was a little too much for her too, but she was clearly enjoying the moment of triumph. The play had been a fantastic production. And she'd helped with all aspects of it.

"You did great," Roth said, holding his palm out to her.

Suki shook her head and gave him a real hug instead. "Thanks for coming."

"We're so proud of you," Roth said. He kissed her hair. "Brice. You were awesome. And tell your mom I want the recipe for the Bugles."

Brice laughed out loud. "It's a family secret. Sorry. Thanks for coming to the show. We couldn't have pulled it off without Suki, our awesome stage manager."

Suki beamed. "Awww, thanks for saying that. The cast is going to Dairy Queen, Dad, so I'll be coming home late."

"Just text Uncle Steve and make sure he knows where you are," Roth said. "But you can go. Just don't stay out *too* late."

"We're all exhausted. So it'll probably be around eleven. That okay?"

"That's fine," Sarina answered.

Roth felt the burner phone in his pocket vibrate, meaning he had a new text. Then it buzzed again. And again.

Worry began to surge inside his chest. He hurriedly fished his hand into his pocket and pulled out the burner phone. About a dozen alerts had been delivered from an unknown number.

Roth felt engulfed by panic. His heart was hammering as he stared at the screen. His mouth went dry.

"Everything okay?" Monica asked, suddenly at his side. He didn't know. He just felt like running.

"Let's get away from the crowd," Sarina suggested. Roth made sure the twins were nearby as Monica and Sarina steered him down the hall back to the open common area at the front of the high school. There were some steps fashioned into an amphitheateresque setting, and he sat down, trying not to totally freak out.

He didn't recognize the number and unlocked the phone to look at the message, which contained about a dozen photo images sent from another phone.

Mr. Roth, this is Illari. I'm in the Yucatán with Dr. Estrada. We arrived in Calakmul two days ago and have been visiting the compound here. We met Ezequiel, who told us what went down that night. His people have been interrogating those who were part of Calakmul's cult. Still trying to find that glyph like we talked about, and we've been asking questions about that too. But that's not why I'm texting. We met this one US family, the Moretti family, who are from Utah. They say they didn't have a clue what any of this was about and want to go home. They also say they know you. Here are some pictures of them. Can you vouch for them?

Roth's heart began to calm as he scrolled through some of the pictures. Roth recognized Mrs. Moretti and the kids. They were wearing dirty clothes and looked pretty scared.

He showed the phone and the messages to Monica. Did the kids know their dad was dead? The ripples caused by Jacob Calakmul would extend for quite a while.

"You recognize them?" Monica asked.

Roth nodded. "Saw them last at Westfall's funeral a year ago. It's them."

"We're still working with State to figure out how to handle the situation down there. Any US citizens being held need to be extradited. Not sure how that is all going to work. But I'll make arrangements to get Moretti's family picked up from the airport or at a border crossing."

"Thank you," Roth said. His stomach was sick again. A few unexpected texts was all that had been needed to send him into an emotional nosedive. It would take time to heal. Time for all of them.

He texted back.

I know the Morettis. Agent Sanchez will work with you to get them back home. Thanks for letting me know.

He put the burner phone back in his pocket and buried his face in his hands. He felt Sarina's comforting hand on his shoulder. Then Lucas hugged him.

"It's okay, Dad. It'll all be okay."

Maybe it would be, and maybe not. An ancient disease was still ravaging the world. Several Central American countries were being shaken up by three Maya angels. A world coup had been disrupted. A prophecy was being fulfilled.

And yet . . . maybe some good would come from all of it? The *kem äm* had the power to change the world. To do spectacular and horrible things.

The future was a big question mark, an unknown. The only thing Roth knew for certain was that his life had become more exciting, more challenging, than in any one of his books. And with his family around him, together again, he was surprisingly okay with that.

AUTHOR'S NOTE

Looking at pictures on the internet is really helpful, but actually visiting locations opens up new opportunities. Before I wrote the climax of this book, I was able to climb the pyramids in the Calakmul preserve and stand in the place where the action happens. Being there helped inspire the ending of the book and the series. I'm so glad I was able to visit.

Travel is a huge part of the inspiration process for me. This series was born from a nightmare I had while visiting Florida. So naturally, I wanted to include part of the state in this final book. I was hoping to include an airboat chase scene in this novel with a jaguar priest getting eaten by an alligator, but it just felt too unrealistic to me! My daughter served a mission for our church in Fort Lauderdale, so I was able to visit many of the cities there. On a separate trip, we went to Washington, DC, and got to visit Ford's Theatre and the Capitol building. I even took a selfie outside FBI headquarters. I tried to get a White House tour, but that fell through. Visiting the different Smithsonian exhibits also helped influence this book.

Because of my writing schedule, I had finished all three books of the trilogy before *Doomsday Match* was even launched, so it is neat to finally be getting feedback on how fans are enjoying this series. I'm so grateful I stepped out of my comfort zone and tried something new. Writing this series has helped me grow as a writer. I don't know if I will ever come back to this world (strange that our world is now part of my menagerie), but I enjoyed the process very much and hope you have enjoyed reading something a little different.

What's coming next? While I was working on Dresden Codex, I began to do some research for a different fantasy world. I enjoy my other worlds very much and still have plans to write more in some of them, but I also like to let my imagination run wild, and it has. I'm thrilled to bring a new series out later this year, called the Invisible College. I've dived into literature that is centuries old. I've been to England and back. I've even been to the Shire, or the village that helped inspire it.

I hope you will stick with me for a journey that will make you wonder. Professor Hawksley and Miss Foster are anxious to meet you.

ACKNOWLEDGMENTS

Tackling a new genre, even though it's a story set in our world, was a lot harder than I anticipated. I like to be as realistic as possible, but I'll confess—most of what I knew about the FBI came from *The X-files*. I've had to do a lot of reading and research to try to get the vocabulary right, and even then, I kept blowing it.

Thankfully, my editorial team continued to bail me out! Adrienne, Angela, Wanda (my resident expert on diabetes, who knew!), and Dan. They've been with me for years and always have insightful comments and suggestions to make my books stronger and more compelling. From ammunition, to time zones, to the history of certain attractions at the Smithsonian, all of this requires a level of fact-checking that most fantasy authors never need to bother with because we can, frankly, invent stuff.

I'm grateful to my readers who stuck with me during this fever dream and for the new readers who discovered me through the Dresden Codex. I hope to visit Germany again and to see the ancient manuscript in person. Without the careful preservation and care from countless individuals, we would not have such archaeological treasures today.

During my trip to Mexico, I visited a monument and statue of Diego de Landa in the city of Izamal (a very cool place, by the way!). I read that Bishop Landa later regretted the destruction of so much history of the Maya. There is so much we still don't know today, but what we do know about them is mind-blowing. I hope you've learned a little more about history from reading this series. History continues to be my biggest source of inspiration for what I write about.

ABOUT THE AUTHOR

Photo © 2021 Kortnee Carlile

Jeff Wheeler is the *Wall Street Journal* bestselling author of more than forty epic novels. *Doomsday Match* and *Jaguar Prophecies* in the Dresden Codex series are the first thrillers he's written since his early years as a budding author, but his many fans think his fantasy novels are thrillers in their own way. Jeff lives in the Rocky Mountains and is a husband, father of five, and devout member of his church. On trips to the jungles of Cozumel and the Yucatán Peninsula, he has explored Maya ruins and cenotes, leading him to dive even further into the history of ancient America and the Spanish conquistadors. There is more to the ball courts than meets the eye. Learn about Jeff's publishing journey in *Your First Million Words*, and visit his many worlds at www.jeff-wheeler.com.